P9-DEP-789

Rachel Hore worked in London publishing for many years before moving with her family to Norwich, where she teaches publishing at the University of East Anglia. She is married to writer D. J. Taylor and they have three sons. Her previous novels are *The Dream House*, *The Memory Garden*, *The Glass Painter's Daughter*, which was shortlisted for the 2010 Romantic Novel of the Year award, and *A Place of Secrets*, which was picked by Richard and Judy for their book club. *A Gathering Storm* is her fifth novel.

Praise for Rachel Hore's novels:

A Place of Secrets

'Rachel Hore's intriguing Richard and Judy recommended read . . . is layered with a series of mysteries, some more supernatural than others'
Independent

'Sumptuous prose, deft plotting, lush settings, troubling personal histories, tragedy, heady romance and even a smattering of eighteenth-century scientific wonderment mark Hore's fourth novel as her most accomplished and enthralling yet' *Daily Mirror*

The Glass Painter's Daughter

'Fans of *Possession* and *Labyrinth* will recognize the careful historical research Hore has undertaken and enjoy the seamless blend of past and present narratives into one beautiful story' *Waterstone's Books Quarterly*

The Memory Garden

'With her second novel, Rachel Hore proves she does place and setting as well as romance and relationships. Tiny, hidden Lamorna Cove in Cornwall is the backdrop to two huge tales of illicit passion and thwarted ambition . . . Clever stuff' *Daily Mirror*

'Rachel Hore knows the tricks of her trade and keeps the pages turning by adding a hint of a past mystery, too. Cleverly done' *Now*

'Pitched perfectly for a holiday read' *Guardian*

The Dream House

'*The Dream House* is a book that so many of us will identify with. Moving from frenzied city to peaceful countryside is something so many of us dream of. Rachel Hore has explored the dream and exposed it in the bright light of reality, with repercussions both tragic and uplifting, adding her own dose of magic. It's engrossing, pleasantly surprising and thoroughly readable' Santa Montefiore

'I enjoyed it enormously and was genuinely disappointed when I got to the end, having read deep into the night to finish it because I couldn't put it down! I was completely drawn into the plot. I thought it a wonderfully evocative and cleverly woven story' Barbara Erskine

A Gathering Storm

RACHEL HORE

**SIMON &
SCHUSTER**

London · New York · Sydney · Toronto · New Delhi

A CBS COMPANY

First published in Great Britain by Simon & Schuster UK Ltd, 2011.
A CBS Company.

Copyright © Rachel Hore 2011

This book is copyright under the Berne Convention.
No reproduction without permission.
® and © 1997 Simon & Schuster Inc. All rights reserved.

The right of Rachel Hore to be identified as author of this
work has been asserted in accordance with sections 77 and
78 of the Copyright, Designs and Patents Act, 1988.

5 7 9 10 8 6 4

Simon & Schuster UK Ltd
1st Floor
222 Gray's Inn Road
London WC1X 8HB

www.simonandschuster.co.uk

Simon & Schuster Australia
Sydney
Simon & Schuster India
Delhi

A CIP catalogue record for this book is available from the British Library

ISBN 978-1-84983-288-5

This book is a work of fiction. Names,
characters, places and incidents are either a product of
the author's imagination or are used fictitiously.

Typeset in Palatino by Hewer Text UK Ltd, Edinburgh
Printed and bound by
CPI Group (UK) Ltd, Croydon, CR0 4YY

For my brother David

Prologue

South London, March 2000

Slipping into the chapel, softly as a wraith, Beatrice found a seat at the back. Aimless organ music was playing, but she hardly noticed, for she was putting on her spectacles and examining the Order of Service the usher had given her. There was a photograph of Angelina on the front, and the sight of it tugged her straight back into the past.

It was a picture she remembered well, a snapshot Beatrice herself had taken in Cornwall, on Carlyon beach, just before the war, when Angie was seventeen. Angie's mother had framed it and kept it on the grand piano in Carlyon Manor. From it, Angelina gazed out across the years, laughing, beautiful, and bathed in sunlight.

As Beatrice stared into those luminous eyes she felt a hot lava of longing and resentment rise inside. She laid the card face down beside her on the pew. She thought she'd mastered these feelings long ago, wrestled them down during many nights of torment. Now she knew that she was wrong: beneath the veneer of good sense, the passions of the past still raged. She closed her eyes, trying to collect her thoughts. She should never have come. But there was someone she needed to see.

Beatrice opened her eyes and looked around. The pews in the crematorium were nearly but not quite full. As her gaze wandered over the rows she noticed they were filled mostly with people of her own generation, the women proper in hats, the old men florid or shrunken inside their dark suits, some, the old war-horses, with medals glinting. There was no one she recognized. Finally, she allowed herself to look towards the front, sitting up a little straighter, craning her neck. At the top of the aisle was the coffin, piled high with blue and white flowers, but her eyes slid over this. Her pulse quickened.

For there they were. It must be them, though it was difficult to be sure from behind. A middle-aged woman with frizzy hair tinted blonde and tied back with ribbon, her crushed-velvet coat of midnight blue cut in a flamboyant style. The man in a crow-black overcoat, his dark hair, Beatrice noticed tenderly, streaked with grey. It was astonishing, she thought, that Tom must be getting on for sixty. And between them, a girl of perhaps sixteen, who kept turning round to look at everything, so that Beatrice had plenty of opportunity to study her pointed chin, her turned-up nose and the lively expression in her stubby-lashed brown eyes. Lucy, it was.

And now the congregation was rising to its feet as the minister, his white robes flying, hastened to the front, and the organist started the first hymn. Beatrice grasped the back of the pew in front for support and tried to focus on the words. But she found no strength to sing.

The comforting words of the liturgy washed over her. She hardly noticed them, so intent was she on watching the small family in the front row. Lucy stroked her father's arm but he barely acknowledged her. There was something lonely about the way he stood, shoulders hunched, head bowed.

And now everyone was sitting down again and Tom was moving to the lectern, so that she saw his face for the first time. So absolutely like his father's. It was the pallor of his skin, the steady way he pushed on his spectacles, his quiet demeanour as he contemplated his audience. But when, finally, he began to speak, his voice was utterly his own, deep and so low she had to strain to catch the words. And what he had to say astonished her.

'My mother Angelina Cardwell,' Tom said, 'was one of the most beautiful . . .' and here he smiled at his wife and daughter in the front row '. . . and certainly the bravest woman I have ever known.' That didn't sound right. She'd never thought of Angie in that light before. Beautiful, yes, but brave? What did he mean? '. . . a difficult life,' she heard him continue. 'The tragic deaths of her brother and mother, her husband's health problems . . .' The volume of the words ebbed and flowed in that soft bass voice. 'It was, I know, a disappointment that I was her only child, and I was always aware of how precious I was.' He glanced up at his audience. 'Many of you will know how she struggled in her later years with illness. This too she bore with great courage, never more so than after the death of my father. Beautiful and brave she was, but I also valued my mother for her loyalty. She was a devoted mother and wife and, as all the letters I've received since her death bear witness, a warm and loving friend. I was proud to be her son.'

Beatrice squeezed her eyes shut for a moment, trying to assimilate all she heard. Devoted, warm, loyal. That's not how she saw Angelina. When she looked up again it was to find Tom Cardwell staring directly at her, a look of slight puzzlement on his face as though he were trying to place her.

At the end of the short service, everyone stood waiting quietly as the electric curtains closed around the coffin. Only Lucy broke the tension with a single sobbing cry and her mother seized her hand with a little rattle of bangles.

It was over.

She watched Tom, his wife and daughter go out first, and Tom take up a position at the door, to thank everyone as they walked out. Beatrice hung back but saw there was nothing for it; she would have to speak to him. She'd rehearsed some words, but now she wasn't sure that they were the right ones. As she waited her turn in the line-up, someone jabbed at her arm and spoke her name. She turned to find a familiar face: a stocky old woman with a raffia hat pulled too tight over wispy grey hair and an expression of malicious pleasure.

'Hetty. It is Hetty?' Beatrice said. Angelina's sister must be in her early seventies, three or four years younger than herself, but she looked older.

'Of course it's Hetty,' the woman said with her usual brusqueness. 'What the hell are you doing here, Bea?' The eyes, it was always the eyes that gave someone away. Hetty's were brown and baleful, and her mouth still turned down. Charmless, that had always been the word for Hesther Wincanton.

'How are you?' Beatrice said, ignoring the rudeness. 'I didn't see you earlier, wasn't sure you were here.'

'Why wouldn't I be?' Hetty said. 'I was her sister.'

'I didn't mean that. I hadn't spotted you – you weren't sitting with Tom.'

'No,' Hetty said shortly. 'Well, never mind all that. I thought I'd warn you not to say anything stupid. You won't, will you?'

'Stupid? What do you take me for?'

Hetty seized her arm and Beatrice felt a spray of spit as the woman hissed, 'Angelina never told him about you, you know. Never.'

Beatrice felt the last shreds of hope blow away. 'Didn't she?' she said faintly. Then she pulled herself up straighter: 'Told whom what?'

'Don't pretend you don't know what I'm talking about. So keep mum. Trust me, it's for the best.'

She might not like Hetty, but Beatrice saw enough urgency in the other woman's face to worry her. She gave her the slightest of nods and turned away.

When she finally reached Tom's side she felt only numbness, knowing she mustn't say what was in her heart. She put out her hand.

'Thank you for coming,' he murmured as he shook it, looking at her, curious. 'Do I know you?'

'I'm Beatrice Ashton,' she said. 'I used to be Beatrice Marlow. A family friend.' She watched his face change. *He knew,* she saw immediately. *He knew who she was.*

With a supreme effort, Tom Cardwell recovered his composure.

'It's very nice of you to come, Mrs Ashton. Perhaps you'd join us for refreshments shortly. I'm sure someone could give you a lift to the hotel.'

'I have my own car,' she said, but already he was turning from her.

'Aunt Hetty,' she heard him say, as she moved on.

'Such a shame my brother Peter couldn't take the trouble.' Hetty's reply carried clear and loud.

'It's a long way from New York, Hetty, and I gather his health isn't good.'

'Well, he needn't expect *us* to turn up for *his* funeral.' She gave a snorting laugh.

'Oh, I don't know,' Tom said.

Beatrice joined the other mourners, admiring the wreaths laid out on the ground. Lucy and her mother, Gabriella, were a little way ahead.

'Oh, this is all so . . . weird,' cried the girl passionately, and started to cry. Gabriella tried to soothe her. Beatrice watched them walk away together into the garden. It seemed she wasn't to speak to them either. No one talked to her. She was a stranger – no, worse, a ghost.

Finally losing her courage altogether, she decided to skip refreshments and looked for the path to the car park.

Later, she was to agonize over her cowardice. If Hetty hadn't warned her, who knows what she might have said to Tom and the effect it would have had. Perhaps it was better for the truth to lie sleeping. After all, who would benefit from it coming to light? Maybe only herself. But hadn't her own mother always enjoined her to tell the truth? A lie leads to a bigger lie, she used to say. It wasn't originally Beatrice's lie, but Angelina's.

Chapter 1

Cornwall, April 2011

'*Please*, Will.'

'Lucy, we're already late. If you girls hadn't taken so long packing up . . .'

'It's not far on the map – look.'

'I can't when I'm driving, can I?' Will's eyes didn't flicker from the road ahead.

'There'll be a sign to Saint Florian soon,' Lucy said. 'I showed you on the way down, remember? Oh, Will, it's only a few miles to the coast. Come on, please. I did say I wanted to go there.' She tried not to sound petulant.

'And we've been busy doing other things all week. Are you going to blame me for that?'

'I'm not blaming you for anything. I just want to see the place.'

'Listen, Lu, we'll go another time, how about that? Jon says let's come again in the summer.' As if to settle the matter, Will touched a paddle on the steering wheel and rock music pulsed through the car, drowning all possibility of conversation.

Lucy traced a finger along the wobbly line of the Cornish coast, with its promise of smugglers' coves and wild head-lands, and privately wondered if there would be a second visit. She'd hardly known Jon and Natalia, the other couple;

they were friends of Will's, and she hadn't even been seeing Will very long. She sneaked a look at him and her pessimism grew. That scowl was becoming an all-too-recognizable reaction to being crossed. He was twenty-seven, as she was, but despite his longish hair and the attractive, unshaven look, which in London she'd taken to mean laidback and open to new ideas, he hadn't turned out that way at all. As for the others, Jon, like Will, was obsessed with finding the best surfing beaches, Natalia with shopping, and Lucy was the only one prepared to walk the cliffs if more than one drop of rain was falling. But as the newcomer to the group, and lacking her own transport, she'd had to comply with their plans. She folded her arms and stared out of the window, trying to ignore the ugly music.

Will glanced at her and turned down the volume. 'You look pretty miserable,' he remarked.

'Thanks,' she said. 'I don't understand why you're so desperate to get home.'

He shrugged. 'I want to get the drive over with. Anyway, there are things to do. I've booked the editing suite this week and I need to go over the brief.' Will was a freelance film editor, and Lucy worked for a television production company as a production assistant.

'You're not thinking about work already, Will?'

'You're lucky having next week off.'

'I feel I've earned it . . . Oh, look!' A road sign had come into view. Lucy sat up straighter. 'The turn-off. Please, Will. It'll only take twenty minutes, I promise. Let's go, *please*.'

Will, who was a little alarmed by Lucy's impetuous side, gave in and swung the driving wheel.

'Thank you,' Lucy breathed, touching his arm. His forehead creased into a frown.

They drove on in silence, the narrow road winding between high hedges. Several times they were forced to pull in to let cars pass from the opposite direction, Will's fingers tapping the steering wheel.

'How much further?' he growled.

'Just another half-mile. Oh, look, the sea!'

They had crossed a plateau and reached the point where the land sloped down to a horseshoe-shaped bay. To the left, high cliffs curved out to a headland with a lighthouse. The view to the right was blocked by a line of Scots pines crowded with rooks' nests. Ahead, the road dipped steeply towards a cluster of whitewashed houses, presumably the beginning of the town.

Another sign, this one pointing right, along a lane behind the pines: '*The Beach and Carlyon Manor*,' Lucy read aloud. 'Will, stop! It's Carlyon!'

Will checked his mirror before jamming on the brakes. 'For goodness' sake, Lu. I thought you wanted the town.'

'I do – but Carlyon Manor, don't you see? That's where Granny lived when she was little.'

Will muttered something impatient under his breath, but turned right anyway. Lucy gazed out of the window at the wild daffodils in the hedgerows and her spirits rose.

Half a mile on, they came to a fork in the road. A white noticeboard detailing parking charges pointed left to the beach. 'Right again,' Lucy said, and the car swerved between a pair of granite posts and along a deep lane, where newly ploughed fields spread away on either side. Then came another bend and a short driveway to the left, to where a pair of high, wrought-iron gates was set in a long stone wall.

'Stop in here,' Lucy said, and Will pulled the car to a halt.

She flung open her door and hurried over to the gates. They were locked and the padlock smudged with rust. She shook them in frustration then gazed through the bars, trying to see a glimpse of the house, but a mass of trees swallowed the view.

Will said, 'Too bad. Get in. Let's go,' and revved the engine, but Lucy had noticed where some stones from the long wall had spilled onto the lane, some way further down.

She reached for her camera bag in the passenger well, swung it on her shoulder and set off at a run, saying, 'I won't be a minute.'

'Lucy!' Will called.

She waved without looking back.

A hundred yards down from the gates she came to the section of the wall that was crumbling. She scrambled up, leapt down into the undergrowth on the other side and pushed her way through a thick belt of trees. There she stopped and stared. Set out before her was Carlyon Manor.

In the photographs she'd found in Granny's box, Carlyon was a long, graceful Elizabethan stone house set amongst elegant trees, its rolled lawns stippled by sunlight. This building was derelict and blackened by fire, its ragged skeleton outlined against the sky, the one remaining chimney reaching up, pitifully, like the wing of a crushed bird. Instinctively, she took out her camera and started to take some shots, wondering all the while when this could have happened. Nobody had ever mentioned a fire.

She scurried across the shaggy grass and the weed-infested gravel. Several steps led up to the front entrance, but some flakes of wood on rusted hinges were all that remained of the double doors. She hovered on the threshold, considering the possible danger, then curiosity got the better of her and she stepped inside.

She was in a ruined hallway that was open, in part, to the sky. She wandered carefully from room to room, stepping over rubble, past twisted shapes of what had once been metal, trying to imagine what it might have been like once, before. It was, she saw, possible to glean the layout of the ground-floor rooms and something of their former purpose. There might once have been a central staircase, she thought, and a gallery, but perhaps that was her imagination.

She stared round at it all in dismay, wondering when the fire had happened and how. From a large room at the back of the house, the rusted vestiges of french windows looked out onto a flagstoned terrace and beyond, a wild garden. They were right on the clifftop here, and between the fluttering leaves of poplar trees glittered the sea.

She turned back to the room. It was the drawing room once, she supposed. The corroded metal innards of an armchair crouched by the fireplace. On the wall above hung the charred shape of what was once a great mirror. She crossed the rotted floor, rubbish crunching beneath her feet, and examined the ruined mantelpiece. It still featured a carved design. She moved her fingers over the lumps and bumps of the burned wood, wondering about the pattern of fruit and flowers. It would have been a stunning piece of craftsmanship. The ghostly remnants of the mirror and the armchair fascinated her, and she reached again for her camera.

Round the rooms she moved in a reverie, taking pictures of anything that caught her eye, trying to imagine the people who had lived here. Sometimes she thought she heard children's voices. God forbid there had been children in the house when this happened. They were gentle voices, though, not sounds of terror, and she came to realize it was just the wind calling through the ruins.

Half an hour later, she became aware that there really was someone calling. Will. She'd forgotten about Will. She picked her way back to the front entrance and looked out across the park. He was standing over by the belt of trees, legs apart, hands on hips. She waved and he began to jog towards her.

'Lucy, what the hell . . .? I didn't know where you were going. You just vanished.'

'I'm so sorry. I forgot the time. Isn't this wonderful?'

He looked past her at the ruin. 'It looks like a dump to me. What did you call it?'

'Carlyon Manor. Where Granny lived when she was young.'

'Very nice,' he said, 'but it must be dangerous. Come on now. We must go.'

She didn't like his hectoring tone, but came reluctantly down the steps. 'I still need to see Saint Florian,' she said and bit her lip, seeing his outraged face.

'I'm sorry, Lucy, but it's just not on. We need to get home.'

He really was furious, and though she resented it she supposed it was understandable. She started to follow him back to the car, but her footsteps dragged; she couldn't dispel the silly notion that the house was calling her back.

Will, she saw, had already turned the car round so that it pointed resolutely in the direction of home. They got in, and when he started the engine she suddenly imagined herself sitting beside him all the way to London, listening to the clangy music, discussing the wretched documentary he was editing, with the town of St Florian, still unvisited, receding further and further away.

They were passing the pines with the rooks' nests now, and Will was signalling left, away from St Florian. A mad idea occurred to her. It wasn't as though she had to get home yet.

'Will,' she said. 'Stop and let me out.'

He hesitated. 'Lucy, please. I'd like to get home sometime today if possible.'

'I'm not coming.'

'What?' His face was a mask of disbelief.

'Look – I've got a week,' she told him. 'I was just going to play about with photographs, maybe get some framed, but I can do that anytime. So I've decided I'm staying here. I want to take a proper look at Saint Florian, see if there's anyone to ask about Carlyon and my family.'

'That's ridiculous. Where will you stay? You can't just decide things like that.'

She rolled her eyes. 'I'll find somewhere.' She reached for her handbag and camera. 'Thanks, Will. For everything. It's been fab.' She leant across and gave him a quick kiss, then opened the door. He sat there, wooden, not looking at her. 'Would you unlock the boot, please? I want my suitcase.'

He gazed at her, his expression anxious and unhappy, saying, 'This is just stupid. Look, I'll tell you what, I'll drive you down to Saint Florian if you're that serious. Then you're coming back with me.'

It wasn't only the tone of voice that maddened her, but the fact that he had no interest in this adventure.

'You don't have to, really. I can walk down. Please open the boot.'

'Lucy—'

'I want to do this on my own.' She knew that now.

A moment later she was standing at the roadside with her suitcase, watching his car speed away.

'Bye, Will,' she whispered.

Trundling her case behind her, with the spring sun warming her back, she set off down the hill towards the town.

Chapter 2

Three months earlier

Lucy's journey to St Florian was one her father, Tom, should have made when he was alive. But he chose not to, and so she was making it for him.

Her quest began one afternoon in mid-January when she visited her stepmother, Helena, in Suffolk. Helena had asked her down from London because she'd been clearing out Tom's possessions and wanted to give her some things.

As Lucy drove her hired car through the stark East Anglian countryside she studied her feelings. It was odd, really, that her long resentment of Helena hadn't eased since her father's death in a car crash the previous June. If anything, it had intensified. She felt sorry for her stepmother, certainly. Anyone seeing Helena's worn expression, her unconscious habit of wringing her hands, would know that she'd loved Tom very much and grieved for him. But Lucy couldn't forgive Helena for taking her father away. She'd hated, too, the fact that Helena, the second wife, the latecomer in Tom Cardwell's life, had assumed the central role in the formalities following his death. As Tom's legal spouse, it was Helena, not Lucy or Lucy's mother Gabriella, who was called to the hospital after the car wreck was found, Helena who took charge of the funeral arrangements, Helena who, in the absence of any will, had presided over the division of Tom's estate, although she'd made no difficulty about Lucy receiving her legal entitlement.

In addition to her own muddled feelings, Lucy had been moved by her mother's intense anguish. By dying, it was for Gabriella Cardwell as though Tom had abandoned her all over again, and she found no comfort in the fact that this time the Other Woman had lost him, too. The two widows were quite unable to meet and share their grief; Lucy gauged that each saw only too clearly in the other what they themselves lacked in relation to Tom, and she was fed up with being the bridge between them.

When Lucy left the car in the quiet lane outside Walnut Tree Cottage, she saw Helena waiting for her at the front door, a willowy figure in a twinset of pigeon grey. 'You're awfully late,' Helena called, her light voice quivery. 'I was getting worried.'

'Sorry, Helena,' Lucy said, feeling guilty. 'I didn't start off till one, then it took ages to get through London.'

'That's all right,' Helena said. 'It's just, ever since your father . . . I can't help being anxious.' Her cheek, when Lucy kissed her, felt dry, and Lucy saw that her matt-brown hair was now tinged with grey, like a coating of ash.

The white carnations Lucy had bought when she'd stopped for petrol were bruised and parched. She passed them across with a muttered apology.

'How thoughtful of you, dear. And I'm so glad you've come.'

'I should have visited before.'

'You're so busy, I know. You've been away, haven't you?' Helena tidied Lucy's coat into a cupboard and led her into the sterile white kitchen. 'Did you say Romania on the phone?'

'Bulgaria,' Lucy replied, watching as Helena arranged the horrible blooms in a cream china vase. 'We were filming a costume drama. I was there for three weeks, on and off.'

In the hall, Helena set the vase on a shelf between two face-less dancing figurines. 'Now, we should start in here, I think.' She pushed open the door to the dining room and her voice trailed to a halt. Lucy saw why. Four ugly cardboard boxes were lined up on the table, spoiling the neat lines of Helena's life.

'They're all bits and bobs of your father's,' Helena said, going over. 'One of the charity shops took his clothes.'

'Yes, of course,' Lucy said quickly. She couldn't bear to think of strangers' bodies filling out her father's suits and shoes.

Helena glanced at her. 'As you know, all his financial affairs are sorted out. There are these and a few things in his study – the books, of course.'

One box was too full to shut properly. On top of a pile of rugby programmes lay a photograph in a silver frame. Helena picked it up and said, 'This was in the bottom drawer of his desk. Wasn't she your grandmother?'

Lucy took it with a tender jolt of recognition. It was of Granny on the beach when she was young – the picture her father had used on the Order of Service at her funeral. It had stood on a bookshelf at home all through Lucy's childhood. But here, it seemed, her father had kept it hidden away, as though he couldn't bear to look at it. Why was that?

'Anyway,' Helena said, 'I'd be much obliged if you'd take all this.'

'I'd love to,' Lucy said. She didn't add that it was hardly Helena's to give her.

As if reading her mind, Helena fixed Lucy with her steady grey eyes and said in her pale voice, 'There never was any question but that you should have it.'

'No, of course not,' Lucy said. She was still staring at the photograph. Her grandmother had been so lovely and Lucy's professional interest was piqued by the knowing sideways look she gave the camera. She'd have been an easy subject for a photographer; it really was true that there were people the camera loved.

'Quite a charmer, wasn't she?' Helena remarked, as though she disapproved. 'Oh, I know it can't be easy for you, Lucy, this situation. I do hope that you and I . . . that we'll continue to be friends.'

'Of course we will.' It would have been cruel to say otherwise, but Lucy sincerely wondered whether friendship would be possible. Not only was Helena nearly thirty years older than herself, but what on earth did they have in common?

'Your father was very dear to me. He seemed so lost and unhappy when I got to know him. He needed me.'

Why? Lucy wanted to ask, but was too proud. A picture came into her mind of her mother's wild weeping after Lucy's father had departed, the blotchy face, the hair frizzier than ever. Helena, apart from the hand-wringing, was always composed, self-controlled. Why had her father come to need this calm, colourless woman?

Key to it all somewhere was why Tom had changed so much after Lucy's grandmother's death, when he'd started to explore the boxes of papers and mementos that she'd left behind. Was it the ordinary processes of grief, or had he found something amongst her possessions that bothered him? Even now, Lucy didn't quite understand. Her father had been an intensely private man with a strong sense of pride and tradition, and rarely talked about feelings. He had always been warm and loving, though, and Lucy couldn't make sense of why he'd cut his ties and set out to remake his life.

*   *   *

After Helena helped her move the boxes out to the car, they drank tea from fragile mugs in the beige sitting room before Helena said, 'Shall we go and look upstairs?'

At the top of the cottage was an airy loftspace that Tom had converted into a study soon after they'd bought the house six or seven years before. As Helena turned on lights and fiddled with the sticking window blind, Lucy surveyed the room. It was the only place in the house where she still sensed her father's presence. His faded navy sweatshirt hung on the back of the door, presumably missed in the charity-shop sweep. There he was, too, in the ordered rows of books, the old mahogany desk in front of the window that looked out onto darkening wintry fields.

Her attention was caught by a photograph that had fallen under the desk. She picked it up. It was of her father's school's first fifteen rugby team, his eighteen-year-old face sweet and eager in the front row. She studied it for signs of the more sombre, introverted man he would eventually become, but saw none. She placed it on the desk next to the computer, by yet another cardboard box.

'Oh, yes,' Helena said, 'you should take that one, too. It's mostly stuff of your grandmother's.'

Lucy pulled up the flaps and looked inside. A yellow ring-bound file lay on the top, and when she opened it she saw notes in her father's small neat handwriting – lists of dates, diagrams with arrows, and a reference to a book about the D-Day landings. Military history then, that was all. Disappointed, she took the file out. Underneath was a big square tin, once used for cake or biscuits, with a picture of a garden on it. She lifted the lid and smelt the scent of roses. The tin contained a jumble of mementos. She closed it again. She wouldn't look at it in front of Helena.

'What should I do with the books?' Helena was at the shelves, straightening a row of old school stories with decorated spines. She looked out of place up here. Tom's study had been his private world. Here he'd spent many hours reading in the big armchair, or at the desk writing, or surfing websites of second-hand booksellers.

'I'd only want them because they'd been Dad's,' she said, 'and I just haven't room in my flat.'

'What about your mother?'

'No. Can't you try that shop in the high street?'

'That would probably be best.' Helena was looking round the room now, wondering what else should be given its marching orders. Her eyes came to rest on the computer. 'There's something else I need to give you, Lucy. Your father was doing some research into family history. It might interest you. I tried to print the document off this morning, but the wretched thing wouldn't work.'

'I'll have a go, if you like,' Lucy offered, curious. She sat down and switched on the computer.

'I guessed his password straight away,' Helena said. 'It's "wasps". ' Tom's favourite rugby team.

Lucy typed it in, smiling, and watched as a series of icons appeared on a black and yellow desktop. Helena pointed her to a file labelled *Cardwell*. A page of text yawned open. Lucy stared at the heading. It was a man's name.

'Who's Rafe Ashton?' she asked.

'You haven't heard of him?' Helena replied, frowning.

'No.'

'Your father said he was his uncle. You must have heard of him.'

'No, I haven't,' Lucy insisted. Great-Uncle Rafe? The name meant nothing.

'I gather he was your Grandfather Gerald's younger brother.'

'I'd no idea he had one. Why wasn't he Rafe Cardwell then?'

'He must have been a half-brother. Anyway, he went missing in the war or something. It's all a bit confusing.'

'I'll take it away and have a look.' Lucy was annoyed that Helena appeared to know more about the family than she did. The printer clattered into life and several typed pages slipped softly into the tray. She tucked them into the cardboard box and, with the box in her arms, gazed around her father's room for what was perhaps the last time.

'I ought to go,' she told Helena. 'I'm due at a friend's house in London at eight.'

'Of course,' Helena replied, but she looked disappointed.

Once on the road again, Lucy quickly forgot about Helena. Her mind was already on the mystery of Great-Uncle Rafe.

Lucy lived in a tiny apartment that her father had helped her buy, not far from the canal at Little Venice in North London. She loved to walk the towpath and watch the barges come and go, sorry that she'd missed the days when they'd been pulled by horses. Nowadays, they mostly carried tourists. The previous year, a series of photographs she'd taken of the area had sold well in an exhibition at a Camden gallery.

So far as work was concerned, Lucy felt at a bit of a crossroads. Photography was her hobby, but she might let it become more. She liked the small TV production company where she worked, but wanted more responsibility. Her boss, Delilah, had been encouraging. 'We're always being asked for short documentaries,' she said. 'Serious themes, women's lives, that sort of thing. Bring me some ideas.' Lucy had tried one or two on her, but nothing that had worked yet.

At twenty-seven, Lucy still hadn't found anyone she'd want to share her life with; being fiercely independent, she wondered if she ever would. Will, whom she had met through work, was the latest in a not very long line of boyfriends.

In the weeks after meeting Helena, when she could bear to, Lucy would lift one of her father's boxes onto the breakfast-table in her flat and take out its treasures one by one. Over his personal things – a carved wooden box containing cufflinks and tie-pins; his favourite LPs with their folk band covers – she didn't linger, putting them out of painful sight and mind in a cupboard in her bedroom, but the photograph of her grand-mother had taken a hold on her. She stood it on the desk and found herself glancing at it as she worked. It was strange, real-izing that the elderly invalid she'd known had once been this beautiful young girl.

Lucy had been dearly fond of her father's mother, but childhood visits to the musty London mansion flat could be something of an ordeal. There was an air of shabby grandeur about the place, an expectance of best behaviour. Angelina Cardwell liked Lucy to dress nicely, which Lucy sometimes fought against, causing ructions between her parents. Her mother Gabriella held that people should be allowed to wear what they liked, while her father argued that best clothes were a form of respect, and that Granny Cardwell liked to see little girls in pretty dresses and proper leather shoes, not jeans and trainers. Since Gabriella refused to accompany Tom and Lucy on these visits, Tom usually won. As she grew into her teens, Lucy came to enjoy the challenge of meeting Granny's high standards whilst satisfying her own colourful sense of style. Granny didn't mind clothes being fashionable, indeed she rather approved.

The three of them would sit together on the over-stuffed chairs and drink tea served by Granny's Polish daily woman, and chat about what Lucy had been doing at school and whether Granny, who suffered badly from nerves and arthritis, was well enough to join some friends on a cruise. As far as Lucy remembered, she never was.

One Sunday afternoon, in a pensive mood, Lucy investigated the box she'd taken from her father's study. Angelina's cake-tin contained a lock of Tom's baby hair folded in tissue; a birthday card he'd made her, drawn in a childish hand; a pair of knitted mittens. She fitted a finger inside one. Had her father really once had hands tiny enough for these?

There were a few letters and postcards he had sent his parents from school, or from holidays. And lots more photographs: only one or two of Tom as a toddler, but several of him as a schoolboy, then a teenager. Here was a photograph of her parents' wedding, a picture of herself aged three in her mother's arms, with the large green teddy she'd famously won at a fairground. All these her grandmother had collected together in this box of memories and it made Lucy feel both sad and happy at the same time to look at them.

She put the cake-tin aside to find what else was in the box. There were none of her father's identity documents, but she supposed Helena would have needed to keep hold of those. There were yet more photographs, from further back in time, a rare one of her Grandfather Gerald as a young man, before he was wounded. She only remembered him faintly, an alarming-looking old gentleman with a scarred face and a glass eye.

An Elizabethan house with high chimneys featured often. In one snapshot an elfin maid was shaking a duster from an open window, in another, a troupe of five children played croquet on the lawn. There were two boys in the picture, one dark, one fair, both older than the girl who was Granny. The youngest child, a glum, square-faced girl, squinted at the camera, pointing her mallet like a rifle – that must be Great-Aunt Hetty. A slender dark girl hung shyly in the background. Lucy had no idea who she could be.

Her grandmother had sometimes talked about the house on the south Cornish coast where she'd been brought up. Carlyon, she'd called it, Carlyon Manor. It was gone now, she'd say. Lucy wasn't sure how. Lucy next unearthed a black and white postcard of a seaside town. *St Florian*, the caption said. That was where Carlyon was, she remembered now.

She went back to the photograph of the children at Carlyon. It was sad to think of the change time had wrought. Granny's eldest brother Edward was dead, killed in the war. Great-Uncle Peter was still alive, but living in Manhattan, and little heard of. Great-Aunt Hetty, a rather grumpy lady whom she only saw on important family occasions, lived in a residential home somewhere, and had been too unwell to come to Lucy's father's funeral.

There was nothing so far about Great-Uncle Rafe. It seemed indeed that he'd been wiped from the family annals. What on earth had he done? Lucy delved once more into the box and brought out a photograph that had caught itself in a corner. She'd almost missed it. As she studied it she felt she was staring into the face of someone she'd known once, long ago, but forgotten. Could this young man be Rafe?

Chapter 3

The Mermaid Inn on the quay in St Florian had been newly painted the colour of clotted cream. On the bright sign, an alabaster-skinned siren lolled in the surf. Lucy smiled at the mischievous look in her eye and walked inside.

The reception area was empty, though a delicious smell of frying butter suggested that someone couldn't be far away. The ping of the bell brought a round-faced young woman with a scrappy ponytail, who struggled through the service door with a parcel of clean laundry and dumped it next to the desk.

'Sorry to keep you, lovely,' she said. 'They're all late with deliveries today. What can I do for you?'

'Have you got a room, please? I haven't booked or anything.'

'You're lucky,' she said. 'We had a cancellation come in this morning.'

The room was surprisingly cheap and the girl showed Lucy up several flights of stairs. It was a poky L-shaped attic with a view of the sky, but Lucy liked the solidity of the old building, the scent of lavender polish. A glance at the tiny shower room and the coffee-making facilities completed her satisfaction. It might be a bit cramped but it would certainly do for a few nights.

'Oh, I'll need to give you some washing,' she told the girl. She'd only brought enough clothes for her week's holiday with Will.

'That's no trouble. There's a bag in the wardrobe. Just put it out for me,' was the reply. 'I'm Cara, by the way. Let me know if there's anything else you need.'

As soon as Cara left, Lucy picked up the television remote control and sat cross-legged on the bed flicking through the channels with the sound off. On the news channel, soldiers moved in tanks through a rocky landscape. After a while, she pressed the off-button and lay back on the pillows, suddenly weary. And all her anxieties rushed in.

Why had she marooned herself here? The reality of what she'd done rose like a bubble in her chest. She'd offended Will – of whom she'd been quite fond, and who'd brought her on a not unpleasant holiday – and was stuck alone in a hotel room, probably miles from any public transport. And for what exactly?

The panic passed. She pulled a plastic folder out of a pocket in her suitcase and consulted the pages she'd printed from her father's laptop. He'd visited the Imperial War Museum in search of Rafe and checked certain National Archive documents. Apart from Rafe's date of birth, 1920, and the bare facts of his schooling and war career, he hadn't found out much – nothing personal anyway. Except something that connected him with St Florian: his mother's sister had lived there.

Inside the folder was an envelope containing the photograph she'd found in the bottom of the box with Granny's things. It was of a very young man, thick fair hair sleeked back, a joyous expression in his sparkling eyes. The photo caught him leaning over a stone wall with his head resting on his forearm. There was no name, yet somehow she knew. The young man looked very like her Grandfather Gerald, but he wasn't Gerald. He must be Rafe.

Over the past three months, Lucy had tried to make sense of

her father's investigations but she'd ended up finding out more about Tom Cardwell than about his Uncle Rafe.

'Did you know about Rafe?' she asked her mother on a weekend visit in March.

Following the divorce, Gabriella had decamped to a small cottage in North Norfolk where she painted great abstract canvases that didn't sell, and more conventional sea scenes that paid her living expenses. Gabriella actually seemed happier and calmer than she had for months. Lucy wondered whether a man named 'Lewin' who owned a local art gallery and whose name Gabriella would frequently drop into the conversation had something to do with this, and if so she was glad. Still in her late fifties, Gabriella Cardwell deserved a little happiness.

'No. Your father was so secretive,' Gabriella said, caressing her beautiful long-haired tabby cat. 'Not like Lewin. We talk about everything.' Lucy was familiar with this line of argument. 'Your father had such a strait-laced upbringing, you see. Those public schools are responsible for so much, and as for his mother – oh . . . a nightmare, so possessive. I saw right away what she thought of me. But despite our differences Tom and I were so happy together, Lucy. So very happy.' She looked appealingly at her daughter.

'I know, Mum,' Lucy said gently.

'It was only when your granny died, and then you left to go to college – not that I blame you, of course, darling – that he sort of changed, got awfully depressed. It was grief, I suppose. Still, we'd have pulled through if that cow hadn't come along.' She cast her eyes to the south, as though Helena, sitting tight amidst her neutral decor in Suffolk, might, even at this distance, be scorched by her vitriol.

Lucy tried to move the conversation forward. 'But he never mentioned his Uncle Rafe?' she said.

'Not a thing. Grandad Gerald was unwell in his later years and he didn't make much sense. I remember that he'd lived in India as a child, because as I told you, I had that wonderful year at the ashram before I met your father, but I didn't know there'd been a younger brother.'

Now, recalling this conversation, Lucy put away the photograph and her notes, picked up her bag and her camera and went downstairs, thinking she'd look round the town. Cara was vacuuming the lobby, but nodded encouragement when Lucy picked up a free tourist map from a pile on the desk.

She walked the tangled streets and looked at the harbour, breathing in the pungent smells of oil and paint and wet rope, and trying to imagine what the place would have been like between the wars. Not so chocolate-boxy for a start. No Spindrift Gift Shop or Surf Girls boutique with pop music blaring; rather, it must have been an ordinary working town with grocer's shops and a baker and boarding-house ladies and fishermen's nets drying in the sun. The parish church would be the same one and might have some memorials, but there wasn't really a graveyard, and when she tried the oak door she found the building locked.

The small museum she came across in one of the back streets might be useful, but the notice on the door said it was closed between noon and 2 p.m., and she was a minute or two too late.

Eventually Lucy bought herself a bag of crisps and a flapjack for lunch and sat on the quay wall to eat, looking at her surroundings and absent-mindedly composing a few photographs. She felt at peace here, thinking how she was connected to the place yet was not of it. No one knew she was here – except Will, of course – and no one was making any demands of her. Her eye was drawn to the boats in the harbour. The tide was surging, and half a dozen small craft bobbed safely within the embracing walls. Along one jetty, a tanned, broad-shouldered young man was tying up his sailing boat – a particularly pretty craft, Lucy thought, with a white cabin and its hull painted the exact pale blue of a robin's egg. A very suitable colour seeing that *Early Bird* was inscribed on its stern. She thought it the perfect foreground for a shot of the harbour.

When the boat was secure, she watched the man step down into it and set about tidying up. She didn't know anything at all about boats but liked the idea of riding the wind and the waves, and being close to the elements. The man fixed a cover across the cabin roof, then slung a kitbag over his shoulder and strolled along the jetty towards her. As he passed they smiled at one another. He had short reddish-brown hair, blue eyes with fair lashes, and a strong, open face.

She finished the flapjack and dropped the wrapping into a bin. All right, so she didn't know what she would do here, but something would turn up, she felt sure. The light was perfect. She began to take some pictures.

The St Florian museum opened again at two, and when Lucy pushed open the door, a man with a grizzled beard looked up from packing tourist brochures into a revolving stand and greeted her.

'Hello,' she replied. 'Is it all right to look round?'

'Of course,' he said, looking at her over his spectacles. 'That's what we're here for. There's no entrance charge – we rely on donations.' He indicated a collection box on the counter. 'There's just the two rooms. We used to be a sweet shop, by the way.'

Lucy fished out her purse and dropped some coins in the box. She could easily imagine the shelves in the bow window being full of jars of candy where now they displayed pretty stones and shells. There was also a small selection of Second World War memorabilia – a gas mask, a ration book, an evacuee's teddy bear.

'Was there anything in particular you wanted to see?' the curator asked. 'The war exhibition is in the back room, and we've *Life of a Victorian Fisherman* as the spring exhibition over there. People are always bringing things in, so we often have a change of focus.'

'I was wondering, do you have anything about Carlyon?' Lucy asked.

'The old manor house?' he said. 'You know it's just a ruin now?'

'Yes, it's so sad. What happened?'

'The fire? I believe it was soon after the war. What's your interest?'

'My grandmother was brought up there. Her name was Angelina Wincanton before she married.'

'She was a Wincanton, was she? Now that was a well-known local name. I thought they must have died out.'

'They practically have,' Lucy said, with a rueful smile. 'Of my generation, there are some second cousins in New Zealand I've never met – and me. My name's Lucy, by the way. Lucy Cardwell.'

'I'm Simon Vine,' he said. 'I don't really have much about the house, to be honest, though there might be something in the storeroom. What precisely were you looking for?'

'Anything to do with the Wincantons, really.'

'Let me see,' Simon said. 'I'm trying to think who I know who might help you, but there really isn't anyone . . . ah. That lady who came in recently – what on earth was her name? Wait a moment and I'll check.'

He went away into the back room where she heard a door open. She followed him to look at the war display. There was more of the kind of thing she'd seen in the window: old clothes coupons, a letter from a soldier to his girlfriend, a black and white photograph of a concrete look-out post, behind which a beach was littered with spirals of barbed wire.

After a few minutes Simon Vine returned, carrying two flat wooden boxes with glass tops. 'Here we are,' he said, putting them in front of her on the desk.

'Oh,' said Lucy, looking with puzzlement. 'They're amazing.' Each box contained an array of insects pinned on to cork: butterflies, their wings as brightly patterned as the day they were mounted; different kinds of moth, a huge beetle – all carefully labelled with tiny strips of paper. 'How does this help me?' she asked.

'The lady brought them in a few months ago. She said she'd caught them round here when she was a girl, so we have a snapshot of natural history from the 1930s, which is rather fascinating. I imagine she'd have some useful stories to tell you. I wrote her name and address down somewhere.' He pulled a foolscap notebook from a drawer in the counter and started hunting through it. 'I bump into her occasionally and I can never remember her name but she always remembers mine, though she must be well over eighty. Hold on.' He checked a label stuck on one of the boxes and flipped a few more pages. 'Here we are. Mrs Beatrice Ashton. And the house is on the road that leads to the cliff path. This lady will certainly be able to tell you about this place before the war.'

'Beatrice Ashton?' Had she heard him correctly?

'Yes. I'll tell you what – are you staying in Saint Florian?'

'Yes, at the Mermaid.'

'Why don't I call in on her on my way home this evening and ask if she'll see you.'

Lucy left the museum and its curator, hardly believing her luck. Beatrice Ashton. Surely the name wasn't a coincidence. Who could she be? Rafe's wife or some other relative? She'd written down Simon Vine's directions to Mrs Ashton's house carefully, her mind awhirl.

She spent the rest of the afternoon exploring the town before returning to the hotel. It felt odd being on her own on a Saturday night, without anything definite to do. Back in her room she slept for a little, then ate an early supper in the hotel bar. She enquired of Cara, but there was no message from a Mrs Ashton. After a last look at the harbour, she went to bed early to read.

At half-past nine Will rang her. 'Oh, you do get a signal there,' he said. 'I tried earlier.'

'What time did you get back?' she asked him.

'About five. Look, Lucy, I'm worried about you. I shouldn't have left you like that.'

'I'm not sure I gave you much choice. And there's no need to be worried, really.' She explained about the possibility of meeting Beatrice Ashton, but he brushed it aside.

'How long will you be there?' he asked.

'I don't know, Will, I just don't.'

He made an impatient sound. 'Well, let me know, and I'll come down and collect you.'

'There's no need for that. You'd be exhausted. I can get a train.'

'Lucy, I insist.'

'Seriously, Will, I don't want you to.'

'I'll ring tomorrow,' he said. 'And see how you're getting on.'

When he'd rung off, she felt angry. She could look after herself. Why was he doing this? She didn't want the pressure; it stopped her feeling free. She bit her lip, thinking, then switched off the phone in case he rang again.

Chapter 4

Lucy heard a distant cry. She'd climbed a steep flight of stone steps and paused at the top to catch her breath, listening to the sound of Sunday church bells. The Rowans, she saw, was set in the hillside before her, half-screened by a privet hedge. High above, a seagull coasted in slow, rhythmic arcs. It cried out again, like a warning.

That morning, after breakfast, Cara had handed her a white envelope, brought by Simon Vine, with *Miss Lucy Cardwell* written on it in black italics. Inside, a short note on thick cartridge paper suggested that she call on Beatrice Ashton at three o'clock that afternoon.

It was five to three. As Lucy pushed open the garden gate, she found herself in a secluded garden. The Rowans was a fine semi-detached house with a white and blue painted frontage and an enclosed glass porch. Patches of spring flowers, saffron, indigo and china white, studded a neat lawn.

NO HAWKERS, NO COLD CALLERS proclaimed a sticker on the front door. Beneath a circle of mullioned glass and a small security spyhole, an iron lion's head snarled. Lucy lifted the ring in its teeth, tapped several times and waited.

The door rattled then sprang ajar, and a pair of brown eyes in a wrinkled face peeped out. The frail hand clutching the door jamb was studded with jewels. 'Lucy Cardwell, is it?'

The woman's voice was musical and strong, the consonants perfectly pronounced.

'Yes.'

Beatrice opened the door to admit her. 'I'm delighted you're punctual. It's not a virtue much in fashion today.'

'Thank you for seeing me,' Lucy said politely.

Beatrice Ashton shut the door and leaned against it as she looked Lucy over, not rudely but with curiosity. She was shorter than Lucy, and slight, with waves of silvery-white hair pinned up at the back in a gold clasp, and regular features in a grave, oval face with a pointed chin. Lucy had the vaguest of feelings that she'd seen her before.

They were in a gloomy hallway where a feeble ceiling lamp struggled to illuminate the dark wood panelling and dingy carpet. In here, it was difficult to believe that it was sunny outside. From the shadow of the staircase a grandfather clock uttered three sombre chimes.

'In here.' Moving slowly, Mrs Ashton led Lucy into a comfortable sitting room where a fire burned in the grate. She went and stood by the french windows. Outside was a small wilderness of back garden, with the hillside rising beyond and the pine trees, with their rooks' nests, filling the strip of sky. On the terrace a couple of blackbirds capered in a birdbath, fluttering water up all around.

'I've been watching these silly creatures,' Mrs Ashton said, smiling. 'They're acting up for us, the little blighters.' She tapped lightly on the glass and the birds startled up but, seeing no danger, resumed their game. 'They know they have an audience. We always have an audience, don't we?'

'How do you mean?' Lucy asked.

'There's always someone to watch us and criticize.' Mrs Ashton, intent on the birds, was bathed in a thin shaft of afternoon light, and Lucy found herself doing exactly what the woman complained of, watching her critically. She must be very old, getting on for ninety and she was well-dressed, in a pale-blue cashmere cardigan and light-grey trousers. A touch of face powder and pink lipstick completed the effect, whilst her flecked nails gleamed with clear varnish.

Mrs Ashton turned to face her and Lucy caught a floral fragrance. It was like opening a door into a past world, a world of golden summer afternoons and teas on the lawn.

'You don't remember me, do you?' Mrs Ashton asked.

'No, I don't.' Though . . .

'Never mind,' the woman said, almost to herself.

'Have you lived in this house long? Mr Vine said you lived in Saint Florian as a child.' Lucy glanced about at the prints of English landscapes, at the pair of faded armchairs before the painted mantelpiece, at the *Daily Telegraph* lying on a side-table, folded to the crossword, a spectacle case beside it. All these and the carriage clock on the mantelpiece might have been there long ago. But some things marked change. A digital telephone sat in its cradle, and on the coffee-table near the dancing flames was a tray with mugs rather than teacups, and a flask with a modern flower pattern. There were touches of the exotic, too – an Orthodox icon on the mantelpiece, African wood carvings. An abstract painting glowed like a jewel in an alcove.

'This was my home when I was a child. My father left it to me when he died, some years ago now, and later I lost my husband. It was time to come back. Lucy.' Mrs Ashton looked up into Lucy's face and the young woman saw toughness there, and pain. 'Tell me why you've come.'

'It's about my father, Tom Cardwell. I don't know if you knew him at all, but he was a Wincanton. He . . . he died recently.'

'I know,' Beatrice whispered. 'Your great-aunt told me. However, only a few months ago.'

'Aunt Hetty? So you do know the Wincantons. Mrs Ashton, you must be something to do with Rafe. I've been trying to find out about him. My father was very interested in him, you see. And I don't know why.'

Beatrice inclined her head gravely. 'I can tell you everything. I very much want to explain things to you, but, you see, it's difficult. You turning up like this – it's a shock.'

'I'm sorry,' Lucy said contritely, by now utterly bewildered. 'I had no intention of causing any trouble.'

'I know you didn't. Don't worry, my dear. The situation is not of your making.'

'You asked if I remember you. Well, I don't, not really. But it sounds as though you knew my father?'

Mrs Ashton stared out of the window as if at something beyond the garden. Finally she said, 'I knew Tommy as a baby. After that, I . . . lost touch with your grandparents.' She frowned and added, with some effort, 'Until Angelina's funeral. I saw you there.'

Her face was so full of anguish Lucy asked, 'Mrs Ashton, are you all right?'

'Yes, yes, of course I am.' She suddenly smiled at Lucy. 'So here you are, Tom's daughter. My dear, it's quite astonishing that you have Angelina's lovely hair.'

Lucy said, 'Thank you. Mum is fair, too. It was always a joke Mum hated, that Dad married late and to someone who looked like his mother.'

'It's not the kind of joke I would find funny.'

'No, exactly.'

'It must have been an awful shock to lose Tom. It was for me, but much worse for you. Your father—'

'Mrs Ashton, I'm a bit confused. How did you know my grandmother? And Rafe. I'm sorry if this sounds unkind in any way, but my family didn't ever mention Rafe and I don't know why. But Dad spent some time before he died trying to find out about him.'

'Rafe was my husband.'

'Oh. And the Wincantons, how did you know them? I'm so sorry if I sound rude asking all these questions.'

'Not at all,' Beatrice said sadly. 'You have every right to ask them. I met the Wincanton family here in Saint Florian when we were children.' Here she smiled, and Lucy had a sudden sense of her as a young girl. 'I first met Rafe on the beach.'

On the beach. Lucy remembered a photograph of girls on a beach in Granny's box, and the one on the croquet lawn with the four Wincanton children and the slight dark girl. It struck her now that Beatrice might have been that girl.

'My name was Marlow then,' said Beatrice. 'Now, why don't we sit down?'

She settled herself in the armchair by the fire that faced the garden and Lucy took the one opposite. She was thinking that this was one of the strangest conversations that she'd had in her life, but very thrilling.

'My help Mrs P. left us tea,' Beatrice said. 'You wouldn't be a dear and pour, would you? I'm not as steady as I was.'

'Of course,' Lucy said, reaching for the flask.

Beatrice pushed a plate of shortbread towards her and said, 'I gather you're staying at the Mermaid. Are you here long?'

'A few days, probably. It's a bit unplanned.' Lucy gathered up her strength. 'Mrs Ashton, I feel I haven't explained myself very well. I came because of a mystery. Dad, before he died, was on a quest. As I say, I don't think he knew anything about his Uncle Rafe until recently, and he became obsessed with finding out about him. I don't know why, but my great-uncle wasn't ever mentioned at all at home and I never saw any pictures of him. Until I found this.' She put her hand into her bag and brought out an envelope. 'Mrs Ashton, is this Rafe?' She passed across the photograph of the boy leaning on the wall.

Beatrice took it and sat absorbed, her face softening. When she reached to give it back to Lucy, the girl saw that her eyes were watery.

'Yes,' she said. 'That's Rafe.'

Lucy sighed. 'Mrs Ashton, would you tell me what happened to Rafe?'

'I can, but it's a long story. I'm not surprised your father was so interested.'

'I don't know what set him off. He loved reading about the Second World War, certainly. He left a whole lot of notes, and boxes of memorabilia belonging to my grandmother. That's why I thought to come here, to see whether I could find out more. The whole thing had clearly been bothering Dad at some level, you see, and I just wanted to try to understand.'

Beatrice said, almost to herself, 'He'd have been too young to remember.'

'To remember Rafe?'

'Yes, and what happened. No, this is silly of me. I'm telling everything in the wrong order.'

'What do you mean, Mrs Ashton?'

'Why don't you call me Beatrice?'

'Beatrice. What wouldn't Dad have remembered?'

Beatrice opened her mouth to speak, but no words came.

Lucy decided to try another tack. 'Mrs Ashton – sorry, Beatrice – I followed up Dad's notes and found out that he'd investigated the War Intelligence archives.'

At this, Beatrice Ashton sat up straight in her chair, looking alert and rather terrifying. Seeing she'd struck a nerve, Lucy went on, 'Dad had found out that Rafe had been in Special Operations during the war – you know, helping the French Resistance or something. Anyway, I don't know exactly how he made the links but he looked up Rafe's file.'

'Rafe's file? Did he find it? What did it say?' the old woman demanded.

'Well, that's just it. He did find it, but it had nothing in it. Nothing in it at all.'

Beatrice sank back in her chair and closed her eyes. Her tone still sharp, she said, 'I'm not surprised that it was empty. They never wanted everyone to know. Too much blame.'

'What do you mean?' Lucy asked patiently. 'I thought all the war files were supposed to be open now. Don't we have a right to know?'

Beatrice's eyes flew open. 'Oh, this "right to know" business! Your generation has no idea how close this country came to disaster and how important it was to keep things secret.'

'I do. I've read about it.'

'Then you'll know of how little importance we were as individuals. Sacrifices had to be made. Sacrifices, yes. We had to put our country before everything, some of us. Before our families and friends.' Her eyes danced black, angry.

Lucy felt lost suddenly, questions and answers writhing around in her mind. She wondered whether Mrs Ashton wasn't muddled in her head.

'I'm tired now,' Beatrice said suddenly, and indeed she did look tired: strained and exhausted. 'There's too much to think about. You'd better come back tomorrow.' She started to push herself up from her chair, but Lucy stayed her.

'Don't worry. I'll see myself out,' she said. She was horrified that she'd made this old lady tired and upset, and indeed, was feeling upset herself. 'Can I get you anything?'

'No, thank you. Well, perhaps a glass of water.' She waved a vague hand. 'In the kitchen. Glasses in the cupboard over the fridge. Oh, and you'll see my pills. Bring them, too.'

Lucy went to investigate. The kitchen was modern and its cleanness emphasized by a dreadful stink of bleach. Lucy selected a glass. On one of the work surfaces was a tray, laid for supper. A note in blobby biro said *Bacon/egg pie and salad in fridge, yoghurt for afters*. A cocktail of pills lay on a saucer. Beatrice's must be a lonely life.

When she returned to the sitting room, Beatrice was lying back in her chair, her eyes closed, and this worried Lucy. She placed the water and the pills on the table to hand and was reassured when Beatrice opened her eyes and sat up.

'Thank you, dear.' She seemed gentle and frail suddenly. Watching Lucy collect her things she surprised her by saying, 'Promise me you'll come back in the morning, my dear? Promise?'

'Of course I will, if you don't think I'll upset you,' Lucy said softly. Beatrice did not reply, and Lucy thought she couldn't have heard. She was about to speak again when she realized Beatrice was struggling with emotion.

Eventually she said, 'I need to tell you the whole story. It's all quite a tangle and I hope I'll be able to tell it straight. But you've asked me about Rafe. Lucy, I loved Rafe Ashton. I loved him more than any man I've met before or since. His story is my story, too.'

Lucy was glad to stumble out into the warmth of the late-afternoon sunshine. In The Rowans, she had felt as if she'd been in another world, a world of the past. Beatrice Ashton had known her father and her grandmother, too. She'd been a friend of her grandmother and had known Tom Cardwell as a toddler, yet Lucy had never heard of her before. She took a deep breath of cool fresh air.

Outside in the lane she stopped to switch on her phone. There was only a message from work that she could deal with later. Nothing from Will. She stuffed the phone back in her bag and considered what to do next.

She glanced up towards the cliff path, where it snaked away into the distance. There was a light breeze blowing off the sea, bringing with it lovely harboury smells. The view was breathtaking up here, of the long headlands protecting the bay, and of the sea. Little waves broke the surface here and there – as a child, she'd been told they were the manes of horses. In the far distance, the bright sky met a bright sea dotted with white sheets of sail.

As she descended to the harbour via the perilous Jacob's Ladder, she thought again about Beatrice Ashton. She'd been drawn to the woman, had sensed warmth and sincerity. There had been a . . . tenderness about her. But steel, too. The woman was terribly bitter about something. Lucy felt a connection. Perhaps she sensed the young girl that Beatrice had once been.

After Lucy had gone, Beatrice Ashton swallowed two pills and sipped some water, then lay back in her chair, waiting for her heartbeat to steady. Her eyes were closed, but she wasn't asleep. Her mind was too active for that. She was thinking about Lucy Cardwell and everything her visit meant. She was lovely, Lucy, with that honey hair, the stubborn chin and the turned-up nose, scattered with freckles. Hers was a beauty of character and strength, not a painted-on prettiness. She looked forward to seeing her again.

Lucy was assured, like many of these modern girls, but there was something a little untried about her, too – uncertain, unbroken. Perhaps something still had to work its way out. Of course, it used to be that bad things happened in families – dreadful things – and everybody shut up and put up with it. None of this talking about it like today. And yet she rather envied them their closeness, today's parents with their children.

She remembered, only yesterday, coming out of her gate to see a tourist with his little daughter on their way up to the cliff path and she'd had a sudden glimpse of herself at the same age, nine or ten. She'd never held her father's hand in that possessive way this little girl did. And he seemed so natural with the girl, explaining something or other patiently to her. Beatrice's parents had mostly spoken to her to give her instructions.

She breathed deeply to calm herself, and was sure the scent of old roses floated in the air. Funny how the house still smelt of them. They had been her mother's favourite: climbing roses round the house and bowls of dried petals in every room. Perhaps the smell had got into the wood. She opened her eyes, for a moment confused not to see the room as it had been long ago, when she was a child, the china shepherdess on the mantelpiece, her mother's French library books neatly piled on the coffee-table, her father's walking stick near the fire, the big wireless where the television stood now.

Perhaps she should never have come back here, should have stayed in Paris after her husband died, but she had never sold the place after her father had left it to her, and the long-standing tenant had moved out and it seemed the right time. She'd just felt a terrific yearning to return to this place where, as a child, she'd been so happy. She'd thought she'd find a kind of peace here, too, but she hadn't, not really. She was aware of the ruin of Carlyon Manor, high above the town, and remembered too much. She'd been made to keep so many secrets and they'd festered. Still, the people involved were mostly dead now. Except Hetty Wincanton, and Peter. There was no real reason to sit like a dragon on its gold.

And now the girl had come, wanting to know things, and she deserved to, though it might be painful for them both. Beatrice smiled without humour. She'd tried to tell some of her story once, after the war, but no one had been interested in the truth then. They'd twisted her words against her. She'd seen what had happened to some of the others who'd spoken out, how they'd been pilloried in the newspapers. But now that so much time had passed and the people with reputations to protect were all dead, there was more genuine interest in uncovering the truth. And yet it wasn't so simple. It was more personal than that.

There were dark places in her mind where she couldn't go, even now. She was frightened of her feelings. *But the truth, Beatrice*, she told herself. The truth was always best. Time was a river, so the poet said, the past flowing on into the future. Her past was dammed in a stagnant pool.

She pushed herself up out of her chair and crossed to the window. Her feet were painful today, as if they, too, remembered. The birds had gone from the drinking bowl, but the carefree sound of their song was all around. That's what she'd loved most, living here as a child – the cries of the birds and the sound of the sea: swishing over the sand, smashing against the cliffs, sucking itself out of secret caves and crevices. It spoke to her spirit.

Lucy walked out along one arm of the harbour as far as she could go and stared out to sea. It was a calm evening and the water shone sleek and opaque now the sun was low in the sky.

She turned to look at the town, spread across the hillside. Far along the cliff she looked for the ruins of Carlyon Manor, but they were hidden by greenery. She remembered what Beatrice had said, so passionately, about her feelings for Rafe. Such a long time ago. A love that survived his death. She tried to imagine feeling like that about someone. She never had, and couldn't imagine that she ever would.

Later, at the Mermaid, she took a history of the Second World War downstairs with her and ordered a drink and fishcakes from the cheerful woman behind the bar, who looked as though she might be Cara's mother. At a table across the room, facing her, a man was making his way through a large helping of cottage pie, engrossed in a magazine. His hair glinted reddish-brown and she observed his slow, careful movements as he ate. When Cara's mother took him a beer he looked up and Lucy realized it was the man she'd seen the day before on the boat *Early Bird*. She liked his tanned face, the cropped hair and the very blue eyes that crinkled up when he laughed at something the woman said. There was energy and strength in every movement. She wondered about him – whether he was staying at the hotel, like her, or maybe he lived in Saint Florian.

He finished his meal and as he walked past on his way out, she tried to see what the magazine was, playing her private game of working people out by what they read. Current affairs, of some sort. She glanced up at him and he gave her his friendly smile. 'Hello again,' he said.

'Hi,' she managed to reply. After he'd gone she read her book for a bit as she ate, then went up to her room. A film she'd helped make was on one of the minor channels, a love story set in wartime France. She remembered how she'd been interested in the real-life episode on which it was based. After watching it for a while she took a shower and investigated the pile of neatly ironed washing that lay on the bed. When she shook out the clean nightdress, a fragrance of roses filled the air.

Beatrice opened the ancient photograph album as she and Lucy sat together at the dining-table the next morning. 'There, that's my father, Hugh Marlow,' she said. The picture was of a young man in a suit and cravat, with a moustache and an intense expression. 'And here's my parents' wedding in 1919.' Hugh, still in military uniform, stood proudly beside a neat, dark girl dressed in white lace.

'Your mother? What was her name?' Lucy asked.

'Delphine. She was French.'

'She was pretty. Where was it taken?'

'Near Etretat on the Normandy coast – do you know it?'

'I've heard of it, that's all.'

'It's famous for its white cliffs, like the ones at Dover. Monet painted them. When I was born in 1922, it was still a small village. My father, a Lieutentant with the Gloucestershire Rifles, was wounded in France near the end of the Great War and sent to a hospital near Etretat. The injury to his shoulder healed fairly easily. It was the lungful of mustard gas that affected him for the rest of his life.'

Beatrice smiled. 'I often used to imagine their first meeting. My mother said he would sit in the hospital grounds when the weather was fine and she noticed how he perked up whenever he saw her delivering fruit and vegetables in a horse-drawn cart. She was the daughter of a local landowner, you see. It's so strange to think about one's parents being young and in love, isn't it?'

'My parents met when Mum's boyfriend's motorbike broke down on the way back from a rock festival. Dad was passing and gave her a lift in this really smart car,' Lucy said. 'He was quite a few years older than her, and wore a suit, and she thought he was pretty cool.'

Beatrice looked delighted at this idea and it was a moment before she returned to her story. 'One January morning in 1919 my mother brought a bucket of early daffodils along with the fruit and veg, but while she was hefting the thing out of the cart, something spooked the pony, the cart jerked forward and flowers and water flew out everywhere. My father staggered over to rescue her. She said she didn't know who must have looked worse – she soaked through and weeping, or he, in bandages and pyjamas, trying to steady the horse. Not a very romantic start, was it? Though I don't know that they were a very romantic couple.'

'That's something my mum complained about – that Dad never did anything romantic. I don't think it was the way he was. But that didn't mean he didn't care.'

'Of course not,' Beatrice said. 'Anyway, they married a few months later. When my father relayed news of his engagement to his parents, there was quite a hoo-ha. Why? Well, for a start my mother was French and a Catholic, and that was bad enough in their eyes. Then, although his family were landowning farmers themselves, somehow Grandfather Marlow didn't consider the fields of Normandy to be as superior as the Marlows' rolling estates in the Cotswolds. My father wasn't the firstborn son and heir, but my grandfather was a controlling sort of man, and the marriage created a rift between them.'

She reached for the fragile album and turned the page. Lucy found herself looking at a traditional French farmhouse with chickens and a dog in a muddy yard. 'That's my Normandy grandparents' house. For a while my father was happy to stay and help out with the farmwork, but the damage to his lungs was significant, and he found it too much for him. As a small child I was carted to and fro across the Channel as my parents tried to find somewhere he could feel settled, with work he could do. I can't imagine what stress it put on my poor mother, she always having to be the cheerful one and buck up my father.'

'And these are your French relations?' Lucy pointed to another photograph, of a family group.

'Yes, these two here are Gran'mère and Pappi. Pappi looks a bit fierce with that beard, doesn't he? He was a kind man, really. Gran'mère was one of those very capable people and she had a lot to be capable about, what with six children and the farm. These three men were my uncles, and the little girls my cousins, Thérèse and Irène. They were a few years older than me, so I was the baby.'

Beatrice then showed Lucy a photograph of Delphine standing next to a dainty little girl with thick dark hair and a shy demeanour. It had been taken in front of The Rowans.

'There, that's me.'

'You looked very like your mother.'

'Yes, I suppose I did. Moving here to Saint Florian, when I was ten, was their final attempt at a new start. My father had got some idea that he would be a writer, and a friend recommended Cornwall as a cheap place to live. They bought this house with Marlow money. Of course, he had to do something else while he made his name, so he scandalized his parents further by taking a job as a clerk in a bank at Saint Austell, and was glad to have it, given the number of people out of work. I have to say, though, that the comedown dented his pride and certainly his temper.'

Beatrice turned another page in the album. An important-looking old man in plus-fours posed by a field of cows. 'That's

Grandfather Marlow,' she said. 'He sent my father a cheque every month. It wasn't so much the cheque – after all, we were always grateful for the money – as the patronizing letter that accompanied it which annoyed my father so much. My mother, who was family-minded, made a point of taking me to visit the Marlows occasionally, which was good of her considering how condescending they could be. And in deference to them, my religious upbringing was a very odd mixture of Anglican and Catholic. She was quite a pragmatist, my mother.'

'It must all have been very confusing for you,' Lucy said. 'That, and moving around, I mean.'

'Oh, I never settled properly till we came to Saint Florian. I went to a local school in Normandy, but not for long enough periods to make friends. When we moved here, I went to a governess with some other girls. I could never invite them round to play, as my father hated noise of any sort. So a lot of the time there was just me – oh, and here's dear old Jinx, my father's dog.'

'Is he a fox terrier?' Lucy said, looking closely at the faded photograph.

'A wire-hair, that's right. Then in the summer of 1935, when I was twelve, the Wincantons came to live at Carlyon, and every-thing changed. This is Carlyon dreaming in the sun. I took it with my Box Brownie.'

And now Beatrice took off her spectacles and leant back in her chair. Her face wore a faraway expression as though she was looking deep into the past.

Chapter 5

Cornwall, July 1935

She'd watched the strange children from the moment they appeared that morning, but they didn't see her at first. Or perhaps they did but were too absorbed in their own company to care about a skinny twelve-year-old girl in a home-made cotton blouse and shorts as she lurked shy as a bird's shadow amongst the boulders and the tidal pools.

She had been lying on her stomach, staring into a pool where fairy fronds of lime and scarlet weed gently undulated and fish darted like shards of crystal. Along the sandy bottom staggered a pink-shelled crab. There was a miniature cave in the rock, scooped out by the sea, and decorated with barnacles and exquisite curled winkles. It might serve as a palace for a tiny mermaid. A sea palace! Beatrice imagined herself very small, with a glittery tail, swimming down with the fish to shelter amongst the snowy pinnacles and the tender anemones. How happy she would be, riding the white seahorses with their coiled tails . . .

A hyphen of electric blue shot out from the cave and pulled her out of her delicious day-dream. One scoop of her net and a moment later the tiny fish was zigzagging round her bucket above a hermit crab and a giant limpet she'd captured in earlier raids.

A shout echoed from somewhere up the beach. She whipped round to see the elder boy come first, leaping out of the dunes, screeching like the Riviera Express, towel, shorts, jersey and shoes all flung to the ground in a heap as he ran down the beach in his drawers. White dune dust flew from his heels, then he gained the harder sand of the foreshore and sprinted on and on, into the wind, towards the sea. Perhaps he imagined the cheers of spectators, for when he finally splashed into the shallows he punched the air in a triumphant gesture then turned as if to an audience, panting, hands on hips.

Now came the others, the younger boy dark and thin where the elder was fair and hearty, struggling out of clothes and sandals. Then he, too, was running, imprinting his own, lighter footprints on the sand, careful always to avoid his brother's firm ones. Next, a sturdy brown-haired girl of perhaps six or seven in a swimming costume. She jumped from a dune, fell, picked herself up, crying uselessly to the boys to wait, then dashed off down the beach after them. Finally there appeared the older girl, straw sunhat in hand, her movements dreamy, serene, her long gold hair blowing out behind like a heroine in a thousand legends and Beatrice, watching, held her breath. The girl picked her way barefoot across the grassy hillocks with self-absorbed grace. Her journey to the sea was winding, for she kept stopping to pin back her hair, examine shells, or simply to whirl about in the wind. Beatrice stared at her, amazed, thinking she'd never seen such a beautiful creature. Reaching the water's edge, where the smallest child waded, the golden girl knotted up the skirt of her dress before paddling in the shallows and waving at the boys, who were already capering far out among the breakers.

'Edward, Peter.' Her cry carried to Beatrice on the wind, bouncing off the cliffs, echoing around. 'Mummy said . . .'

Beatrice couldn't make out what Mummy had said but imagined it to be something about not going out too far. But the boys dived like dolphins under the waves and kicked spray at one another and ignored their sister who gave up after a bit and instead helped the smaller girl draw pictures on the sand with driftwood. Beatrice returned to her pool and concentrated on levering a blood-coloured anemone away from a rock.

'Hello there!'

When she looked up again, the golden girl was coming towards her, glowing with life, her hair flying out everywhere. Beatrice rose to her feet, brushed sand from her shorts, and waited for the girl to reach the rocks.

'What are you doing?' the girl called, placing a bare foot on the lowest rock and craning her neck to see. 'Ouch. Can I come over?'

Beatrice looked down at her own sensibly sandalled feet and said doubtfully, 'If you want.' The golden girl plotted her way painfully across the barnacled rocks. She was like the mermaid in the story Beatrice often read, who was given human legs but condemned always to feel she walked on knives.

'Oh, you've got an an-em-one,' the girl cried, reaching her and peering into the pool. 'I love an-em-ones! Their mouths are like people's when they kiss you.'

Beatrice gazed at her in astonishment. She considered the talcum-powder pecks her English grandmother gave her and the smacking kisses from her French relations and thought their mouths were nothing like anemones. She hated it worst when people pinched her cheeks as though testing whether she was fat enough to eat. She imagined they must find her disappointingly scrawny.

The girl was talking away in a quite uninhibited fashion. 'I have to say an-em-one slowly because I nearly always call them anenomes. It's Greek. Mummy's name is Oenone and that's Greek too. Some people don't know how to say "In-ony", because it's spelt funny.' She laughed, her face open, happy. 'Edward, he's the biggest, does Greek at his school so he always says words right. I wish he wouldn't laugh at me, though. It's not my fault girls don't do Greek or Latin. I think it sounds more fun than boring old geography. At which Miss Simpkins says I just don't try. What about you?'

Beatrice was startled at this long, complicated speech, but managed to say, 'I like geography,' as she loved examining maps and saying the strange names of cities and rivers to herself, but sensing the girl's annoyance she added quickly, 'Well, some of the time.' She was torn, frightened of displeasing this extraordinary girl by disagreeing with her, but still sore from a recent misunderstanding when her mother believed her to have lied. 'Always tell the truth, *Béatrice*,' she had remonstrated in her accented English. 'Even if it makes trouble. Your integrity is the most valuable thing.'

She was relieved to see the girl was still smiling. Close up, Beatrice could see her large clear blue eyes and just the faintest smattering of freckles across her creamy skin. She must be the same age as herself, or slightly older – thirteen, perhaps – already tall, with long languorous limbs. She held herself confidently, too. Her shirt was tight across her chest, and when she crouched down to poke about in the bucket, there was something self-aware about the movement. 'I'm sorry, do I talk too much?' she said, her face now an appealing frown. 'Nanny says that empty vessels make most sound. Gosh, I say, look at that stripey fish. It's so pretty I could just eat it up. Not literally, of course. I mean, it's just a heavenly blue, don't you think? I love all animals but horses best of all.'

'Oh, so do I!' Beatrice couldn't help bursting out.

'Do you keep a horse? We have two, but they're Mummy's, though I'm allowed to ride Cloud. He's only a pony but it's quite true, Jezebel does bite. Cloud's name is Claud really, but Cloud is a grey – which means white – so it suits him so much better. Don't you agree?'

Before Beatrice could admit that, no, her family didn't have horses, nor was it likely they'd ever have one in a thousand years, a boy's deep voice called, 'Angie!' and she saw the other children hurrying towards them over the sand. They waited in a line, where the rocks began. The little girl said, 'Angie, you've got to come. Now.'

Edward, the eldest, who studied Greek, stood arms akimbo. He said, 'Good afternoon,' to Beatrice in a polite, very grown-up way. Then to Angie, 'I say, would you and Hetty go and get our shoes and things. I vote we go round to the other cove.' All five of them looked to where a passage of bare sand had opened up between the sea and the jagged rocks of the headland. 'I want to find that cave Daddy told us about.'

Peter, the next in age, was examining a small cut on his arm. When he glanced up at Beatrice his black eyes were expressionless, unreadable. She stepped back, flustered, and her foot knocked the bucket. 'Oh, watch out, silly,' cried Hetty. They all saw it rock then settle.

'What's your name?' Angie asked.

'Beatrice,' said Beatrice, pronouncing it the English way.

'Goodbye, Beatrice. Look, Hetty, stay here with the boys. I'll be quicker. You'd better not go without me, Ed,' she warned. She set off up the beach in the curious loping stride of someone not used to running. Hetty stared into Beatrice's pail and then up at her stolidly, before turning and following her brothers back to the shoreline. There Edward filled time by practising cartwheels on the sand and Peter hurled pebbles into the waves with what Beatrice considered excessive force. Up by the dune, good-natured Angie could be seen stuffing towels, clothes and shoes into a straw bag. She hurried back to her siblings and the four of them ambled over towards the other cove, not even turning to wave to Beatrice.

She'd visited the other cove with her parents, but had been repeatedly forbidden ever to go there by herself because it got covered up so quickly by the tide. It occurred to her now that she should have warned the children, but they were already too far away to hear.

She watched until they were out of sight, then turned back to her task, hauling her bucket over to the next big rockpool. There, three pretty pebbles gleamed in the depths and she almost forgot about the children as she fished these out one by one, thinking they'd look well in her collection box at home. Then she sat back against a boulder, took an apple and a greaseproof package out of a shoulder bag and ate ginger biscuits while she made notes in an exercise book about her afternoon's finds. She drew the fish and a picture of a mermaid swimming in the palace she'd imagined. Then she put away the notebook and spent some time fishing for a particularly elusive crab in a large shallow pool, the surface of which kept being ruffled by the breeze. It would be a good hour before she needed to return home to tea.

The sun crept across the sky. The tide was on the turn now. She could feel the tension of it, sucking and pulling in secret places under the rocks. She wondered idly where the other children had got to and whether they knew about incoming tides. Edward was older; she thought he must know. She'd wait for a while longer just to see, but she'd be in trouble if she were late home.

She stared over at the passage to the next cove. It was narrower than it had been. Every now and then, a wave would nearly reach the jagged black rocks of the headland. But then several would fall short and she'd decide she was being hasty.

Time to go. She swung her bag across her shoulder, lifted the bucket of sea creatures and the net and started up the beach, but each step was reluctant. When she reached the far side of the dunes and gained the path back to St Florian, something made her turn round. A cry, she was sure it was a cry. It might be one of the children. She couldn't go on, couldn't just leave them there in danger.

She left her things by the path and retraced her steps, but when she reached the place where the passage had been, she saw that the sea had nearly covered it. They hadn't come back. They'd be drowned.

She eyed the vicious rocks, imagining where her hands and feet could fit, and looked down in dismay at her soft hands. She wouldn't have to go very far – if she could just see the children and warn them . . . She placed her sandalled foot on the lowest ledge and began to climb.

Chapter 6

Oenone Wincanton, whose name was pronounced 'In-ony', came to tea with Beatrice's mother the next day. Beatrice skulked in the hall, listening at the door.

'Your daughter is obviously a tomboy. Ah, the dear thing, she sounds just how I used to be.' Angelina's mother gave a delicious rippling laugh and Beatrice couldn't help smiling. 'I had brothers, you see, and the things we used to get up to would simply make your blood freeze. That's why you must let me help. Don't worry, your little Beatrice will turn out beautifully with me, you'll see.'

Beatrice narrowed her eyes. What did Mrs Wincanton mean by help?

'But you know where we found her, *madame*,' she heard her mother say in her accented English. 'On the cliff! It makes my heart stop to think of it. Anything dangerous or daring and she cannot resist.'

When Beatrice had failed to return home the previous evening the Marlows had sounded the alarm. A search party found her as it was growing dark, clutching for dear life to a rocky overhang, unable to go either up or down, soaked by icy spray and terrified, while the Atlantic Ocean churned beneath. Oenone Wincanton had been with them.

'All your little girl would say was, she wanted to save the children. So plucky of her. No reason for her to have known

about the steps, of course. It's impossible to see them if you
don't know where to look.'

Beatrice knew now that a secret set of steps, cut into the
cliff, led up from the second cove to the grounds behind
Carlyon Manor. The Wincanton children had simply climbed
them and had been home safe and dry twenty minutes after
they'd disappeared from Beatrice's sight. How foolish she
felt.

She slumped against the panelling and hurt her elbow on a
shelf. 'Ow!'

'Who's there?' Her mother's heels tapped on the wooden
floor. Beatrice scrambled into the dining room just in time.

'*Béatrice*?' her mother's voice called into the hall.

'She's in there, the minx,' Cook said, appearing at the kitchen
door with a fresh pot of tea. She scowled at Beatrice.

'*O ma fille*,' Delphine Marlow said, scrutinizing the girl.
She never frowned – frowning caused wrinkles, she liked to
say – but Beatrice *felt* her frown. 'Run up and brush your hair,
mignonne. Madame Wincanton would like to see you.'

In the drawing room, Beatrice wasn't sure where to put
herself so she hovered by the fireplace, standing first on one
leg, then on the other, and peering at the visitor from under her
lashes. Oenone Wincanton looked Beatrice up and down with
an amused expression. She was so lovely and elegant, the girl
thought; you could see where Angie got her good looks. Mrs
Wincanton's hair was honey-coloured, but a couple of shades
darker than her daughter's, and piled up in an artless coil –
not fashionable at all, but beautiful all the same – and her eyes
were a pure blue, like pieces cut out of a sky. Beatrice realized
where she'd seen her before: racing a dainty bay mare across
the shoreline, with an older, soldierly-looking man on a great
black hunter in hot pursuit.

She wasn't wearing her riding habit today, but a trim tea costume in navy and white. Pearls gleamed at her ears and her throat. She laid down her cup and saucer and patted the sofa beside her. Beatrice shuffled over and slid onto the edge of it, her hands hot under her thighs until, seeing her mother's *moue* of displeasure, she took them out and folded them on her lap. The *moue* transformed itself into the faintest of smiles.

'Your mother tells me you like horses,' Mrs Wincanton said, her eyes merry. 'We have two. Perhaps you'd like to come and see them sometime?'

Beatrice glanced up at her mother for guidance. Her mother looked away. What was going on?

'What else do you like, Béatrice?' Mrs Wincanton pronounced it in the French way, as her mother did. 'Such a pretty name. Your mother says you do your lessons well.'

Beatrice recalled the disinfectant smell of the rooms above the dentist's surgery in the town, where Miss Tabitha Starling had been teaching her and two other local girls at a big round table in the window overlooking the back of the inn.

'I like natural history,' she said haltingly, not used to undivided adult attention.

'Ah yes, Angelina told me about your rockpools,' the woman replied. 'Very commendable. You speak French, of course, you lucky thing. And I gather your governess lived in Germany for a while before the war? I wish Angelina took more interest in languages. Now that would be useful. Miss Starling's lessons must have been rather pleasant.'

Their lessons – arithmetic, English, geography and history, with a little German and natural history thrown in – were interestingly taught but were occasionally interrupted by chilling screams of pain from the surgery. But now poor Miss Starling was ill with her nerves again, and with the start of the long summer holiday upon them, had decided to go and live with her widowed sister in Weston-super-Mare.

Mrs Wincanton pulled on a pair of white gloves and remarked, above Beatrice's head, 'Mrs Marlow, I imagine she'll do rather nicely. Speak to your husband about the matter and let me know what you decide. The sum involved will be quite modest, I assure you.'

Beatrice, bewildered, stumbled out a reply to Mrs Wincanton's, 'Goodbye, dear,' and trailed out behind them into the hall. Cook opened the front door, and beyond the garden gate could be glimpsed the sleek black wing of a motor car. After they'd watched it bear Mrs Wincanton away, Mrs Marlow touched Beatrice's hand and whispered, 'Well, *ma petite*, I can't think what your father will say.'

'Say about what, *maman*?' Beatrice asked. 'I don't understand.'

Her mother pressed her palms together, as though in prayer, though she wasn't outwardly a very religious woman. 'Mrs Wincanton would like you to go to Carlyon Manor every day to be a companion for her daughter Angelina.' She went on, 'You would join her and her little sister in their studies from September. A Miss Simpkins lives at the house and teaches every morning. The boys will naturally be away at school and Mrs Wincanton says Angelina needs the company of suitable girls of her own age. There is only one month between the two of you.'

'Oh!' She would be with Angelina. She could not think how to respond. What had she – thin, shy Beatrice – to offer lovely, golden Angelina? The girl seemed older than her; indeed, if her birthday was in August she was a whole school year ahead. If they were going to school, that is.

'I'll talk to your father', Mrs Marlow sighed. 'I hope he will agree.'

*   *   *

Days of argument followed.

'It is a marvellous opportunity for her,' Delphine would say.

'We'll be beholden to them,' Hugh would object. 'And she'll start expecting to live the high life.'

'Oh come, that's nonsense – not our little Béatrice,' she would counter.

Eventually Hugh Marlow gave way, astonished at his wife's unusual insistence.

It was early in July when Beatrice was first invited up to the house. Her mother went with her. Up the cliff path, then a short walk alongside a field of ripening corn to a lane that ran between stone hedges to the gates of Carlyon Manor. Beatrice yearned for the house until they rounded the bend of the drive, then there it was, a wide expanse of Cornish granite with diamond-hatched windows, high chimneys and a slate roof. They passed a croquet game, abandoned on the front lawn. As they neared the front door their footsteps slowed, and though she said nothing, Delphine held her daughter's hand more tightly.

A little maid with beady eyes, like a jenny wren, admitted them. 'The mistress is still out riding,' she told them, and showed them into the drawing room to wait. Beatrice, who had never been in a place so splendid, gazed at the sunlight dazzling off the electric chandeliers. The french windows stood open and beyond were lawns and flowerbeds and swaying trees.

'May I go out in the garden?' she asked her mother.

'No, *mon amour*, we are not invited,' said Mrs Marlow, tenderly brushing a lock of hair from her daughter's face. There was a great tarnished mirror over the fireplace and Beatrice wandered across to make faces in it, though she was barely tall enough to see. She noticed the carved mantelpiece itself and ran her fingers over the pattern of leaves and flowers and fruit, wondering at the warmth and smoothness of the wood. Then her keen eyes spotted a carved insect hidden amongst the petals of a flower. It was a bee, its wings spread wide, and so delicately wrought she could see the markings on them. She traced its shape with a fingertip, thinking that because it was so small perhaps she was the only one who had ever noticed it. When she took a step away from the mantelpiece, the bee could hardly be seen. She was still marvelling at this idea when the door opened and Mrs Wincanton, in riding breeches, burst into the room. She was breathing quickly and her colour was high.

'I am sorry, Mrs Marlow. It's so glorious out on the beach, I quite forgot the time.' She cast her hat and riding crop on a chair. Her bright gaze passed over Beatrice in her neat brown dress and black lace shoes, then she realized what she'd been looking at. 'Oh, have you found our little bee? I'll tell you the story about him.'

Mrs Wincanton pulled the bell-rope by the fireplace. Whatever the story she'd been going to tell, it was forgotten, for a sinister rumbling noise had started up somewhere above their heads. Beatrice and her mother looked at the ceiling in alarm, but Oenone Wincanton was unperturbed. When the jenny wren maid appeared she said, 'We'll have tea now, Brown. Would you take Miss Beatrice up to meet the children? I gather from the ghastly row that they are somewhere about?'

'Upstairs, mam, all of 'em. Miss Hetty's worriting the life out of that poor dog, and now the boys are playing skittles in the corry-dor. The butler's been up to speak to them twice about their behaviour, but they don't take no notice, mam.'

'Oh, never mind. I'll deal with them later. Boys will be boys,' Oenone said to no one in particular, with a little laugh. She gave Beatrice's shoulder a light pat and said, 'Go with Brown,

Beatrice. I'm sure you'll have a very nice time, whilst I speak to your mother.'

With a pleading look, ignored by her mother, Beatrice followed the little maid out to the hall and up a wide wooden staircase. At the top a long landing stretched right and left into darkness.

'Look out, miss!' Brown cried, and pulled her to the wall as a missile came hurtling out of the gloom and sent a pile of wooden objects crashing at the other end.

Roars filled the air: 'A triumph!' and 'Ed, you foul cheat. Your foot was over the line.' And then came the sound of a struggle. Brown's high voice piped above the general mayhem, 'Master Edward, Master Peter, get up, both of you, you've got a visitor.'

Edward appeared first, scrambling to his feet, wiping his arm across his perspiring face and laughing. 'Beatrice.' He reached for her hand and shook it heartily. 'I'm so sorry. I'm afraid you arrived at a bad moment. Pete, get up, will you, you storming great idiot.' Peter, still sprawled on the floor, muttered, 'Hello.'

Brown pulled herself up to her full four feet ten and said, 'You're to look after her, do you understand? Show her round. Now where's Miss Angie?'

Edward propelled Beatrice into a large untidy schoolroom with no carpet, overlooking the back garden, where the sea could be glimpsed sparkling beyond the trees. Here, too, all was chaos. At a table by the window, Angelina sat reading a crumpled magazine and eating an apple. A gramophone spat out scratchy dance music, and little Hetty, mousy hair flying, was on her hands and knees, chasing a large shuffling personage in and out of the table legs and shouting, 'Jacky, come here. Jacky!' It took Beatrice a moment to realize that Jacky was an Old English Sheepdog done up in a dress and bonnet. It looked up shamefaced at Beatrice, who felt a rush of pity. Hetty pushed past it, growling, and crawled over to Beatrice, showing gappy teeth. 'Guess what I am, guess what I am,' she shrieked.

'A dog?' Beatrice asked.

'Wrong. She's a crocodile,' delivered Peter, rolling his eyes. 'She's always a ruddy crocodile. She's obsessed by crocodiles.'

'No, I'm not. Today I'm an alligator,' Hetty shouted with indignation. 'And Nanny told you not to swear.'

'You're not an alligator, you're a little prig.'

'Oh, shut up, all of you!' Edward roared over Hetty's cry of rage. 'Can't you see you're terrifying poor Beatrice.'

'How can anyone get peace and quiet to read?' cried Angie, slapping her magazine shut and getting up from the table. 'Honestly, all of you. What must you think of us, Beatrice?' She smiled lazily, pushing back a wavy lock that had escaped from her plait, her large blue eyes dreamy.

A short stout woman in a navy uniform bustled in from the connecting room, her face half-hidden by the stack of board games she was carrying. 'Children,' she ordered, in a soft, cracked voice that was lined with steel. 'Too much noise. Your mother won't stand for it.'

'Mother won't care. Nanny, do stop fussing,' Edward said, with the casual confidence of the eldest son who could do no wrong. 'Look, we've got Beatrice.'

'Oh,' Nanny said, putting down the boxes on the table. 'So you're the one. Let me look at you.'

Everybody became quiet as she perused poor Beatrice, who felt her face flush. She twisted her arms together and looked down at her feet, trying to wish away the clumpy black shoes. Angie, she'd noticed, had pretty ballet slippers. Of course she would, no matter that the toes were worn. Beatrice felt no envy, just humility in the presence of beauty.

It was Angie who took pity on her, stepping forward to give her an awkward hug. She smelled deliciously of soap and apple. 'Don't mind the others,' Angie said. 'They've got no manners. I'm glad you've come. The boys are perfectly horrid, but it's awfully boring when they're away at school.'

'There's me,' shouted Hetty, in high dudgeon. 'I'm still here.' Peter made a grunting noise behind her.

Angie pressed her perfect lips together in a complicit smile that meant girls of six didn't count. Hetty, seeing it, gave an un-alligator-ish pout. Beatrice smiled back at Angie, feeling her heart open like a flower. Ed kicked a piece of chalk, which Peter stamped on. The dog sat down and began to scratch in a vulgar fashion.

'If everybody's finished,' Nanny said severely, 'you may show Beatrice round Carlyon.'

'The gardens first,' Ed said. 'We'll make Brown happy and take the skittles outside.'

'No, the kitchen. I'm hungry.' That was Hetty.

'You were very greedy at breakfast,' Nanny told her. 'You don't need anything else.'

'Let's take her to the cesspit,' Peter sang out.

'Don't be rude, Peter,' Angie replied. 'We'll go to the stables first, don't you think, Bea? I want to show you Cloud.'

'Yes, the stables,' echoed Beatrice. *Bea*. No one had ever given her a nickname before. She thought of the tiny wooden insect nestling in the carving in the drawing room, behind which was a story.

'Busy Bea,' said Hetty.

'Brown Bea,' said Peter, looking at Beatrice's dress.

'Bees aren't brown, Pete. Bumblebees are gold and black.'

'Some are brown,' Peter argued, glowering at his brother.

'Beatrice doesn't bumble, she's a honey bee, aren't you?' Angie took her by the hand.

'They're very brown.'

'Still, I think I like honey bees best,' she said.

'So do I,' said Beatrice.

It would be two months before lessons began in September. For Beatrice the time crawled. Once or twice over the summer she was invited up to the house and these were wonderful exhilarating times. Then came one baking hot day in early August when Angelina turned thirteen, and Beatrice was invited to a picnic on the beach, but everyone was out of sorts for some reason. She was confused to see that Angelina's eyes were red-rimmed, her lovely mouth turned down. Ed got them all playing cricket on the damp sand above the shoreline.

Peter performed a splendid catch. 'You're out, Angie,' he insisted, and the girl threw down the bat with a wail and marched up the beach to where Mrs Wincanton was packing away the picnic. Beatrice saw her cast herself in her mother's lap and Oenone hug her tight as she wept inconsolably.

Hetty saw Beatrice's puzzlement.

'Daddy was s'posed to come today,' she explained importantly, 'but he telephoned to say he isn't and that's why she's upset. Angie feels things very deeply, you know. That's what Mummy says. Nanny says it's bad for her to be overwrought. I don't know what that means, do you?'

'It means,' said Peter, pursuing the ball as it rolled past, 'that you're a sneak who listens in to grown-ups' conversations.'

'Shut up, Peter,' Hetty cried, and Peter pretended to shy the ball at her, then grabbed her instead and forced sand down her neck.

'Hey, pack it in, Pete,' Edward said, coming to rescue Hetty. Beatrice had often noticed that he was the peacemaker, effortlessly defusing tension.

By the time the others trooped up to fetch their towels to swim, the regulation hour for their food to settle having passed, Angie looked more cheerful. Beatrice overheard her tell Edward, 'Mummy says he might come next week instead.'

After the children had splashed in the waves for a while, they lay on their towels on the beach sharing bottles of home-made lemonade while behind them on the dunes their mother read a book.

'Bowl me a few balls in a moment, Pete?' Ed said.

'S'pose,' Pete said, grumpy.

'Don't you like cricket?' Beatrice asked him.

'It's all right,' Peter said, with a shrug.

She saw that being good at games came naturally to Edward. He was kind, too, and a natural leader, at ease with everybody and everything, the complete antithesis of poor Peter. She watched Peter's face, pinched and unhappy, when Angie questioned Edward about school, and Ed told them stories of cheats and swaggerers, of brutal initiation ceremonies and bullying masters. These were, she sensed, not things that happened to Edward, but she wondered if Peter knew about them all too well.

The following Saturday, Beatrice's mother said to her husband at breakfast, 'I hear Michael Wincanton is coming down from London this weekend. That will be lovely for the children.'

'Ah, our Honourable Member,' Hugh Marlow said, folding his newspaper in order to read an article about Germany's growing air force. 'I'd like the chance to ask him what he believes this Herr Hitler is up to. I don't think we can trust the fellow for a moment. What sort of a title is Führer anyway? Ridiculous nonsense.'

Beatrice said, 'Why doesn't Angie's father live at Carlyon Manor?'

'Don't speak with food in your mouth,' Delphine said. 'He does, but he often has to be in London. When one governs the country, there is little time for holidays.'

At last August turned to September, and now when Beatrice visited the house there were big leather trunks gaping hungrily in the boys' bedrooms, and Nanny and Brown sewing laundry labels on shirts or packing books and piles of ironed clothes. Whilst Ed practised kicking a rugby ball about the grounds, Peter went for walks on his own and grew listless. It wasn't hard to work out that he didn't enjoy school.

And suddenly, like the house martins that had nested under the eaves of Beatrice's bedroom all summer, they were gone.

Lessons started the following Monday.

As Angie had confided to Beatrice, Miss Simpkins wasn't a bad old stick, though plain of face and a little portly, it could not be denied, and her stockings tended to gather in frumpy folds on her thick ankles. She was kind, but her patience was not endless.

Angelina managed her well, making up for her own lamentable lack of interest in everything except drawing and music by being charming.

'I wish I were as clever as Beatrice,' she'd say, when their governess chided her for failing to rote learn her French verbs.

'Angelina, it's not cleverness, it's application you lack.'

'But I try and try and try. I *do*. And I think I've got them all in my head and they simply fly out again.'

'I would suggest that you hadn't learned them thoroughly the first time. Now try the written exercise again, and this time, remember what I told you. There's a pattern to the endings if you take the trouble to look for it.'

'It's not as if we'll ever need to speak Frog,' Angelina muttered. 'And it's utterly unfair that Beatrice knows it already.'

'Only the spoken language, dear, and she's not quite perfect there. Remember, I studied the language in *Paris*. She needs to work as hard as you do on the grammar. Now, girls, poor Hetty has been waiting ages to read to me, so please continue the work by yourselves then try the reflexive verbs.'

'They really aren't hard,' Beatrice told Angie at luncheon in the nursery. '*Je me suis couchée à huit heures*. It means I put myself to bed at eight.'

'Do you? Well, who else would do it for you?' Angie said sulkily. 'Don't you think it's so silly?'

'Angie, it doesn't matter whether it's silly or not, it just is like that. I'm only trying to help you.'

'I know. Good old Bea. I'm sorry. Will you forgive me? It must be awful to have to put up with someone as stupid as me.'

She would look so sorrowful, Beatrice always forgave her. Immediately and fully. If Angelina didn't smile at her, it was as though the sun had darkened.

And always there were the horses.

'Here you are again, miz, like a bad penny,' Harry, the weatherbeaten old groom grumbled as he carried another straw bale into Jezebel's stall and cut it open with his pocket-knife, but Beatrice saw he didn't really mind.

So often was she to be found in the stables, feeding Cloud handfuls of sweet hay, stroking his nose, that sometimes Harry saddled up the pony and let her sit on the beast whilst he led them round the cobbled yard on a long rope.

'Sit up, miz,' he ordered her. 'Grip him with your legs there. Don't hold the reins all sloppy. Show him who's boss.'

'Oh! He is!' Beatrice giggled, as Cloud bucked his head and she snatched at the saddle, thereby losing the reins, but after several of these sessions in the yard she learned confidence and how to control him with a gentle kick and the slightest tug of the bit in his soft mouth.

'You'll do, miz,' was as good as a compliment from Harry. 'We'll try a trot next time if you're ready.'

Beatrice nodded shyly, but Harry caught her happiness all right. 'Get yourself a thicker pair o' trousies or you'll be sore,' he told her, as he helped her dismount.

She often visited Cloud and Jezebel on her way home. She loved to watch Harry groom them, or was content to stand and stroke them in their stalls, seeing their muscles twitch and the way they flicked their tails against the flies, breathing in the sweet smell of their manure. She whispered secrets to them, satisfied that their snorts and whinnies passed for conversation.

Often, on her walk over the cliffs in the mornings, she would glimpse Oenone Wincanton on Jezebel, prancing along the beach, sometimes with the military man she'd heard the other children refer to as 'Rollo', or cantering across a field in the distance, woman and horse moving as one, and she yearned to be there, too.

Angelina, by her own admission, was a sack of potatoes on a pony, but she too loved Cloud and was sometimes to be seen riding away, Harry on Jezebel beside her, as Beatrice set off on foot for home.

There came a day when Beatrice was practising rising and falling to a trot that Mrs Wincanton appeared unexpectedly in the yard. Harry wheeled Cloud to a halt. Beatrice was worried that she was doing something she shouldn't with her secret riding lessons, but she needn't have been.

'Oh, bravo!' the woman cried, applauding. 'You have a natural seat, Bea.' All the family had caught this nickname. Only Miss Simpkins, the governess, persisted in calling her Beatrice, sometimes in an Italian accent – *Bayatrichay*. 'Like Dante's lost love,' she sighed, her eyes soulful, thinking perhaps of her own fiancé, buried far away in Belgium.

Mrs Wincanton had come to tell Harry to saddle up Jezebel at four. She wanted to ride across the next valley to see a friend who'd had a baby. Orders given, she said, 'Don't let me delay your lesson any longer,' and strode away, hands in pockets, singing a gay little tune to herself.

Not long after this came the surprise. One afternoon Beatrice found Harry sweeping out an empty stall. 'Wait until tomorrow,' was all he'd say, winking at her, and the next day there was a third horse standing quietly there, a sturdy skewbald pony with a gentle face. Her name was Nutmeg. 'She's so you and Angelina can ride together,' Mrs Wincanton told Beatrice. 'And for Hetty to learn, too, when she's older.'

Beatrice stumbled out her thanks. Nutmeg might not be white with a flowing mane, like the horses of her dreams, but with her black and brown patches she was still adorable.

'Daddy's coming today,' was how Angelina greeted her one Friday morning in November. Her cheeks were even pinker than usual and her eyes sparkled with excitement. 'Mummy's driving to meet him at the station herself and he's staying for a whole three days. I've told Mummy we must have no lessons on Monday but she said we should wait and see.'

'Why doesn't he live here, with you?' Beatrice asked. 'Does he have to work in London all the time?'

'He's in the government. He has to be in London because of running the country. It's very important, Mummy says. You can't always be going off in case the Prime Minister needs you to do something, like stop another war or pass a law . . .' She waved her hand in a vague fashion.

Beatrice thought it sad that running the country meant you couldn't be with your family. 'Why don't you all go and live in London then, with him?'

'I don't know,' she said, a rare frown creasing her brow. 'We did before, but not any more. It's something to do with here being Daddy's um . . . consistency, and that's why some of the time he's here he'll be going off to meetings with farmers and people. And there's a dinner tomorrow night here with *thirty guests* coming and Mummy's awfully busy and doesn't want us getting under her feet.'

There was indeed an hysterical air about the household. All morning, as the older girls puzzled over long division and took turns reading from *Julius Caesar*, carts would arrive with vegetables, vans with meat or fish on ice. Doors slammed, Brown's high-pitched voice was heard complaining, and Mrs Wincanton called out instructions about moving furniture. With the sound of each new visitor, little Hetty, who was supposed to be practising her handwriting, dropped her pen and ran to the window. Finally, she knocked over the inkwell.

'Oh, you wretched child!' cried Miss Simpkins. 'You've got it all over you!'

Beatrice hoped against hope that there would be lessons on Monday, or she'd never meet the Hon. Michael Wincanton. Would he be tall and dark like Rollo Treloar, she wondered, the man who rode with Oenone Wincanton, or sturdy and fair like Edward?

'Is Major Treloar coming to dinner tomorrow?' she whispered to Angelina when Miss Simpkins was cleaning up Hetty's spill. Did she imagine the way Miss Simpkins's hand stilled for just a moment on the exercise book?

'Rollo? I really don't know.' Angelina stared at William Shakespeare as though actually trying to commit the script to memory. 'I'm not sure Daddy cares for him much.' Beatrice wished she'd never asked the question. Angelina was hiding something from her again. Sometimes she couldn't fathom this family.

'We really should get on, girls.' Miss Simpkins's tone was granite. 'Hetty, go at once and find Nanny and change your blouse. I've never known such a clumsy hoyden, in all my born days.'

There were lessons on Monday, but Beatrice did not see Angelina's father.

When Beatrice arrived it was to find Angelina almost wild with misery and Miss Simpkins could do nothing with her.

'He's gone back to London,' Angie said at lunchtime in the stableyard, when Beatrice asked.

'I thought he was going to be here today.'

'So did I. I don't want to talk about it.' But after they'd been petting the horses for a bit she softened. 'Daddy said something had come up. He came to say goodbye, very early. I was to tell goodbye to Mummy because she was still asleep. But when I gave her the message she looked upset. Then she went out riding.'

'With Major Treloar?'

'No, on her own. Rollo did come to the dinner – but I was right about Daddy not liking him. I heard him and Mummy arguing because she'd invited him.'

'Did you go to the dinner?'

'No, but Ed and I were allowed to greet the guests. There was one terribly amusing man, awfully flirty, and I'm afraid I lied and told him I was fifteen and Bea, you'll never guess, but he said he didn't believe me, that I looked at least seventeen. I laughed like a drain. He was awfully old, twenty-five or some-thing, and then Mummy spoilt it by sending me up to bed.'

Beatrice found herself looking at Angie in a new light. The man had been right about her looks. Her figure was distinctly curvy, and when, almost unconsciously, she played with her hair, pushing it back off her face, it seemed an adult gesture. Beatrice's was still the body of a child, but lately she'd noticed a tenderness about her nipples, one of several symptons of a sea change. Her mother had made embarrassed murmurings about something unpleasant being likely to happen and when it did she was to come at once and tell her. But it was Angie, pink-faced and self-important, who first whispered to her about 'the curse' and how much it made one's belly ache.

October 1936

It was soon after Beatrice's fourteenth birthday, and *The Times* was full of General Franco's victories in Spain, when Hugh Marlow suffered a heart attack. The doctor, sent for in the middle of the night, arranged for his transferral to hospital in Truro where he remained for a week. Mrs Wincanton insisted that Beatrice come to stay at Carlyon. She also lent Mrs Marlow her driver every day so that she might visit the invalid.

Whilst troubled about her father, Beatrice enjoyed actu-ally living at Carlyon. Everyone was particularly kind. Brown would call, 'Chin up, miss,' whenever she saw her, and the cook-housekeeper, Mrs Pargeter, pronounced her a 'poor little lamb' and turned out chocolate cake and toffee apples at regu-lar intervals to 'keep the spirits up'.

Above all she loved the ritual of breakfast, helping herself to porridge or boiled eggs or fresh toast from the array of silverware on the sideboard and sitting where she wanted at the big table with its fresh white cloth. Oenone Wincanton would come in late from riding, drop her gloves on a chair and eat her breakfast standing up, pacing the room. Then she'd be off for the morning or the day, often as not, on mysterious missions in her husband's constituency that might involve taking enormous quantities of ribbon or something else for which she'd practise reading a typewritten speech as she drank her coffee. On one occasion they returned home after a nature walk on the cliffs with Miss Simpkins to find the house filled with ladies gossiping and drinking tea, some clustered about a leathery man in wire-framed spectacles, tweeds and facial whiskers. 'This is Professor Stanley, girls,' Oenone said, bringing Angie and Beatrice into the circle. 'He's given us a most affecting talk about the pagan temples of Ephesus, haven't you, Professor?' The girls took the first opportunity to escape upstairs in fits of giggles, Angie declaring, 'It was like shaking hands with a bat.'

When she'd previously stayed overnight at Carlyon, Beatrice had been given a spare room, but this time she was glad to share Angie's big bed. She'd never shared a bed before – and found that in the darkness, the confidences came easily.

'Do you love your father?' Angie asked.

'Of course,' was Beatrice's automatic response. She'd never thought about it before, but now Angie had made her, she realized she didn't know. What did love mean? She didn't want him to die, of course, and she was used to his physical weakness, his demands for attention. Her mother was often explaining to her that her father had given the best of his strength for his country during the war. He had done his duty at great personal cost. The war must have been bad, she knew, because sometimes her father shouted out in the night and once her mother appeared in her room to reassure her that it was only a bad dream. But the result was that Hugh Marlow had little attention to spare for his daughter. He relied heavily on his wife, and the endlessly patient Delphine tried to meet his every need. Beatrice had never thought about her relationship with her father before. She only knew one thing for certain: she loved her mother.

'Why, don't you?' Beatrice whispered back. 'Love your father, I mean, not mine.'

'Course,' Angie said, and her voice was husky. 'It's just that I never see him. Well, hardly ever. We always used to live in London. We have a big white house with a view over a lovely park where Nanny used to take us. But then it all went wrong. Ed says that they quarrelled, and they agreed we should all live here more. It's not fair. I mean I like it here, especially now I've met you, but I did like London. There are always things happening there, and lots of other children and wonderful parties, much better than here, and the shops, you should see the shops, full of all the things you could ever think of. Beautiful clothes and toys, and Mummy would take us to tea at lovely hotels like Brown's and Claridge's. She must miss it all. But I miss my father so much, that sometimes I feel like . . . like running away and taking the train up to London and finding him.'

'Why don't you?' Beatrice replied, excited by this idea.

'As if I had the money!' Angie said. 'Anyway, he'd have to send me back. I couldn't live with him all alone. Though Ed says he stayed there once when he had an exeat from school and Daddy wasn't alone for dinner. There was a woman there called Grace. I wonder if Mummy knows about Grace. Ed says I'm not to tell her.'

Angie sighed in the darkness. Beatrice tried to think what to say. The grown-up world floated just beyond their vision, full of secrets and puzzles. After a while she realized Angie was crying.

'Oh, don't,' she whispered, touching the other girl's shoulder and was thrilled when Angie rolled over and lay in her arms, sobbing softly. 'I'm sure everything's all right. It must be that he's very busy and can't come here very much, like you said.'

'I miss him so much,' Angie gulped. 'If you could meet him then you'd know.'

Beatrice thought of her own father, but could only remember the sour look he had given her last week, before his illness, when he'd arrived home unexpectedly and slipped on the ball she and Jinx had been playing with in the hall. She hadn't seen him since his heart attack. The hospital had been judged by her mother 'no place for a child'. She tried to squeeze out a tear, just one tear, for him, as she pictured him pale and sort of dead-looking in a narrow bed with crisp white sheets, but it was only when she remembered her mother's anxious face that tears came.

It was during this stay that she met Angie's father for the first time. He arrived one afternoon and immediately departed again to a meeting, his wife told the children, with local tin miners about a proposed mine closure. He returned shortly before dinner, and when Beatrice was introduced to him she suffered such a fit of shyness she could do little more than shake his hand and answer 'yes' or 'no' to his questions, blushing all the while.

She'd never met anyone before who exuded such a strong physical presence, a sense of authority, and she found it rather thrilling. She finally plucked up the courage to meet his gaze and saw humour in his hazel eyes, and warmth.

He left for London again the next morning. Late that

afternoon, Mrs Wincanton called Beatrice into the drawing room.

'Sit down a minute,' she said. 'I'd like to talk to you. Have you enjoyed staying with us?'

'Oh yes,' Beatrice said. 'It's been lovely.'

'Well, we've enjoyed having you,' Mrs Wincanton murmured. She smiled. 'But you'll be pleased to hear that you're going home. Your mother telephoned from the hospital a few minutes ago to say that your father has been discharged. So you must run up and pack, and Pengelly will drive you back after tea.'

Beatrice's face must have betrayed her sadness because Mrs Wincanton looked at her tenderly and said, 'Don't you want to go? You are a dear little thing. I'm so glad we found you, you've been so good for Angie. She needs somebody steady and sensible. You know, she's sometimes . . . a little nervy.'

Beatrice nodded. She was proud that Angie's mother was pleased with her. She waited uncertainly, wondering if the woman wanted her to go now, but when Mrs Wincanton stood up, it wasn't to signal that the interview was over. Instead she went to take a cigarette out of a box on the mantelpiece and lit it, then draped herself elegantly against the fireplace, contemplating Beatrice. She smoked, Beatrice saw, as though she wasn't used to it, holding the cigarette clumsily in her slim fingers and pursing her lips to exhale. 'Beatrice,' she said, 'Bea, do you mind being called Bea?'

'I rather like it.' She couldn't help glancing at the carving. Mrs Wincanton followed the line of her gaze.

'Oh yes, our own little bee, I had been going to tell you about him. This house belongs to my husband's family, Beatrice. The bee is the Wincanton family symbol. There was some Wincanton in Tudor or Stuart times who did something particularly plucky in one of the Cornish rebellions, I'm not sure which, the Cornish always seemed to be rebelling against something. And the chief rebel, Lord Somebody-or-other, was telling him what a brick he was when a bee landed on the Wincanton ancestor's sleeve and someone cried, "It's a sign!" Something like that, believe it if you will. Anyway, here is the little creature, and here's the family motto.' She traced a Latin tag carved along the rim of the mantelpiece with her finger. 'Michael assures me it means brave and faithful, and we'll have to take his word for that.'

'It is a honey bee, isn't it?'

'I suppose it might well be. A dutiful member of a hive.' She laughed and threw her cigarette into the grate. 'Not very much like the current generation of Wincantons at all.' She contemplated Beatrice for a moment then said, 'In fact, you suit the motto better than the rest of us. How strange.' She reached out and took Beatrice's hand. 'I sense you'll be a faithful friend to us, and to Angie in particular. You're almost a part of the family, child. Now,' she rumpled Beatrice's hair and said, 'you must be going back to your own family. Your mother's missing you. Off you go!'

And Beatrice went, pondering the conversation. Although Oenone Wincanton had asked nothing specific of her, why did she feel that, with all those veiled hints, a pact had been asked of her? All that talk about faithfulness and duty. It was silly. Being Angie's friend was no effort at all. She liked pleasing Angie and was grateful to the girl's mother for her kindness. If Angie's mother chose to put another cast on it, that was nothing to do with her.

The Rowans, April 2011

'At the time,' Beatrice Ashton said, 'I forgot about this conversation, for I was racing up the stairs to pack. Suddenly, I badly wanted to see Mother and Father and Jinx again. For things to be normal and ordinary . . .' She smiled and trailed to a halt, a soft expression on her face as she relived those events of so long ago. She was telling her story so vividly that Lucy was spellbound.

The girl glanced at her watch and was surprised to see that two hours had passed. The only interruption had been the arrival of Mrs P., a pleasant local woman in her sixties, who could be heard clattering about in the kitchen. Seeing that Mrs Ashton had a guest she'd promptly insisted on finding Lucy something for lunch.

Lucy said, 'It's extraordinary hearing stories about Granny when she was a girl. She told me some things – that she loved Carlyon – but the part of her childhood she talked about most was when she was younger. I suppose her mother and father were happier together then when they all lived in London. She had dancing lessons and amazing children's parties with conjurers and magic lantern shows and fancy dress.' She didn't like to tell Beatrice that Granny Angelina had never mentioned sharing lessons with a shy little half-French girl.

'Perhaps we all need a part of our childhood that we think of as golden, a time we imagine that we were completely happy,' Beatrice murmured. 'Well, mine was Carlyon.'

'My mum used to take me to stay with some art college friends in Wales every summer,' Lucy said, remembering. 'I had a brilliant time with their children. You wouldn't believe the things we got up to. It seemed like paradise compared to primary school in London.'

'Where was your father while you were there?'

'He ran his own business and never gave himself holidays.'

'Any holiday we had,' Beatrice said, 'was staying with one side of the family or another. My father liked home and routine best.'

Chapter 7

Hugh Marlow came home but he was sadly weak. When, after several days in bed, he was able to get up, he was pale and exhausted and could hardly leave the house. The manager at the bank did his best to keep the job open. After all, Marlow was valued by 'our classier customers' and was 'one of our heroes'. When he'd recovered a bit more, Beatrice's father tried working half-days, but even this tired him and as a result her mother wore a permanently strained expression. The doctor visited once or twice, then there came several evenings when Beatrice lay awake to the sound of arguing in the drawing room beneath. One phrase her mother uttered frequently and with mounting exasperation was, 'Write to him, Hugh, please, and just see what he says.'

In the end, it seemed that the terrible letter was written, for one Saturday the postman left one of the familiar thick white envelopes with a Gloucestershire postmark. It lay looking ominous all morning on the tray in the hall until Mr Marlow returned from work and opened it.

No one told Beatrice what it contained, but soon after that Hugh Marlow handed his notice in at the bank, and the monthly white envelopes became the most looked-for event in the household, opened by Beatrice's father with a mixture of fury and relief. But there had to be economies, it was explained to her. Less good cuts of meat from the butcher, a fraying

Rachel Hore

winter coat patched up to last another year. For a while Mrs Marlow took in pupils for French conversation, though this so disrupted her husband's new routines that eventually it had to stop. Beatrice felt the household grow increasingly dismal, her mother and father wrapped up in one another more and more. Apart from schooling and meals and bedtime she began to come and go as she pleased.

Much of her time she chose to spend at Carlyon Manor.

When lessons were over, she went riding or rambled over the cliffs with Angie, or was driven to take tea with other girls, daughters of Oenone's local network of acquaintances, well brought up, county types, for the most part, who were rather in awe of Angie's glamour and who nervously suggested games of cribbage or croquet, whilst guessing rightly that they'd bore their Wincanton visitor. There were birthday parties, too, and, as summer came round, picnics, to which Beatrice sometimes found herself invited. But, conscious of her parents' reduced circumstances, the plainness of her clothes, and the fact that she could never return these invitations, she knew she acted shy and awkward with the others. She did earn, though, the distinction of being good at dares. If there was a wall to climb or cartwheels to turn, she would try harder than anyone else, so getting Bea to perform became a regular entertainment at some of these gatherings. She got on with it grimly, but it gave her no pleasure, and sometimes she elected not to accompany Angie, even when she was specifically invited.

It was one such afternoon in June of 1937, her fifteenth year, that she remained behind at Carlyon, reading on the terrace and fortified by sips of Cook's cloudy lemonade. She heard a car draw up outside the house. Surely it was too early for everyone to return? Mrs Wincanton had dropped Angie at a party at a neighbour's and gone on to Truro in search of new shoes for Hetty, after which they were meeting friends for tea.

There came an exchange of voices – Brown the maid's and a deeper, male voice – and then a man stepped out through the french windows. He was dressed in a camel-coloured suit and shiny brown brogues. It was Angie's father. Beatrice half-jumped to her feet, clutching her book to her chest.

'Beatrice, hello. They tell me you're the only one here. No, no, don't get up. Didn't they get my message, the blighters?'

'Nobody said they received one. Really, I'm certain they weren't expecting you. Angie wouldn't have missed you for anything.'

'No, of course she wouldn't.' He settled himself on a chair near hers, dug out a pipe from his jacket, blew through it and filled it with tobacco, tamping it down with his thumb. He was a broad, muscular man in his early forties, with a handsome, cleanshaven face and sandy hair. She watched him light the pipe, then shake out the match. Every movement imparted masculinity, strength and purpose. He regarded her thought-fully through a wreath of smoke and she crossed her ankles, feeling self-conscious.

'I had a less busy patch, thought I'd motor down for a few days. Is everybody well?'

She had met the Hon. Michael Wincanton MP several times now and he'd always been polite and warm enough, but she usually hung back, knowing that he really came to see his family. Today was the first time she'd found herself alone with him. She searched about desperately for topics of conversation, about what everyone had been doing, nervous that she'd bore him.

'And how's your father?' he asked. She was touched that he remembered, but stumbled out that he was managing quite well. All the time, she was aware of his eyes on her, a slightly amused look on his face. She was getting used to men noticing her. It made her feel awkward. When she woke up in the morning, sometimes it felt like bits of her had grown in the night. This man made her feel slightly uncomfortable, as though her hem was down or her hair was a mess. She wriggled under his gaze.

'What's that you're reading? Anything good?' he asked, but when she showed him the novel he didn't seem that interested.

'You said you were less busy,' she asked bravely. 'Is Parliament still sitting?'

'No, we're in recess, though there's business to attend to here. It doesn't do for a Member of Parliament to neglect his constituency or he won't get re-elected. Now, when do you suppose my wife will return?' He stood and began to pace about and Beatrice was rather relieved when he announced he was going up to change. Later, after the others came back, he insisted on his own driver taking her home. That night she dreamed about him: big, warm, masculine, with smoky breath.

The next morning, Mrs Wincanton telephoned to say that lessons were cancelled, and the following day when she arrived at Carlyon, the place rang with nervous tension. Then the blow fell.

'Daddy's taking us to Scotland for the summer,' Angie cried. 'We're to stay in a real castle.'

On further enquiry it turned out that the castle belonged to friends of the Wincantons, Lord and Lady Hamilton. Lady Hamilton – Aunt Alice – was an old schoolfriend of Oenone's and was Angie's godmother. They were to spend July and August up there. The staff at Carlyon were to be put onto board wages, though Mrs Pargeter had agreed to go to Mrs Wincanton's aged parents a few miles away because they'd recently lost their cook. All these arrangements had been made, it seemed, in the twinkling of an eye, and Beatrice was dismayed to find that she was to spend the summer on her own.

Several weeks passed, the loneliest weeks Beatrice had ever experienced, for she'd grown used to companionship and now it was gone. After the first few days without Carlyon, without Angelina, the tenor of her parents' routine became unbearable. Wherever she drifted in the house she was in someone's way, and she took to going for long walks with Jinx over the cliffs or down to the beach. Cornwall was starting to get busy with summer visitors. Sometimes when the tide was low she'd take that forbidden passage to the less visited next cove, where she'd become absorbed in the rockpools there because it was quieter. But she'd no longer imagine mermaids and palaces. Instead, like a good student, she'd draw fish and birds in her sketchbook, or if it was warm in the sun, sit and read novels from the pile Miss Simpkins had lent her, then when the tide was coming in she'd urge Jinx up the narrow steps cut into the cliff and pass home along the fringes of Carlyon's gardens.

Her mother had started to encourage her to play tennis at the club further up the hill, where she joined the fringes of a group of the sons and daughters of families Delphine met through charity work or her French conversation lessons. They were friendly, not as grand as the Wincantons' friends; they invited her to picnics and birthday treats, but still she didn't feel a part of it all. The Wincantons had spoilt her for that.

When the weather was bad she found herself holed up in her bedroom at home, reading, or arranging and labelling her nature collections. Sometimes she was summoned downstairs to amuse her father by playing chess or reading to him. In the evenings they all sat together listening to the news of the Japanese invasion of China, whilst Delphine sewed and Hugh Marlow played endless games of solitaire, and Beatrice seethed with frustration and loneliness. And every time the postman came she hoped there'd be something for her. Sometimes there would be: a letter or a postcard badly spelt but enthusiastically written by Angelina, with a picture of a stag on it from Hetty.

Beatrice felt empty, yearning. There was a space to fill.

And then Rafe came.

Late July brought more visitors to St Florian, though because it was tucked away, and the beaches were small, it didn't attract the big crowds. Still, the town was busier than usual. Small children hunted crabs in the rockpools at low tide, the jolly sails of boats skimmed the sea and the Italian ice-cream man set up his barrow on the quay.

One afternoon of intense heat and stillness, Beatrice took Jinx for a walk on the beach, seeking coolness by the water. Delphine had gone to bed complaining of a headache. Hugh was playing bridge at Colonel Brooker's, a new development that 'at least gives him an interest,' as his wife said. Beatrice imagined the middle-aged men sitting round the table talking of the days when they'd diced with death in the trenches rather than gambling away small sums at cards. Yesterday's men, all of them. Another war was coming, but it wouldn't be theirs.

She passed a group of boys of about sixteen, playing cricket on the sand, far too absorbed in their game to notice her. When she reached the sea she pulled off her sandals and walked in the shallows, throwing pebbles into the sea for Jinx. They reached the headland that separated this cove from the next. The tide hadn't gone out far enough yet to reveal the passage, but she looked for the jagged rock where she'd got stuck that far-off day two years ago and saw it as an important moment now, for it had brought her Angelina and a life at Carlyon.

She stopped as close to the rocks as she dared, watching the waves dash against them and swirl back, dash and swirl, then whistling to Jinx, turned back, thinking she'd find the narrow path over the other headland and walk down to the town and buy an ice cream.

As she neared the cricket game she saw the boys had spread out across the beach, the reason quickly becoming obvious as a tennis ball hurtled past her into the waves. 'A six,' cried the batter, a heavy red-haired boy she vaguely recognized as James Sturton, a local boy who frequented the tennis club. Jinx leapt into the sea, seized the ball and ran off with it along the beach.

'Flipping heck, Sturton,' cried the bowler. 'You nearly took her head off.' He wheeled round and strode across the sand towards Beatrice. 'Sorry, miss,' he called. 'You're not hurt, are you?'

'No, not at all,' Beatrice said. He was tall for his age, this boy, loose-limbed and graceful, with sleek, butter-coloured hair and a thin, sunburned face. A stranger, but with something of Ed in him, that public-school gloss, and, in the concerned way he looked at her and smiled, utterly familiar.

'Jinx,' Beatrice said severely, and they both looked at the dog, who opened his mouth in a teasing smile, thus dropping the ball, then snatching it up again, ready for a good chase.

Beatrice called him. He ignored her. The boy lunged towards the dog, which pranced further away. They spent several minutes, calling and coaxing, in Beatrice's case, or sprinting and rugby tackling in the boy's. The other boys watched, laughing, the large boy, Sturton, taking the chance to sprawl on the sand and mop his flushed face with a handkerchief. 'Come on, you lummoxes,' the fair-haired boy shouted to his friends. 'Give us a hand.'

After several minutes Jinx allowed himself to be caught and the fair-haired boy wiped the ball carefully on his shorts before raising it in triumph.

'I'm so sorry.' Beatrice clipped the dog on the lead and said, 'He's got awful manners, hasn't he? I hope he hasn't spoilt your game.'

The boy gave Beatrice a mock bow. 'The fault was ours, or more specifically, Sturton's. He could bat for England, could Sturton, but his sixes would knock out the umpire.'

Beatrice hardly heard the sense of his words, so intent was she on the sound of his voice, and the warmth of his gaze. She imagined he must spend a lot of time on the playing-fields to be so sun-browned, and she marvelled that it made his eyes seem so blue.

He was putting out his hand now. 'How do you do?' he said. 'Ashton. Rafe Ashton.'

Beatrice managed to get out her own name and shook his hand. It was as though a warm current passed between them.

'See you around, Beatrice Marlow,' he said. 'Bye, Jinx-boy.' And he was striding back to resume his game.

I'm already forgotten, Beatrice assumed, but as she led Jinx past the temptation of the spinning ball and towards the path to the harbour, Rafe gave her a smile that assured her otherwise.

'Arlene Brooker has her sister's boy staying,' Mr Marlow remarked, reaching for the condiments. 'Rafe Ashton. He's sixteen – a nice-looking lad. I met him with Larry Sturton's boy at the Brookers' today. Turns out Rafe's at Winchester with James.' Beatrice's father didn't notice his daughter's interest in this conversation. He began to eat in his usual irritating way, nibbling his food off the fork in fussy, catlike movements.

Delphine spread her napkin on her lap and began to sever fat from her chop. 'Arlene Brooker has told me about Rafe and his older half-brother. A dreadful business. Her sister's been widowed twice already and has married for a third time. They were in Paris with her last husband, but this one's stationed in India, somewhere in the mountains – where would that be?'

'Kashmir, I reckon,' her husband said.

'Yes, Kashmir, that was it. The boys used to stay with their grandfather in the school holidays, but do you remember Arlene telling us that he died at Easter? Gerald, the older boy, he's at Sandhurst, but Arlene said she could take Rafe. I imagine he'll be in Cornwall often.'

'I think I saw him this morning,' Beatrice plucked up the courage to say. 'Playing cricket on the beach. And one of the other boys was definitely James Sturton.'

'It's a pity they're all boys,' said her mother. 'It would be nice to have more girls for you to play with.'

'I don't mind, *maman*.' She wasn't keen on meeting strangers of either gender. But she thought she'd like to see something more of Rafe.

For the next few days she walked on the beach or up to the tennis club or shopped for her mother with a continuous sense of hope that she might see him.

The Brookers' villa was up on the plateau near the tennis club, and Beatrice would walk past the house trying to appear as though she were not avidly looking for Rafe. One afternoon when she loitered, pretending to find early blackberries in the hedges, she was sure it was his voice she heard in the back

garden, laughing and talking, though she could only make out
the odd word of whatever adventure he was recounting.

It was three mornings after their first meeting that she saw him
on the beach again, this time swimming. A wind had got up, and
Rafe and James Sturton were surfing the waves with handheld
boards. When he saw her he splashed his way to shore, where he
rubbed his back vigorously with a towel as he asked her questions.

'Do you live in Saint Florian?'

'Yes.'

'All the time or just the holidays?'

'I live here all the time,' she told him. 'Do you remember the
first house you come to when you walk back that way?' She
pointed to the dunes and he looked and nodded. 'That's where
I live. It's called The Rowans.' She was surprised at how easy
she found him to talk to.

'Do you know the Brookers, my uncle and aunt?' he asked,
pulling the towel around his shoulders.

'Yes, I think you met my father recently,' she replied. 'He
plays bridge with your uncle.'

'That was your father? What a coincidence.' He laughed.

'I'm sorry you can't go home,' she told him.

'Don't be. It's not bad here, and I'm hoping to see my mother
at Christmas if my stepfather gets some leave. I haven't seen
her for a year.'

He looked wistful so she said quickly, 'I hope you do.'
She did feel sorry for him, separated from his family, but his
thoughts had already moved on.

'I say, do you play tennis?' he said, his face brightening,
and when Beatrice nodded, 'We must make up a foursome.
Sturton's got a sister who plays, don't you, Sturton?'

'What's that?' James Sturton had waded out of the sea and
now stood puffing beside them, like a friendly walrus.

'Tennis. Your sister and Beatrice here. We must do it. I'll send you a note.' He was shivering with cold and excitement, his eyes full of light and happiness. And yet, there was a vulnerability there, too – she'd seen it. Something in the twist of his smile. She wanted to tell him it was all right, everything was all right. Because she could see it hadn't always been so for him.

The next morning she'd arranged with old Harry to ride Cloud, and it was as she was pulling on her riding boots that an envelope slipped through the letterbox. She beat Jinx to snatch it from the mat, read her name and wrenched open the front door in time to see Rafe's retreating back. He was dressed in shorts and an old shirt, with a towel draped over his shoulder. 'Rafe,' she called, and he turned, his sensitive face breaking into a smile when he saw her. He glanced at her boots and breeches.

'You're going riding?' he asked, unnecessarily, bending to rub Jinx's rough coat, and when she nodded, said, 'Let me know if you can play tennis.'

'Wait a moment,' she said, scrabbling open the envelope. 'Tomorrow afternoon? Um,' she said, trying to be offhand like Angie, 'yes, thank you, I can.'

'See you up there,' he said. He looked at his watch and the sun flashed on the metal. 'Must hurry. We've bought an old canoe.' His eyes gleamed with humour. 'Sturton'll probably scalp me if I don't show to help him carry it.' He pulled the gate shut and she heard his whistle as he passed back down the lane.

Beatrice stood on the doorstep, listening to the whistle and the wail of gulls, feeling the sun on her face. It shone from a cerulean sky. The air was warm and thick as honey. Time slowed. Whatever happens, she told herself, I must always remember this moment. She'd pin it in her memory like one of her butterflies. Take it out to look at, if she needed to remind herself what pure happiness was.

On the way up the cliff path, half an hour later, she turned to look down on the beach. Two boyish figures were struggling to launch a cumbersome canoe in the surf. She watched, laughing, as one gained a seat and the other scrambled in, only for a wave to strike them broadside, capsizing the craft. There was a rush to rescue the paddles before they tried again. Then they were afloat, and coursing through the waves onto calmer water. She turned and laboured on up the path, larksong heralding her ascent.

Harry had got Cloud saddled and ready for her. She thanked him, but refused the offer of his company. 'I'm fine with him now. He knows me.'

Harry grunted, but Beatrice knew he wouldn't let her go if he wasn't sure. She mounted Cloud and he shortened the stirrups for her and remarked, 'Don't go too hard in this heat, he won't like it.'

'Of course I won't, Harry. Don't worry.' He stood back and she set off at a walk, out of the stableyard, down the lane, heading for the meadows on the brow of the cliff. Cloud, his flanks quickly damp with sweat, was reluctant even to break into a trot, but she urged him on. Away from the shelter of the trees the afternoon sun beat down. She wouldn't ride for long. She turned along the cliffs, above the sea, where there was the slightest of breezes.

The world vibrated with a long rumble of thunder. The pony hesitated and his ears switched back. Beatrice glanced up, whispering calming words, and was surprised to see that the horizon ahead was vanishing into a dark haze. As she gazed out to sea, she saw black clouds rolling towards them across the water, yet still, immediately below, the sea sparkled in sunlight. Soon, she noticed the birds fell silent. A draught of cool air began to blow, and on it floated a faint scent of rain. As she watched, the brightness leached from the sea below, leaving it dull as liquid lead. Horse and rider toiled along the wide band of cliff behind the trees bordering Carlyon, and as they passed the secret steps down to the second cove, she realized a storm was coming – coming swiftly, too. They'd ride as far as the next promontory, she decided, then turn in time to gain home before it reached them.

They plodded on, the pony sluggish, Beatrice watching the dark haze surge nearer, inking out the sky, cloaking the sea. White light flashed. A splash of rain struck her cheek, then another. The goal was reached and she wheeled the horse round. Nose to home, he grew more eager, breaking into a trot. Even so, by the time they reached the turning back to the stable, a stinging wind was blowing. She pulled up and took a final look out at the swelling sea. There was a sailing boat, flying before the wind, heading round the point to St Florian harbour. Further out, a small rowing dinghy inched towards the shore. She watched it for a moment, thinking it had better hurry, then came another great roar of thunder. Cloud reared in alarm, then charged forward in a wild gallop, ignoring his rider's instructions, sensible only of stable and safety.

Beatrice dropped the reins then hurled herself forward, throwing her arms round his neck, gasping at him to stop. Some instinct told her to kick off the stirrups, so that when, finally, she fell, it was cleanly and into a yielding if prickly hedge. There she was caught, scratched and weeping, till bit by bit she worked herself free. The rain started in earnest now, great drops slapping her face and bare forearms, and the whole countryside vanished in thick mist that lit up and thundered.

As she stumbled towards the stable she thought, Poor old Rafe and James Sturton on the beach, having to lug that great canoe back home . . . and then, with a stab of almost physical pain, she made the connection.

It was still sinking in, this realization, when a huge figure formed out of the mist ahead. For a moment she was terrified, then saw it was Harry, enveloped in oilskins.

'Thank God you're safe, miz,' he cried, reaching her and seizing her shoulders, his breath coming in great gasps. 'Your face. Are you all right?' She touched her cheek and blood and rain flowed down her fingers.

'Just scratches,' she said above the noise of the storm. 'From the hedge. Is . . .?'

'Cloud's safely in his stable. I was that worried – you could have fallen anywhere. Run with me now or you'll catch your death.'

'Harry, no.' Her teeth were chattering. 'The beach. You've got to come. Trouble. A friend of mine. There's another boy, too.' She wasn't making sense.

'You're soaked through, Miss Beatrice.'

'I don't care. We've got to hurry. They're out in a boat. They won't get back in time.'

She stared into his weathered, rain-blurred face and he saw her urgency. 'Wait a moment,' he cried, and disappeared back into the mist. When he returned, long minutes later, he carried a second oilskin and a coil of rope.

The beach was deserted. The sea, good-tempered such a short time before, was a raging beast. They heard its angry roar, then, running down the beach, met huge waves that dashed the shore, clawing up towards the dunes. Beatrice stared into the tumult, and uselessly cried, 'Rafe!' but could see nothing through the rain and spray.

Moments passed, then Harry gave a shout and rushed into the waves, where she saw him clutch at something. It flipped up in his grasp and she saw its large solid shape – like a coffin, she thought. It was the canoe. He had it, now, wrestled it into the shallows and levered it upright. It was empty – what else did she expect? She helped him drag it out onto the sand.

'We'll find them, miz,' Harry said, and strode back into the sea. Together they waded up and down the shoreline, searching and calling, then he turned and said, 'You must go for help. The nearest house.'

She did not like to leave, but knew she must. She stared one last time through the stormy waves. The rain seemed to be lessening now, and an ethereal gold light suffused the air. The worst of the storm was passing. Then the light caught something in the water, a brief flash of silver and a long pale shape in a breaking wave and it was gone. The wave crashed and there the shape was again. With a cry she rushed towards it.

She struggled, was sucked down across sand and stones, pain, darkness, then up again, her lungs bursting. As she lurched to her feet, whooping for air, she was struck by something softly solid, felt cloth and hair against her skin. She grabbed at the body and, wrapping her arms around it, held on for dear life. Crying to Harry for help, she braced herself, digging her feet into the shifting sand. Harry reached her now and with the help of a following wave, they heaved the body onto the beach. It was shrouded in water, a lifeless thing. Harry rolled it onto its back and she gave a howl. It was Rafe.

Harry knew what to do. He felt for a pulse then tipped back the boy's head and bent to breathe air into his mouth, again and again. Nothing happened for a long time, then suddenly Rafe lurched forward and began to retch. Beatrice helped Harry to turn him onto his side, where he lay coughing and sobbing.

The grey limbs were flushing faintly now and his eyes fluttered open. She knelt to stroke his face, crying, 'Rafe, Rafe, come on, it's all right,' and he rolled onto his front, confused and terrified.

She felt Harry's hand on her shoulder. 'Leave him. He'll be all right. Go for help, now. I'll find the other one.' And this time she rose, shivering, and ran back up the beach, through the slackening rain.

Chapter 8

They searched for James Sturton until nightfall, returning again at dawn. It was his father who found his body, washed up by the tide. It was unimaginably awful. He was sixteen, their only son.

When she heard the news, Beatrice fled upstairs and wept on her bed until, bruised and exhausted from her ordeal, she fell into a troubled sleep. Around two in the afternoon she was woken by her mother to be told that Mrs Brooker, Rafe's aunt, had telephoned. Rafe had been asking for her.

'I can't go,' Beatrice said, burying her head in her pillow.

'Béatrice, you must.' Delphine came to sit on her daughter's bed, and softly stroked her hair. 'Sometimes we must do things we don't want to, because it is our duty. And you, who have been so brave in rescuing the boy, must go to help him now.'

She helped Beatrice up from the bed, washed the girl's scratched face and brushed her hair as though she were little again, then found her a fresh dress from the wardrobe.

'Do you need me to come with you?' she asked, as Beatrice opened the front door, but Beatrice shook her head and stepped out into appalling bright sunshine. She walked to the Brookers' house as though in a trance, aware that only yesterday she'd have been at a high pitch of excitement to be invited there. Not today. The summer blazed on all around, but a page had been turned in their sunny lives, and the story had gone dark.

'Ah, our young heroine,' Mrs Brooker said when she opened the door. 'Rafe will be so happy to see you, dear.' She was a good ten years younger than her burly husband, elegant and bony like a greyhound. 'He's taking it very hard. Seems to think the whole thing's his fault for some reason. He's out in the garden. Supposed to be resting, of course.'

Rafe was sitting hunched up on a bench, tossing an old tennis ball from hand to hand. When he saw Beatrice he stood, pocketing the ball and drawing his forearm across his eyes. She saw at once that he'd been crying. His face was blotched and puffy and he had a bruise on his forehead, but seemed otherwise uninjured. 'The doctor said he'd be right as rain,' Mrs Brooker said, twisting the rings on her manicured hands. 'Now I expect some lemonade will make everybody feel better. And Cook's made a chocolate cake to die for . . . Oh, silly me!' She saw Rafe's disbelieving face, and turned and hurried into the house.

'She means to be kind,' he said. He sat down again, pulled out the tennis ball and turned it in his hands. 'I must thank you, Beatrice. They all said you've been a brick. Saved my life and all that. What can I say?'

'You don't need to say anything,' she said, sitting next to him. 'It was Harry who knew what to do.'

'Poor old Sturton.' His voice ended in a squeak and his face screwed up, his shoulders shook and he began to sob. Beatrice put out a hand and touched his arm. To her surprise he turned towards her and she found herself pulling him into her embrace and he was crying noisily into her neck. 'Sorry,' he muttered between sobs. 'I'm so sorry. I wish my mother was here.'

For a minute or two they sat like that, she stroking his hair as her mother had stroked hers, immensely moved. He must feel so alone. She didn't imagine Mrs Brooker to be much use, and the Colonel was nowhere to be seen. Rafe needed her. No one had really needed her before, not even Angelina.

Soon he grew quieter, then drew away. 'Sorry,' he said. 'I've funked it. Don't know what you must think' He dragged a handkerchief from his trouser pocket and blew his nose.

'It's all right, really it is,' she said, but they were both embarrassed now and sat without looking at one another.

'I'm to see his parents,' Rafe said dully. 'Don't want to, but of course I must. I don't know what to say to them. I should have stopped us going out so far. It's my fault really. All my fault. It's always my fault.'

What a strange thing to say. Beatrice thought of that moment she'd seen the canoe from the top of the cliff, with the storm coming, and not known what it was. Perhaps she ought to have recognized it and to have raised the alarm then. An abyss of guilt opened in her mind. The hell of guessing what might have been. 'It's not your fault, Rafe,' she said desperately. A phrase Mrs Wincanton used came to mind. 'Really, you can't take on so.'

'But it was my idea, buying the canoe. I talked him into it.'

'You couldn't have predicted the storm. It took everyone by surprise.'

'You don't understand,' he said, turning and looking straight at her, his eyes wild. 'It's always my fault. It's like a sort of curse.'

'What do you mean?' She was almost glad when, at that moment, Arlene Brooker emerged carrying the tray of lemonade and the cake to die for.

They saw each other most days after that. There was the

terrible afternoon of James Sturton's funeral. Most of the town turned out for it, and James was buried in the cemetery on the hill above St Florian, while bumblebees blundered in the long grass. It was a drowsy afternoon when in life he might have played cricket or wandered in the countryside whistling his tuneless whistle. Instead he was laid to sleep for ever in the earth, alive only in the minds of those who knew him as a clumsy sixteen-year-old boy with a lopsided smile, a dusting of freckles, a passion for rugby and a dislike of book-learning. Beatrice's mother had told her she needn't upset herself by going to the graveside, but she went anyway to support Rafe, and as she stood at the back of the crowd thinking about all the things in life that Sturton would never see or do, the tears dripped down her face.

Life went on in its unfeeling way. They played mixed doubles at tennis, but not with Sturton's sister. Rafe came to tea at The Rowans and Beatrice sat stiff with anxiety in case her father was rude or, worse, cold and uninterested. Thankfully, even he responded to Rafe's polite friendliness, his handsome open face and his happy sensitivity to others.

'You were in the war, sir?' Rafe asked, and his respectful manner was genuine. 'My father was, too.'

'Your uncle tells me he got an MC,' Hugh said, a bit grudgingly.

Rafe nodded. 'He saved some of his platoon by leading them through a minefield. I wish I could remember him, but I don't.'

Beatrice was intrigued to catch her parents exchange meaningful looks. Then her mother said, 'Of course you don't. Now, Rafe, you'll have some more tea?'

'I feel sorry for your generation,' Hugh Marlow continued, discarding the cucumber from his sandwich. 'There's another war coming, you'll see, and it'll be worse than the last.'

'I hope you're wrong there, sir,' Rafe said, his expression alert. 'My uncle says we should stay out of it, that Herr Hitler's not interested in fighting us.'

Beatrice's parents again glanced at one another, and Mrs Marlow's face was troubled. 'I don't think it'll be as easy as that,' her father said.

Her mother smoothed her skirt and shook her head. Beatrice had heard them talk in anxious tones about letters from the family in France. These described the surge of refugees passing through Normandy to board ships to England and America, recounted stories of persecution and brutality that the refugees brought with their meagre possessions out of Germany.

'This will be everyone's war, I think,' Hugh Marlow said solemnly. 'England expects every man to do his duty.' He pushed back his chair and went to tap the barometer on the wall with his knuckle. 'High pressure,' he said. Rafe watched, sensibly making no comment.

But nor did he let the subject lie. Another day, as they walked on the beach with Jinx, he said, 'Suppose your father's right?'

'What would you do, if there were to be a war and you were old enough to fight?'

'I'd fight,' he said, pulling himself up, suddenly looking older than his sixteen years. There was a strange light in his eyes that made her shiver. Seeing her face he said, 'But don't worry. My uncle says Mr Chamberlain will sort things out. You'll see.' And he picked up a stick and hurled it across the beach for Jinx to chase.

Beatrice watched him tear after the dog, his long legs lithe and golden, his shirt unbuttoned, blowing in his wake like wings. She liked to study him when he dozed in the sun, noting his hair to be the exact old gold of corn waiting to be harvested, the glow of his pale brown skin; fascinated by the pulse that throbbed in his throat. Since that day in the Brookers' back garden they'd not touched except by accident. That matter had never been mentioned again, but Beatrice remembered it, and treasured it when she lay sleepless during the hot August nights. His skin had smelt salty; even the slight tang of sweat had not been unpleasant, but rather alluring.

Sometimes they talked of deeper things: of his mother, far away in India, whom Beatrice guessed he missed more than he ever had courage to say; of his father, dead when Rafe was only six; of the older half-brother, now at Sandhurst. Beatrice felt a channel of sympathy flow between them.

More often he spoke of that boys' world full of thrillingly shocking things that Edward had once described: of sadistic schoolmasters and swaggering bullies, of freezing dormitories and trouncing other schools at rugby, of despised homesickness and the boredom of lessons.

Sometimes they talked about the future, as if war would never happen.

'I'd like to be a doctor. A surgeon, of course. I fancy cutting people up and moving their insides about to see how they work.' Rafe was reclined against a sand dune, his arm shielding his eyes from the sun.

'It sounds dreadfully bloodthirsty. Aren't you supposed to cure people?' Beatrice, sitting beside him, watched the sand ants bear away crumbs from their picnic.

'I expect I'd have to. Aunt Arlene says Mother writes of me joining Father's old regiment after Oxford, but I'm dashed if I'll go and leech my life away in the Colonies somewhere. No, I want to stay here.'

'In Cornwall?'

'Well, England. I hate India.'

'You mean, you don't like your stepfather.' Beatrice started tickling his neck with a piece of grass.

'Stop it.' He pushed it away, opened his eyes and sat up.

'Stop what, talking about your stepfather?'

'You know what I mean.' He looked furious now. He always did when his mother's latest husband was mentioned. Beatrice thought the man sounded perfectly ordinary. It was the idea of him replacing his father that he couldn't take.

She remembered the way her parents had looked at each other when Rafe's father had been mentioned. 'Rafe,' she said, 'what happened to your father? I mean, how did he die?'

He looked away into the distance, then down at his hands. Finally, he spoke. 'I don't really remember, but Gerald says that I found him. He once told me the whole thing was my fault, you know.' She saw in his eyes the evidence of some awful horror and it frightened her.

'I don't know what you mean,' she whispered.

'I was only six. I must have blotted it out. We'd come back from Paris for the summer. Gerald tells me I found him hanging in the barn.'

'Hanging?' Still she didn't understand. No one had talked to her about anything like this before.

'He killed himself, Bea. The man who got a medal for bravery went and did a cowardly thing like that.' Rafe's voice squeaked in rage now. 'Gerald says I should have found him earlier.'

'That's stupid.' Beatrice stood up. She could think of nothing else to say. All this was beyond the comprehension of her sheltered life.

Rafe saw she was distressed. 'Come on,' he said. 'Let's go for a swim.'

She remembered later that Rafe hadn't asked her what she would do with *her* life. Nobody had ever asked her, in fact, but change was in the air.

The future must be decided. Next August, 1938, Angie would be sixteen, Beatrice, the month after. There was only this one more year of sharing Miss Simpkins. Her parents hinted at various possible ideas. Miss Simpkins had suggested Beatrice be sent away to a proper school for three years, an enlightened one that prepared young ladies for university.

'And what would Beatrice do after university? Become a governess?' her father sneered, when her mother mentioned this.

'Mrs Wincanton has talked of her coming out with Angelina. They're sending Angelina to school in Paris in September, to finish her.'

'And quite how would we afford all that razzmatazz?'

'She would stay with them in London. I suppose there would be the matter of dresses and expenses, but it would be a great opportunity for her, Hugh. We could send her to Normandy for a few months first, to stay with my family. She must do something. What will there be for her here in Saint Florian?'

'We can't send her abroad. The Wincantons can do what they like, but I say the political situation is too uncertain.'

'Perhaps you are right, but I don't know what we shall do with her then.'

'Isn't anybody going to ask me what *I* want?' Beatrice said crossly. Her mother raised her delicate eyebrows.

'And what would you like, Beatrice?' her father said in a voice heavy with irony.

She thought about it. What she would really like was for everything to stay the same. For this summer to go on. For Rafe not to go back to school. That couldn't happen, of course, but she was unable to imagine anything else.

'Go to London maybe?' she said finally. 'With Angelina.'

The more she thought about it, the more the idea grew. She began to daydream about life there, the streets of great white houses she'd seen in films. Trams and buses, the Houses of Parliament and Buckingham Palace, and the dressing up and the parties, though she wasn't certain she'd enjoy the parties. Angelina's father lived in Kensington, she'd been told this. She supposed they'd all stay with him and that sounded very glamorous.

But there was still a year, another glorious year to live through before any of that need be decided. She enjoyed her lessons with Miss Simpkins, had devoured greedily the books the woman lent her, the works of Jane Austen and George Eliot and the Brontës, though the novel by Virginia Woolf was puzzling her. Her father had grudgingly let her borrow some of the leather-bound volumes of Charles Dickens from his study, and a beautiful edition of Gilbert White's *Natural History of Selborne*.

Near the end of the holidays, Rafe was invited to stay with a schoolfriend up-country for a week; though missing him badly, Beatrice spent the days on her old hobbies, collecting insects, pressing flowers and searching rockpools. Sometimes she rode Cloud. And sometimes now there were outings. Her father, who appeared stronger this summer, occasionally borrowed a motor car from a bridge partner, and they'd drive up to the north coast, where the cliffs were higher and crueller and the jagged rocks cradled pools teeming with species she'd not come across in St Florian. Once, she found a great dead blue jellyfish washed up on the beach. She crouched over it, flicking through her book. The picture she found showed the animal's triangular sail, *like an old Portuguese caravel boat*, the description ran. She looked out to sea, imagining how sinister an armada of the venomous creatures must look approaching over the waters. Later, she watched an old man carrying the corpse on a spade to bury it further up the beach.

Late August 1937 brought the Wincantons home, their father with them for a short while, and two little girl cousins for Hetty to play with. Receiving the summons, Beatrice hurried up to the house. Although she was greeted rapturously by everybody except Peter, she noticed at once that things were different. Angelina was growing up fast. It was as though the awkward stage had passed her right by and Beatrice was left behind. She was taller, with an unfashionably full figure, and the old dreamy expression on her face had turned knowing and slightly amused. Something had happened to her in Scotland.

Once they were alone in Angelina's room, Beatrice quickly found out what.

'Look,' Angie said, showing Beatrice a postcard. It was a photograph of a young man in ceremonial Highland dress. 'The Hamiltons had their nephew Bertie to stay. It was simply too thrilling,' she whispered, clutching Beatrice's arm. 'He wouldn't let me alone. He trailed around behind me wherever I went and everybody remarked on it. And no one would believe I wasn't out yet and Mummy let me stay up for dinner, and Aunt Alice got a maid to do my hair. And two nights ago Bertie asked me to go for a walk in the grounds after dinner and I let him kiss me. I wanted to see what it was like, you see.'

'What was it like?' Beatrice asked, at once horrified and intrigued.

'Oh, once we sorted out where our noses should go it went awfully well. Look, hold still and I'll show you. No, it's best if you close your eyes.' And she pulled Beatrice into her arms and pressed her mouth slowly and carefully onto hers. Beatrice, stiffening at first, opened her eyes wide in surprise. An exciting warm feeling started somewhere in her throat, spreading through her breasts and down through her whole body. She became acutely aware of the heaviness of Angelina's arms, the familiar smell of her, the gold hairs gleaming on her arms. She broke off, pushing her away.

Angelina stood back, laughing. 'You're supposed to kiss me back, silly!' she said. 'We must practise. It'll be important if we're to get anywhere with men. Come on, don't look like that.'

'Like what?'

'Like Granny Trevellian when S.E.X. is mentioned. Your mouth all wrinkled up like a prune.'

'It's . . . very strange, that's all. Didn't it, well, encourage him?'

'Only a little. I wouldn't want to marry him or anything. He's awfully serious, you know. He would look at me like a mournful dog. I couldn't bear him following me around all my life. Fortunately Mummy came out to look for me so I was quite safe. We had such a marvellous time there. Oh, dinners and shooting parties. And Ed shot grouse, though Peter wouldn't.'

Beatrice saw that Angelina wasn't ever going to ask what she'd been doing, so she thought she'd better say it herself. 'I've met someone, too. His name's Rafe.'

Angelina's limpid eyes grew wide. 'Oh Bea, goodness, your letter. It all sounded too dreadful for words. Is it that boy? Not the one who died, of course, the other one? Everyone said you were so brave. Mummy heard *everything* from Deirdre Garnett's mother.'

Beatrice, who was still trying to blot out that awful day, sat down on the bed and said glumly, 'I wasn't brave at all. If old

Harry hadn't been there I don't know what I should have done.'

'Still, you helped rescue someone, that's what's wonderful. And now I suppose he'll be grateful to you for ever and ever. What's he like, anyway? Is he good-looking?'

'Oh, Angie, is that all you think about?' Beatrice said with a groan. 'I suppose he is. He's very nice and easy to talk to.'

'We must all meet him then,' Angie said. 'There, that's settled. You must bring him up to Carlyon. I'll ask Mummy to fix it.'

'He's been away, but he should be back today. And he'll be going to school soon, so it'll have to be quick.'

'Ed and Peter will be leaving next week. I know – bring him tomorrow. I'll ask Mummy if he may come for tea.'

'All right, ask her,' Beatrice replied. But the thought of sharing Rafe made her nervous. Part of her desperately wanted to show off the Wincantons, but she feared, too, that then he wouldn't be just hers any more. He'd be swallowed up by them. Though that was nonsense. He wasn't really hers at all. They'd been thrown together, that was all. He had a mother in India and a brother, and dozens of friends. And he'd be going back to school soon, and then he'd forget all about her.

Angie fitted the photograph of Bertie Hamilton into the corner of her dressing-table mirror, humming to herself. The picture wasn't destined to remain. The next day Peter found it and ribbed his sister so horribly that she tore it up in a fit of pique.

The visit was, from Beatrice's point of view, a disappointment, but Mrs Wincanton afterwards declared it to be a great success.

Rafe was enthralled by Carlyon. He paused as they walked round that all-important corner of the drive. 'Golly,' he said, and whistled.

As they waited in the hall for the Wincanton children to be winkled from various reaches of the house and grounds, he wandered round, studying the portraits of long-dead Carlyons, passing a hand over a carved newel post, calling Beatrice over to find St Florian on an old framed map of the county.

The drawing-room door opened and Ed appeared first, elbowing Peter to keep back. He and Rafe shook hands, instantly at ease. 'We've an Ashton in our house at school, haven't we, Pete? George Ashton.'

'No relation, I'm afraid. Not that I know of, anyway. There don't seem to be many of us Wiltshire Ashtons left. But, I say, did we play you last autumn at Eton? I seem to remember—'

He broke off for Beatrice to introduce him to Mrs Wincanton who had finally arrived, carrying a basket of fragrant roses and lifting a floppy sunhat from her head. 'You must be Rafe. Welcome to Carlyon, dear. We've heard all about you. The girls are about somewhere.' She glanced back through the drawing room and they all held their breath at the lovely silhouette of Angelina, framed by the french windows as she paused on the threshold to call to the little girls still somewhere in the garden.

'They're not taking any notice,' she said, coming into the hall. 'Oh hello, you must be Rafe.' Beatrice was dismayed to see how Angie looked sideways at him under her lashes, and he stumbled out a greeting as he shook her hand.

'Why don't you show Rafe round?' said Mrs Wincanton, laying down her basket. 'I'll let Cook know about tea.' She disappeared through the baize door to the kitchens.

Rafe was still staring at Angie, but Ed touched his arm. 'Come and see the games room,' he said, and they drifted off with Peter trailing unhappily behind.

'Well, that's the last we'll see of them for a bit,' Angie declared, making a *moue* at Beatrice. 'Let's go out and find the girls. Hetty's got a beastly dead blackbird and they're having a funeral. It's horribly ghoulish.' Beatrice followed her, her spirits sinking. They passed Angie's sketchbook lying open on the grass, half a dozen crayons spilled carelessly about. Down by the belt of trees, three small figures were crouched over something on the ground like midget witches from *Macbeth*.

As they approached, Hetty straightened and called out, 'Do you think a poem would be all right, Ange? We've never been to a funeral. We don't know what to do.'

'Beatrice has, haven't you, Bea?' Angie said. Beatrice, remembering the awful day when James Sturton was buried, said quietly, 'I'm sure a poem would suit. Or a favourite hymn.'

It was after they'd finished scattering petals on the mound to Hetty's jolly rendering of 'All Things Bright and Beautiful' that they saw the boys coming towards them across the grass. How alike they all were with their cowlicks of hair and their schoolboy swaggers, hands in pockets.

'We're going to the beach, if you lot want to come,' Ed called. 'Mother's put back tea and we're lending Rafe some togs.'

'Do you mind, you girls?' Rafe asked Beatrice and Angie, shading his eyes against the sun. His gaze fell on the little mound and for a moment his expression hardened. Then he looked at Beatrice and smiled. She smiled back, feeling a little happier.

'I don't think I'll swim, Rafe, but I'll come down with you all,' she said.

Whilst the others raced upstairs to change she stayed to watch Mrs Wincanton arrange roses in the drawing room, collecting up the leaves for her on a sheet of newspaper. Finally they lifted the vase onto the great carved mantelpiece, where the flowers' reflection in the mirror doubled their magnificence. Mrs Wincanton lit a cigarette and stood back to admire her work.

'It's so clever of you to have found Rafe,' Mrs Wincanton said. 'He's a very suitable young man. Ed needs someone of his own age here. I'm afraid he's getting a little bored with coming every holiday.' She balanced her cigarette on the mantelpiece in order to adjust an errant bloom. 'So sad,' she said. 'You're all growing up so fast.'

'They do seem to get on well,' Beatrice said, a little wistfully. She remembered, too, how beguilingly Angie had looked at Rafe, and how Rafe had responded.

Mrs Wincanton started gathering up the newspaper with the discarded leaves inside. 'Look after the little girls going down the steps,' she called as everyone assembled on the terrace. 'Oh, thank you, Bea.' She took her cigarette from Beatrice.

'It was singeing the mantelpiece,' Beatrice said, and went to join them.

On the beach, Rafe was the perfect guest, solicitous with every-one in turn. He swam with the boys, helped bury the little girls in sand, moulding them mermaid tails and maidenly bumps for breasts, which made them giggle so the sand fell off. He hunted in rockpools with Beatrice. Only with Angie did he act unnaturally. Angie didn't seem to mind his stammering attempts at conversation, but looked at him with luminous eyes. She laughed at the sandy mermaids then sat in the shade to sketch them.

Rafe and Beatrice walked back to St Florian together in the cool of early evening. He spoke eagerly of the visit.

'Ed's planning to go up to Oxford, too,' he said. 'Saint John's, though. I expect I'll look him out. Balliol's only round the corner. A good chap, Ed – the brother's not bad. And the little girls are pretty sporting.'

'I'm glad you like them all,' she said. 'I think they liked you.'

'And Angie's . . . well.' He whistled and her spirits fell. Worse was to come. When they reached the gate of The Rowans, he said, 'I can't see you tomorrow, Beatrice. I'm afraid my aunt's taking me back to school early. We're to stay with some cousins on the way.'

'Oh.' She'd already daydreamed about their last day together, of all they might say to one another, and now it was spoiled.

He gently fumbled for her hand. 'Beatrice,' he said, 'if I write to you, will you write back? I don't get many letters, you see.'

'Of course I will.' Happiness radiated through her.

'This summer, it's been awful – with poor Sturton, I mean – but in other ways it's been the best I remember. You can't believe how dreary it was with my grandfather. Not his fault, poor old man, he did his best, but I don't think I could face another game of chess ever again.'

She nodded, unable to speak for emotion. He was going away. But he'd come back to her, she was sure of that.

'I'll see you at Christmas, I expect.' He squeezed her hand once more. 'Goodbye, Bea,' he said. He gave her a sudden clumsy hug and was gone.

The autumn of 1937 was measured out by the postman's visits. Beatrice kept a look-out for him from her window, and when she saw him wheeling his bicycle up the steep lane she would make the most ridiculous bargains with fate – if he reached the gate in the next ten seconds then there'd be a letter. But did it count if he hadn't touched the gate before the time was up, but stopped outside to rummage in his bag? She'd ponder this fine point as she rushed downstairs.

'You're very interested in the mail these days,' Hugh Marlow would say. 'Oh, there does seem to be something here for you . . . postmark Winchester.' He'd tease her by holding the letter high, trying to get her to jump for it. She'd turn away scowling. 'Here, catch,' he'd say, and throw it in the air.

'Hugh, don't be unkind,' Delphine admonished, but Beatrice would simply take the letter, snatch up her schoolbag and slip out of the door, hardly muttering goodbye. How she ever managed to reach Carlyon on a letter day without falling over the cliff on the way, was a wonder, so deep would she be in Rafe's scrawled pages.

He was an amusing, if irregular correspondent, the letters full of dramatic accounts of rugby matches and practical jokes, but sometimes there were serious, even tender comments, too.

Sturton is much missed, one early letter said. *He was our best prop forward by a mile and he made us laugh and didn't mind being the butt. No one can believe he's gone. Some days I hate myself for I still think I'm to blame.*

After the arrival of a precious letter, Bea had to force herself not to immediately post a reply. She felt she shouldn't seem too eager. Angie's tuition had its uses. 'You should always make boys wait, Mummy says.' Angie was showing by example. She'd had several passionate letters from the young man she'd met in Scotland, and these she read out to Beatrice, rolling her eyes and clutching her chest mockingly. Beatrice laughed despite herself, but she disapproved of Angie taking ages to scrawl a couple of lines of reply or sometimes sending nothing at all.

'You're so cruel. Someone should tell him you don't care,' Beatrice said. She vowed never to read Rafe's out to Angie.

The Scottish boy's letters grew plaintive, then ceased.

Chapter 9

Cornwall, April 2011

'At the beginning of 1938,' Mrs Ashton told Lucy, as they finished the lunch Mrs P. had prepared for them, 'the news was full of Hitler's calumnies, but in this house most of the conversation was about my future. Two things finally put my parents off choosing the same route for me as Angelina. One was the uncertainty of the situation in Europe. Many girls went abroad anyway, but my parents were a fearful sort. Even in peaceful times they would have worried. Adolf Hitler provided a useful excuse.

'The second concerned a visit from our governess, Miss Simpkins. She felt passionately that my schooling should continue beyond the summer. I was extremely able, she told them, and it would be a waste to give up now. My parents discussed the various options endlessly above my head. As ever, the main obstacle to any ambition was lack of funds. Finally, my father agreed once more to swallow his pride and write to his father on the matter.

'To his amazement, my grandfather replied with a generous offer. They would pay the fees for me to attend a reputable boarding school for girls near their home in Gloucestershire. It would mean spending my exeat weekends with them, but they were happy to receive me, and I would go home for the long holidays. And so it was settled. There was the small matter of an entrance test, of course, but somehow, with Miss Simpkins's help, I muddled my way through that and was offered a place to start the following September, just before I turned sixteen.'

Lucy asked: 'Didn't you mind that you weren't going to Paris and London?'

'You might be surprised, but no. I wanted to see those places, but in the end, I didn't think I'd be good at being finished and then all the fuss, people staring at me and whispering about my looks and my background, how much money my father had, that sort of thing. I knew I'd be found wanting on all of these fronts. And part of my mind was now always on Rafe. I liked to think of him studying at Oxford, and me being a few miles away at school, studying too. I tried not to think of his tales of bullying and petty cruelty, and thought that was probably just boys for you. It might seem hopelessly unrealistic to a modern girl like you, but I really believed that we were meant for one another and that we'd be together one day. When he was ready I would be there waiting for him. I just knew, Lucy. I loved him so much it hurt.'

Lucy smiled. 'I've never felt that way about anybody,' she said. 'Boys came and went when I was in my teens. None ever made me think, *This is the guy I'll be with for ever.*'

'Quite. But I'd had such a protected childhood. I existed in a cocoon, wrapped in daydreams. It's dangerous to be too much alone with an imagination.

'The last summer term of tuition at Carlyon was a queer one. Miss Simpkins, whilst doing her duty by little Hetty, turned most of her attentions to me, to prepare me for school. Angie drifted through our lessons, making little effort. She was bored with the schoolroom, bored with being treated as a child. Anyone could see that. She talked endlessly about September.

The school she'd be going to in Paris, the other girls who might be there. Who might chaperone them on the journey. And there was great excitement when a letter arrived from Lady Hamilton offering to present Angie at court in the 1939 season.

'She clearly hated lessons, hated being stuck in the country. She longed for city life and excitement, to live in her father's big white house in London and go to parties every night. There was an anxiety about her longing that was unsettling; it was as though whatever she was given she would always still want the moon. I think her father had done that to her, with his absences and the confusing way he'd treat her when he was there, flirting with her, but taking little notice of her as a person. Thoughts of London were all bound up with him and the glamorous life she thought she'd been excluded from by her parents' rocky marriage.

'Of course, none of this ended up quite as planned. Germany invaded Austria in March 1938, and there was much uncertainty about whether Angie should go to Paris at all. In the end she went, but when Hitler annexed the Sudetenland and Mr Chamberlain returned from Munich at the end of September brandishing a piece of paper that everyone knew was worth more than the promise written on it, her family rather wished she hadn't.'

Beatrice was quiet for a moment and Lucy prompted, 'And you went to school.'

'Not right away, no,' Beatrice replied sadly. 'But that was nothing to do with Hitler. During the summer holidays, I was volunteered by my mother to help with a children's party at the tennis club. Several weeks later I woke with a fever and a terrible headache. By the end of the day I could hardly move, everything ached all over. The doctor was summoned and now it was my turn to be transferred to hospital. I'd caught polio, you see, from some child at the party.'

'Polio? But that's serious, isn't it?'

'Your generation doesn't know about polio, thank God, the fear the word engendered.'

'I know we're immunized against it. The vaccine used to be given on sugar lumps.'

'But not until after the war. Polio has been eradicated from large parts of the world now, but back then it was a terror.'

'It's a virus, isn't it?'

'Yes. Along with diphtheria and TB and a host of other nasties, it was a potentially fatal illness. I remember my mother's obsession with hygiene throughout my childhood. I wasn't to drink from the same cup as other children, I must wash my hands before meals, I mustn't take food that someone else had touched. Polio could be a devastating disease. If it got into the central nervous system it could paralyze or worse. I was lucky, since the version I got was relatively mild. But even after two weeks in hospital I was in bed for three months at home and very weak for some time after that.'

'I suppose you were kept in isolation.'

'That's right. Rafe used to write me letters and send me little presents, but all the summer holidays he was forbidden from seeing me. When the worst was over, we'd have conversations, he standing in the front garden, me at my bedroom window, but even this tired me.'

'So no school.'

'Not until after Christmas. Instead I stayed in this house and frankly I was glad to. It was a long, slow recovery, but recover I did.'

Looking at Beatrice's straight-backed figure, Lucy could well imagine that determination had been a major factor in that.

Beatrice picked up the battered photo album they'd been looking at earlier and turned the pages. When she got to the

very last page she stared at it awhile, before passing the album
to Lucy. The picture was of herself. She was posing with her
back to the camera, looking over her shoulder, so one could see
the trail of the long dress and the little gauze train.

'You look really beautiful,' Lucy breathed.

'Don't I?' Beatrice said, with a touching trace of pride. 'That
was taken at Carlyon Manor at Christmas 1938. I'll tell you
about it tomorrow, but what was set in motion at that party
proved far more devastating than any illness in my life.'

After leaving The Rowans, Lucy walked up the cliff path and
took the turning for the beach. Twice a day, she thought, the
tide washed everything away as though it had never been, but
it was still easy, standing in the dunes, to imagine all the events
that Beatrice had described. How the sea, today tranquil, could
turn to fury in a moment, and take a cruel revenge on two
unwary boys presuming to ride it in a fragile craft.

The tide was rising now, so she could not pass to the other
cove and look for the secret steps. Instead she chose to cross the
other headland, as Beatrice had often done, in the direction of
the town. She paused at the highest point to see St Florian laid
out before her, its buildings a colony of limpets clinging to the
hillside. Down in the harbour the tide was rousing the boats
from their sleep in the sand.

She set off downhill, eventually finding a steep flight of
mossy steps between two houses. Young Beatrice must have
walked down here, too. The passage emerged above the
quay, and across the little harbour, she saw the man she'd
seen in the hotel bar last night standing on *Early Bird*, getting
her ready for sea. He straightened and looked right over at
her, and waved. She walked across, her hair streaming in the
wind.

'Hello, again,' he called up to her, as she drew near. He had a clear, low voice with a slight lilt.

'Hi, I love your boat.'

'She isn't mine, but thank you.' He was threading a rope through an eyelet in a sail. 'I thought I'd get out while the tide was right,' he said. He secured the rope and stepped up onto the quay to meet her. 'I'm Anthony,' he said as he shook her hand with a firm grip. 'We keep nearly meeting, don't we? Do you live here?'

'I'm Lucy. No, I'm staying for a few days. Are you at the Mermaid, too?'

'I was just eating there. They do good comfort food.' He studied her for a moment then said, 'This might sound a bit forward, but would you like to come out in the boat with me?'

'Me? Now?'

'Why not? I've got some spare kit.'

'Oh, I don't sail. You wouldn't want a novice, would you?'

'Sure,' he said. 'You can swim, can't you?'

'Yes, though I hope I wouldn't need to. Really, though?' The idea was growing on her.

He looked her up and down, as though gauging her size, then stepped down into the boat and opened a locker. He brought out a pile of oilskin tops and trousers. She looked at them in dismay and said, 'Will I need all those?'

'It's very blustery out there.'

'I won't fall in,' she replied.

'Fine,' he said in a mild tone, but his expression was set, 'though take it from me, you'll be glad of them in this wind. You can use the cabin to change in.'

'I'll change at the hotel,' she said, just to be stubborn.

'As you like.' His eyes were merry now.

She took the armful of clothing and walked away, aware that he was amused by her. Quite why she was doing this, she didn't know. Her wretched impulsive nature again. Her mother had warned her about not getting in strangers' cars, but did boats count, too?

She was ready in ten minutes and returned to Anthony feeling self-conscious. 'I look like a penguin,' she told him, splaying her feet, and he laughed. Her sleeves were too long and she had to roll up the legs of the trousers above her canvas shoes. He couldn't resist a grin, but seeing this made her chin go up.

'Here, you'll need this,' he said, as he passed her a buoyancy aid. It looked like a padded waistcoat.

'Is this right?' she said, pulling it on.

'Zip it up and the belt goes . . .' he said, standing close to make an adjustment, 'like this.'

Everything went wrong from the moment she stepped into the vessel. 'Sit down, no, over here, you're rocking the boat,' he commanded. She moved, wobbled and clutched at a wooden pole, which swung free, nearly knocking her over. 'Ouch,' she cried.

'Are you all right? Now, mind the boom or it'll get you again.'

He gave her a rope that was tied to the sail and she sat down. 'The boom,' she repeated. There was a whole new language here. He started up the engine and they motored out between the arms of the harbour in a cloud of fumes. A cold wind struck immediately and Lucy gasped. They set off for the centre of the bay.

'Right,' Anthony cried. 'If you take the tiller, I'll get the sails up.'

'I don't know what to do,' she said.

'Just hold this. If you want to go right move it this way – left, that way. Straight to go straight. Keep her into the wind. You'll pick it up easy.'

They swapped places. She pulled and pushed the tiller arm and the wind blew them in little circles. 'Hold it still, will you?' he said.

'I can't,' she replied.

'Try, or we'll end up in the drink.'

Eventually she got the hang of it and Anthony got the sails up and turned off the motor. He thrust the end of a rope at her and said, 'Right, grab this and change places. Now.' They did a stupid dance, trying to pass one another.

'Don't let the boom go,' he shouted and she pulled on the rope, panicking as the strength of the wind filled the sails. The boat whipped along, the rope sawing at the skin on her fingers. 'There's some gloves in that locker,' he said, but she couldn't move to get them and now the boat was tearing towards rocks.

'Ready about,' Anthony shouted. 'Pull the rope hard.' She did, and the sail flapped in the wind. 'Now. Duck! Watch the . . . oh hell.'

The swinging boom this time hit her on the side of the head as the boat wheeled round. She cried out with the pain. 'Keep hold of the rope,' he cried. 'Haul it in! *Haul it in!*'

'I can't. Everything hurts. Stop shouting at me.'

'Here, take the tiller. Hold it steady.' He reached for the rope and pulled the sail tight, then hitched the rope round a convenient cleat and returned to take the tiller.

'Right,' he said. 'Untie that rope and hold in that sail for dear life. When I say "ready about", hold it firm, I'll move the tiller and the bow will swing round. Then watch out for the boom which will move across the boat. And that's the moment you tighten the rope and hold on for dear life. Got it?'

'Yes,' she said, crossly, rubbing her face on her sleeve. 'Just stop shouting at me.'

'I'm not shouting, I'm giving instructions.'

'You could at least say please.'

He looked at her in astonishment, then his expression turned to a comic urgency as he cried, 'Ready about. For God's sake, *do it!*'

'*Please,*' she shouted back, but ducked under the boom just in time and hauled on the rope.

'*Please* and bloody thank you,' he said, and she sat up straight and smiled.

'You are something else,' he said finally.

She was starting to enjoy it now, the excitement of the wind and the spray dashing her face, the flight of the craft skimming through the blue-green water. She was freezing, but getting to the stage of numbness where it was starting to feel warm. She closed her eyes and was relaxing a little when he shouted, 'Ready about, again. Please.' And she pulled the rope and got the sail across just in time.

They were right out to sea now, far from land and she didn't like to think of the fathoms of water beneath. It was an act of faith, this, being on a boat, working with the weather and the capriciousness of the sea. No wonder sailors were a superstitious lot. What else did they have but the signs of the sky and the water and the hints the gods gave them? She looked back the way they'd come. St Florian was a scar of white and grey on the flank of the land.

It was on their way back that the disaster happened. They were nearing the harbour and Anthony ordered her to swap places again and hold the tiller while he reeled in the sails. He was just coming to reclaim his seat and Lucy stood up to swap over, but she let go of the tiller too early. A great gust of wind blew the boat round and she wobbled, screaming. She grabbed the nearest object, which happened to be him; he stumbled, roared and fell over the side.

'Help, what do I do?' she shrieked at the empty water. After a long, long moment he surfaced, gasping, still holding tightly to the rope, and clutched the side of the boat.

'Sit down!' he spluttered. 'No, over there. Now lean out that way.' With a supreme effort he managed to haul himself back in. He didn't stop to recover, but seized the tiller and brought the boat under control. His eyes were steel and she was afraid to say anything. They entered the harbour and slipped quietly into their mooring.

She waited until he'd tied up before saying meekly, 'Anthony, I'm terribly, terribly sorry. It was my first time. I didn't know what to do. I should have listened to you.'

She was relieved to see a slow smile spread like a flame across his frozen face. His eyes sparkled and he started to laugh.

'What?' she said. 'What? Tell me!' Then she started to laugh, and soon they were both helpless with laughter.

'Please,' he said. 'Please. Oh, wait till I tell the boys that.'

'What boys?' she asked, but he was still laughing.

Finally he said, 'Go on, you go and get changed. I'll finish up here.'

She climbed up onto the jetty. 'Thank you,' she called down. 'Buy you a drink in the bar later?'

'I'm staying in a borrowed house till Sunday,' he said an hour later, taking a draught of the local bitter. They were sitting opposite one another at a wooden table in front of the hotel, the evening being mild. 'It was my friend's boat, really, but it doesn't get used much now. I thought you did very well, by the way.'

Lucy almost choked on her lager in surprise. 'Don't be daft. I was a disaster.'

'No, really, for a first-timer. You kept your head.'

'And tipped the skipper in. Surely they used to make you walk the plank for that.'

He smiled in that way she liked, which illuminated his face. He was a little older than her, she thought, but not by so much. His tanned skin and short, sun-bleached reddish hair signalled long hours spent outdoors. She sat, chin in hand, watching him roll a cigarette and light it with slow, capable movements. She wanted to ask him about himself, but she sensed a barrier.

'So you're on holiday?' was the question she settled on.

'That's about it.' He stared past her, out to sea. Finally his eyes met hers. 'I'm an Army officer. Just finishing home leave after a long stint in Afghanistan. Reporting for duty again Monday.'

'Oh,' she said.

'You're frowning. What are you thinking?'

'Just that it sounds a bit more important than TV film production.'

'That's what you do?'

'Yes.'

'What sort of thing?'

'Historical drama at the moment. With the odd documentary thrown in.'

'Which is the kind of programme I enjoy watching when off-duty. Therefore vital to the world.'

'You know what I mean.'

'Yes.'

She hesitated for a moment then said, 'Have you had an awful time?'

Again, that far-off look out to sea. After a moment he nodded. He took a long drink of his beer. 'It's good to be home, to sit on an April evening by the sea.' His eyes crinkled. 'Hey, what about you? Holiday?'

'Not really – well, sort of. I mean, I don't have to be back at work till Monday either, but this trip was a bit unplanned. I'm trying to solve a family mystery.'

'That sounds interesting. A skeleton in the cupboard?'

'Possibly, yes. My granny's family used to live here. In Carlyon Manor up the road.'

His face betrayed surprise. 'That burnt-out place? I walked past it the other day.'

'The man at the museum said it happened a long time ago.'

'Oh, I've met him.'

'He's been very kind. Fixed me up to see an old lady who turns out to be my great-aunt by marriage.'

'And she's got a story to tell?'

'A fascinating one. I'm on the trail of a great-uncle who disappeared in the Second World War. My father was obsessed with the mystery, and I'm trying to find out why. She's still telling me about it all.'

'What did your great-uncle do in the war?'

'I don't know exactly. Something to do with Special Operations.'

He nodded slowly. 'I've read up a bit about that. Would I have heard of him?'

'I've no idea. His name was Rafe Ashton.'

'Rafe Ashton. No, it doesn't ring any bells.'

'His official file was empty.'

'Was it now? Cover-up by our people, do you suppose?'

'It looks like it.'

'Let me know if you want me to sift around. See if I can find anything through my channels.'

'I will,' she said. 'Thank you.' She brought out her purse.

'It's definitely my round next,' he said.

'No, I'll buy,' she replied, 'but it's not that. I was looking for this.' She handed him one of her business cards.

'Lucy Cardwell,' he read aloud. 'Blue Arch Studio. That's you?'

'Yes, that's my mobile number. And my email.'

He pulled his wallet out of his jacket and stowed the card away safely then gave her his contact details.

'Well, Lucy Cardwell,' he said, 'it's definitely my round. And I'll bring out the menu – unless you've got other plans.'

Later, in her hotel room, she checked her phone and found another message from Will. He was beginning to sound impatient and she knew she couldn't pretend any longer. It wasn't fair on either of them. She called his number, and when he answered they had one of those stumbling conversations at the end of which both parties were in agreement that things weren't working. It was, they decided, best that they return to being friends.

After switching off her phone again, Lucy was surprised to feel not sadness but a soaring relief. She lay down on her bed and thought of the time she'd spent with Anthony, their laughter when they'd regained the safety of the quay – and she smiled.

Chapter 10

Today, Tuesday, a large flat cardboard box had joined the photograph albums on Beatrice's table. Beatrice coaxed off the lid, lifted several layers of tissue paper and shook out a gorgeous dress of silver slashed with midnight blue, onto which was sewn a small train of a pewter-coloured gauzy material.

'It's the dress from your photograph. How wonderful,' Lucy said, stroking the soft garment. 'To think it's survived so long.'

'It's lovely, isn't it?' Beatrice said. 'My mother made it. The rows we had over the fittings! I was so cross and fidgety, having to stand still with pins sticking in me, that she lost her temper one day and threw it into the dustbin. That shocked me. I had to creep out and rescue it and apologize.'

'Was it made for a special occasion?'

'The Wincantons threw a party at Carlyon Manor two days before Christmas 1938. It was, I'm sure, Oenone Wincanton's idea. She felt, no doubt, that her chicks were starting to fly the nest, and wanted to mark the fact. I think she also felt sorry for me. My life had come to a temporary halt, you see. I was still weak and thin, and I had a slight limp from my illness. And I was going away to school, not somewhere marvellous abroad or having a season. The party was like a consolation prize, my only chance at coming out. Rafe was invited and a whole host of young people from local families. Even Michael Wincanton graced us with his presence. After all, there were appearances to keep up, no matter how stormy their marriage was in private.'

As an honorary member of the family and because Angelina begged her to help her dress, Beatrice arrived at Carlyon early, driven by her father in his borrowed car, her dress wrapped in tissue in a box on her lap, her mother's only good jewellery tucked safely in a vanity case on the back seat.

Brown, who admitted her, said, 'Thank God you're here, miss. Maybe you'll put some sense into that young lady. I don't know what they've been teaching her in France, but it certainly ain't good manners. Find your own way up, miss, would you, or Cook'll have me guts for gaiters.' And she fled through the green baize door.

Beatrice stood in the hall for a moment, listening to the tension that crackled through the house. From the dining room Mrs Wincanton could be heard giving orders. Bless the butler nodded a greeting as he passed through with a callow youth in train, each of them bearing a tray of champagne flutes. From the floor above emanated a girlish shriek of temper followed by a throaty laugh. Angie and Peter. Picking up her luggage with a sigh, Beatrice went upstairs.

She reached Angie's room in time to see Peter sauntering out of it, hands in trouser pockets and with a sneery smile pasted on his face. When he noticed Beatrice, his expression went blank in that strange shy way he had. Muttering, 'Hello,' he dodged past her.

'Hello, Peter.' He'd grown appreciably since she last saw him at the beginning of the summer. Sixteen he was now – taller, the coarser, adult features beginning to form. Where Ed was assuming the best side of each of his parents, his mother's temperate blonde beauty and his father's handsome physique, the leaner Celtic looks of some more remote ancestor were blooming darkly in Peter. His cleverness, though, and the moody air were all his own. Beatrice felt awkward with him and pitied him in equal measure. She had gathered from comments Ed let drop that, though no longer bullied, Peter lacked friends at school and that his shyness and surliness drew unfair comparisons with his elder brother. Ed clearly felt sorry for him and had done his best to protect him. Now Ed had gone up to university Peter was alone and no one was certain how he fared.

'Go away!' Angie cried, when Beatrice knocked on the half-open door.

'It's me,' Beatrice said, going in.

'Thank heavens you've come. No one here has time to help me with my dress.' She was standing at the basin in petticoat and stockings. On the bed lay the most beguiling confection of pale green satin and froths of white lace.

'Oh, Angie,' Beatrice cried, fingering the silky fabric. 'It's beautiful.' She helped Angie pull it over her head, aware of the girl's warm back under her fingers as she fastened the column of tiny buttons. The cut of the gown flattered Angie's curves perfectly, and against the green her skin glowed luminous, without a flaw. The fashionably natural waves of her honey-coloured hair needed merely the flick of a brush. Soon pearls gleamed at her ears and throat.

Beatrice stood back to see the effect. Manners or no, Angie had certainly acquired a kind of allure abroad, a sophistication. She looked perfect.

'How am I?' Angie asked, twisting and turning to see her reflection in the big cheval mirror.

'Wonderful,' said Beatrice. 'The dress is lovely with your hair.'

'Now it's your turn,' Angie said happily, and Beatrice opened her box and took out her precious dress.

Moments later, Beatrice took her turn by the mirror, a curious expression on her face.

'Oh,' Angie said, staring at her. 'I think I'm going to cry.'

It was the first time Beatrice had seen herself full-length in the dress and she couldn't believe that the stranger who looked back, rather a beautiful stranger, was herself. The blue and the silver glimmered against her glossy dark curls, highlighting her pointed ivory face and bright chestnut eyes. Her mother's sapphire pendant lay on her collarbone, and she clipped on the matching drop earrings. They pinched her ears madly, but the pain must be borne. She slipped her feet into the silver kid sandals her mother had bought in Truro.

'You're not little brown Bea any more!' Angie whispered. The face looking over Beatrice's shoulder in the mirror did not show admiration so much as envy, and Beatrice was shocked. But when she turned to look at Angie the expression had been smoothed away. All was as serene as before.

'Come on,' Angie said, handing her some gloves, and they went downstairs together.

The hall was already full of men in dinner jackets and women in opulent dresses divesting themselves of coats, hats and fur wraps, taking glasses from the young boy's tray, noticing the wonderful Christmas tree covered in candles before moving into the drawing room to be greeted by Mr and Mrs Wincanton.

As the girls came down the stairs, they were received by a sea of admiring faces. They were looking not just at Angie, but at both of them – blonde and brunette, light and dark, a pair of opposites, but both lovely.

Just then, Bless opened the front door, and there on the doorstep stood Rafe.

He paused on the threshold, looking from Beatrice to Angie and back to Beatrice, who smiled at him shyly, but it was Angie who pushed forward to greet him.

'Oh, Rafe, you're nice and early,' she said, taking his coat. 'Don't we all look grown-up?'

'You both look very well,' he stammered, and blushed. His eyes said 'stunning' and Angie laughed, one of her golden infectious giggles.

'Thank you. So do you, doesn't he, Bea?'

Rafe, too, was all grown up, tall and dashing in formal dress, his fair hair soft in the light of the candles. As they helped themselves to champagne, Beatrice couldn't keep her eyes off him.

'Well met, Ashton!' called Ed, coming across and clasping Rafe's hand. And turning to Angie and Beatrice, 'I say, you girls look . . .' He trailed to a halt.

'Don't they?' Rafe said, the first rush of champagne hitting its mark.

'Shall we take you to Mummy and Daddy?' Angie asked. She was looking at Rafe, who immediately presented his arm to escort her. Beatrice pushed away her disappointment to take Ed's.

'Darlings!' Oenone said, as they passed into the drawing room. 'So lovely. And boys, you look so handsome. Where's Peter, by the way? Is he down?' No one seemed to know.

'Who are these exquisite young things? I don't remember inviting them,' Michael Wincanton said. Angie squealed delightedly. 'Oh, Daddy, don't be silly,' she said, and leaned to kiss him. Over his daughter's shoulder, Mr Wincanton looked Beatrice up and down with open appreciation. He reached to clap his son on the shoulder and to shake hands with Rafe.

They moved past Angie's parents, further into the room, where they merged with the other younger visitors, the children Ed and Angie and latterly Beatrice had played tennis and shared dancing lessons with, whose birthday parties they'd won prizes at and who were now, many of them, at their first proper adult party, awkward, spotty and gangly, most shy and self-conscious. The girls grouped together in little giggling groups for safety, peeping at the boys, who squared up to one another like young bucks clashing antlers, ignoring the girls.

'Beatrice, that's such a clever dress,' said Deirdre Garnett, large-framed and deep-voiced. 'No one would guess about your poor legs.' Everyone heard her and everyone immediately stared at Beatrice's skirts, as though wondering if she wore callipers underneath.

'My legs are completely fine, thank you,' she said in her coldest tone. 'The doctor says I'll be perfectly all right.' She'd liked to have added, 'Which is more than I can say about you and your fat hips, Deirdre,' but of course didn't.

She wandered off crossly to where Rafe was standing by the fire, already deep in discussion with Ed, who loved talking politics. 'I say we should stop him now, before he gets the idea anything goes.'

'But we're hardly prepared for a war,' Rafe replied. 'My uncle says we don't have the weapons or the planes.'

'We're rearming like mad,' Ed said. 'My father reckons we'll be ready for him.'

'Oh, you're not talking about war tonight, are you?' Beatrice said. Rafe was glancing across the room and when she followed the line of his gaze she realized he was watching Angelina. Angie was whispering into the ear of a man Beatrice didn't know, a rather obviously good-looking man in his forties, with a moustache and an overly familiar manner.

'Who's that?' Beatrice asked.

'Oh, some businessman my father knows from the local Party. He's been coming to the house rather a lot recently to see my mother.' Ed's eyes were unreadable, but the undercurrent of his voice was disapproving. Whether this man came to see Oenone or her daughter, he clearly had what her father called 'an eye for the ladies'. She remembered the tensions that Oenone's previous admirer Rollo Treloar had once caused and hoped that there wouldn't be another row between Angie's parents.

'I told Mother I'd see where Pete's got to,' Ed said, excusing himself.

'Here, let's find ourselves another drink,' Rafe said, and they moved out into the hall where Bless filled their glasses, and from there to the library, cosy with its crackling fire, dark red curtains and old leather chairs. 'I'm glad I've got you alone,' Rafe said. 'There's something I must tell you. I had a letter. Mother's on her way home.'

'When? Oh, Rafe, surely that's good news!'

'She'll arrive early in the New Year. Everybody's so worried about the international situation it seems sensible. But the thing is, Bea, I'll be spending the holidays in London from now on. That's where my stepfather has a place, you see. I won't be down here so often. That is, I'll try to come, but it's not going to be easy. We'll still be friends, of course, won't we?'

Beatrice felt all her energy draining. She would be away at school, then in Gloucestershire with her grandparents, or here. She wouldn't see Rafe unless she went to London. Suddenly it was as though she was looking down a long, grim tunnel that wound she knew not where.

'Are you all right?' he asked her anxiously.

'Yes,' she lied, but she felt the corners of her mouth turn down. 'But I'll miss you, Rafe.' She couldn't help herself. Her throat prickled.

He leant forward and with a finger lifted a tear from her cheek. 'Bea,' he said. 'Oh, don't cry. We'll still see one another, I promise.'

She tried hard not to weep, but all the frustration and worry of the last months was surging to the surface. She'd felt so trapped. So bored. Sometimes she'd believed she'd be at home for ever, looking after her parents as they grew older and with her father getting more unwell and more tetchy. These were her thoughts, but instead she said, 'I'll miss our holidays together.'

'Don't, please,' Rafe said. 'Something will turn up, you'll see.' He put his arm round her and hugged her and she laid her head on his shoulder. His grip tightened. They stood together a moment or two, then he released her and said gently, 'I'll tell you what, why don't you go up and wash your face, then we'll find a bit of supper.'

She nodded, unaccountably disappointed. She walked slowly up the stairs, unable to control her tears now, then blundered along the corridor to the bathroom, which mercifully was unoccupied. She dabbed cold water on her face, dried it on the wafer-cotton towel, quickly patted her hair into place, then sat on the side of the bath staring glumly into the distance. Rafe didn't see her as anything but a friend. She couldn't blame him, not really. He had the whole of his life before him, university and a career, maybe as a great doctor. And now she would be part of his past, not his future. To stop herself crying again, she pinched herself hard, then after one more look at her tragic face in the mirror, unlocked the door. By the stairs she paused, then turned back. She should fetch a spare handkerchief from her case.

As she opened the door to Angelina's room, she caught a movement in the darkness further down the corridor. 'Hetty, shouldn't you be in bed, dear?' she called. 'Oh, it's you.'

Peter moved out of the shadows.

'What are you doing up here?' Beatrice asked. 'They've been looking for you.'

'Have they? Not very hard then. I've been in my room all the time.' He came and stood in the doorway, watching as she searched for the handkerchief. Angelina had left her bedside light on, and it cast strange shadows across the room.

'Why don't you go downstairs?' she asked. 'What's the matter?'

'I could ask the same of you.' He followed her into the room and she pitied him his awkwardness, in an evening suit that was too big for him, the tie hanging awry. He knocked against the dressing-table, upsetting Angelina's glass bottles. 'Damn.'

'Oh, I'll see to it.' She went over and started to put everything straight.

He pulled at his collar, irritated by its stiffness. They stared at each other in the dressing-table mirror. Two miserable faces.

'You're the same, aren't you,' he said finally. 'They get to you, don't they?'

'Who?' she asked, puzzled.

'All of them. They're so . . . self-absorbed, aren't they? Ed's not so bad, he can't help having to be responsible, but Father and Mother and my bloody sisters.' He looked around the room and now she saw it as through his eyes. Discarded clothes were strewn over the floor, a couple of fashion magazines lay open on the pink and white frilled eiderdown; Angie had spilt a box of face powder on the floor by the basin and not bothered to clear it up. Beatrice hadn't thought about it before, how Angie moved through life assuming that someone else would always clear up after her. Was this what Peter meant? Her own little case and the box for her dress, she had set neatly against the wall, ready for when the Brookers' driver came for her and Rafe at midnight.

'Peter, what's wrong?' she asked. He had a wild look about him. 'Why don't you come down?'

He shrugged. 'I'd rather be tortured on a rack. What would I say to all those people? I hardly know them.' She saw he hated the whole idea of the party, the small talk, pretending to look as though he was enjoying himself. 'And that man,' he muttered. 'How my mother has the nerve . . .'

'Who do you mean?' But again she read his mind. The bold-looking man with the moustache. It must be Oenone he came to visit. 'How do you know, Peter?' she asked him. 'You might be wrong.'

'I know, all right? I've seen them together, Brent Jarvis and my mother.' And he uttered a word she didn't know the meaning of, but it sounded horrid.

'Don't, Peter.'

'Why are you defending her?'

'She's your mother. She loves you. And she's always been kind to me.'

'That's what you think, is it? Bea, she's just using you. They're all using you. They use everybody, don't you see?'

'That's a horrible thing to say, Peter. You must be ill or something.'

'No, it's the truth. They all want power in their own crooked little ways – my father in his Cabinet, my mother out here, doing whatever she likes, and Angelina's worst of all. Watch out for Angelina. If she sees someone else wants something, she takes it. She can't help it. She has a need to be the centre of attention.'

Beatrice stared at him, her mind working, suddenly remembering the way Angie had looked at her in the mirror, her behaviour with Rafe this evening. She put her hands over her face as if to shut away the image. Peter was twisting everything, that was all. His hatred was poisonous.

'I don't believe you,' she said, her voice dull.

'Yes, you do.' She felt him come close. He pulled her hands away roughly. 'Look at me,' he said, and she did. The anguish on his face was dreadful to see. 'Believe me.'

'Peter,' she said, desperate. 'You've got it wrong. They love you and care for you. They've been worrying all evening where you were. Didn't they find you?'

'Ed came up, and Mother,' he said. He chuckled. 'They knocked and called a bit, then when I didn't answer they went away. As I say, they didn't try very hard. I don't fit in, you see. Don't play the games they play.'

'That's silly,' she said. 'Childish.'

'Don't be unkind!' he cried. 'Not you, too.'

'No, of course I won't be, Peter, don't worry, it's all right.' But he was looking at her so tenderly now it frightened her. She'd always been wary of him – his moods, his cutting comments – and now it was as though he stood open before her, and she saw his unhappiness down to the core. Poor Peter, the misfit. He slumped suddenly on the bed beside her, rolled over and buried his face in the eiderdown. She put a hand on his shoulder to comfort him as Rafe had tried to comfort her only half an hour ago. She knew he was wrong about his family. They did love him. They were loyal. They loved her and had been kind to her. Angelina had her faults, of course she did, but that was understandable. She was vulnerable, too. Beatrice didn't mind that Mrs Wincanton had made her Angie's guardian angel, she was proud to do it. And now Peter needed her help, too.

She coaxed him to sit up and it helped her to be strong. 'Peter, come on. Your tie's all crooked – there. Let's go down, then, well, maybe you would take me in to supper.' She'd said she'd go with Rafe, but Rafe would surely understand.

When they got downstairs, it was as though someone had turned on a bright light and she saw everything more clearly. She realized that her hostess and Brent Jarvis Esquire kept a too deliberate distance from each other, that Mr Wincanton had disappeared altogether. As for Angie, Rafe came up, full of apologies. 'I waited a bit for you, then Angie asked me to take her in for supper. I hope you don't mind.'

Beatrice shook her head dumbly.

After supper, Peter drank glass after glass of wine and shadowed Beatrice like a silent black dog, though hanging back from the dancing and the carol-singing round the piano, which was played by Jarvis. She was glad when midnight came and the car arrived to take them home. In the back seat, Rafe held her hand all the way and talked about the Wincantons, how pretty Angie had grown and what a good chap Ed was. On and on. Beatrice could hardly bear to listen.

Everybody was going away. After Christmas, Rafe travelled to Southampton to meet his mother off the ship, then accompanied her to London. On the first day of 1939, Beatrice walked up to Carlyon Manor to say goodbye to the Wincantons. The household was in a flurry of packing up. Angie, after much debate, was to return to Paris for a short time at least, Peter was set for school, Ed for Oxford. Only ten-year-old Hetty and her mother would remain, and they, too, would be moving to London in March for the start of the season. Beatrice wandered through the untidy rooms, sensing that a whole era of her life was coming to an end.

There was her own packing up to do, her mother furiously sewing name-tapes on the blouses, tunics and cardigans that arrived in the post. Two days into January her father drove her to his parents in Gloucestershire – the first time she'd met them for several years. In their lovely house of golden stone also lived her uncle and aunt and three younger cousins. Her grandparents' household was a formal one, Mr and Mrs Marlow growing elderly now, and Beatrice's Uncle George, Hugh's elder brother, had taken over the management of the estate. She liked the gentle rolling countryside and the villages of mellow stone, liked being part of a busy family household and being treated as a grown-up, dressing for dinner every night and being introduced to guests as though she were a young woman, no longer a child. The cousins were rather sweet, twin girls of eight and a younger brother of six. Their mother, Aunt Julia, was Uncle George's much younger second wife, his first, Sylvia, having caught tuberculosis and died around the time Beatrice was born. Julia was a jolly, friendly woman with a passion for hats and days out. She immediately took Beatrice under her wing, taught her to style her hair more fashionably and gave her face powder and lipstick.

Several days later, her father drove her to Larchmont, a girls' school twenty miles from her grandparents', and for the first time in her life she was left alone amongst strangers.

Larchmont was not one of those schools designed to teach genteel young ladies accomplishments. Rather, its Headmistress had founded it shortly after the Kaiser's war to give girls who might need to earn a living an academic education.

Beatrice was relieved to find that although she was a little behind in geometry and algebra, Miss Simpkins had served her splendidly in all the other subjects she must take for her School Certificate. Lessons in a class of intelligent girls, mostly eager to learn, were a delightful new experience. The boarding, however, she hated.

The school was situated in a converted mill, and a very long narrow room under the eaves held the forty boarders in a single dormitory with no privacy but the blankets under which they slept. The bathrooms, too, were communal. Whilst in many ways enlightened, the Headmistress had no truck with individualism. Solitude, apart from the rule of silence in the library to foster private study, was deemed unhealthy, and once studies were over, the girls were expected to play team games in all weathers, or to join in the weekly cross-country runs. Beatrice, because of her illness, was excused all these, but since to be different at Larchmont meant social ostracism, she quickly became determined to drive the weakness from her limbs. This didn't stop a small group of girls seeing her as odd and freezing her out of their activities. In time, she found her place, swimming in the middle of the shoal, determined to be no different from the other nervous fish swimming about her. It was to be another lesson in survival and she learnt it well.

She and Rafe wrote to one another regularly. He was happy that his mother was home, but the first surprise of the year was that he gave up Oxford, which seemed to be down to difficulties with money. *My stepfather has arranged for my inclusion in the next intake at military college. There's nothing I can do.*

At the end of March, Beatrice went home to Cornwall. On the evening of 26 March, the family listened to the devastating news that Hitler's troops had invaded Czechoslovakia. Beatrice's father leant forward and turned off the wireless. 'Well, that's it then,' he said, his eyes blazing with a strangely satisfied light. 'Even Chamberlain can't ignore that.'

'What do you think he'll do?' Delphine asked, her dark eyes huge in her pale face with its halo of prematurely greying hair. 'There's still a chance, isn't there? He wouldn't attack France or us. Why would he do that? Why should we have to fight him?'

Hugh Marlow took out his pipe and started to pack it with tobacco. 'We can't stand by and watch, my love, as he ravages other nations,' he said. 'It's a moral principle, as simple as that. And it could be us next.'

Chapter 11

'Never mind the people of Czechoslovakia,' Beatrice Ashton told Lucy. 'Never mind the inexorable road to war. For Angelina, it was as though nothing had happened.' She rooted about in a shoebox and brought out a small packet of letters, one of which she extracted and passed to Lucy.

'This was all she could think about when Prague fell under the jackboot.'

Lucy took the sheets of folded paper, the top one engraved with an address in Queen's Gate, Kensington. The letter was written in her grandmother's rounded hand, quite easy to read.

Darling Bea,

Two nights ago, I was presented!! It was the most exciting night of my life. You should have seen my dress – apricot and silver brocade with the most darling little buttons and a long shimmering train and a feather headdress that was a nightmare to put on. Aunt Alice lent me the lace gloves she wore when she was presented to Queen Mary. I really felt like a princess. We drove in the Hamiltons' car to the Palace, and the crowds, dearest, they pressed up against the windows to look in – quite alarming it was, yet exciting at the same time. There were dozens of other girls and we all had to stand in a group in a huge echoing room, till the King and Queen arrived, then wait simply ages until our names were called. There was so much to remember to get right. I was terrified

I'd make a mess of my curtsey – you know how clumsy I can be,
and my dance teacher had quite despaired – but I don't think I
wobbled too badly. The King looked well enough, if a little stern,
I thought, but the Queen was very sweet and gracious and asked
about my father, whom she remembered meeting once at a dinner.
And next Tuesday is my dance and I'm a bag of nerves. I wish you
could be here, Bea, and not at your mouldy old school. It's all so
thrilling. I hardly think about Carlyon one bit, though of course I
miss the dear horses and I miss you, my darling.

Lucy handed it back to Beatrice. 'I see what you mean. I
suppose she was still very young. She told me once about being
presented. She made it sound as though it was one of the greatest experiences of her life.'

'You're a kind girl and you're right, I'm not entirely fair
to her,' Beatrice said, replacing the pack of letters in the box.
'Our lives had to go on in the usual way, after all, and those
debutantes all felt that it was their turn, their moment. It was
what they'd been bred up for. It's all too easy to be disapproving, looking back. My parents took a great interest in the
political situation. Many people weren't so well informed. But
as the year waxed on there was such an odd atmosphere – on
the wireless or when you talked to people. It was as if we
knew we were walking towards disaster but could do nothing
about it.'

'I read somewhere that that sort of situation can make people
eager to grab life and live for the moment,' Lucy said.

'I suppose that's it. The danger imparted an urgency to
everything. And so the debutantes danced and flirted, and I,
who was only able to read what Angie wrote about it, I missed
it all.'

July 1939

For two months now there had been no letter from Rafe, just a postcard of Nelson's Column that arrived at school at the end of June with a *Hope all well, having a splendid time, will write soon* scrawled on the back which falsely raised her expectations. She wrote back to him immediately, a long gossipy letter about her school life, and looked every day after that for a reply, but there was nothing and she was cast down. Then term ended and her father came to fetch her.

Home was dull. Her parents were pleased to see her, of course, but they'd got used to being without her. Delphine was using Beatrice's bedroom as a storeroom. There was a strange winter coat mothballed in the wardrobe, and a stack of Parisian fashion magazines – her mother's private weakness – under the chest-of-drawers. Bea found one or two acquaintances to play tennis with, and exercised the horses for old Harry, but with the Wincantons away, St Florian's felt empty.

The letter from Angie landed on the mat at home a week later. She picked it up with a feeling of foreboding, hearing the postman's mournful whistle and the squeak of the garden gate.

'I'm taking Jinx out,' she called to her mother. On a whim, she set off, not for the beach, but up past the tennis club, where a path led alongside a field of ripening grain. By the tennis courts was a bench where she sat and took out the letter. The place had a deserted feel about it. Behind her, Mr Varcoe, the groundsman, was re-liming the lines on the grass courts.

The envelope smelt of scent and stiff elegance, and opened easily. She read it twice, which was necessary, for the sentences rambled about in Angie's careless manner.

Darling Bea,

Thank you for yours of last week. It's funny to think of you being back in Cornwall. How are Cloud and Nutmeg and Jezebel? I do miss them, but I'd rather be here. You wouldn't believe what a marvellous time I'm having. Last night Katie Halpern's dance was in a gorgeous garden near Hyde Park with strings and strings of gold and silver lanterns and a band on a platform like a boat in the middle of a tiny artificial lake. The night before, we sat through a performance of A Midsummer Night's Dream *in Regent's Park, and of course I wished I'd listened a bit more when Miss Simpkins made us read it, but, heyho, it seemed difficult and boring then, not magical and funny. I must tell you, I often see Rafe and his brother at parties. They both look terribly dashing in their officers' uniforms. Gerald's already a Captain, and a lot of the girls are mad for him, but the talk is of him getting engaged to Katie. Rafe is awfully sweet to me and we often speak of you. Mummy's asked for Carlyon to be ready at the beginning of August so I'll look forward to seeing you for a few days then.*

Beatrice sat for a long moment, lost in thought. Gradually she became aware of the normal sounds of summer around her. Birds singing, Mr Varcoe's pottering, someone sawing wood a couple of gardens away. Jinx lay panting, waiting patiently for his walk. There was nothing to suggest that life was any different from five minutes ago and she couldn't say exactly how, but it was. Something had shifted. The thought of walking back home to her parents and continuing with the routines of her life seemed completely impossible.

Jinx gave a little bark to remind her he was there.

'Yes, all right,' she told him. She made herself stand up.

She'd go on, that's what she'd do. She'd walk Jinx through the fields and go home and then she'd think what to do next.

She refolded the letter carefully and slotted it back in its envelope. She stared at her name, distorted by Angie's rounded scrawl, and felt a quick shaft of anger. Quickly she tore the letter to shreds, which she thrust deep into the Brookers' privet hedge. This badly scratched her hand, but she welcomed the pain. Only when she unclipped Jinx's lead, by the field, did she notice the gathering beads of blood.

The Wincantons came in August as promised. Well, Oenone and her children did, but they were often busy with visitors and Beatrice felt uncomfortable about inviting herself up. Some days, though, she was asked to the house and went eagerly, trying to make herself believe that all was the same as it had always been. And it was – on the days when it was just Ed and Peter, Angie, Hetty and Bea again, and they went riding or swimming, or simply hung about the garden, squabbling about who cheated at croquet.

Angie and Deirdre, the large-boned girl who'd been tactless about Beatrice at the Christmas party, shared a birthday picnic on the beach. Beatrice indulged her new hobby, taking pictures with a camera she'd bought.

But there were times when she saw that her old relationship with the Wincantons had changed. One day she was foolish enough to call at the house without an invitation and found that a party of young people, three men and a girl, had arrived by car from London the evening before. Though Angie asked her to join them, the invitation was graceless and Beatrice quickly regretted accepting. Ed and Peter weren't about and Angie treated her rather distantly. She found herself hanging around on the edge of the group, feeling gauche.

There was a single bright point. One of the men caught her admiring the motor car, which was dark green and sleek.

'Is she easy to drive?' Beatrice asked.

'I'll show you what to do, if you like,' he said, opening the driver's door. 'Hop in and I'll get her going.'

The moment when the car first rolled forward under her control was terrifying. She stalled immediately.

'Left hand down,' he cried, when they were off again. 'Now straighten.' They took off down the drive, and out into the lane, to the cheers of the others.

'I say, you're jolly good for a girl,' one of the other men said, when they were safely back at Carlyon once more. Her spirits soared.

Still, she was glad when the visitors all left, though her hopes to have Angie to herself were quickly dashed. A few days later, it was Ed and Angie's turn to go away to a houseparty and though Beatrice and Peter played some desultory games of tennis at the club, the atmosphere was gloomy.

Finally, near the end of August, came the longed-for letter from Rafe. She ran upstairs to read it alone.

Dear Bea,

I'm sorry I've been a shabby correspondent, and that we haven't met for so long. I often think of you and St Florian. How are your honourable ps and my sainted aunt and uncle? It all seems another, faraway world. I'm billeted near Hyde Park now. It's not what I would have chosen, a bit dull, but the life's not too bad. I don't see my people as much as they'd like. The old man's home from India as well now. His regiment have found him a desk job here in London. I suppose something is going to happen sooner or later, that's what everybody says, and then maybe things will liven up. I wish it would get on with it if it's going to. It's the waiting that's bad for everybody.

Let me know if you come to London, and I'll see if we can meet.

Yours as ever,

Rafe.

She read it several times, repeating the *Yours as ever*, to herself, trying to squeeze meaning out of it.

Two weeks later, at the beginning of September, Rafe's wish was granted. Hitler's tanks rolled into Poland and the Allies delivered their ultimatum. Two long days passed and the world held its breath.

Sunday 3 September was a gloriously sunny day. Beatrice accompanied her mother to Mass, which Delphine had got into the habit of attending recently. They emerged as the clock on the Anglican church tower struck eleven, and were climbing the Jacob's Ladder, when she glanced up ahead to see the alarming vision of Hugh Marlow prowling at the top, clearly agitated.

'Hurry!' he shouted to them. 'For God's sake, hurry up!'

'What is it, Hugh?' Delphine cried, but he didn't reply, just stared wildly at the sky and gesticulated to them madly.

'What's the matter?' Delphine panted as they reached the top.

'Confound it, haven't you heard? We're at war. I've closed all the windows. I expect they'll be here soon.' He checked his watch and looked again at the horizon. Beatrice and Delphine looked, too. The sky was a deep, glorious empty blue, all the way to eternity.

A horrible mournful wail started up somewhere below in the town. A woman began screaming – a thin, passionless sound.

'It's the siren. Come on.' He hustled them back to the house where he fussed about fitting their gas masks and they sat fearfully in the sitting room waiting for the bombs to drop. Instead, some fifteen minutes later, the all clear sounded. They waited twenty minutes more. No roar of plane engines, no explosions. Nothing happened.

'Well, that's it, Beatrice. You won't be going back to school.' Her father looked white with exhaustion, but triumphant, too. At last something was happening in his quiet, sequestered life.

In fact, she did go back, but only once it was apparent that the bombs weren't coming any time soon. The next few days were a manic whirl of preparation. The Brookers lent their gardener to dig a hole for an Anderson shelter. Cook stationed buckets of water in every room – whether against gas attack or fire even she didn't seem sure, but Jinx made a right mess drinking from them. Mrs Marlow began to stockpile tins and bottles in the garden shed and boiled up several preserving pans of blackberry and apple for jam.

A week later, two dozen evacuees arrived off the train from London. 'We're not having one,' Hugh Marlow said, banging the marmalade pot down on the breakfast-table. 'Not with my condition. There are plenty of others who can take one better than we can.'

'Oh, Hugh,' was all Delphine said, spreading her napkin with a loud flap. She wouldn't look at him, and later, took him his coffee without speaking, banging the study door behind her. In the middle of the morning she went out. When she returned, she was holding the hand of a skinny five-year-old boy with a badly repaired hare lip. At the sight of Jinx the boy gave a terrified whimper and hid behind Mrs Marlow's skirts. 'This is Jamie,' she told her husband and daughter defiantly. 'He was the only one left. Someone had to take him, Hugh, and I know my duty.'

Beatrice gazed at Jamie, his thinness, his grimy city skin, in astonishment. But what was more astonishing was that her mother had openly gone against her father for the first time in their marriage.

Hugh Marlow merely shot his wife a look of scorching resentment and without a word marched into his study and closed the door.

That night Jamie wet the bed. Every morning after that, Delphine, with the expression of a martyr, came down the stairs with a bundle for the wash, Jamie creeping after her with a tear-stained face. After a fortnight, his mother, skinny and sharp-nosed, from whom no one had heard a word the whole time, pitched up without warning to fetch him home. Hugh Marlow had managed the whole time by ignoring the child entirely.

England grew tired of waiting for Hitler's bombs, and normal life – of a sort – resumed. Shortly after Jamie left, a letter arrived announcing that Larchmont School would reopen. Beatrice, returning by train this time to conserve petrol, was conscious of being almost the only person carrying a gas mask. This was at her father's insistence. It was the day she turned seventeen.

Chapter 12

In December 1939, near the end of term, Beatrice received a
letter with a London postmark and in a hand she recognized
at once as Oenone Wincanton's. Pushing away her toast, she
tore open the envelope. As she read she felt herself fill up with
happiness.

*Will you come and stay with us in Queen's Gate for a few days
before Christmas?* the letter ran. *I think it would do Angelina good
to see you, and of course we'd all love the pleasure of your company.
I wrote to your mother last week and received a reply this morning
agreeing to the plan. I gather your aunt might accompany you to do a
little shopping. Do say you'll come!*

Letters flew back and forth and all was quickly arranged.
Then she wrote to Rafe.

*I'm coming to London for a few days. Is there any chance of you
getting away? Do telephone me at the Wincantons' house. I'm sure
they won't mind.* She dipped the pen in the inkwell, thought a
moment, then added boldly, *It would be so lovely to see you,* then
quickly signed it, *Yours truly.* She sneaked out to the postbox
herself rather than leaving the envelope in the tray in the hall
where the other girls might see it and tease her. Would he even
receive it, let alone reply? She'd not heard from him for a while.

Her trunk was packed and sent ahead to Cornwall, but
she felt a little depressed about the meagre items in her small
London suitcase. The one evening gown she had with her – the

splendid party dress being much too showy for weekends at her grandparents' and therefore left in Cornwall – was very ordinary for London. Suppose they dined out or went to a show, what then?

Aunt Julia, being a woman of discernment, solved the problem. Sitting opposite Beatrice on the train up to London, she leant forward, eyes merry in her pretty, girlish face, and said: 'I'd like to buy you something nice to wear. A little Christmas present, if you like.'

When they reached Paddington she took Beatrice straightaway to a perfectly lovely shop in Bond Street, all hedged about with sandbags, where they had remarkably little trouble finding Beatrice a form-fitting evening gown in pale brown silk-satin and a pair of white lace gloves. Flushed with triumph, they took a bus to Harrod's, where they were delighted to find most of the usual Christmas fare – nuts, fruits, candy – if at quite a price. Aunt Julia took some time choosing dolls for her daughters and a model steam engine for her son, whilst Beatrice, with money from her allowance, bought pretty boxes of sweets to supplement the gifts she'd made for her family in sewing lessons.

It was her first proper visit to London, apart from to change trains at Paddington, and she was overawed by the hugeness of it. The air was cold, but clear. 'It makes such a difference to everything, now no one can afford to drive,' Julia remarked.

A maid who wasn't Brown opened the door of the white Regency house with black railings in Queen's Gate, which was the Wincantons' London home. Beatrice turned and waved down to Aunt Julia in the cab. Julia blew her a kiss and the cab pulled away.

Beatrice found herself in a big, chilly, high-ceilinged hall, greeting Jacky the dog, who looked uncertain of himself, being a country bumpkin in this elegant urban environment. To the right, a graceful staircase curved up out of sight. As she handed over her case and her coat, she was disturbed to hear raised voices. It proved only the first indication that something here was wrong.

She hugged to herself the thought of Rafe, safe, familiar. She yearned for him to be in touch. 'Nobody's telephoned for me, have they?' she asked the maid.

'No, miss, I don't think so,' was the reply.

Just then, a door at the back of the hall flew open and Angelina stormed out, her normally serene features distorted with anger. This turned to surprise at the sight of Beatrice, who, in turn, stared back, amazed.

'I'd no idea you were here,' Angelina murmured, coming forward.

'Only just,' Beatrice replied shyly. They pressed cheeks quickly. Angie smelled of face powder and expensive scent. *How grown up she looks*, Beatrice thought, *with her scarlet lipstick and her hair waved like that*. She had felt smart in her neat navy day dress and simple white clutchbag, but next to Angie she felt a plain jane.

'When did I see you last?' Angie was asking. 'Simply ages ago, anyway.'

Beatrice was hurt by this vagueness. 'August, of course. At Carlyon. I say, do you remember that picnic you and Deirdre had and how awful we all felt afterwards?'

'Did we? What happened?'

'Why, yes,' Beatrice said in puzzlement. Was Angie doing this on purpose? 'On your birthday. There was something wrong with the fishpaste sandwiches and we were all dreadfully ill.'

'Oh, I do remember now. It seems a lifetime ago – before the war. Did you see Deirdre in *Country Life*? I can't believe with her homely looks she's the first of us debs to get engaged.' She took Beatrice's arm. 'Come and see Mummy.' Her voice lowered suddenly. 'You won't believe it, but she's only just told me that you were coming. I'm simply furious with her. She says she forgot. *Forgot?* No, it's quite deliberate. She won't leave me alone.'

Beatrice followed her, feeling close to tears. Why hadn't Mrs Wincanton told Angie she was coming? And oh, the idea plunged her into misery – was that what they'd been quarrelling about? Her coming to stay?

The odd feeling of being a pawn in some unknowable game did not leave her.

'Beatrice!' Mrs Wincanton was sitting at a huge diningroom table, surrounded by cardboard boxes of all sizes and in various states of disembowelment. As she rose to greet Beatrice, a large ball of string rolled from the table onto the floor near Angie. Angie stood and watched it, arms folded, expression petulant. Beatrice stepped over, picked it up and passed it to Mrs Wincanton, feeling embarrassed by Angie's behaviour.

'Thank you, Beatrice. Always so helpful.'

She glared at her daughter. Angie glared back.

'My ladies have been here packing Christmas boxes,' Oenone explained, 'for little Jewish children.'

'Who don't actually celebrate Christmas,' Angie said. 'Daddy laughed like a drain when he heard that one, Bea.'

'Your father, as usual, is infuriating. Jews still have to eat at Christmas. And wash, one would hope. Plus, many of them are homeless. And if you'd helped, Angie, instead of swanning about, the job would have been done more quickly. Instead,

I'm still tying up boxes and hardly had time to tell you about Beatrice.'

'That's nonsense.'

'Angelina. Your rudeness – and in front of our guest.'

'Beatrice isn't a guest, Mummy, she's part of the fur— family.' She smiled at Beatrice, who forced her mouth to turn up at the edges. She couldn't remember Angelina ever being as bad as this. Grown up. Glittering. Beautiful. Hard. Spoilt.

'Mummy, we mustn't embarrass poor Bea. Shall I ring for tea?' Without waiting for a response she went over to the fireplace and with an arrogant swoop of her hand, pressed an electric bell.

'Bea, dear, would you mind putting your finger here while I tie?' Mrs Wincanton asked. 'We'll take tea in the drawing room,' she told the maid when she appeared.

'Yes, mam. And Mr Wincanton telephoned to tell you he's dining out, mam.'

'Oh, did he? There'll be the four of us for dinner, then. I believe Peter's train is due in at five. That'll be all.'

'Mummy, I was going to the James's. You didn't tell me about Beatrice coming. Remember?'

'Well, you'll have to un-go to the James's. Tell them there's a war on and you're wanted here.'

Angie gave an exasperated little screech, but she turned on her elegant heel and marched out of the room. There came the impatient tones of her trying to get through to the James household on the telephone.

'Last one,' Mrs Wincanton said, and Beatrice obediently placed her finger on the knot. 'Then Bless can move them ready for the van tomorrow. The morning room would be best, I think.' She piled the last box with the others, glanced towards the door and said in a low voice, 'I should like to have the opportunity of a private word, Beatrice. Perhaps you'd come to my room before dinner?'

'You've seen how she's become,' Oenone Wincanton said, balancing a cigarette in a diamond-studded holder on an ashtray on her dressing-table. 'Of course you're only young once and I was hardly an angel myself, but I'm worried about her. She does rather play the field, and one's reputation . . . It doesn't look well with the dowagers. So protective of their darling heirs.' She gazed at herself in the mirror, and taking up a silver-backed brush, touched it to her hair in two or three places. 'I imagine she'll marry young and then she'll be some-one else's problem.'

Angie's mother still looked beautiful, but faded – more unhappy, thought Beatrice, who was sitting on a bedroom chair behind, sipping a tiny glass of sherry and darting little glances about. Interestingly, although the Wincantons were living all together, there was no sign of any of Michael Wincanton's possessions in the bedroom.

Oenone's languid eyes – so like Angelina's – met hers in the mirror.

'That's a very pretty dress, Bea, did I say?' She tapped the long ash from her cigarette and took a lengthy drag of it. The smoke coiled out from between her dazzling red lips as though she were a dragonness. 'You're becoming a very graceful young woman.'

Beatrice felt the blood flow to her face. 'Thank you,' she stammered.

'I thought you might talk some sense into her – you know. You're a calming influence. She listens to you.'

'I don't think she does, Mrs Wincanton.'

Oenone turned round on the stool to face her. 'Still, I'd like you to try,' she said simply, and there was no mistaking the order. Then, 'Shall we go down?'

So that was why she'd been invited, Beatrice thought bitterly, as she followed Oenone down to the drawing room. Not for herself, but because she was good for Angie. Perhaps that wasn't fair on Mrs Wincanton; it was just that she was so hurt by Angie's coldness.

At least she might hear from Rafe. And at the thought of him a great longing swept over her. And now they were entering the drawing room and here was lovely Angie, glowing like a goddess in amber velvet, coming to coo over Beatrice's new dress in such a friendly way that Beatrice instantly forgave her earlier rudeness. Then a thin dark figure emerged from the shadows by the book-lined walls. Peter.

'Hello, Beatrice,' he said, putting out his hand. He was taller than she remembered, though he'd never be tall, but his gaze as ever met hers then skittered away. The old nervous habit.

'How are you, Peter?' she asked, responding with the usual feelings of pity and wariness.

'Not so bad,' he replied. 'I say, I wasn't expecting to see you. Quite a surprise.'

She couldn't tell whether he thought it was a nice one or not but decided to be optimistic.

'Your mother was kind enough to invite me,' she explained. 'It's my first proper visit to London, you know.'

'Is it, by Jove,' he said, perking up. 'Well, perhaps I can take you about a bit tomorrow. A lot of the museums have opened again – you might have heard. Though some of the best pictures have been sent away.'

'Thank you,' she said politely, unsure whether to accept or not. There would still be the second full day free if the opportunity arose to see Rafe. If he was in Town, which she rather supposed he couldn't be. She glanced at Angie and her mother. 'Did you have particular plans for me, or should I go with Peter?'

Angie shrugged. 'Doesn't worry me if you do. I've a dress fitting in the morning and Mummy, I've simply got to meet Felicity Wheeler for lunch or she'll blank me. I've put her off three times already.'

'Well, if Beatrice doesn't mind,' Oenone said, a little doubtful. 'I'm afraid Peter's a bit of a bore when it comes to pictures and things, Beatrice.'

'All those Italian Old Masters he likes,' Angie said. 'Either pious rolling eyes or scenes of torture.'

'They're not all like that,' Peter said. 'There are some more modern pieces. Will it bore *you*?' he asked Beatrice, with heavy irony.

'I'm sure it won't,' she replied hastily, 'though Aunt Julia said I should be certain to see Madame Tussaud's.'

'Oh lordy, really? Well, if you must. In the afternoon perhaps, when you're fed up with high art.'

'The Chamber of Horrors. More scenes of torture,' Angie groaned.

'Just because you only like pictures of pretty landscapes and animals.'

'And what's wrong with that?' This bickering continued until the maid came in to announce dinner.

The atmosphere at dinner was as fragile as the crystal glasses. The Wincantons, it seemed, lived more formally in London than in Cornwall, though the food wasn't up to much. A clear soup like fatty water was followed by overdone beef – Mrs Wincanton complained at the salty gravy – and whoever made the apple pie had a heavy hand with pastry. The beloved

Mrs Pargeter, Beatrice learned, was left behind in Cornwall and the Wincantons were between cooks in London, the old one having, in a fit of patriotism, gone off to make aeroplanes. Ed was flying them in Sussex. It was the one moment of the meal when they were all united in warmth, talking about Ed, his fearlessness, his recent promotion, and how they worried about his safety.

They had just risen from the table when Mr Wincanton arrived home, apparently having dined at his club. His appearance in the drawing room – broad, manly, in a cloud of tobacco fumes, exuding his glamorous aura of power and mystery – affected each of the party differently.

Mrs Wincanton, pouring coffee, didn't bother to look up.

'Good evening, everybody,' he said, throwing his newspaper on the chair nearest the fire, which Beatrice realized now had deliberately been left vacant. 'Ah, the traveller's returned, I see. Hello, Peter. A pleasant journey, I hope?'

'Hello, sir,' Peter muttered, standing to shake hands with his father. 'Yes, not bad.'

'Daddy!' Angie squeaked like a little girl.

'Hello, Princess,' he said, his glance hardly resting on his daughter. 'Ah, Beatrice, or should I say Miss Marlow?' He took her hand in both of his and Beatrice felt herself go red under his searching gaze. 'And how are your parents? Well, I hope? Your father's written to me a number of times about local defences. I'm glad someone's on the case, I must say.'

He finally relinquished her hand and moved over to the drinks cabinet. 'Peter, some brandy?'

'No, thank you, sir.'

'How was your day?' Mrs Wincanton murmured, but she seemed more interested in turning the pages of a first-aid manual than in her husband. 'Is the country still running?'

'Interminable meetings and administrative bloody-mind-edness,' he replied, splashing amber liquid into a tumbler, swilling it round and taking a large mouthful, as though it were medicine. 'If certain people would stop defending their own patch and start defending the country instead, we might find some way of stopping Hitler.'

'How very frustrating,' Mrs Wincanton said vaguely, and frowned at something in her book. 'Is that really how you manage an amputation? It all looks a bit tidy to me,' she said to herself.

'Which department are you concerned with?' Beatrice asked Michael Wincanton, her voice betraying her nervousness, and she regretted asking, because he looked at her so shrewdly, she felt he could see right through her.

'General War Office duties at the moment, my dear,' he said gently. 'And never mind what I said just now, we're making headway. Now tell me about your school. Are you happy there?'

'On the whole,' Beatrice said, hating to be turned into a schoolgirl again. 'But . . . I suppose I'd like life to begin.'

'It'll begin soon enough,' he said, narrowing his eyes in a way that she found disturbing, and he swallowed the rest of his drink. 'Now if you'll all excuse me, I've some paperwork to do. No peace for the wicked. Oenone, there might be a telephone call for me later. Please make sure it's put through to the study right away.'

'Of course, dear,' was the weary reply.

Angie said, 'Oh, Daddy, there's a letter from Hetty on the mantelpiece there. She's desperate to come home.'

'Well, she can't,' Mr Wincanton said. Picking up the envelope, he extracted the contents, read it quickly and smiled at something in it. 'No,' he said, putting it back. 'Germany could strike at any time. She's safer in Devon with her cousins. Don't worry, Angie, Nanny will look after her.'

'I wondered where Hetty was,' Beatrice said when Mr Wincanton had left the room. 'Is she well?'

'We haven't heard otherwise,' Oenone said. 'Though I gather there's some measles about.'

Beatrice had been given her own small room at the back of the second floor of the house. The fire wasn't lit, and she was slipping, shivering, into bed when there came a knock on the door. 'Are you awake?' Angie said, peering round. She floated in, swathed in broderie anglaise, and perched on the bed, knees drawn up, like a runaway angel. 'Goodness, it's chilly in here.' She frowned and Beatrice watched her nervously.

'It's no use pretending,' she told Beatrice severely. 'I know you and Mummy have something cooked up. Out with it.'

Beatrice felt a stab of anger. 'I have nothing cooked up with anyone,' she said. 'Your mother invited me and I thought it was a social visit and that you must know about it. That's all.'

'She's got you as a spy, I know she has. She hardly lets me do a thing these days.'

'Angie, I am not a spy, all right? I've no idea what's going on between you, but I'm not getting involved.'

'But she's asked you to, hasn't she?'

Beatrice shrugged. 'What if she has?'

'You're in her clutches, I can tell.'

'Oh, don't be ridiculous. You make me wish I hadn't come.'

Angie stared at her for a moment, then her expression softened. 'I'm sorry,' she said, and gave one of her most dazzling smiles. 'It's just everything's so deathly at the moment.' She stood up and started walking about the room, peering into

Beatrice's washbag, admiring herself in a long mirror, and finally swooping on a tiny framed photograph of Rafe that she found in the suitcase Beatrice regretted having left open. She studied the picture thoughtfully for a moment, seemed about to say something, then didn't, and put the photo down.

'So,' Angie said, wrapping the candlewick bedspread around her shoulders and sitting on the bed again, 'you're stuck with Peterkin all day tomorrow.'

'It's very kind of him,' Beatrice replied, wondering what was going on behind Angie's mild expression. Angie's fingers traced around the printed roses on the eiderdown.

'Isn't it?' she said. 'Well, perhaps you'd come out for dinner later at Quag's. Dickie's bringing some friends. Have I told you about Dickie Bestbridge? He's an absolute scream. Listen, I'll tell Mummy you've lectured me and that I've promised, hope to die, to be better, then maybe she'll get off our backs.'

'All right.' Beatrice smiled, with relief. The cloud had passed. Angie shrugged off the bedspread, came over and kissed her cheek, then padded out of the room, not quite closing the door behind her. Beatrice climbed out of bed and pushed it shut. There was something wrong with the latch, so to keep it closed she turned the key.

The next morning there was still no call from Rafe. Beatrice and Peter trailed about the National Gallery, Peter deploring the sad gaps on the walls.

'Where've they put everything?' Beatrice asked.

'I don't know. My father thinks somewhere in Wales. I've got this vision of a cave in the mountains, where King Arthur's sleeping, hundreds of paintings stacked up all around him.'

She laughed, then said more soberly, 'He's supposed to wake in England's time of need, isn't he?'

'Perhaps that'll come before too long. It's unnerving, this war-that-isn't-a-war. I wonder how Ed's getting on? He hasn't written lately.' He looked around the room. 'I say, if you've seen enough pictures, let's get a bite of lunch, then catch a bus back to Kensington. The Victoria and Albert's rather splendid.'

Peter was much nicer away from his family, Beatrice thought. He'd lost that hang-dog look, and when he was talking about things that interested him – pictures and antiques – he became quite animated.

They ate sandwiches in a Lyons Corner House, where Beatrice admired the nippies rushing to and fro and tried to imagine what it would be like to work in a job like that. She'd like to do something useful once she'd finished with school, but the question was what. Anything but go back to St Florian and live a suffocating life of seclusion with her parents, she knew that much.

'I suppose I'll have to try and get a commission,' Peter said miserably, when they discussed the future, 'unless Father can find me a desk job. I couldn't stand to stay at home. I'd go mad. Beatrice, why did you come?'

'I wanted to see the museums,' she replied, knowing exactly what he meant but not sure of the reason behind his question.

'No, why did you come to stay? You know my mother's up to something.'

'Yes, I do,' Beatrice said, wiping her fingers on her handkerchief. 'But it's all right, I can manage her.'

'Thank the lord for that,' he said. 'We're no good for you, any of us.'

'You said that before. Don't be silly,' she said.

'No, I mean it. You're too nice for us Wincantons, Bea.'

'Well, thanks very much.'

They hardly spoke on the journey up to the Exhibition Road, both a bit out of sorts after this conversation. Looking down from the bus Beatrice considered how calm and ordinary everything seemed. She'd expected people to be fearful, to see more evidence that invasion was expected any day. Yet there was little, apart from the ubiquitous piles of sandbags, the blackout paper and the odd boarded-up window, to suggest that this wasn't like any other Christmas. Occasionally she saw men in uniform, but not as many as might be expected. Every now and then she'd glimpse the back of one who looked like Rafe and would will him to turn round so she could see his face. Every time one did, she was disappointed. Why hadn't Rafe replied to her letter? Had he been sent away somewhere?

When they reached Knightsbridge it started to sleet. Feeling unaccountably melancholy, she watched the blobs of melting snow shuffle down the window.

The V&A cheered her. It was delightful, she decided, as they moved through the rooms, Peter in a world of his own as he studied the objects and read the labels, she drifting after him in a pleasant haze. When they emerged, a little before three, the sleet was worse, and as they descended the steps, she slipped in slush and fell, scraping her leg on the sharp edge of the stone.

'Are you all right?' he asked, helping her up.

'I think so,' she replied, examining her calf. 'Blast!' Her stocking had torn, and the graze underneath was already beginning to smart and well with blood.

'Oh,' he said, too young and inexperienced to handle the matter. 'I say, will you really want to do Madame Tussaud's with that? We can always go home, you know. It's not far from here.'

She looked again to judge whether the tear was very obvious and decided it was.

'We could take a cab,' Peter said anxiously. 'Mother's given me enough.'

'Why don't I stop off quickly and change,' Beatrice said. She could find out if Rafe had called, and if he hadn't, well, it would be miserable to sit indoors listening for the phone. 'I'd like to see the waxworks.'

The cab drew up outside the house in Queen's Gate.

'I'll wait here for you, shall I?' Peter said. She hobbled up the steps, not needing to knock because the little maid had seen the cab and opened the door right away. She wore a curious expression on her sharp little face.

'I'll be going straight out again,' Beatrice told the girl, keeping her coat, and on the way upstairs wondered whether the maid had been about to say something but then hadn't.

She went to the bathroom and dealt with her graze, which was more extensive than she'd thought, but at least had stopped bleeding, and she was lucky to find a roll of plaster in a cupboard. Her stocking looked as though it might be repairable so she washed it out and hung it on the chair in her bedroom, before finding a fresh one in her case. All the while she was dogged by an awful sense of unease.

It was when she came downstairs that she noticed for the first time a military great-coat hanging on the stand behind the front door. She stopped still, her hand on the banister, thinking about this. Then, through the closed door of the drawing room she heard a man's voice, low, followed by a woman's careless laugh.

At that moment the little maid appeared downstairs. She was clutching a dustpan and started in surprise when she saw Beatrice. 'Sorry, miss, I didn't know you were there.'

'Is there a visitor?' she asked the maid, and again, was shot that curious expression.

'Yes, miss, didn't I say?' she replied. 'That man you kept asking about if he'd called. Well, he's here.'

'Is he?' Beatrice cried. Rafe was here! 'Why didn't you tell me? How long has he been here?'

'Miss!' the maid warned. But Beatrice, who'd been waiting so long, was down the last few stairs and across the hall, pausing only briefly to knock before walking in.

Rafe and Angie were sitting together on the sofa facing the door. Angie was lying back, relaxing. Rafe sat on the edge of the seat, close to her, intimately close. His fingers were interlocked with hers. The pair looked up at Bea in surprise. Bea stared back at their intertwined hands. What were they doing?

'Bea,' Rafe said, loosing Angie's hand and getting up. 'I thought you were out. I mean—'

'Well, I was. I've just come in. Actually, I'm going out again.'

'How are you?' Rafe asked.

'I'm very well,' she said.

'Come and sit down, Bea,' Angie said, almost purring. 'What have you done with Peter?'

'He's outside in the cab.' She explained what had happened. 'I'll tell him to come in, if you like,' she said, getting up and going to the door, then hesitated. She still had that picture in mind of those hands, Rafe's and Angie's, intertwined. She didn't quite understand, and yet she thought she ought to.

'I didn't know you were coming,' she said to Rafe.

Rafe said, 'I'm sorry, I telephoned and only Angie was here. She said to come and wait, so I did.'

She knew him too well. The slight blush, his look too steady. She wanted earnestly to believe him but couldn't quite manage it. *Angie knew I wasn't due back till late afternoon.* This fact was inescapable.

'Are you all right?' Rafe asked.

'Yes, of course I am,' she said.

'Oh, this is silly. I'll get Peter,' Angie said, wrenching open the door and marching out. A moment later Bea heard the taxi move away and Peter followed Angie into the room.

'Ashton,' he said. 'It's good to see you.' He seemed nervous, as though the air were charged with a strange current.

'I'll order some tea,' Angie said, stepping over to the bell. Later, Bea arrived at the exact word for the expression on her face. It was smug.

Rafe left around six, soon after Mrs Wincanton arrived home, greeting him with enthusiasm. 'I'm afraid I'm due back on duty,' he told her. 'I'd have loved to stay longer.'

'I'll write to you, I promise,' he said to Beatrice when she saw him to the door. After he'd left she leant against the front door and tried not to cry. When she returned to the drawing room, Oenone and Angie were arguing about Angie's social arrangements. Peter muttered some excuse and disappeared past her upstairs.

'I hope Peter looked after you today,' Mrs Wincanton said, taking off her gloves. 'Oh dear, obviously not. What have you done to your poor leg?' Beatrice assured her that she was all right and Mrs Wincanton went off to change.

Angelina was reading the *Bystander* and smoking a cigarette as though nothing had happened. Beatrice looked for signs of guilt or anxiety in her, anything that would give reality to the scene she'd broken in on that afternoon. Perhaps it was all some sort of dream, she thought wildly, or perhaps the whole thing meant nothing at all. Maybe it hadn't to Angie, that would be typical, but she knew in her bones that Rafe would not have been acting lightly.

Just now, Angelina seemed more bothered by the fact that her mother had forbidden the outing to Quaglino's. She threw her magazine on the floor with a sigh.

'I'm quite sure Richard Bestbridge is not the kind of companion Mrs Marlow would regard as suitable for her daughter,' Angie said, mimicking her mother. In fact, as Beatrice understood it, the reason was more complicated. Her mother had bought tickets for the Priestley play and booked a table for them all to have supper out first.

Angie yawned. 'Excuse me,' she said. 'I can't think why I'm quite so tired. Must be the thought of *Music at Night*. How did you get on with Pete earlier? Did he bore you to death?'

'Not at all,' Beatrice replied, a little stiffly. 'He knows so much. It makes one feel very humble.'

She walked upstairs in a trance. Normally she'd have been enchanted to see a show, but not tonight. They got to the theatre somehow, but she hardly concentrated on a word. Her mind's eye was on a more dramatic tableau. Angie, Rafe, those clasped hands, the adoring expression on Rafe's face – yes, it had been adoring, she knew that now. Round and round in her head the picture went. She felt sick.

'Are you all right, Beatrice?' Oenone Wincanton asked her in the interval. 'You look a little peaky to me.'

'Just tired, thank you,' she lied. 'I'm really enjoying it.'

When she went to bed she locked the door again. The last thing she wanted was Angelina, coming in with her questions and her confidences. She lay awake for some time. Downstairs, doors opened and closed. There were footsteps and deep male voices, then Oenone's laughter. She must have drowsed, for when she awoke, she heard the front door bang with a solid, final sound. More footsteps, people going to bed, then just darkness and silence. No, there was the slightest sound. There, again. Someone was trying the door of her room. 'Beatrice?' A male voice. Low. She said nothing and waited fearfully for whoever it was to go away. Eventually the floorboards creaked, and somewhere nearby a door closed. It was a long time before Beatrice slept, and then, it was fitfully.

She rose early, packed, and departed before breakfast. The letter she left Mrs Wincanton was brief but polite, her excuse admittedly a weak one, that she felt she ought to get home as she hadn't seen her parents for months.

There were recriminations. Mrs Wincanton wrote her mother a hurt letter, saying she hoped they hadn't offended Beatrice. Mrs Marlow wrote back apologizing for Beatrice's rudeness and blaming her daughter's being out of sorts on exhaustion.

Then, the day before Christmas, a letter arrived for Beatrice from Rafe. She took it upstairs and read it in her bedroom, her tears splashing onto the paper.

Chapter 13

All Christmas she was not herself. Christmas Day passed in St Florian with the usual rituals, her mother attending early Mass before accompanying her husband and daughter to the Anglican service, then the fussing over a pair of pheasants Mr Marlow had been given by Colonel Brooker, and which he insisted that his wife carve carefully to pick out the shot. Beatrice pinched the palm of her hand, listening to his whining voice with a rising anger. How could she care about food when her world had come to an end?

'Cheer up, won't you?' her father remarked as he served himself his wife's famed duchesse potatoes and she rose, threw back her chair and ran out of the room. A few minutes later her mother found her sitting on her bed, staring dully at the floor.

'Whatever's the matter with you?' she asked Beatrice. 'You won't say why you came home from London early and you've been rude and miserable ever since.' The girl did not reply so she went back downstairs. Delphine didn't know that her daughter held a letter hidden behind her back, the letter from Rafe. The phrases floated in Bea's head. *It was wonderful to see you,* but also, *I realized when I saw Angie again the depth of my feelings for her. It was like a light going on in my head. Bea, I will always value you as my dear, dear friend who saved my life and has been saving it ever since with your friendship and reassurance . . .*

'Don't you see?' she wanted to shout at him. 'She doesn't really care, she just wants you to be in love with her. She needs adoration.' It seemed so clear to Bea now. She hated Angelina for casually reaching out and plucking Rafe. Because she could. Because it was easy. Did she really despise Beatrice so much, or care so little for her? What could Beatrice do or say? Nothing, without losing her dignity. Nothing.

After a while she recovered herself sufficiently to go back downstairs. She resumed her seat under her father's baleful glare and muttered, 'Sorry.'

'Our dinner's getting cold, young lady,' was all he said. 'For what we are about to receive, may the Lord make us truly thankful.'

They had been invited to the Brookers' for tea and party games. Beatrice tried hiding behind the excuse of a headache but her mother, who was worried about her, insisted she come and be cheered up by Charades and Consequences. She wasn't. After tea came the reading of a poem entitled 'Bombers over Bethlehem', written by another guest, Mr Cyril Thatcher, St Florian's resident poet, which really proved the limit.

'Much more of this, is there?' Beatrice heard her father whisper to her mother and was relieved when they left shortly afterwards to walk home under the wintry stars.

In January she returned to school a different girl to the one who'd left full of bright-eyed expectancy before the holidays. Everybody noticed how withdrawn she was, how she took no interest in her work or anything.

'Beatrice Marlow, we hardly hear from you.' Her science teacher dragged her out of her thoughts. 'Will you tell us the four types of Arthropod, if you please.' Brought back to the reality of the chalk-dusty classroom, and the inquisitive eyes of the dozen other girls in black pinafores, she stuttered out an answer that was more or less correct, and the lesson moved on. But when the bell went, Miss Hardwick held her back and asked, 'Is there anything wrong, dear? Such dark shadows under your eyes. Are you sleeping properly?'

Beatrice was not sleeping at all well. Her dreams revolved around memories of Rafe and Angelina, the jagged nightmare snapshot of them sitting together on the sofa, or sometimes another, that she was searching for him in the dark, howling, stormy sea, and this time not finding him.

'You're talking in your sleep again, Marlow. Do shut up,' Hilary Vickers drawled one morning, not unkindly. Hilary, an earl's grand-daughter, possessed a natural air of authority. She considered the other girls at Larchmont beneath her in the social scale – she was probably right – and effortlessly assumed charge. But Beatrice was grateful to her, for in her desire for control, Hilary had stamped out some of the culture of cattiness, and this year the others seemed to respect the aura of 'keep your distance' that Beatrice had woven round herself.

Winter gave way to spring, but she hardly noticed through her blur of misery. Another letter arrived from Rafe, extoling Angie's sweetness and she couldn't bring herself to reply – did he really not understand how deeply he had hurt her?

Just before Easter, there was a letter from Angelina. When she read it, Beatrice felt nothing. Part of her had been expecting it all along. Rafe's regiment had gone abroad, Angelina wrote – to France, she thought. Before he embarked he'd asked her to marry him. She had told him she would, but hadn't finally decided.

Slowly, Beatrice's anger grew. Angie seemed to be treating something as serious as a proposal of marriage as lightly as an invitation to tea. Worse was the knowledge that Rafe was possibly in the front line and there was nothing she could do but hope and pray that he'd be all right. She considered writing to him via his regiment, indeed twice started letters, but found she couldn't keep her anger off the page. He wouldn't need that from her at the moment.

Two weeks after Easter, important news began to arrive from Europe. The war had finally got underway and it wasn't going well for the Allies.

Hitler invaded Norway. In May his troops swarmed into Belgium and Holland. Allied troops fled to Dunkirk and were rescued by a heroic flotilla of little boats. France lay open to the enemy, her borders inadequately defended. In the end they were easily breached. On 22 June 1940, France surrendered to the enemy.

Delphine's anguish was terrible. Her letters to Beatrice became long, distracted scrawls, betraying anxiety for her family, distress at the lack of news. Beatrice, too, was troubled, thinking not only of Rafe, wherever he might be, but of the vulnerable elderly couple, her grandparents, in their isolated Normandy farmhouse. Pappi was known to be excitable and, as her mother wrote, quite capable of resorting to his rifle if upset. He wouldn't have a chance against German soldiers. At least his sons, Delphine's brothers, were nearby.

Exams loomed. Somehow, Beatrice mustered some spirit and got through. Two and a half weeks to the summer holidays. Still she did not know what she was going to do with herself. Her parents expected her to return home to St Florian for the holidays, but to what? Their suffocating lives, locked into the roles of invalid and nurse? The knowledge that up the road lay Carlyon Manor with all its memories and dashed hopes? Going home meant going backwards. A whole summer of this, then back to Larchmont for the final year. For what, when the future was so bleak, uncertain? She badly wanted to do something useful now, not least something that would occupy her thoughts.

It was two weeks before they broke up that news came, in a letter from Angelina. Beatrice took it outside and sat in the sun on the sloped roof of the air-raid shelter to read it, but was unable at first to take in what it said.

I thought you'd want to know at once, Angelina had written. *Rafe is missing.*

At once she was plunged into further misery. No one knew if Rafe was alive or dead. In the confusion after the Fall of France it was difficult to gauge what had happened to many stranded troops. There was nothing anyone could do except wait for more news.

Waiting. As Germany sealed off Europe to the Allies, and Italian troops surged into Northern Africa, Britain was isolated. Fear of invasion clouded everyone's thoughts. As for Beatrice, what could a seventeen-year-old schoolgirl possibly do about anything?

It was Hilary Vickers, the earl's grand-daughter, who saved her, telling her about the horses.

'My cousin's working there. They take horses and ponies that have been brought in for Army use, dozens of them, and train them to pull wagons or carriages for ceremonial duties, then most are sent abroad. Some are fine animals – it's awful to think of, actually. All Daddy's lovely hunters are gone. It was the first thing he did after war was declared. "I'm too old to fight Hitler," he told us, "but by God my horses will do it instead".'

The place in question was a remount depot in Leicestershire. Beatrice wrote to them before she could have second thoughts, outlining her experience at Carlyon's stables and asking if they'd have her. A week passed without any word. Then came a letter from a Captain Browning, a contact of Hilary's cousin.

You are required to present yourself at the Superintendent's Office at 0800 hours on 7th July. Since there is no accommodation for females on site, I have arranged for you to lodge with a Miss Catherine Warrender, The Poplars, George Street. She expects you the evening before.

Bea read this with a mixture of excitement and dismay. What had she done? She wrote at once to her parents, and the letter resulted in a summons to the Headmistress's study.

Miss Pettifer, a tall, thin woman with an imperious air, folded her hands in her lap and regarded Beatrice thoughtfully.

'I received a telephone call from your mother this morning,' she said. 'She was in a state of some agitation, and when she read me out the letter you'd sent her, I understood her disquiet. You're only seventeen, Beatrice. I was imagining that we would have the pleasure of your company at Larchmont for another year, and that you'd take your Higher Certificate, but it appears that you have other plans.'

'Yes, Miss Pettifer, I'm sorry.'

'Do explain yourself. It appears that you, an educated young woman, wish to work with, er, horses?'

'Yes.' Her gaze slipped past the Headmistress, to the tranquil country garden outside. Somewhere nearby, the comforting sounds of a tennis game could be heard.

'I want to be useful,' she told Miss Pettifer. 'I can't stay here. I just can't.' She couldn't find the words to explain that she felt enclosed, trapped by boarding school, but that nor did she want to go home. In all honesty she didn't see where her future lay. All she knew was that she wanted to get out, to go some-where and do something.

Miss Pettifer studied her for a long moment. Finally she said, 'Beatrice Marlow, you're an able girl, very able. In normal times I'd have said that you should try for university. But these are not normal times. And I detect that for some reason, you are not happy. What makes you think you'd feel better doing what is only likely to be rough, manual work?'

'I don't know that I'd be happier. But I love horses and it would be doing something. Not being stuck here – I mean, sometimes I feel I'm going mad.'

Miss Pettifer smiled. 'I hope we aren't so terrible a place.'

'No, of course not, I'm sorry.'

Miss Pettifer sighed. She opened a drawer and took out a sheet of writing paper, then unscrewed her fountain pen. When she had finished the letter, she passed it across the desk to Beatrice.

'You'll need this reference,' she said. 'I'll speak to your mother and explain that we can't force you to stay, especially since you've been offered war work. But be sure to write to them every week. They worry about you.'

'I know,' Beatrice whispered.

'You're an unusual girl,' Miss Pettifer said. 'But resilient, I think. I remember, when I was your age . . .' The Headmistress, who had always seemed so poised, gave her a girlish smile. 'But life is different for women now. Perhaps you will have chances that I never had. Beatrice, I sense your path may not be smooth. "Follow the truth." That's what we try to teach our girls here.'

'The school motto,' Beatrice said.

'That's right. But I must give you another piece of advice.' She leant forward slightly. 'Follow your heart.'

Beatrice nodded, not quite sure what she meant, but felt a thrill pass through her all the same.

'And now I think our little interview is over. You'll attend lessons for the duration, and when you do leave, it'll have to be quietly. I don't want to unsettle the other girls.'

'Of course. Thank you, Miss Pettifer.'

'Perhaps you'll find time occasionally to write. I like to hear how our girls get on.'

Beatrice nodded, and shook the outstretched hand.

She took the letter up to her dormitory, intending to pass it on to Captain Browning unread, but when she made to place it in her drawer she saw that the envelope was unsealed. Miss Pettifer, perhaps, had intended her to know its contents. *To whom it may concern*, it started. She read on, amazed.

I would like to commend to you most warmly Beatrice Marlow, a pupil at my school for the last two years. She is one of the most naturally intelligent young women I have come across, in addition to which she has a strong sense of duty and loyalty. I find in her diligence, physical toughness and a quiet strength of character. I sense she will do great things.

Dizzy with astonishment, Beatrice read it again. For the first time in her life she felt she was someone who mattered.

Chapter 14

'Bert's vicious; you've got to watch him. Look what he did to me a few weeks back, the tinker.' The girl, Tessa, pulled her overall down her shoulder to show Beatrice a puckered bite wound marring her creamy shoulder, still livid. 'Didn't half hurt, I can tell you.'

'That's awful,' Beatrice said, looking up nervously at the great bay horse in his stall. 'What's with matter with his eye?' The horse flicked his ears back and watched them warily out of one rolling eyeball. The lid of the other drooped. Now she was growing used to the gloom of the stable she could make out long scars on his flank and chest. 'Why, the poor old thing. Who did that?'

Tessa shrugged. 'He's an old cavalry charger. Came off the boat from India. He's not the only one to be badly treated there. No wonder he likes to get his own back on humans.'

'How could anyone do that?' Beatrice whispered, putting out her hand to the animal, but Bert backed away.

'Careful,' Tessa said. 'It's shameful, that's what it is, hurting an innocent beast.'

They moved on past him to the next stall. 'This one's Sunny. By name and nature.' Tessa rubbed the nose of a gentle grey mare. 'Yes, you're a darling, aren't you? And them two over there –' a pair of quiet draught horses '– are Pip and Wilfred.'

Beatrice patted them and stared along the long line of stalls, wondering how many horses there were in here – two dozen perhaps, and this was only one of many rows of shelters at the depot.

It was her first day. She'd arrived by train at the Midlands market town the previous evening and found her way easily to the address Captain Browning had given her. Miss Catherine Warrender, her landlady, lived in a pretty, pebble-studded townhouse, the short front garden rampant with hollyhocks. Miss Warrender herself was a tall, heavily built woman in her fifties, with a deep, cultured voice and a cheerful disposition. She knew Colonel Flanders who was in charge of the depot, which is why she'd been asked to put up Beatrice. Beatrice liked her at once and liked the comfortable bedroom she was given, which looked out onto a small orchard with a beehive, and a pair of tethered goats, later introduced to her as 'my girls, Moony and Belinda.'

'Dinner's at seven and the water will be hot at six. I expect you'll like to wash and change after you've been with the horses.' Miss Warrender left her to unpack.

Dinner, it turned out, was prepared by Miss Warrender herself, as was everything else in the house. Beatrice discerned that she'd fallen on hard times and was probably grateful to have a lodger.

Today, Captain Browning, fortyish, pale and flabby, had given her several forms to sign before handing her into the care of an ageing NCO with a rough countryman's face. This was Sergeant Dally, the head groom.

Sergeant Dally had greeted her without meeting her eye. As she walked with him across the stableyard he remarked, 'We don't want women here. They upset everything.' Then he left her with this local girl, Tessa Hill, one of only two other females at the depot.

'Don't let 'im get to you,' Tessa whispered, seeing Beatrice's stricken face. 'Once the men see we do the work same as them, they treat us all right,' she said. 'Oh, and you have not to mind the language.'

Tessa helped Beatrice pick out the smallest pair of overalls from the store, though these were still baggy on her, and was now showing her the half-dozen horses and ponies she was being allocated to feed, muck out and groom every day. 'And that's before the exercising and the training, I'm warning you,' she said. 'Come on, we'd better get started.'

Beatrice loved the job at once, though it was hard physical work and she got very tired. Sometimes, waking in the mornings, her legs and hips felt weak and tingly, a result of the polio, she supposed, and she'd lie there willing herself to get up. That was the only time she allowed her thoughts to crowd in.

The work did help keep her mind off things, in particular the awful dragging anxiety about Rafe. It was always there, in the background, but most of the time she was too busy or too tired to think about it. Sometimes she asked herself why she'd come, and it gradually dawned on her that she'd been running away, just running, without knowing where she was running to. It wasn't a bad place that she'd found herself. She didn't know how long she'd stay here, but for the moment it suited her.

The majority of the horses were being trained to pull heavy wagons. Tessa didn't know where they would end up; maybe in terrain where trucks couldn't go, it was supposed, or where there was no petrol. Some would become police horses, and some of the more aristocratic steeds would be used for ceremonial duties.

It was pointless, Beatrice quickly discovered, to become too attached to her animals, for the easier ones like Stanley, the big hunter, would stay for as little as a few weeks, before being loaded into one of the trailers and taken off heavens knew where. It would have to be enough for her to know that she was giving them a short period of kindness before some possibly dark fate overtook them.

There were one or two other men who shared Sergeant Dally's world view, but most of them did accept the women without question. Sturdy Tessa was a farmer's daughter of nineteen with a furze-bush of fair hair, and well used to sharing heavy work with men. The third woman, Sarah, was a different kind altogether: dark-haired and mysterious. Probably in her late twenties, tremendously voluptuous, there was a sad, brooding air about her. She was pleasant to Tessa and Beatrice, but didn't brook confidences. While over their lunchtime sandwich and cups of strong sweet tea Tessa talked enthusiastically about Ted, her childhood sweetheart, who wrote postcards to her from an RAF camp in Kent where he was ground crew, Sarah said nothing, but stared into the distance and turned a gold ring she wore on the fourth finger of her right hand. There was one thing everyone valued about Sarah: while the girls were all devoted to the animals in their care, Sarah seemed to have an uncanny ability with them, quieting even the most nervous and badly treated. It was as though she understood them. Even Bert never tried to bite Sarah.

They were out in all weathers. The horses had to be exercised and Beatrice quickly became familiar with the local network of country roads and bridleways. Then there was the training.

The problem, inevitably, was Bert. One morning, a fortnight after she arrived, Sergeant Dally decided Bert should be tried on a wagon for the first time. Beatrice was nervous, but she didn't dare show it. She muzzled him, and by holding him on a short rein and firmly coaxing, managed to wheel him round and back him into his place next to Stanley. After a couple of false starts, she led them successfully about the field and was pleased with his progress. Stanley was clearly a calming influence.

The watching Sergeant wasn't satisfied, though, and it wasn't long before he strode across and commanded, 'See how they go with you riding upfront.'

'I don't think he's ready for that,' Beatrice said carefully, but Dally's rough reply was, 'Do as you're ordered,' so she shrugged and climbed into the driver's seat while Dally held the horses' heads.

She fumbled with the reins, but before she was ready the Sergeant shouted, 'Away you go,' then to her horror, he struck Bert on his imperious rump. The horses surged forward with such a jerk that Beatrice had trouble keeping her seat, and for a moment she lost all control. She held on for dear life, the wagon bumping from side to side and the shaft in front swinging about and hitting the horses. She righted herself quickly, crying out, 'Stop!' and pulling on the reins, but the only effect this had was to make Bert rear in a sudden panic and she felt the wagon fly up too. The shaft hit her in the face before she was tipped onto the ground, the wagon just missing her. She was aware of the horses struggling, whinnying with pain and panic.

A hue and cry started up; people came running.

'Are you all right, miss?' a man's voice, then the shaft of the wagon was lifted off. 'Don't try to move,' he said. 'Where do you hurt?' She couldn't see for the blood running in her eyes but felt firm fingers on her neck, searching for the pulse, then brushing back her hair to examine the wound.

She could hear a woman's voice now, Sarah's, soothing the horses, and the clink of their bindings.

'How are you doing?' came the man's voice. She opened her eyes and found herself focusing on a kind face with eyes the same chestnut colour as her own. The name Shaw, Corporal Shaw, drifted through her mind before she passed out.

On the doctor's orders, she spent two days in bed. On the morning of the third day she awoke feeling much better, though her forehead was still swollen and bruised and it hurt to breathe. She struggled out of bed and when she went to draw the curtains was met by an amusing sight. Miss Warrender, clothed in white from head to foot and wearing her gas mask against a cloud of smoke, was collecting honey from the hive. The goats, removed safely to a far corner, gazed astonished at the sight.

Beatrice dressed as quickly as she could and went downstairs. There she was watching from the kitchen window, nursing a cup of tea, when her landlady bustled in carrying a frame of dripping honeycomb.

'My dear, are you sure you should be out of bed?' Miss Warrender asked, pulling off her gas mask. She began scraping the honey onto a large metal tray, stopping only to remove the odd trapped bee with a teaspoon.

'I feel a great deal better,' Beatrice said. 'Oh, there's one on your arm, look. And another on your back. Stay still.' And she trapped the sleepy bees one by one in a tea towel and shook them off outside. When she returned, it was to find one more insect drowsing on the table. She marvelled at the smallness of it, the plainness, before catching it up in the cloth.

Miss Warrender, scraping away, said, 'It's wonderful to think that something so small and insignificant has such an important place in the world. If it didn't perform its duty then fruit and flowers wouldn't be pollinated and we wouldn't have this lovely honey.'

'And what if it didn't do its duty?' Beatrice said from the doorway. 'Would the other bees punish it?'

Miss Warrender appeared to consider this. 'I don't know. They might turn on it. But it always *does* do its duty. What it's created to do.'

'I expect you're right,' Beatrice said. 'Now if you'll excuse me I ought to get off to work.'

'You shall not,' Miss Warrender said, washing honey off her hands. 'You took a terrific bash, girl, and this is your first day up.'

'But I feel fine. Just a bit shaken.' The bump on her forehead did throb, though.

'You're not stepping outside my front door till the doctor's seen you again. You could have been killed, you know – that's what he said.'

'Did he? I don't remember. Miss Warrender, I must thank you for looking after me.'

'Not at all. It takes me back to my days driving ambulances at the front.'

'Really?'

'I was with the FANY over in Belgium. You will have heard of us – the First Aid Nursing Yeomanry. We saw some awful things. But it was the most thrilling time of my life. You wouldn't know when you woke up in the morning what you might have to get through that day.'

Through conversations over dinner, Beatrice had gleaned small nuggets of information about Catherine Warrender. That she'd been born in a big house with servants, but her father had died when she was fourteen, leaving only debts, and the family had moved to this townhouse; that she'd nursed her mother through her final illness; that she taught first aid to local volunteers. But of her inner life she gave little away. Beatrice saw her love of her garden and of animals – she could often be heard calming her 'girls' with soothing nonsense as she milked them or fed them soft-scented clover hay. She was a woman who did her duty willingly and without complaint.

'I'm so grateful for your kindness,' Beatrice told Miss Warrender now, and she felt the warmth of affection in the woman's smile.

'I think you are much better, Beatrice. I'm so relieved. You're a brave girl with those horses. By the way, a Corporal Shaw has been here asking after you.'

Beatrice heard her, but as from a long way off. In a sharp flash of memory she was seeing Sergeant Dally strike the terrified Bert with his crop. And the vicious expression in the Sergeant's eyes.

Her mistake was to have said anything.

Pudgy Captain Browning listened to her carefully with a blank expression on his face, then took a piece of rough paper out of a drawer and wrote something on it.

He said, 'I'll speak to him about it. You can go now.'

'But,' she broke in, 'aren't you going to ask me any more about it? Isn't there a procedure?'

'I said I'd speak to the Colonel about it. And he'll do as he sees fit. We haven't had any trouble before now with the *ladies*.' He gave the word a little mocking emphasis. She thought perhaps he hadn't fully understood.

'Look, Captain. Sergeant Dally struck the horse. He knew Bert was difficult. He must have known how the poor boy would react. But I think he wanted to hurt me. He doesn't like me, I can tell.'

All that happened was that everything got much worse for her after that. If there was ever a tricky or particularly dirty job, Sergeant Dally would be sure to pick her out for it. He'd criticize everything she did, too. She spent a long afternoon with Stuart Shaw, the man who had rescued her, training some of the pedigree mounts for ceremonial duties, laughing and chatting with him as they rode round a muddy field to tinny brass band music from a wind-up gramophone, but it was only her that Dally shouted at when a horse put a step wrong. She tried to take it all without comment, biting the inside of her lip to stem the anger, leading the animal away without a backward look at the two men.

Tessa had little sympathy for her. 'Surely you know,' she told her crossly as they filled the mangers with hay and lugged pails of water for the horses to drink, 'Dally and the Colonel go right back. Dally was his batman in India. Probably saved him from a tiger or an armed tribesman. No one can say a word to him against Dally.'

'Someone might have told me that before,' Beatrice said, forlorn.

'It's not just that, though. They're not used to us women here. They think we're weak if we complain.'

Beatrice felt tears prickle, but imagined Tessa would think her silly, so she blinked them away. Later, when she was alone, she was sure the horses sensed her unhappiness, for Sunny nuzzled her shoulder and Pip and Wilfrid watched her, solid and patient. A bucket broke, spilling feed everywhere. 'Oh, fidget!' she cried. Snatching up a broom, she began sweeping it up with brisk angry strokes.

A shadow fell across the floor, and she looked up to see

Stuart Shaw standing in the doorway. He had changed out of his overalls and his shirt lay softly open at the neck.

'Sorry if I startled you,' he said. He stepped over to pet Sunny, who was everyone's favourite. 'Oh, you know I've got something, do you?' he told the pony, as she nudged at his jacket. He extracted a couple of runtish apples from a pocket and fed her one. The other he balanced on the gate of Bert's stall, where the charger rolled his eyes at it for a moment before taking it into his mouth.

'Thank you, he's enjoying that,' Beatrice told Stuart. Though comfortable with him, she felt intensely aware of his interest in her. He helped her shovel up the sweepings, then waited as she hung up her overalls.

'I pass your lodgings. I'll walk with you, if you like,' he said.

She waited while he collected a battered bicycle from the side of the office. It was a warm evening, and the song of a pair of skylarks took her straight to the fields above St Florian. For a moment she imagined it was Rafe walking beside her, not a near-stranger, and she struggled against a wave of sadness.

'I felt sorry for you with Dally.'

'Don't.'

'I wanted to say something.'

'You'd have got into trouble yourself.'

'Yes,' he admitted. 'But it was so . . . unnecessary.'

'I'll survive,' she said. 'Do let's talk about something else. Where is it you live?'

'I stop with my aunt, out at Micklehurst,' he told her, naming a village a couple of miles away. 'Coventry's home, though.'

'Coventry. Where did you learn to ride then?'

'My mother's father owned a farm near Micklehurst and my sister and I often stayed with him and rode his horses.'

Slowly, she unwound his story. His father was a canon at Coventry Cathedral. Stuart had intended to go to Cambridge to study law, but then war came and he'd joined the Army instead. Three months into training and he'd been stood down with suspected tuberculosis. So here he was, 'in limbo' as he put it, neither discharged from the Army nor able to take an active part.

'Several months' bedrest, then they decided working here would be best for me. Healthy country living. Can't say it's what I signed up for. Not when the country's in such a hole. You know, you're the best thing that's happened here so far.'

He was nice, Beatrice thought, and she enjoyed the attention, but when they reached Lavender Cottage and Stuart asked, 'I say, you wouldn't come out with me sometime?' she felt a dragging reluctance. 'There's a dance at our village hall next Saturday.' He looked so pleading that in the end she said yes.

She and Miss Warrender listened to the news after dinner that evening. It was all about the planes battling high in the skies for Britain's very soul. Ed might be in one of them, but she hoped he wasn't. Always at the back of her mind she wondered if Rafe was all right. Nobody had heard anything more, according to Angelina's last letter, in which she had also told Beatrice that she was thinking of joining the Wrens.

Miss Warrender was sewing some shapeless garment out of a piece of summer curtain. 'He seems a pleasant young man,' was her comment on Stuart, when Beatrice told her about the dance, 'but I must insist on your returning by eleven. Your parents would be anxious.'

Beatrice knew Miss Warrender was merely doing her duty, but she was already beginning to feel restless here in the back of beyond. It had suited her needs to come nearly two months ago, but now she was starting to ask herself where it was all leading.

She did go dancing with Stuart. Miss Warrender helped her shorten one of her long dresses and lent her a bicycle, a monster of a machine with a squeaky back wheel that announced her presence as she passed through woods and farmlands to meet him. The hall was packed with people from miles around, all drinking and dancing, laughing and falling in love. 'No one would think there was a war on,' Stuart said to a perspiring young sailor who commented on the crush. 'It's *because* there's a war on, mate,' the other called back. 'We'll show them!' He punched the air. Them, of course, meaning the Germans, now daily expected to swarm up England's white cliffs with knives between their teeth.

August was nearly gone and the lanes were strewn with dusty straw from harvesting. Sunny the grey pony, Pip and Wilfred the draught horses, had departed several weeks before. It twisted her heart to say goodbye. Beatrice had accompanied their trailer to the station and urged them up a ramp into a goods carriage. 'Liverpool, they're going,' the guard had told her, as he fastened the doors. She turned away with a sigh. The docks then, and abroad to who knows where.

Sarah, too, had gone. In the middle of August, Captain Browning told her that a man calling himself her husband had come enquiring for her; at this news, her sallow skin had paled. The next day she didn't show up for work. Tessa was sent to her lodgings to find out where she was, only to be told that she'd fled in the night, a month's rent owing.

Two other women arrived at the depot, local women Tessa was at ease with and who took Sergeant Dally in their capable stride. Beatrice, however, was still given the more difficult horses to deal with.

'Take it as a compliment,' Stuart advised. 'Dally thinks Bert's ready to move on.'

And, indeed, the scarred charger would now wait quietly for the wagon to be attached, and pull it smartly round the field. It was all down to her patient coaxing, but she didn't think Dally was impressed.

Matters were growing tense between her and Stuart, too. She kept him at a distance and hated seeing the desperation in his eyes when she finally had to say, 'I'm too young for anything serious,' and turn her face away when he tried to kiss her. She liked him, but it was Rafe who filled her thoughts.

And then one evening when she returned to Miss Warrender's there was a letter waiting from Angelina. For some reason she felt a terrible sense of foreboding. *Not Rafe*, she prayed, *please not Rafe*. She took it out into the garden and sat on a seat under an apple tree. Moony came and gently butted her knees.

It wasn't Rafe, but Ed. *We've had the most dreadful news*, Angie had written. *Mummy thinks you might not have heard. He's been killed. His plane was shot down two weeks ago. Naturally we're all distraught.*

For a moment she could take in no more. Closing her eyes, she allowed her mind to fill with images of Ed, as a glorious boy running into the sea, handsome and poised at the Christmas party, his head thrown back laughing. A golden lad. The delight of his parents, the firstborn, sacrificed for King and Country. She started to cry and it was a while before she could return to the letter.

His commander wrote to Daddy, a lovely letter. It seems he'd been flying back to base after a difficult but successful mission. It was a stray enemy plane that got a lucky strike. Lucky for them, that is. His co-pilot managed to bail out, but Ed went down.

'Are you all right out there?' Miss Warrender called from the kitchen door. When she saw Beatrice's face she came instantly to find out what was the matter. 'Oh, you poor thing,' she said when Beatrice told her, and comforted her with tea and brandy.

Later Beatrice told her, 'I must go to London. I can't stay here. You've been so kind, but there's got to be something more I can do.'

Miss Warrender regarded her with a wistful expression. 'I wish you would stay, dear, but I'm not surprised you're restless – a bright young girl like you.'

'I've learned so much here, Miss Warrender.' Looking back now over the last eight weeks, Beatrice could see how the experience had restored her, made her grow up. She'd done something on her own initiative far away from family and friends, and that was good – but she'd never be happy working for someone like Sergeant Dally, and everywhere she went she seemed to feel Stuart's pleading eyes on her. She knew he was good and kind, but she still thought first of Rafe.

'Can you drive?' Miss Warrender asked suddenly.

'Um, yes,' Beatrice replied. She remembered the previous summer at Carlyon, the young man who had taken her out in his sleek green motor car. 'Why?'

'I've an idea,' Miss Warrender said. 'It's only a suggestion, but I could write to my old friend Gamwell, if you like. I'm sure the FANY would be pleased to have a girl of your quality.'

Chapter 15

'I'm sorry to interrupt, but what was the . . . er . . . fanny?' Lucy asked, thinking the word sounded a little embarrassing.

'*Is* not was,' Beatrice replied proudly. 'The FANY Corps still exist, you know. We were considered the classiest of the women's uniformed services. FANY stands for First Aid Nursing Yeomanry, but no one ever called us that. They were originally set up in 1907 as a first-aid link between front-line troops and the field hospitals, and were very active in the First World War. Young women of independent spirit like Catherine Warrender, who wanted to "do something to help", might become FANYs and often found themselves in France or Belgium working in conditions of extreme danger.'

'I hadn't heard of them before,' Lucy said. 'Is it part of the Army?'

'It was for a while during the last war. The organization has always had a fierce sense of its own identity, which for me was part of its appeal. The traditional armed forces were suspicious of us. They thought we were a bunch of mavericks, because we didn't have defined duties. It was considered rather shocking, too, that we were allowed to carry firearms, which the other women's services weren't – most unladylike, you see. And the organization was quite selective. They didn't take just anyone.'

'But you got accepted.'

'I did, thanks to Miss Warrender and my Headmistress's smashing references. The FANY was under the umbrella of the ATS by then, the Auxiliary Territorial Service – the more properly established women's branch of the Army – but FANYs still held onto their distinctive identity and leadership and we were jolly proud of that, I can tell you. You never knew what you might end up doing as a FANY – driving VIPs about or being sent to Egypt to help with Intelligence, which is what happened to my friend Mary. We were very flexible.'

'What did you end up doing?'

'I'll tell you in a moment. But before I started, an extraordinary piece of news came through. I had letters from both Angie and my mother about it. Rafe had been tracked down in an Oflag – an officers' prisoner-of-war camp – in Bavaria. Everybody felt extraordinarily relieved that he was alive and, according to Red Cross reports, in good health, but we knew conditions must be dreadful.'

'What had happened to him? How had he got there, I mean?' Lucy asked.

Here Beatrice put up her hand. 'All in good time, dear.'

She sat back and closed her eyes and Lucy said, 'Are you all right?'

The old lady's eyes fluttered open. 'Of course I am.' The hands of the little carriage clock had reached three o'clock. She said, 'I might take a short nap now, but would you be free to come back this evening? Half past six perhaps? Mrs P. said she'd leave enough for both of us for supper.'

Today it seemed natural for Lucy to visit Carlyon, following the path up the cliff. It dipped down when it passed the beach and rose steeply again on the other side. Soon she was high above

St Florian. Another path led right, inland. This must have been the route Beatrice took so often. It skirted fields, then twisted round to meet the wall, then she came to the lane and eventually to the gates of Carlyon itself.

It struck her as odd now, that the house had been left in its tumbledown state for so many years. Perhaps Beatrice would know who owned it now, and why the house hadn't been cleared or rebuilt. Or maybe Simon at the museum could tell her.

This time it was different, wandering through the ruins, knowing now about her grandmother Angelina's family; the different personalities, the things that had happened in these rooms. Here, she imagined, standing in a long narrow room, to the front, was the dining room, here the hall, where her grandmother had first met Rafe. She liked the drawing room best. She went once more to inspect the charred remains of the wooden mantelpiece, the carved design of fruit and flowers. The section where the bee must have been was there no longer, but she could imagine where it was, and the young Beatrice finding it. The Latin motto was unreadable, too. The glories of the Wincanton family, such as they had ever been, had passed.

She walked back to the clifftop and stood for a moment looking out across the water, studying the dots that were little boats. One of them might be Anthony's. That one, perhaps, with the blue-ish tinge. If it was, could he see her? She waved, just in case, but it was too far away to see if anyone waved back.

She was about to walk back to St Florian and the hotel when she remembered something. Directly below must be the little beach that would be cut off by the high tide. Perhaps she could find the secret steps. When she walked further along the cliff, she found a gouge in the clifftop that seemed to be the start of a path. Stepping down into it, she could see that a path did indeed exist, set between rocks and winding down out of sight. She followed it a little way, feeling perfectly secure – until she came to a sharp bend and made the mistake of peeping over the edge. The view fell away to the beach, thirty feet below, and her stomach lurched with fear. She sat back against the cliff wall and stared at the sky to steady herself, but the puffs of cloud moving so fast overhead made her feel dizzy and she had to close her eyes.

After a minute or so, she felt strong enough to return to the clifftop and set off back to St Florian.

'I don't know who owns Carlyon,' Beatrice said, 'or why no one has ever built on the site. Perhaps your Aunt Hetty would know.' It was a cool evening and she and Lucy were sitting before the fire with glasses of pale sherry.

'I haven't seen her for years,' Lucy said. Whether it was the effects of the sherry or the atmosphere of the room, she felt curiously cut loose from her normal life. 'I'm not even sure where she lives.'

'Not very far from here, actually. As I say, she wrote to me about Tom. The address on the letter was Saint Agnes. That's up on the north coast.'

'I'd no idea,' Lucy said, surprised. 'We never saw much of Hetty. Dad and she weren't particularly close. I don't really know a lot about her – she didn't marry or anything, did she?'

'No, I never heard that she even got close. Not the sort, perhaps. She worked as a publisher's copy-editor for many years. Was rather good at it, I understand. She loved Cornwall. That must be why she returned here.'

'When did you last see her?'

'Not for ages. Angelina's funeral . . . and before that? I can't remember. Hetty sees me as the enemy, I think. I was surprised when she wrote to tell me about Tom. I wonder,' Beatrice said, as though to herself, 'if her intention in writing was to be cruel.'

'How do you mean?' Lucy asked.

Beatrice, sunk in thought, didn't answer, but her ringed hand tapped on her glass. She was cast in a pensive mood for the rest of the evening, and Lucy tried not to intrude. At the same time she was touched by how pleased Beatrice seemed to be that she was there, as they ate their simple meal together. She asked Lucy about her work and about her schooldays.

'I've never met your mother,' Beatrice said, 'though I did see some very attractive seascapes by her in a gallery in Norfolk once, a number of years ago. Does she still paint?'

Lucy explained about Gabriella's work and her new life; her bewilderment concerning Tom leaving her.

'I still can't understand what went wrong,' she said. 'He and Mum had always been happy together, I'd thought. They'd had difficult times, but I never thought they'd split up. Mum used to get very annoyed when Dad had one of his low periods. It frightened her that he'd never explain what he felt about things, but then Mum can get a bit over-anxious at times. He definitely changed after Granny's death, but I don't know why.'

'Maybe when I've finished my story you'll understand a little more,' Beatrice said.

'What do you mean?'

'I need to explain it all to you properly or it won't make sense.'

When Lucy left, promising to visit the next day, it was nearly dark. Returning to the hotel she looked in the bar for Anthony, but he wasn't there and she was disappointed. When she went to bed, she lay awake for a long while, her thoughts swirling in her mind. Tomorrow was Wednesday, halfway through the week she'd given herself here. She was completely caught up in Beatrice's story, but what did she mean when she said Lucy would understand more? This quest had started with Rafe. She was beginning to suspect that it was actually all about her father, Tom.

Chapter 16

London, November 1940

Beatrice placed the mug on the counter. The old man took it carefully, warming his hands on it and taking noisy sips of tea. His fingers poked through worn gloves, the nails ridged and rimed with dirt. 'Brass monkey weather tonight,' he remarked, as though he were passing the time of an ordinary evening. 'Hope it freezes the balls off Jerry.'

The air-raid sirens began to howl once more, great mournful beasts in a primeval landscape.

'Take cover, hurry up,' a warden was shouting. A young woman with a toddler struggling under one arm and clasping a large bundle with the other, stumbled out of the smoky night. She passed the mobile canteen, and before she vanished through the gateway that led to the shelter, Beatrice saw, with a prick of pity, that tears were pouring down her cheeks. Beatrice hoped someone inside would help her.

'Well, I'll be off, my darlin',' said the old man, replacing the mug on the counter. He nodded his thanks and made his way with tortuous slowness towards the shelter.

Three blasts of a hooter split the night. Danger overhead. Next came a sinister drone of engines. Beatrice was always comforted when the anti-aircraft guns started up, though they didn't block out the evil sound of the approaching enemy planes. 'Let's get out of here, Mary,' she shouted to her companion.

As with icy hands she worked the mechanism to lower the serving-hatch, she watched the beams of light now sweeping the sky, picking out the dismal silhouettes of broken buildings all around.

'Hurry,' Mary said, slamming a tin of biscuits into a cupboard, and they ran across the cobblestones to the massive warehouse beyond like two mice, and entered through a small door in its flank. They found themselves in what Beatrice privately called the pit of hell, but which many of its thousands of occupants probably thought of as home.

Beatrice had been driving the canteen round the public air-raid shelters during the Blitz every third night for the previous month, since she'd finished a short period of training for the FANY. There were daytime duties, too, sometimes with the canteen, at other times driving a small ambulance taking patients to and from the First Aid Post where she was based.

She'd taken cover in the Whitechapel warehouse, an unofficial shelter, a number of times now, but she could never get used to its hollow vastness, nor, once her eyes grew used to the gloom, the awe-inspiring sight of the thousands of people quietly waiting in its belly, listening to the crump of the bombs, the cracks and crashes of disintegrating buildings outside. In the low light she could see them now, sprawled amongst their possessions on blankets and mattresses, beneath the lines of arches that stretched in wave after wave beyond her vision. A couple of months ago, out in the Leicestershire countryside, she'd never have been able to picture something like this in her wildest imagination. Already, at eight in the evening, some were asleep. Others passed the time knitting or reading, or simply staring at nothing. A handful of the younger people were playing cards and chatting quietly, but if their games got too loud there was always some angry voice to shush them.

Once, recently, someone had got up a sort of cabaret in a space in the middle, with an accordion player and a girl dancing, but the sombre spirit of this place must have made its disapproval felt, because the performance was desultory, and they packed up after half an hour. Any who walked the aisles to visit the latrines or to visit a friend did so quietly, with head bowed. There was no joking, none of the community singing that took off in other shelters. It was something about the monolithic nature of the building, Beatrice thought – it was like a giant mausoleum that crushed all human hope and laughter. The people had claimed it from its owners as a place of safety, and although it deigned to share its loneliness with them, it was making no concessions.

Mary was sitting against the wall beside Beatrice. With her head tipped back, her perfect profile gleamed palely in the gloom. Her eyes were closed, and with crossed arms she held her great-coat tight around her willowy body against the cold. No one could look at Mary and doubt that she'd been tipped for Deb of the Year only eighteen months back, in a different London. Now look at her, Beatrice thought with an affectionate smile. Modelling Army breeches with soot on her nose and a tin hat hanging off her arm.

Bea's thoughts moved naturally on to Angelina. She'd met up with her, of course, soon after she'd received that awful letter about Ed, taking a couple of days' leave from the depot to travel up on the train.

It had been hard, very hard, to walk up the steps to the house in Queen's Gate and ring the bell, not only because it was now a house of mourning, but because the last time she was here it had been the scene of such anguish for her. That had been only nine months ago, but in so many respects it was a different world. The only thing that hadn't changed was her feelings for Rafe. The freshness of that terrible moment of realization hit her again as she waited for the door to open. Then it did open and at the sight of Angelina's grief-stricken face she was swamped not with jealousy but pity.

'Oh, Bea, thank God you've come,' she said, opening her arms and clinging to Beatrice. Her hair was limp and unwashed, her face blotched from crying. She still smelt faintly of apples. It was the old Angelina. The one she'd grown up with and loved, the one who needed her.

'Of course I came,' Beatrice said, hugging her, her own tears starting. 'Of course. Angie, I'm so sorry. Poor, poor Ed.'

In the drawing room Oenone was standing by one of the windows, watching some children play hopscotch in the street, a vacant expression on her face. Bea went forward hesitantly and said, 'Mrs Wincanton.'

Angie's mother turned. 'Oh, Bea,' she murmured. 'So glad you've come. Awful, isn't it awful.' She kissed her, but her mind was somewhere far away.

'Mummy, why don't you come and sit down,' Angie said, going to her, but her mother waved her away.

'No, I'm all right,' she said, and continued to watch the children, a sad smile on her face.

'I'll show you the letter, Bea. Mummy, may I?'

'What, dear?'

'Show Bea the letter from Wing Commander Lewis?'

Oenone Wincanton gave a shrug.

'Is she all right?' Bea whispered. Angie fetched an envelope from the mantelpiece and they sat together on the sofa where she'd seen Angie with Rafe those few months ago.

'The doctor's been giving her these dreadful pills. She doesn't sleep, you see,' Angie said in a low voice. 'Daddy's no help. He's never here. And no one seems to know what Peter's up to. Daddy fixed him up running errands for one of his government friends and now he's been given some desk job.' Great tears splashed on the envelope.

Bea took it gently from her, withdrew the letter inside and read it. It was a masterly expression of sympathy. The man had known Ed personally. She sensed his own grief and anger at the loss of this brave and beautiful young man. *He gave his life that we might be free*, was his final sentence, and despite her own sorrow her heart lifted. That was what it was all about, selfless love for others. It was what it *had* to be about, or what was the point of it all?

'I want him back,' Angie sobbed beside her. 'I just want him back.'

Bea put her arms round her and held her tight.

Later, she asked carefully, 'Has there been any word about Rafe?'

'No, of course not, or I'd have told you,' Angie said, her voice dull. 'Nothing.'

Two months after this conversation, there had still been no news. And now, sitting in the gloom next to Mary, listening to the planes and the bombs, Beatrice said a small prayer for him.

An hour passed. There had been no bombs for a while. The gunfire became more sporadic, and soon died out altogether once the throb of aircraft engines had faded.

Mary whispered, 'Shall we see what it's like outside?' and the two of them got up and made their way over to the door.

'Now then, ladies,' said the warden guarding the entrance. 'Where do you think you're going? We haven't had the all clear yet.'

'Open the door, please do,' Mary begged. 'They've gone, you know they have, and we simply must get on to the next shelter.'

The warden eventually let them out, grumbling about falling masonry and saying that young ladies these days didn't know what was good for them. Mary thanked him with one of her very dazzling smiles and he grunted and shut the door behind them.

It was a terrible world they passed into, back-lit by fire, the air filled with billowing smoke and dust, through which shouts and screams could be distantly heard. With coats pulled up over their chins and gloved hands protecting their eyes they felt their way out of the little gate, feet crunching on glass, to where the canteen mercifully still stood intact. They stood for a moment, contemplating its thick coating of dust and debris with dismay.

Just then came a cracking and groaning like a tree in a high wind. They looked up in time to see, a few hundred yards away, a building disintegrate in mid-air and tumble into the street.

'If we'd gone that way a couple of minutes earlier—' Beatrice started to say.

'Don't,' Mary stopped her. 'We'll have to take another road.' When the latest dust had settled, she opened the passenger door and seized an old towel, with which she started to brush the mess off the windscreen. Then they both climbed aboard and Beatrice fired up the engine.

'Down to the river, don't you think, if we can get through?' She edged the vehicle forward and drove down a side alley, the weak headlights picking out lamp-posts and a pillarbox daubed with white paint. They emerged into a broader highway that they were able to follow for a time, then turned left towards the river. Ahead, a blazing building cast a dancing light.

'Look out!' Mary shouted, and Beatrice jammed on the brakes just short of a large crater. They both got out. Beatrice shone her torch down inside it. A taxi had tipped in and lay, wheels presented to the sky, like a large dead insect. The driver's door was open and though they called, no one seemed to be left inside.

'We could just about get round here,' Bea said, strafing the pavement with her torch beam. They returned to the van and she wound down the window to check how close they were to the crater as they mounted the kerb and carefully drove past.

Further up the road they came to a scene of frantic activity. A stretcher was being loaded into an ambulance. Several bodies lay by the roadside, half-covered with blankets. At least one, Beatrice saw with dismay, was a child. Firemen played jets of water on the flames and various people were sifting through rubble. A warden gestured them to go on, and Mary opened her window to speak to him. Somewhere a man was shouting, 'Mrs Cardew? Mrs Cardew!' in desperate tones.

They arrived at the next shelter soon after, parked by the entrance and set about heating water and cutting sandwiches. Mary walked back to serve the rescue workers whilst Beatrice served the queue of people from the shelter. Everywhere cement dust was settling on people's heads and shoulders like snow. Near the entrance to the shelter she glimpsed a pair of dray horses, as stoic as Pip and Wilfrid, eating from nosebags, hardly bothered by the disturbance around.

'Shall we move on?'

By half-past ten the skies remained quiet and clear, and the queues had gone. Beatrice and Mary packed up their van and drove on to the last shelter on the night's watch, stopping occasionally to feed emergency teams. Sometimes they'd find a road impassable and Beatrice had to turn the van in the darkness and seek an alternative route. Given the blackout, the fact that there were no street signs, and because bombs had altered the look of everything anyway, it was easy to get lost if you didn't have a good nose for direction. It was one of the things Beatrice had quickly had to acquire.

There were other things she'd learned too: how to keep calm in an emergency, how to hold herself together and carry on in the midst of terror and carnage – and she'd seen some terrible things. She'd discovered in all this that she had a great desire to help people, and felt a tremendous loyalty to this community who were nightly enduring appalling experiences of death and destruction. When she had time to think about it, which was hardly ever, she looked back on her life at school with amazement. It was such a short time ago, but it was as though she'd been another person then.

Around five o'clock in the morning, while it was still dark, people came to queue for breakfast. It was seven before the two girls left the canteen near the First Aid Post in the Mile End Road, and flagged down a bus to take them home to an ATS hostel in Bloomsbury. Here, they stumbled upstairs to the room they shared with two others, already up and out, peeled off their dusty uniform and climbed into their bunks. Beatrice fell asleep instantly and did not even dream.

The following night, she was woken in the small hours, not by an air raid, but by stones rattling on the window. 'Your turn,' came Mary's groan from the lower bunk. Beatrice slid down from her bed, tiptoed downstairs and opened the back door. A small slight figure slipped inside.

'Thanks, you're a brick,' Judy whispered, shivering. She smelt gorgeously of Chanel No. 5 and foreign cigarettes.

'Good time?' Beatrice was yawning.

'Marvellous.' Judy gave a delicious wiggle as she took off her shoes. 'Took ages to find a taxi back, though.'

Together, they crept upstairs, determined not to wake Matron.

'Come with me tonight, Bea, do! Dougie's bringing some pals.' Judy, who'd been preening in the mirror, twisted round to show her pretty face lit with excitement. 'You'll moulder away if you're not careful.'

'I do go out – I went to the pictures last night.' She'd accompanied Rosemary, the fourth member of their dormitory, who'd declared herself 'off' men following a broken romance with a Polish Spitfire pilot.

'Don't tell me, *Gone With the Wind* again.'

'I like *Gone With the Wind*. But no, last night it was *Rebecca*.' She'd felt dreadfully homesick seeing the Cornish setting.

'That's exactly the same thing.' Judy addressed her reflection as she dragged carmine lipstick across her mouth. 'You're happy to watch love affairs on screen but not to find any of the real thing for yourself. What's the matter with you?'

Beatrice, reading on her bunk, closed the book and sighed. 'All right,' she said, swinging herself down. 'I'll come, though I don't imagine I'll know anybody. What are you doing?' Judy had thrown open the cupboard door and was rifling through dresses. 'We have to wear our uniform, Ju.' Rosemary had recently got into trouble with Matron on this matter and been barred from an evening out. Judy, however, broke every rule in the book, if she could get away with it, and she usually did.

'This'll do – catch,' Judy said, throwing over a long pale-blue dress of her own. 'You put it on in the nightclub, silly. Hurry up,' she commanded, 'and I'll do your hair, if you like.'

It was nine o'clock when they joined the queue for the night-club, a large cellar below Leicester Square. Sleet was coming down fast, and once they finally got down the stairs, Beatrice was more than happy to follow Judy through the crowds to the ladies' powder room. There they changed into their dresses and repaired their make-up. Fair little Judy, in figure-hugging scarlet, stood out from the dowdy navy and khaki of the other girls jostling for space at the mirrors, but Beatrice, too, in her borrowed dress, was subject to the odd approving look.

When they were ready, they pushed their way through to the bar where Judy had spotted her boyfriend ordering drinks. His pleasant, boyish face lit up.

'Judy, darling. And Beatrice, what angels you look. Where's Guy gone. Guy? Girls, this is Guy Hurlingham from the mess. Now what will you have to drink?'

Beatrice liked Dougie, whom she'd met on a previous occasion. Whilst he and Judy chattered away she shook hands shyly with the other man. Guy Hurlingham was tallish and well turned out, with a Captain's pips on his shoulder and a musical lilt to his voice. He was a few years older than her eighteen years, with clever, slightly foxy features. His glossy dark hair contrasted with very pale skin.

He offered her a cigarette, which she declined, then lit his own with graceful movements. He had a quiet way about him which some people might have thought stand-offish, but which Beatrice sensed was only reserve. She wondered whether Dougie and Judy were deliberately pairing them off and felt a little annoyed with Judy for not warning her.

'Are you on leave like Dougie or just up for this evening?' she asked.

'We're both on twenty-four-hour passes,' he replied. His voice was deep, almost gravelly. 'Came up from Aldershot this afternoon.' His smile was slow and serious, but no less genuine for that. 'You're billeted with Judy here, I gather. What sort of a place is it?'

'The hostel? It's two big terraced houses knocked together,' she replied. 'Rather a rabbit warren, with Matron prowling about like a vixen.'

'You poor bunnies!' he said and she laughed.

'We're pretty good at creeping past her. It could be worse. The place feels comfortably solid in a raid. We sleep in the basement when it's very bad.'

'Which I know it has been. I say, it looks as though that party's leaving. Shall we?'

They hurried to secure one of the plush banquettes that lined the red-silk-covered walls while Dougie and Judy trailed after with the drinks. The whole place was so wonderfully glamorous, Beatrice thought, liking the crimson velvet curtains and the burgundy carpet glowing in the low light. She was glad she'd come. The band was playing a slow number and several pairs of dancers were drifting about on the dance floor. Before long, Judy and Dougie got up and joined them, leaving Beatrice and Guy to guard the drinks. After a minute or two the music turned lively, and they had to sit quite close together on the sofa to hear one another speak.

'I haven't known Dougie long,' Guy told her. 'He's a cheerful fellow, isn't he? I enjoy his company.' Being from Wales, he said, he didn't know many people in London, though he hoped to look up an old school pal who'd written to say he was in Town.

Dougie and Judy were coming back now. They'd met some other friends, and soon there was quite a crowd roosting around their table. An extraordinarily beautiful Italian-looking girl with a sardonic expression perched on the arm of Beatrice's sofa and talked to a stocky young Flying Officer, some story about her brother. Then she mentioned the name of a school and Beatrice couldn't help interrupting to ask the young man, 'You were there? You didn't know anyone called Wincanton, did you? Their sister is a friend.'

The Flying Officer looked dismayed. 'I should say I did. Ed Wincanton was in my year. You heard the news, I suppose?'

'Yes,' Beatrice said sadly. 'Poor Ed.'

'You know the parents, obviously,' he said. 'How did they take it? Badly, I expect.'

'Awful,' she said, and it rushed back, her meeting with Angelina, Oenone's devastation.

'And his brother was a couple of years below. Peter, I think his name was.'

'That's right. You haven't come across him recently, have you?' Beatrice asked. 'No one seems to know quite what he's up to.'

'I remember Peter Wincanton,' the Italian beauty cut in. 'He came to stay with my brother once. I thought him rude.'

'I don't think he meant to be,' Beatrice said. 'He's shy, you see.'

'Most awkward. What does the father do now?' the beauty asked. 'Isn't he in the government or something?'

'I think he's a Minister in the War Office,' Beatrice said. 'It's a bit vague.'

'Who knows what anyone does these days,' said Guy, who'd been listening to the exchange. 'No one will tell you anything.'

The band had struck up a popular number, and two by two the group peeled off to dance.

'Would you like to?' Guy said. Beatrice wondered if he was merely being polite.

'I really don't mind sitting out. I've two left feet, I'm afraid,' she told him.

'And I've two right ones, so we'll match,' he said, smiling. 'Come on.' They danced to two lively numbers before the music turned slow again. 'Shall we try this?' Guy said, and when she demurred he gently pulled her to him. She closed her eyes as they drifted dreamily. It was easy in here to forget the fear and the horror for a while, just to feel the music and the comfort of someone's arms around you. Then she remembered he was a stranger and the feeling was lost.

When the song was over, they went back to their seats. The young Flying Officer from Ed and Peter's school reappeared. The Italian beauty had vanished. Dougie started on some anecdote about a friend Guy and Judy seemed to know.

'Would you like to dance?' the Flying Officer asked Beatrice and it seemed impolite to refuse. Nick, she thought that was his name. He led her round the floor in an uncomfortably brisk fashion and asked her how she knew the Wincantons.

'We were neighbours in Saint Florian,' she told him.

'I wanted to tell you,' he said in her ear. 'Peter. I didn't like to mention this in company. A pal told me he's doing something frightfully hush hush. His father got him the introduction. I don't know if it's true, but it's rather interesting if it is. Clara's right, he is rather a strange chap.'

Beatrice resisted the temptation to pull away. Peter had to be defended. 'He's shy, I told you. And a little unhappy, I think. He's always been rather kind to me, actually.'

'Has he?' Nick said, staring at her. 'Well, I'm pleased to hear it. I'm sorry if I've said the wrong thing. I intended no offence, you know.'

'None taken,' Beatrice said, but knew she sounded cool.

As soon as the dance was over, she thanked him quickly and started to walk back to her seat.

'Air raid. AIR RAID. AIR RAID,' a stout warden was hollering. 'Out you all come, gentlemen and laydees. The fun's over for now.'

There was a great fluttering as people searched for bags and coats and began to swarm to the exits. A few didn't move at all. One couple continued to sway together on the dance floor, as if welded to one another, though the band had stopped playing.

Beatrice found herself caught up in a surging tide of humanity squeezing up the bottleneck of the stairs and out into the square, where they finally heard sirens. She saw Judy, briefly, a few yards away, but then she was borne out of sight by the crowd. Someone took her arm. 'Beatrice,' Guy said in her ear. 'I thought we'd lost you.'

The atmosphere was surprisingly gay. A party in front were rather the worse for drink, the men joking and the girls shrieking with laughter as they stumbled along the road in the direction of the Underground.

'Looks like we've lost Dougie and Judy altogether,' Guy said, looking about.

'I saw they were with one another, at any rate. Look, there's a side entrance through here,' Beatrice said, hoping it would be less busy, and she led them along an alleyway and then down a flight of steps just as the hooter sounded for 'danger overhead'.

Down on the platform they had to step round the regular occupants, who'd already arranged themselves for the night. The atmosphere was raucous here, with singing and laughter. Eventually they found a few square inches of space in a passage and Guy folded his great-coat for them both to sit on. They waited together, feeling the air sucking and blowing about them, whether from trains or explosions, Beatrice couldn't tell. Every now and then the whole edifice around them shuddered in a terrifying fashion and everybody would cry out in fear. Guy's hand felt for hers and she clutched it tightly. When someone passed them tea from a Thermos, they shared the cup. Later, he put his arm around her and held her close.

After what might have been an hour the message was handed down that the all clear had sounded, and the more temporary residents started getting up and gathering their possessions. When Beatrice and Guy emerged into Leicester Square, it was to see that it had escaped the bombs altogether. And there were Dougie and Judy waiting for them where the railings would have been, had the authorities not taken them away for scrap.

'We thought you'd spot us all right,' Dougie said. 'Don't know what you think, but I'd say we've seen the best of this place tonight. Would you girls like to come on with us? We're kipping with a pal near Manchester Square.'

'I'm up for it,' Judy said. 'How about you, Beatrice?'

'Is it far? What about Matron? We'd need to be able to get back to Bloomsbury afterwards,' Beatrice said. They'd get a terrible ticking off if Matron realized they'd been out all night.

'Honestly, that woman treats us like children,' Judy muttered, but the complaint was half-hearted.

'It's only a little way north of Oxford Street, practically round the corner from you,' Dougie wheedled. 'We'll see you get home safe, I promise.'

It was getting on for midnight when they stepped out of a taxi into pitch darkness. Tinny dance music swirled in the misty air and when a front door opened to disgorge party guests, a feeble yellow light was cast briefly across the pavement. Long enough for Beatrice to take in a terrace of white-painted houses, the end one on the left roofless, like a broken tooth, exposed to the sky.

Dougie knocked on the door of one to the right of the party house. There was no response. 'Perry must be out,' he told the others. He foraged under a window box, produced a key and got the door open.

'He showed us where everything is so we'll make ourselves at home, shall we? Ah, here we are, come in.' They walked into a hall where the light didn't work when Dougie tried it, and through a door to the left.

It had once been grand, Beatrice saw, looking round the drawing room with its crumbling plaster decoration and its faded velvet curtains. Now it smelt terrifically of damp, there was a great crack down the front wall, and the striped paper was dark with mildew. The music from the party next door ebbed and flowed through the dividing wall.

Dougie vanished and when he returned he held two half-bottles of whisky to his chest. Guy, meanwhile, set about switching on lights and an electric fire, and the girls were coaxed finally into unbuttoning their coats. Dougie splashed whisky into tumblers and sat on one of the sofas with Judy snuggling into him, while Guy and Beatrice shared the other. Guy brooded unhappily and Beatrice wondered how long it would be before she could go home.

After Dougie refilled everyone's glasses, to Beatrice's horror he pulled Judy to her feet and said, 'We're going on a wander. See you later, I expect.'

Beatrice and Guy listened to them tramping noisily up the stairs, Judy shrieking with laughter, then came the sound of a door slamming. Alone now with a stranger, Beatrice huddled into a corner of the sofa, unable to think of a thing to say. Guy cleared his throat and moved a little closer. He said, 'Shall we? If you want to?'

It took her a moment to realize what he meant. She shook her head fiercely. 'No,' she said. 'No.'

Guy looked relieved. 'I didn't think so,' he said.

'It's just . . . not me,' Beatrice stammered.

He smiled, all his nervousness gone, and now she thought how nice he looked.

'Thank heavens for that,' he told her. 'I'm afraid I'm a bit out of my depth with girls like Judy.'

'I'm awfully fond of her,' Beatrice said, her face warm from whisky and embarrassment.

Guy lit a cigarette and said, 'Dougie's crazy about her. Bores us all rotten about it. Look, I heard you say earlier you hail from Cornwall. I know the place a bit. Used to holiday in Newquay with my aunt, in fact. Which part are you from?'

And Beatrice found herself telling him about St Florian and about her parents and her early childhood in France, and in return he described his upbringing on the Welsh borders near Hay, where his family were landowners and farmers. The lilt in his voice became more pronounced when he spoke of two elder brothers, of a little sister who'd died of meningitis. After boarding school in Malvern he'd applied for a commission a year or two before war broke out. His company, like Rafe's, had been in France, and he'd been evacuated from Dunkirk, being picked up by a Hythe fisherman. 'Forevermore I'll associate the white cliffs of home with the stink of fish and oil,' he said, with a smile. 'But don't think I wasn't grateful.'

'I have a friend who was in France.'

'He's alive?'

'Yes. He was taken prisoner. But we haven't had news of him for a long while now.'

There was silence between them. So much of this war was about waiting, about not knowing, Beatrice thought, and hardly daring to hope.

The music next door stopped abruptly, to be replaced by the sound of voices raised in argument, then a woman's angry squeal. A door slammed and people spilled onto the street, where they talked and laughed and shouted goodbyes, then all was quiet.

Eventually, Guy said, 'Oh, not again. Listen.'

Somewhere far away, the sirens were howling. Soon came the dull thud of bombs. This lasted for a tense few minutes, then there was silence.

'It's after two. I ought to get Judy home,' Beatrice said, looking at her watch.

'I'll tell them.' Guy went to holler up the staircase, and eventually Judy and Dougie reappeared, dishevelled and sheepish-looking.

'We'll walk you home, won't we, Doug?' Guy said, reaching for his coat.

Outside, the temperature had dropped several degrees further and the girls, tired and hungover, were soon shuddering with cold. Fortunately, when they reached the main road, it was to see a taxi drawing up. Two women fell out, and one began arguing with the driver until the other said, 'Let's give him what he wants, Kath, I'm beat.' She slapped some coins into the man's hand and hauled her friend away.

Dougie stalled the driver and snatched open the rear door. 'Hop in, girls,' he said.

'Goodbye,' Beatrice said to Guy. 'I enjoyed this evening.'

'So did I,' Guy said, taking her hand.

As the taxi bore her and Judy away, and the men were lost to the darkness, she was visited by the fear that she'd never see him again.

'You liked him, didn't you?' Judy said, yawning. 'I thought he'd be your sort.'

'Whatever sort that is,' Beatrice replied. 'But I don't know that I'll see him again.'

'I think you might,' Judy said. 'In fact, I'd bet on it.'

'Dougie's very keen on you,' Beatrice said.

'Yes. It's no good though,' said Judy, in a small voice. 'Dougie's married already. And his wife won't give him a divorce.'

Christmas slipped by and 1941 crept in. Apart from the night of 29 December, when the whole city was set aflame, the raids had become more sporadic. Although Londoners continued their established nightly routines, some settling into their garden shelters, others crowding into the Underground stations, others merely staying in bed and hoping for the best, that relentless terror, which visited with every twilight, felt easier to bear, and a patched-up version of normal life resumed.

Guy telephoned Beatrice at the hostel a few days after their first meeting and they had dinner together a week later in a busy restaurant above Regent Street. She found they talked easily to one another. Beatrice was impressed by his quiet strength of character and simple decency. He spoke sympathetically about the men he led, and she sensed his devotion. Endearingly, he possessed a dogged belief that right would win over might, that they would prevail in this war. Beatrice wanted badly to believe him.

In turn she spoke of her work, the long nights at the shelters, the days when she could drop with tiredness. How sometimes she helped the rescuers, though she could hardly bring herself to describe some of the things she'd seen. The worst was when a family's garden shelter had sustained a direct hit. She and Mary had driven past immediately afterwards and stopped to help. The sight of the mutilated bodies of the three young children, laid alongside that of their mother on the pavement, was something she would never forget.

'The father came home from work when we were bringing out the little girl . . .' She shook her head, unable to continue. Still, from his intent expression and the tender way he touched her hand, she knew Guy was trying to understand and that was all she required.

They met whenever they could after this, though it wasn't easy. Once he didn't turn up at their trysting place at all, and Beatrice returned to the hostel after two hours of waiting, and spent a night of worry, only to learn the next morning that he'd been stuck for hours on a train, unable to contact her. She was disconcerted to realize how much she was coming to look forward to their times together. It wasn't as though she'd forgotten Rafe. Quite the opposite. She carried her love of him deep inside, along with a continuous prayer for his safety – and always she had to remind herself that Rafe belonged to Angie.

Guy calmed her, held her steady. It was a gentle love, this one, built for her on friendship rather than passion, but she knew from the hungry looks he gave her that Guy wanted her, and from his tender solicitousness that his feelings ran deep. Gradually she found herself responding and would long for their meetings.

Late in February 1941, he began to hint that his company would soon be on the move. 'I can't predict when,' he told her, 'just that it's the rumour.' Their meetings from then on felt snatched and intense. Every moment together might be their last for a long time.

Once or twice, she went with him to Perry's house, where he and Dougie usually stayed when they came up to London. Once, she met Perry – a harassed, thin-faced young man who

worked nights on air defence, which explained why he was
rarely at home. Although she and Guy shared passionate
embraces on Perry's sofa, he would never go what her friend
Mary called 'too far'. Having heard tales from some of the ATS
girls, this puzzled her, but she was too inexperienced in such
matters to discuss it with him, unsure of the protocols. Later
though, when she was snug in her narrow bunk with its prickly
blankets, she would lie burning with longing for him, and it
would be some time before she settled to sleep.

Soon after the second of these occasions, he asked her nervously if she would come away with him and she said she would.
One Saturday morning in the middle of February, she took a
train down to Hastings, through countryside sparkling with
frost. He was there on the platform to meet her, and though she
took his arm calmly enough she felt sick with nerves.

'Are you hungry?' he asked.

'A little,' she lied, but she was happy enough to pick at a fish
pie in a restaurant on the high street, watching him dine more
heartily on a steak pudding that was more suet than meat.

In the afternoon, they wandered along the seafront until they
reached a small hotel where the receptionist met Beatrice's eye
with a discreet smile as she checked their booking. The room
had a sea view but was shabby, with ill-fitting windows that
rattled in the wind. A fire burned in the grate, but the heat went
straight up the flue rather than warming the room, so they
undressed quickly and got directly into bed. She kept her eyes
closed at first, enjoying his caressing fingers and the surprising feelings of her awakening body. 'Wait a moment,' he said,
turning from her briefly to take something from the bedside
cabinet. Whilst he fumbled with himself she put out her hand
and stroked his chest, wondering at the strange hardness of the
muscle, leaning to kiss the soft skin above his collarbone. When

he was ready he took her in his arms once more and rolled gently on top of her so he was looking down into her eyes.

'I love you,' he whispered, 'you know that, don't you?' and it seemed right and natural when he slipped inside her and soon they were moving together, slowly at first, then more urgently. 'Oh, Beatrice,' he whispered finally and she clung to him tightly until the delightful waves of warmth subsided. Afterwards they lay entwined without speaking and she felt tender and happy and loved. They dozed as the windows rattled and the wind roared in the chimney. Later, giggling and half-dressed, they took turns to creep along the corridor and use the bathroom.

Next morning, as the train bore her away from him, she was overwhelmed, as at their first meeting, by an awful sense of loss. Her body, raw from the closeness of his, already needed to feel him again.

After this short weekend, they snatched hungry moments alone together whenever and wherever they could, and the knowledge that at any time his orders might come gave their meetings a sweet urgency.

It was one Thursday evening early in March that she was summoned to the telephone in the draughty hall of the hostel. It was Guy.

'Bea, they've put us on embarkation leave. Forty-eight hours. I'm afraid this is it. Listen. I must go home to my folks. It wouldn't be fair not to. I wondered if you would come with me? Could you? I'd like you to meet them.'

'Go to Wales? Guy, no – I mean I'd love to meet your parents, but I don't imagine it's possible. Not at this short notice.'

'Will you ask?'

'Of course I will.'

As she feared, her request for leave was turned down. She didn't tell Guy what her Commanding Officer said. 'If he were your fiancé, of course, that would be a different matter. But I feel a line must be drawn here. You're so very young. And we simply can't spare you at present. We're so stretched with the other girls away.'

It seemed a long time before he came to the telephone.

'Bad news, I'm afraid,' she told him.

'Damn.' She heard him breathe down the crackling line. 'Did you tell them it was important?'

'Of course,' she replied. 'Judy hasn't had any luck either. Our C.O. will only give me Saturday afternoon off. Can't we meet on your way back through London?'

He was late, a whole hour late, and she waited alone at a table in the gallery of the nightclub, peering through the railings, in case there was anyone she recognized amongst the dancing couples below. Twice she had coldly to tell some chancer that she was waiting for someone. Lateness, missed meetings, these were something everyone was used to now, but tonight it worried her more than usual. She was struggling to tamp down the fear that perhaps she'd never see him again when her attention was caught by a man in uniform walking round the edge of the dance-floor. There was something familiar about that bright fair hair that made her think of Rafe.

'Bea. Thank heavens, I thought you might have given up waiting.'

She swung round. 'Oh, Guy.' The fair-haired man vanished from her mind. Guy was at her side, warm, very much alive and out of breath. As he bent to kiss her cheek she smelt rain and cigarettes.

'I'm sorry, darling,' he said. 'The usual kind of story. The train packed up for twenty minutes just before Paddington, then when I finally got on a bus it couldn't get past Bayswater because of a bomb.'

She clung to him, suddenly desperate not to let him go. 'It's all right,' he soothed. 'It's all right, darling girl. I'm here now.'

Without letting go of her hand, he pulled out a chair and sat down, then, when a waiter came, set about ordering. As usual, when the food came he ate hungrily, while she hardly noticed what she was eating. Instead she tried to imprint the sight of him on her memory, his broad shoulders, his handsome pointed face, the light glinting off his dark hair, still damp from outside. There was always that air of stillness about him, an aloneness, as though he didn't register being in a crowd. She was so glad to see him, but could not shake off that feeling of apprehension.

'How are your parents?'

'They're very well, thank you,' he told her. 'And horribly brave about me going away. When I said goodbye I could see my mother had been crying, but I knew she wouldn't want me to mention it.' He stared at his food, unseeing for a moment, then said, 'They've two little urchins to stay, sent down from Liverpool. My mother looks tired, though, and she's worried enough about Clive . . .'

'He's your eldest brother? The pilot?'

'That's right.'

'I suppose the urchins must take her mind off things.'

'Oh yes. They're bright lads. Common, of course, and one can't understand a word they say. They get up to tremendous mischief. My father had to whip them for throwing eggs in the barn.' He laughed. 'Don't suppose they'd ever seen hens before.' He pushed his plate away and lit a cigarette. There was something on his mind, she sensed.

'When do you go?' she said in a low voice.

'We embark at Portsmouth tomorrow sixteen hundred. I don't suppose you'd be able . . .'

She shook her head sadly. 'Tonight is all we have,' she said, and again he felt for her hand. She was annoyed to feel tears prickle and looked away, blinking furiously. 'Where are you going? I don't suppose you can say.'

'The rumour is it's desert khaki, that's all I know. Should be a deal warmer than here!' She didn't smile at his joke and he added weakly, 'Cheer up!'

They were both silent for a moment, and she found herself once more scanning the dancers below. It was getting very busy now, and the air swirled with smoke and heat and heady music. She remembered the man she'd glimpsed earlier, the man with the bright gold hair who looked like Rafe, but she couldn't see him now.

She glanced up to see Guy was studying her, an awkward expression on his face. He reached into his breast pocket and extracted a small packet, which he opened to reveal a delicate ring with a stone that shimmered sapphire blue.

'Oh, Guy,' she said, staring at it. 'It's beautiful.'

'It's only paste, I'm afraid. I'll get you something better when I can.'

'I don't mind, really I don't.' She turned the box so that light from the chandeliers flashed off the stone, and experienced a rush of love and relief.

'You know what I'm saying, my darling, don't you?' he said, his voice hoarse. 'We can't know what will happen, but I'd like to think that you're here, waiting for me. We've known each other such a short time, I understand that, but I . . . I've never been more sure of anything in my life.'

She stared at the ring, and looked into his dear, kind face. She could be happy with Guy, she saw that. It was as though a light poured down into her mind, illuminating pictures of their future together. After the war. A house surrounded by fields, children as mischievous as the evacuee urchins. Was that to be hers? Here, in the heat and urgency of this moment, the scent of desire was spiced with the fear of death. There was no chance for reflection, no time for careful thought. There would be waiting enough when he was away, time to consider.

'Oh yes, Guy,' she breathed and allowed him to push the ring onto her finger, where it sat quite snug.

'I love you,' he said, taking her hand. 'You've made me so happy.' And, not minding where he was, he pulled her suddenly into a passionate kiss. A group of soldiers on the next table clapped and whistled, until they pulled apart laughing.

'My dear girl. I suppose I ought to speak to your father,' he said. 'I wish I'd met your parents. What do you think he'll say?'

'Let me write to him and tell him all about you,' she replied, smiling gently. 'Then we can visit them together, when you're home.' At least Guy's family background was one her father would recognize. And her mother? Well, maybe once she'd had grand hopes of their connections with the Wincantons, but lately Delphine was so focused on her husband and her worry about her family in France, Beatrice imagined she'd forgotten such petty concerns long ago.

'You must write to me every week,' Guy said. 'I want to know exactly what you're doing, so I can picture you. Oh, and I must have a photograph. It's only fair since I've given you one of me.'

'I brought one with me,' she said, and searched in her bag. It was the portrait they'd taken of her when she joined up; she didn't like it much. 'The others I have are of before the war and I look like a child.'

'You certainly don't now,' he said, smiling meaningfully.

'Did you tell your parents about me?' she asked.

This question wasn't answered because it was then they were interrupted. 'Beatrice, there you are!' It was Judy, making her way between the tables with her usual talent for disturbance, dragging Dougie by the hand. 'Hello, Guy, darling. We've been looking for you everywhere.'

'I hope we're not intruding,' Dougie said, seeing their faces, 'but you did say you might be here, Guy, and we took that as an invitation. Heavens, it's crowded tonight.' He addressed the soldiers on the next table. 'Are you chaps needing all those chairs?'

Whilst he sorted out seats, eagle-eyed Judy saw the ring and pounced with a gasp of delight. 'Dougie, look, he's only gone and done it!'

Dougie swung round. 'Guy, my dear boy, congratulations. And Beatrice, how wonderful. It couldn't happen to a nicer pair,' he cried, pumping Guy's hand and kissing Beatrice. Judy sent him off to find the manager and in due course he returned with a dusty bottle of champagne and a clutch of glasses.

Everyone was staring. The group of soldiers behind broke into a cats' chorus of 'For they are jolly good fellows,' which clashed badly with 'Oh Johnny', being struck up by the band below and Judy, her eyes gleaming with fun and bubbly, giggled and wept by turns. Meanwhile Beatrice and Guy sat quietly smiling, embarrassed at the fuss, holding hands under the table.

Had she ever felt so happy? A picture came to Beatrice's mind. That hot summer's day in the front porch at home, the morning before Sturton's tragedy, when she'd felt so rapturous. This, too, was happiness, yes it was, but a different kind – more steady, grown-up, she supposed.

The soldiers returned to their beers and Judy and Dougie started an amiable squabble about money Judy had apparently lent him earlier to pay for supper. After a while they got up to dance. Guy excused himself and Beatrice sat alone in her bubble of happiness. She watched Judy and Dougie descend the stairs and join the dancers, wishing they could share the same happiness. It was too crowded for them to move about much, but that didn't cramp Judy's style. Beatrice laughed to see the fiery little red-clad figure spinning Dougie about, Dougie having to apologize to everyone they bumped into, their friendly smiles winning immediate forgiveness.

Then she saw again the man with the fair hair. The bubble of contentment burst. She knew him now, for certain. But it couldn't be him, it absolutely couldn't be; he was missing somewhere in France. He was dancing with a blonde woman in a Wrens uniform, a woman who looked horribly familiar. As she stared, waiting to be certain, the woman threw back her head in laughter.

Beatrice rose to her feet and mouthed, 'Angie!' It was Angelina, and she was dancing with . . .

'*Rafe* . . .' she whispered.

Then came a great crashing sound, and her world exploded in a roar of pain and terror.

Chapter 17

The blast from the bomb had blown her completely across the gallery to the wall against which she sat, surrounded by a tangle of furniture, rubble and glinting glass. She was fighting to breathe; then, with a great whoop her lungs filled with air – not air as she knew it, fresh and life-giving – instead hot and seering and noxious. She hurt all over, but seemed to be in one piece. Looking up, she saw a great hole in the roof, and beyond, the night sky, coruscating with light. She moved her left hand to push herself up, but felt a sharp pain as something pierced it, and snatched it back. Somehow she struggled to her feet and glass cracked under her feet as she started to work her way through the chaos towards the one surviving staircase.

She passed the edge of the gallery with its twisted railing and looked down. Where the dance-floor had been was now a pile of rubble. Already dark figures with torches moved through the devastation, searching and calling over the screaming. Now she started to remember.

'Guy.' Her lips formed his name. Which way had he gone?

She heard a groan, felt a hand grasp her ankle. 'Help me,' a man said. Not Guy, but one of the soldiers who'd serenaded them earlier. She heaved at the table that pinned him down and he crawled out, then both did their best to help any others they could make out in the dim light. One woman lay still, her face gleaming pale, her eyes glassy, forever looking upwards. Beatrice had seen that look too many times, out on the streets. She closed the woman's eyelids and passed on by.

The gallery glowed suddenly with soft light. 'Anyone up here?' Two wardens had climbed the staircase and began to guide people down. 'Slowly now as you go, miss,' one said. 'No need to panic now, nice and easy.' As if in answer, the sound of hysterical sobbing started up somewhere nearby. Beatrice made her way down the stairs, her limbs shaking.

'Bea, thank God.' Guy was at the bottom, having stumbled through the mess to meet her. She fell the last couple of steps and he caught her, grasping her tightly. 'Come on, let's get you out of here.'

'No,' she said, remembering the others. The vision came to her of Rafe, and Angie, her head thrown back in laughter.

'Judy, Dougie,' Guy said. They stared around.

Bodies and debris lay everywhere, the little flames from searchers' cigarette lighters like wake lights all around. A pale torchbeam fell across the scene and for a second Beatrice caught a glimpse of red halfway across the room. Judy's dress. 'Oh no, Guy,' she gasped, and began to stagger over to it, though glass and splintered wood tore at her legs. Someone else had got there first.

The man was stooped over Judy's body. Beatrice saw with horror that he had Judy's little clutch bag.

'Get away from her!' she shrieked, grabbing at the bag, but the man snatched it away and scrambled ratlike into the shadows. She bent and clawed through the rubbish to uncover Judy's face, and as Guy's little lighter sought it out, screamed in horror, for half Judy's head was sheared away. She turned and pressed her face into Guy's chest.

'Beatrice,' he said. 'Calm down. We must get out.'

But then they saw Dougie, the front of his jacket sodden with blood. She crouched down and felt for his pulse. It fluttered madly like a trapped moth, and even as Guy shouted to a pair of men carrying a stretcher, it stilled. 'Dougie!' she whispered, uselessly. The stretcher-bearers veered away.

'Beatrice, come on,' Guy ordered.

Panic fought in her chest. *Get a grip*, she told herself fiercely. She'd seen scenes like this so many times in the Blitz, had cursed the German pilots and the puppet-master who pulled their strings, but never before had the bombs hurt anyone she knew; never had she felt it was personal.

She remembered something else. Rafe and Angelina were here somewhere. She'd seen them, hadn't she? Or had that brief moment of recognition been something she'd dreamt whilst unconscious?

Again Guy urged her to leave.

'Wait.' Quickly she grasped at a shred of material, part of a curtain, maybe, laid it over Judy's face and whispered goodbye. It was all she could do. She was shaking with the shock of it all, but now Guy was taking charge, pulling her away.

As they passed near the back of the room by the staircase she'd just come down, she saw them finally in the dim light. A fair-haired man, bending over a woman lying in the rubble. He called to them.

'Help me, for God's sake!' At that second a ray of light caught his face.

Beatrice breathed in sharply. 'Rafe,' she whispered. She pulled Guy over towards them.

It was definitely a woman he was tending. Her uniform was ripped and dusty.

'Angie?' Beatrice said, kneeling down. 'Rafe, is she all right?'

He twisted his head to look at her, frowning.

'Oh,' she said. It wasn't Rafe at all.

'She's breathing all right,' he told her. 'Angie, Angie, darling, it's Gerald. Can you hear me?'

Angelina was coming to now. She raised one arm to her face and began to shake with silent sobs.

'Angie,' Beatrice said, 'it's Bea. Don't worry, dear, we'll get you out of here.' She was checking her for injury as she'd been trained, but all the time her mind was trying to take in the man who wasn't Rafe, but Rafe's half-brother Gerald. He was bigger than Rafe, broader, somehow, and though he had the same fair hair, she thought it must grow differently, not pushed up at the front like Rafe's. Angie, fully awake now, sat up, then leant over suddenly and retched.

'Oh God, Angie,' Gerald said. 'Here.' He felt in his pockets for a handkerchief and wiped her mouth. 'Come on, I'll help you up. Let's get you safely out.'

'My head,' she said, as he lifted her to her feet. 'Killing me. Bit groggy.'

The stretcher team had arrived now, but Gerald waved them away, and something about the gesture reminded Bea of Rafe.

Guy was there, and together the two men eased Angie onto a chair made of their arms. A warden went ahead to pick out a route.

'All dead, poor buggers,' she heard someone say as they passed. She tried not to look at the splashes of dark liquid tracking up the steps. Halfway up, a silk handbag lay in a glistening black puddle.

The square was a mad chaos of people and skewed vehicles, doors thrown open. What was most awful was the dark and the silence in which they worked. Along the pavement in the shadows lay a long row of bodies, some barely clothed. A man in a torn dinner jacket was being loaded into an ambulance. A very young girl in a dancing dress knelt grieving in the street whilst a warden tried to comfort her. Gerald and Guy sat Angie on an upturned crate, where she was briefly examined by a woman in a nurse's uniform who told her there was nothing badly wrong with her, she should just go home. Gerald caught the blanket someone flung to him and wrapped it round her shoulders while Guy tried to find a taxi. There were none for ages and ages, and then they were lucky.

As he handed Angie into the cab, Gerald said to Bea, 'You called me Rafe in there. You're Beatrice. Rafe used to speak of you.'

'Yes.'

'And your friend is Captain . . .'

'Hurlingham,' said Guy. 'Guy Hurlingham.'

'This is a pretty poor show,' Gerald said to Guy by way of greeting. 'I'll get Miss Wincanton home. Don't feel you two need to come.'

'No, I'd like to come,' Beatrice insisted. 'I must see that she's all right.'

'Bea, perhaps we should call it a night,' Guy said. 'You must go if you want, but I should only be in the way.'

'Don't be silly,' Beatrice said, sticking out her lower lip. 'I need you with me.'

'What are we doing, gents?' the taxi driver asked.

'Queen's Gate,' Gerald said briskly.

They all squashed into the taxi, Guy and Beatrice opposite Angie and Gerald. Angie looked as though she was about to be sick again but fortunately wasn't.

As they moved off, Gerald said to Beatrice, 'He's often talked of you, my poor brother. I wonder all the time how he is. We haven't had any news for months.'

He smiled at her, but it was a more cautious smile than Rafe's ever were. She lifted her hand and examined her ring. How strange to see it on her finger.

Angie recovered sufficiently to take notice. 'Bea,' she whispered. 'That's pretty. Does that mean . . . ?'

'Yes,' Bea replied.

'Oh, I'm so pleased for you, darling,' Angie said, making to lean forward to embrace Bea. Instead she sank back, clutching the side of her head. 'I must learn not to do that,' she said.

Beatrice sat back and closed her eyes, then as her head swam, regretted it. Her ears still rang from the explosion and bits of her ached. She couldn't tell what she looked like, but if the others were anything to go by, dusty and dishevelled. Not that she cared. The image of Judy lying in the rubble rushed into her head and she gasped and felt herself start to shake. Guy, beside her, put his arm round her. He must be feeling much the same. She turned her head into his shoulder and he held her tight. All of a sudden she felt warm and safe, and then came a selfish rush of thankfulness that she was alive.

When they reached the house in Queen's Gate, Mrs Wincanton came downstairs in her dressing-gown to answer the door, and when she saw her daughter, clothes torn to shreds, hair matted with blood, she screamed. 'My God! What's happened to you?'

Angie pitched forward into her mother's arms.

It was Gerald who carried her up to her bedroom. Beatrice, following, helped Peggy the maid clean Angie up and get her into bed while Oenone could be heard down in the hall trying to get through to the doctor on the telephone.

Dr Strumpshaw duly came and did various tests before declaring Angie to be slightly concussed from a nasty crack on the head, and saying that she should be watched, though he didn't think any serious damage had been done. By this time, however, Mrs Wincanton had wound herself up into a dreadful state. The thought of losing her elder daughter as well as her son seemed to her a real possibility, and it was only with the greatest difficulty that she was calmed down and made to go to bed with a sedative.

Downstairs, the telephone was ringing again and somebody answered it.

Tired beyond measure, Beatrice stumbled downstairs to see the doctor out.

'And where is the man of the house tonight?' he said.

'I don't know,' Beatrice replied. She was too loyal to say that in her experience he was rarely home.

The doctor frowned. 'You'll be staying here then, I trust? They need someone reliable.'

Beatrice bit her lip, her exhausted thoughts going round and round. It was their last night together – hers and Guy's – but Angie needed her. Either way, if she wasn't at the hostel in the morning there would be a row. 'I don't know what to do,' she told the doctor. 'I'm on duty in the morning.'

'You won't be, you know. Telephone first thing and tell them. You've been through a terrible experience and we can't have you collapsing at your post. That won't do anyone any good. Besides, as I say, you're needed here. In fact, I insist. Shall I write you one of my notes?'

'That would be marvellous,' she said. She took him into the drawing room where there was a writing desk. There they found Gerald and Guy, still waiting patiently.

'That was Mr Wincanton on the telephone,' Gerald said. 'He'd heard about tonight's blast and wanted to know whether his daughter was home safely. How is Miss Wincanton?' he asked the doctor anxiously.

'Nothing that a few days' rest won't solve,' the doctor said as he wrote. 'But she won't be going back to the Wrens for a while.'

'I should think not. Now, I ought to be getting back to barracks, Miss Marlow,' Gerald told her, 'if there's nothing more I can do here. Mr Wincanton left me with the distinct impression that he'd be home as soon as he could find a cab. That might be a while, so I'm glad that you're staying.'

'What about Angie's brother – Peter, I mean?' Beatrice asked. 'Isn't he here?'

'I don't think he lives at home at the moment,' Gerald replied. 'Angie told me there had been some difference of opinion.'

'Oh,' Beatrice said. She wasn't that surprised.

'I can give you a lift if I'm going your way,' the doctor said to Gerald. 'My next port of call is Oxford Street.'

'Thank you,' Gerald replied. 'If you could drop me at Marble Arch.'

Beatrice and Guy exchanged glances. 'Guy,' she said, 'I think I must stay here tonight. I'm sorry.' She knew at heart she shouldn't leave Angie; not when Oenone was under sedation.

He nodded. 'Of course you must.' She thought he looked as exhausted as she felt. A great bruise was blooming across his cheekbone and his eyes were rimmed red. Whenever he moved, his uniform shed puffs of dust.

'Perhaps I can prevail upon you for a lift, too, sir,' Guy said to the doctor. 'I'm staying with a friend north of Oxford Street.'

'The more the merrier,' the doctor said. While Peggy the maid fetched their coats, Gerald went upstairs to say goodbye.

'Bea, what's the number here?' Guy said. 'I'll be leaving Perry's early, but I'll telephone you first.' She wrote it down for him.

'Thank you, Guy, for everything.' He took her hand, and once again she felt the pressure of the blue-stone ring.

'I'm so sorry,' she whispered. 'I wish we could be together tonight.'

After the men had gone, and while Peggy was making up the bed in the room she had slept in last Christmas, Bea wandered wearily along the corridor to see how Angie was. The bedside lamp cast a warm ring of light, by which she saw the girl was dozing. Her breathing was steady, though once she mumbled and frowned as though in pain. Beatrice watched her for a while, arms folded, her thoughts chasing round and round her head. Despite the doctor's calmness, she was worried about Angelina. The girl had clearly been hit hard by the bomb-blast and the vomiting was not a good sign.

And mixed in with the concern for Angie was something less worthy – suspicion. Maybe going dancing with Gerald was innocent enough, but something about the intensity of Gerald's concern told a different story. Gerald was in love with Angelina. The more she thought about it, the surer she was. And Angie? Who knew what her feelings were. Angie loved to make people love her. It made up for something, that's what Peter had said. But it could be terrible for the people concerned. Bea's heart ached for Rafe, far away, a prisoner undergoing who knew what suffering, living on hope of home and the girl he'd left behind.

It was nearly two and Beatrice was getting ready for bed when she heard Angie's father return. She threw on a lady's dressing-gown someone had left hanging behind the door and went downstairs. Michael Wincanton was in the drawing room pouring himself some brandy. He came over to her at once.

'Beatrice! Bloody awful time I had getting home. I'm so sorry. How is she?'

'Angie has slight concussion. And the doctor's given Mrs Wincanton a sedative.'

'Good God, Oenone wasn't in it too, was she?'

'No, no.' She explained briefly.

'Such a relief that Angie's safe. I went down to Leicester Square as soon as the news broke. A bad business. Blood and jewels all over the place. Saw several chaps I knew. One was looking for his daughter. And found her, unfortunately.'

Beatrice sank down on the sofa, very weary now and close to tears. Michael came to sit next to her. He smelt of brandy and expensive cigars. She pulled the dressing-gown tighter around her.

'There were some other friends of mine in there,' she managed to get out. 'I can't bear to remember . . . Dead, both of them.'

'My dear girl,' he said. He laid his hand on her knee in what might conceivably have been a gesture of comfort. 'I'm so very sorry. Here, have some of this to steady yourself.' He handed her his brandy and she took a couple of sips. It tasted awful but after a moment she relaxed into its warmth. He began to stroke her knee very gently. She fought a temptation to lean against him and thought about Guy.

The hand moved up her thigh.

'Don't,' she said, and twisted away. 'Angie's asleep now. And I'm in the spare room, I hope that's all right. I'll hear her if she needs me.'

'Of course, of course,' he said. He was still very close to her, a powerful, disturbing presence. 'I must thank you, Beatrice. You've been a brick tonight.' His voice was low, caressing, but there was something else there, too. Sincerity. She was surprised.

Michael Wincanton had never paid her much attention as an individual before. She knew that the way he was looking at her now was the way he looked at most women, as though assessing what they might be like without their clothes. And she wasn't surprised to know that women responded. Her body was all too aware of his attractions, but she would never give in to him.

'You know, you've changed a lot, Beatrice, if I might say so. Come out of yourself. You were always such a shy little thing. I couldn't tell what my wife saw in you, frankly. That's the one good thing about this bloody war. It brings out the best in people.'

'The best and the worst,' she said, somewhat surprised by his honesty. 'You know there were men going among the bodies tonight, stealing dead people's valuables. How could anyone do such a thing?'

'Desperation, perhaps? Some of those men have nothing, not even a roof over their heads. But you're right. There are always the few who'll capitalize on someone else's misery. That was a filthy job tonight. Eighty killed, someone told me. I can't think how you all made it out alive. This chap she was with, Rafe's brother. What d'you know about him?'

'Not very much. Had you not met him before?' Perhaps he and Angie weren't so close after all.

'He's been to the house once or twice to take her out. He seems all right, but I thought it was Rafe she was keen on, poor chap. She's been very cut up about what's happened to him. I've made enquiries, of course, but there's no particular news of him.'

'Yes, poor Rafe.' She couldn't look at Michael Wincanton in case he should read what was in her heart.

Angie's father was studying her carefully now. 'What is it you're doing at present?' he asked. 'With the FANY, I mean.'

She told him about the mobile canteen and the little ambulance she drove for the First Aid Post.

'You've some French, haven't you?' he said.

'I was born in France, so yes,' she replied.

'Of course, I think I knew that.' He drank down the rest of his brandy, not taking his eyes off her. She expected him to explain his question, but he didn't. So she surprised him with one instead.

'How is Peter?'

'Peter? As far as I know he's all right. He's taken a room in a friend's house, I gather. We don't see much of him, but he turns up sometimes when he's hungry.'

She remembered what Dougie's friends had said about the 'hush hush' work, but something closed about Michael Wincanton's expression warned her off asking.

When she finally got to bed that night, she took care to lock her door again.

The next morning, Angie's condition had improved. She seemed herself again, and had some colour in her face, while complaining that her head still ached. Oenone, on the other hand, was very pale, with pouches under her eyes that powder couldn't conceal. Still, she seemed well enough to take charge of her daughter's care and personally took her breakfast up and sat with her as she ate. Beatrice too was eating when Guy telephoned.

'How are you?' he said. Then: 'Listen carefully. Can you meet me at Waterloo station? I have to be on the ten o'clock train to Portsmouth.'

She arrived at ten to, and pushed her way through the crowds onto the platform. For a while she couldn't see him through the hundreds of people and started to panic.

'Bea,' he said behind her, and she turned and found herself in his arms, and then they were kissing, stopping only to gaze at one another, as though to drink in every memory.

She'd vowed to herself to be strong for him, but she could hardly bear it. 'Take care of yourself, darling,' she begged him. 'Don't do anything reckless, will you? I need you back here safe.'

She helped him onto the train with his kit, and he kissed her one last time, and then the guard's whistle sounded and the train started to move. She watched, waving, until the train was a blob in the smoky distance, and then her tears erased the blob.

She walked back to Bloomsbury, every bombed-out building now serving to remind her that others were suffering worse than herself in this war, back to the hostel where Judy's possessions had already been packed up, her bed stripped, and where she found Mary, once nearly Deb of the Year, weeping for her lost friend.

Chapter 18

Over the next fortnight Beatrice became a frequent visitor to the house in Queen's Gate. Angie's recovery was slow, and with her mother in such a fragile, nervous state, they needed her there. There was some talk of bringing Nanny up from Devon, but that meant Hetty would have to come, too, and Mr Wincanton declared that to be a bad idea whilst the bombing continued. Poor Hetty. Beatrice privately thought the girl, who must now be twelve, received little attention from her parents, but no one else in the household seemed to make anything of it. She was in a place of relative safety with her aunt – Oenone's brother's wife – and her cousins; Nanny was with her, and all her material and emotional needs were deemed to be supplied. What more could she ask of them? No, there was nothing Beatrice could usefully do about Hetty.

After spending the first two days in bed, Angie was judged well enough to be brought down to the drawing room, where she reclined in a nest of pillows on the sofa and complained to anyone who would listen. Reading tired her and made her head ache. Friends who telephoned or called to the house apparently tired her, too, and since they all wanted to talk about what she referred to as 'The Event', going over and over the names of those killed or injured in the blast and whose funeral had been most lavish, which depressed her, she told Peggy to turn them away.

Paradoxically, she welcomed Beatrice's company. Because she had gone through the tragedy with her, Angie said that she understood. Beatrice learned not to refer to 'The Event' except obliquely, and instead they chatted about more cheerful things such as Beatrice's engagement. Angie approved of Guy, whilst appreciating that she might not have seen him looking his best on the night of 'The Event'. She got it into her head that he was right for Beatrice. 'Very steady and clearly fond of you.'

'Goodness, that does make him sound stodgy,' Beatrice said, a little crossly, and couldn't help thinking of Rafe, who Angie clearly had thought more interesting.

Rafe was another subject off-limits, she discovered. No one had heard from him or about him, and despite Michael Wincanton's enquiries, no one learned any more. What Beatrice saw quite clearly, even if Angie didn't, was that the girl was definitely transferring her affections to Rafe's brother.

Gerald came often. Her first impressions of him were borne out in subsequent meetings. Taller and broader than his younger brother, he had none of Rafe's quick energy, being rather more serious and cautious. He had a natural air of authority about him, and Beatrice wasn't in the least surprised to hear that he was in line for promotion to Major. He seemed to be working on something that necessitated him remaining in the country, for there was never any talk of him leaving. The cautiousness was related to a stubborn streak, too. She saw it first several days after 'The Event', in a conversation with him about whether Angie was well enough to go outside.

Beatrice said that she was. 'The doctor thinks a walk in the fresh air would do her good.'

'I don't know, it seems a bit soon to me. That was quite a blow to the head that she got. How do they know there's no lasting damage?' Beatrice sensed his care of Angie, but was also well aware that Angie played up to this. She might be chattering away to Beatrice one moment, asking about Guy's family and what they did, then, hearing Gerald arrive, would sink back on the pillows and assume a wan expression.

Gerald would draw up a chair, sit and gaze at her tenderly. 'How are we today?' he'd ask, stroking her hand.

'Oh, a little better, I think,' Angie would whisper. 'I managed a bit of soup at lunchtime and I'm sure it's done me good.'

Beatrice would grimace at Angie over Gerald's shoulder, but it had no effect. Angie knew how to play her advantage all too well, and Beatrice would have smiled if she hadn't been fed up.

What she was upset about, of course, was the thought of Rafe, a prisoner in a foreign land, probably holding some ethereal vision of Angie in his mind to keep him going. Gerald must know that Angie had an understanding with his brother, even though there had been nothing officially announced. Beatrice wasn't sure what Angie now felt about Rafe. Sometimes she almost hated Angie, believing her to be fickle and playing with people's feelings. Whether she was just toying with Gerald because Rafe wasn't there, she didn't know. That would be the worst thing of all. As for her own feelings, she'd found Guy now and it was much easier than she'd once thought it ever would be, to put away her own memories about Rafe. She cared desperately about what happened to him and prayed for his safety, but at eighteen, with all she'd been through, she was a vastly different person from that shy, devoted young girl who had been so convinced that Rafe belonged to her and her alone. Still, it was horrible to think that Rafe might only be keeping himself going by thoughts of Angie, when Angie was making love to his brother.

A week passed before Beatrice felt Angie was strong enough to be confronted on the matter.

'You do lead the poor man on. It isn't really fair, you know.'

Angie was playing Patience, for which she was ill-suited. She laid down a jack and said, 'Gerald? Oh don't worry, Bea. So what if I do? He likes it.'

'But you shouldn't play with people's feelings.'

Angie was silent for a moment, then said, 'But perhaps I'm not. Though frankly, I don't think it's any of your business. Damn, no more aces. This stupid game never works out.' She slammed down the remaining cards on the table.

Beatrice was so hurt by this rudeness she couldn't think of anything to say for a moment. Angie went on, 'I hope you're not going to be a dull old matron now you're due to be married. Don't go getting stout, will you?'

'Oh, for heaven's sake,' Beatrice snapped. Through the window, she saw a little family passing, an exhausted woman trundling a pram full of possessions, the baby carried by one of the two skinny children who were trailing behind. It was awful how one was becoming inured to such sights. At least they were still alive. Someone, somewhere would probably look after them.

'And now I've made you cross, Bea,' Angie said. 'I'm so sorry I'm such a wretch. Do come and sit down and I promise I'll be nice.'

'I ought to be going,' Beatrice said, which was true. She was on duty in Mile End later in the morning, and she had some errands to do on the way.

'But you'll come again soon?'

Angie looked so pleading that Beatrice gave in. 'If you want me to.'

'I do,' Angie said gravely. 'You're the only one I can really talk to.'

'There's Gerald,' Beatrice was unable to resist saying.

'Oh, you know what I mean.'

'When does the doctor think you can go back?'

'To the Wrens? Next week maybe.' She made a face, then said, 'It is very boring being an invalid. It'll be more fun back in Dover.'

It was the last week of March 1941 that Sandra Williams, Beatrice's Commanding Officer, looked up with a smile as Beatrice arrived at the First Aid Post.

'Well, you're a one,' Williams said. She waved an official-looking letter. 'Who've you been making up to, in high places? You'll get us ordinary folk into trouble.'

'What do you mean?' Beatrice hastily reviewed the last couple of days for what she might have done wrong. For one thing she'd forgotten to demobilize the canteen on her return the night before last; she'd been so tired lately, draggingly tired. Perhaps last night's crew had complained.

'It's an awful nuisance, you realize. I'll have to find someone else to do your shifts.'

'Oh, Williams, I'm so sorry about the blasted rotor arm. It won't happen again, I promise.'

'You really don't understand, do you? It's nothing you've done wrong – well, at least I don't think it is. Someone's obviously asked for you. You're being transferred.'

'Transferred where?'

Williams passed her the letter. 'An R. Newton at Senate House wants to see you at ten o'clock tomorrow morning. He'll tell you your new duties. Here, read it and wonder.'

She became a driver for the Ministry of Information, and quickly established that one of her regular passengers would be Michael Wincanton. Being only a Junior Minister he was, she knew, supposed to take whichever driver was available when he needed one, but that didn't stop him from requesting her.

'You know the way, do you?' he asked the first time. He'd told her to take him to an address in Knightsbridge.

'Of course,' she replied, 'though it would be useful if you could point out the building.'

He settled back in his seat. 'I expect you were surprised to be transferred. There was a vacancy and I merely suggested your name.'

'I just do what I'm told, sir,' she said, trying to keep her voice as neutral as possible, but he didn't seem satisfied with this answer.

'Most commendable. Still, people work best when they're happy.'

'I was very happy driving the canteen,' she told him, trying to turn off the car heater. It was a lovely spring day and the heater, probably stuck at the 'on' position all winter, was suddenly redundant. She couldn't get the lever to budge. 'It felt like helping people – you know, ordinary people.'

'Well, this is important war work. Very important.'

'I didn't say it wasn't,' she told him. The truth was that she didn't like the thought of being under his eye. She felt there was something he wanted of her.

After driving a canteen through the back streets of the East End in the middle of the night with bombs falling around her, the actual mechanics of this job were easy. Other aspects were not.

Occasionally she'd be required to report first thing to the house at Queen's Gate, to take Michael Wincanton to offices in Westminster or Whitehall, where presumably meetings were going on, though naturally he never spoke of what.

One evening, however, she received a message at the hostel, instructing her to pick him up early the next morning from an address in Cadogan Gardens. 'Stay in the car,' she was told. 'He'll look out for you and come down.' She didn't know who lived there, but when she was searching for the house, she noticed a woman's pale face watching from a top window. The woman turned as if to speak to someone and moments later the street door opened and Michael emerged. When he thanked her for coming so promptly she replied, 'I merely follow my orders,' in her coldest tone, feeling a rush of loyalty for Oenone. He appeared gently amused by this rather than cowed by her disapproval.

'It doesn't suit you to look sour, you know,' he said.

'My expression is neither intended to please or displease you,' she snapped back.

'I would hope that was the case.' His voice was hard now, and contained a warning. 'After all, you're not paid to express your opinion.' It was the only time he was ever curt to her and she felt her face flame as though he'd struck her.

Late one evening, soon after this, she was summoned to pick him up from a restaurant in South Kensington in a lull after a raid. The woman was with him. She was expensively dressed and the car filled with her musky fragrance. She spoke only once, 'Michael, you'll telephone to me about Friday?' in a light voice with an upper-class accent, when Beatrice stopped outside the flats in Cadogan Square. She was to take him on to Parliament Square. It was, she supposed, some emergency meeting.

'I'm sorry to trouble you so late, Beatrice. There were no taxis,' was his only explanation but she would not speak to him, only nodded.

Usually when she drove him, he'd sit in the back and look through papers for whatever engagement he was on his way to, and they wouldn't talk, but sometimes, especially in the evening, they'd converse quite companionably. He had that coaxing way with him; it was difficult not to respond.

'Have you heard from your fiancé lately?' he asked once, in May when the news in all the papers was the evacuation of the British from Crete. She was so surprised, she almost drove into a truck parked on the road.

'No,' she said and then twigged. 'Why, was Guy's regiment going to Crete? I thought it was Egypt.'

'No good asking me for details,' was his mysterious answer. 'It's not my area,' but this was enough to brood on. British casualties had been heavy in Crete and it was true, she hadn't heard from him for some weeks. Since Guy had first embarked, there had been two letters, with some phrases blacked out by the censor's pen, and three postcards: one a view of Cape Town with Table Mountain rising out of the mist behind, and two sepia scenes of camels in the desert and a souk. They'd been enough to assure her that he was alive and well, and she'd been able to imagine his ship sailing down the west coast of Africa and up the other side to Egypt.

She'd thought of contacting his parents to ask if they'd heard anything, but she'd never even spoken to them and didn't know how they'd respond. She assumed that they must know about her – Guy wasn't a secretive person – but she wasn't sure what he'd told them about her.

As for Michael, she couldn't discern what his 'area' was, though she tried to do so from the passengers he brought with him. He seemed to have a wide web of contacts. Once or twice he had Free French officers with him and on one occasion when he was dropped off first and she was by herself with two of them, she was amused by their light-hearted attempts to flirt with her, delighting them by answering in their own language.

Once, accompanying Michael, was a stocky Scottish soldier in his mid-forties with a moustache and bright eyes that seemed to take in everything. Beatrice's interest was piqued when they started to discuss none other than Peter Wincanton.

'He's a sharp boy, that lad of yours, very useful. I must thank you for pushing him my way.'

'Glad he's of use to you. He's been something of a square peg up to now.'

'He's certainly not that with us. Or if he is, well, our department's the right shape for him. You know the new division. Bunch of square-pegs. We need to be.'

Michael Wincanton laughed uproariously at that.

Beatrice wondered what they were talking about. She hadn't seen Peter Wincanton since he'd taken her to look at paintings at Christmas, 1939. She wondered what his job was, but knew there was no point asking. Her duty was only to drive.

At the hostel, life was much as before, but without Judy. Mary had been moved to other duties and wrote to say she was being sent abroad. A Yorkshire girl named Christina had taken Judy's bunk. Everybody talked obsessively about food. The girls fantasized about it. Successful U-boat attacks on convoys in the North Atlantic were having significant effects on supplies. Christina, being a country girl with a healthy appetite, was finding it hard to adapt to margarine, and the tiny portions of fatty roast and watery sausages Matron was able to get out of the meat ration. At least they were all sleeping better. The night air raids had largely abated now, though there had been lulls like it before, so no one dared quite relax, and the mobile canteens still did their nightly round of the shelters.

On evenings off, she went out with some of the other girls, but mindful of her engaged status she avoided the wilder parties. Even with a ring on her finger she could not escape men's attention. None made much of an impression on her. And recently, there was another reason more important than all the others. Beatrice strongly suspected she might be pregnant.

Her periods had always been irregular, and when she missed one in March she thought nothing of it. A slight spotting of blood in April reassured her, though the tiredness, and the tingling in her breasts was disturbing. Guy had assured her that he'd dealt with that side of things, that there was nothing to worry about, and she continued to believe this. June came and she carried on as normal, though the waistband of her skirt began to dig in and her jacket felt tight.

One evening, when she was changing, Christina was lounging on her bunk, turning the pages of a magazine and watching her in a way that was a tad too curious.

'Is there something you're not telling, love?' the girl said, not unkindly. 'You look like my married sister does when she's starting a bairn.'

The Army doctor, perhaps unused to women patients, was neither gentle nor a gentleman. He probed her most private places with unnecessary roughness, so she felt invaded, and though she'd turned the stone of her engagement ring inwards to make him believe she was married, he saw through the ruse easily and spoke to her without meeting her eye. The baby was probably due in November, he said as he washed his hands. She looked healthy enough to him, but should come again in a few weeks' time. Meanwhile, she might like to be thinking how on earth she'd support a child in wartime unless her fiancé was able to make an honest woman of her. Good morning – next, please!

The receptionist was kinder and told her how she should present her medical certificate to claim a green ration book in addition to her ordinary one and explained how she could book into a state maternity home. Beatrice thanked her, thrust the certificate into her bag, and pushed her way out of the waiting room into the sunshine. Her thoughts were so confused, she didn't know what to do or where to go, and a short while later, she found herself in a little park edged with flowerbeds that someone was still managing to tend amidst the general chaos. She sat down on a rickety bench, stared at a statue of a cherub holding a birdbath, and tried to calm her rising panic.

Another person was growing inside her. This baby was part of Guy, and, whatever happened, she knew she cared about it passionately. She would write to Guy at once and tell him, and he'd make it all right. There would be explanations to the authorities and to both their parents. Her imagination failed her there, as to what all the parents would say. Anyway, he'd come back as soon as he could and they'd be married and life would blossom. Differently to how she'd imagined – somehow the mental pictures of the country cottage and the children had been set in some golden future after the war, not during it – but she'd raise the child as best she could. She placed one hand on her abdomen, in the place where she imagined the baby was growing, and said a little prayer, a prayer that was half a promise.

She wrote to Guy that very evening. As she slipped the envelope into the postbox, addressed to that official catch-all address in Whitehall, she wondered again where he could possibly be. Michael Wincanton had hinted Crete, but the British had been heavily defeated there and so she hoped he was wrong. Or maybe he had been, but he'd escaped back to Egypt. If so, she wondered how long the letter would take to reach him there.

The next thing was the most difficult – to find somewhere of her own to live. She couldn't imagine how she'd pay for it once the baby came, but she'd think about that later. The hostel, full of prying eyes, simply wouldn't do any more.

'Angie? It's Beatrice.' She had telephoned Angelina at her Wrennerie in Dover, intending to suggest that they meet. It seemed important to tell Angelina face to face about the baby. She wanted her support. But Beatrice and her secret were swept away by the tide of Angelina's news.

'Bea, darling, I'm so glad you've telephoned. I'm so excited I have to tell you straight away. I'm getting married.'

'Married? Who to?' Part of her still believed that Angie was faithful to Rafe.

'Oh, Bea, don't be a spoilsport, you know who. It's Gerald. He's been pestering me for weeks for an answer.'

'Oh.'

'I know what you're going to say – that it wouldn't be tactful, with Rafe being away – but we don't know when he's coming back. It might be years.'

'Angie, that's a horrible thought.' But Rafe would be hurt, surely. She wondered if Gerald felt guilty about Rafe.

'Well, there it is. And I want you to be my bridesmaid,' she continued. 'Mummy is thrilled, of course, though the wedding's to be in only three weeks. That's when Gerald can get leave.'

Beatrice couldn't imagine Oenone Wincanton being thrilled about anything. When she had last seen Angelina's mother, in April, she had still been very melancholy over Ed and the fact that the rest of her children were gone in one way or another. However, she imagined Oenone would be pleased. Gerald, if not of high birth, was a sound catch and clearly adored Angie. What's more, he had got his promotion to Major and if he wasn't the son of an earl, who really minded these days.

'I'd be delighted to be your bridesmaid,' she told Angie. She wondered how she'd find a dress that would fit her. 'But I don't know whether you'll want me. I've got some news of my own, you see.'

Chapter 19

St Florian, 2011

'Angie and Gerald were married one lovely July day in 1941 in the Church of St Margaret, Westminster,' Beatrice concluded. It was Wednesday afternoon, and she was tired from talking. Pouring the tea Lucy had just made, she added, 'Very exclusive. You need special connections to be married there. I think with Angie it was her godmother, Lady Hamilton. Or perhaps Angie's father had pulled strings. I forget which, but I was the bridesmaid. Angie didn't mind about the baby.'

She sipped her tea.

Lucy, who had been sitting quietly for a while, said carefully, 'Why would she have minded? I'm sorry, but I'm finding some of all this quite hard. You don't always make Granny sound a very nice person.'

'She wasn't sometimes, Lucy. But nor was I. I look back on myself then and think how naive I was. Everything was black and white to me, and that must have been very annoying to someone like Angie. I loved Rafe and saw him as mine in a curious kind of way. But I realized in time that Rafe was his own person; he owed me nothing, he was free to fall in love with whom he liked. And Angie clearly found him very charming – which he was; the most dear and charming man you could ask for.'

'Do you think she was in love with him when she said she'd marry him?'

Beatrice thought for a moment. 'I think she might have been in her own way, but it wasn't a lasting thing, rather something delightful and of the moment. And then she met Gerald and he really was the man for her. The bomb blast – it changed her, made her grow up a little, and Gerald was part of her doing that. Being very steady and dependable, he enabled her to settle down.'

'Do you think he made up for her father being so distant?'

'I do, yes.'

'I feel quite sorry for her. And for you, of course. You were both so young.'

'We were, and having to deal with the most horrific things. However, when it came to relationships we were so awfully innocent.' Beatrice's expression hardened. 'But feel sorry for Angie? I find that very difficult.'

The old lady levered herself out of her chair and went to look out of the window. 'It might rain later,' she murmured, 'and Mrs P.'s left the towels on the line. I don't suppose you'd mind . . . ? It's the reaching up I can't do.'

'Of course I wouldn't mind,' Lucy said, jumping up. 'I'll get them in and then leave you for today. I'm sure I've tired you enough.'

'I've enjoyed talking to you, dear, but I do admit to feeling a little weary,' Beatrice agreed, sitting down once more. 'However, you must promise me you'll come tomorrow.'

After Lucy had gone, Beatrice sat for a while, remembering that wedding so long ago. It had indeed been a beautiful day. Angelina had worn a rather gorgeous ivory-lace dress of her mother's, and had borrowed an apricot-coloured tea-gown for Beatrice, which Beatrice had had to let out. Gerald, in uniform, looked very proud and adoring. At the reception, held in a hotel nearby, Beatrice met Rafe and Gerald's mother, Amanda Armstrong, for the first time and thought her cool and elegant, though perfectly gracious. The poise cracked slightly when Beatrice asked if there was any news of Rafe. There wasn't, and she wished she hadn't mentioned him as Rafe's stiff, soldierly stepfather marched over and steered his wife away. For a while Beatrice stood alone, fighting back tears. Later, she caught Angie's little bouquet when it was thrown, and stared down at it.

Gerald and Angie had two days' honeymoon and after that, Gerald had to return to his regiment. Angie, being married, stood down from the Wrens, and they rented a cottage in the Kent countryside, near London for her and close enough for him to visit once a fortnight or so, which was as much as he could get away.

As for Beatrice, her life continued as usual, though something odd and disturbing did happen.

Since the Fall of France, her mother, Delphine, had not been able to communicate with her family in Normandy. In August she suddenly received a message on a small strip of paper from one of her nieces in Etretat, Thérèse. It had been somehow secreted to England and posted anonymously from London. It bore the awful news that Pappi had been killed by German soldiers, apparently over a misunderstanding.

Delphine sent the message on to Beatrice with a letter of her own, an outpouring of grief.

Beatrice had to drive one of the French officers that week, and she resolved to share the message with him, to ask him whether it could be true. He was an older man with a sad face, as though he felt the full weight of his nation's humiliation. There was something about the way he held his hands – broad, countryman's hands – one clamped over the other on his cane like a shepherd's over his crook, that made her trust him.

They'd talked in his native language as she drove. He was from the Ardennes, she discovered; his family's village had been one of the first to be overtaken by the German forces as they pushed their way into France and he'd only just managed to escape.

When they stopped in traffic, she fumbled in her pocket for the tiny strip of paper, and passed it to him, saying, 'Excuse me, but may I ask what you think of this letter.' She told him how she'd got it.

The officer found his spectacles and frowned as he worked out the tiny writing. 'You say this is from your cousin?' he asked.

'Yes,' Beatrice replied.

'Well, I am most sorry about the news it contains. Your grandfather was killed.'

'For stockpiling food, concealing it from the authorities. But my cousin says it was a misunderstanding.'

The officer's bloodhound eyes met hers in the driving mirror. He looked sadder than ever as he passed back the letter. 'I am indeed sorry, *mademoiselle*,' he said. 'But this kind of story is why I am here. This struggle belongs to us all. There is no mercy in Nazi justice, no room for doubt. This is why those who resist are in such danger.'

'But would they have no pity? He was a very old man. Old and ill.'

The officer leaned back, uttering an oath. 'This is why we resist,' he said fiercely. 'For all the grandfathers. Please convey my condolences to your mother. Tell her to thank God she has you bravely doing your part here.'

'A little, pathetic part,' she said angrily.

'Add up all the little parts . . .' he made a broad gesture with his hands '. . . and we will win this war. Always remember that. Do your best and believe.'

Remember . . . Beatrice had remembered. She'd kept that little letter and had it still, at the age of eighty-eight. For years, memories were all that she'd had, and some of those she wished she could forget.

Her gaze fell on the small pile of laundry that Lucy had rescued from the line and folded. She was a lovely girl, Lucy; Beatrice was becoming very fond of her. She was surprised at her shrewdness, too. She'd thought that in telling Lucy her story it was she, Beatrice, who was enlightening Lucy. Instead, some of the things Lucy said made Beatrice think. That business about looking at events from Angie's point of view. She'd never really thought about it before, didn't want to. She'd always thought her own version the only one.

She stood, scooped up the pile of washing and slowly made her way with it upstairs.

Lucy walked down the steps to the harbour, where she sat in the window of a quiet café and ordered hot chocolate. She sprinkled some bits of marshmallow on top and watched them settle into the foam. She was thinking about everything that Beatrice had just told her, and realizing that she hadn't properly considered before what her grandparents' generation had endured in the war. She thought of Beatrice being alone, frightened and pregnant. A feeling of disquiet was stirring in her about the way the story was unfolding.

She looked up to see Anthony striding past, his holdall hefted on his shoulder. Forgetting her thoughts, she knocked eagerly on the glass. When he saw her, he ducked through the low doorway of the café.

'Hello. You again!' he said.

'Were you coming or going?' Lucy said, pushing away her cup.

'Going. I thought I could get out on the water for a couple of hours. Like to join me?'

The sea was choppier than last time, and there was a biting wind out on the bay. But it made her feel exhilarated, alive. This time she was better at swinging the sail round at his instruction; she thought they worked well as a team. They went right out into the open sea where, looking back, she could see quite a length of the coastline.

'There, that's Carlyon!' she cried, pointing to the shell of the manor house on the crest of the hill, and he turned the tiller so they could keep it in view.

Even now, it had a kind of dignity, like the ruins of a church or rather, with its high chimneys, a small palace. Now she saw it from this angle, lonely, abandoned, its charred messiness softened by misty distance, she felt a strong connection to it. And sorrow that it was a piece of her history that had been taken from her before she even knew about it.

'How did it happen?' Anthony called. 'The fire, I mean.'

'I don't know.'

When they returned to the harbour, it was she, this time, who stepped up onto the small jetty with the mooring rope. She helped him tidy up, though her hands and face were frozen. The warmth had gone from the day, but a golden light played on the water.

'Come back to my place for some tea, if you like,' he said when they'd finished.

*　　*　　*

The house was one of a terrace of white-painted houses huddled halfway up the hill, not far below Beatrice's, over-looking the bay. The glass of the porch was rimed with salt, its shelves arrayed with leggy spider plants and dusty geraniums.

Inside was tiny, a hallway with two small rooms on one side, a kitchen at the back, stairs up to two bedrooms and a little bathroom. Coming out of the bathroom Lucy glanced through the open door of the back bedroom. Anthony's duvet was straight and smoothed, his nightclothes neatly folded on the pillow. She smiled, remembering how, in contrast, her bed at home always looked like a mare's nest.

Downstairs, he'd already laid his sailing kit over plastic chairs to dry under the small back verandah. He handed her a huge mug of toffee-coloured tea and she sipped it quickly, though it scalded her, glad to feel the heat course through her limbs.

When they went to sit in the living room he seemed too large for the space and the tiny old armchairs. Perhaps he was used to cramped quarters. She stole a look around. A laptop, several books and DVDs, a couple of magazines were stacked on the coffee-table, though there was plenty of space on the bookshelves. The place gave the impression that he was bivou-acking, that at a moment's notice he might have to sweep everything into one of his big holdalls and rush away. The way he sat, too – on the edge of the chair, knees apart, lean-ing forward – suggested restlessness, but she liked the steady manner in which he studied her.

'Whose place is this?' she asked.

'It belongs to the parents of a friend,' he told her. He explained that they were kindly letting him stay there rent free. 'And I can use the boat, too.'

'Where's home for you?' was her next question. Did she imagine the shadow that crossed his face?

'Near Hereford, I suppose. Do you know that part of the world?'
She shook her head.

'The countryside's lush green hills, idyllic, really. My mum's parents were farmers and I spent a lot of time with them when I was a kid. Dad retired from the Army a few years back and they bought a place nearby.'

'Nowhere to call your own then?'

'No. I don't know where I'd go, though I suppose I'll have to decide sometime. How about you?'

'Oh, I bought a flat in North London a few years ago. The edge of Camden. I fell in love with round there, you know, the canal, the boats, the markets.'

He smiled, briefly, then the smile seemed to cut off and a faraway look came into his eyes. Puzzled, she stood, putting her empty mug down on the table, feeling she ought to go. But he looked up at her and suddenly he seemed himself again, warm and friendly.

'Are you doing anything later?' he said. 'I haven't got much in the fridge or I'd offer to cook, but maybe we could have something out. If you feel we've had enough of the Mermaid, there's a pub near the headland that does food – posh fish and chips, steak and kidney pies. What d'you say?'

'It sounds tempting,' she said. She longed to, but wondered whether she should. Their lives were so different. There was no reason they'd meet again. Yet she trusted him . . . felt as though she'd always known him. And she sensed that he accepted her for what she was, without even knowing her. How did that happen between people? You recognized something in each other. What if she were mistaken?

He was waiting for her answer and she knew what she wanted to say. 'Yes. I'd like that.'

*　　*　　*

The pub turned out to be very olde worlde, with brass tele-
scopes and fishing nets decorating the walls. It was still quiet,
being early, and Anthony was sitting at the bar talking to the
barman and didn't see her arrive. He wore a soft jacket, cream
shirt and dark jeans and she realized again how attractive he
was, the cropped hair suiting his handsome tanned features.
He saw her and greeted her with a smile that lit his eyes.

'Hello,' he said. 'What'll you have to drink?' He pulled out
a stool for her.

Whilst the landlord fetched her lager, Anthony passed her a
menu. They both decided on the same thing – fish and chips.
Lucy, despite his insistence on paying, pushed a ten-pound
note into his breast pocket. They took their drinks and sat down
at right angles to one another at a small table in the window
where they could both view the sea. She'd brought her camera
with her, and placed it on the floor under the table.

'I thought I might take some pictures later,' she explained,
'when it starts to get dark.' The sun was low and the rain
Beatrice had anticipated had never materialized. Rags of black
cloud were dotted about the sky, but they didn't look as if they'd
amount to anything. She might get some dramatic images.

'Tell me more about your work,' he said. 'What kind of thing
do you usually like to photograph?'

In response she reached for her camera and showed him
some of the pictures she'd taken over the previous few days.

'They're good,' he said.

'I take cityscapes, too,' she said, and told him about her exhibition about Little Venice. 'And anything to do with water. I like
the life of it. What it does with light.'

'I wish I had your skill,' Anthony said. 'Some of the places
I've seen in Afghanistan, I'd love to photograph them. And
the people; their faces stay in the mind. How they put up with

everything, Christ knows.' He passed her camera back to her. 'Do you have a website? I don't have internet access here, but when I get back I'd love to see what else you've done.'

'It's on the card I gave you.'

He found it in his wallet. 'Don't worry, I'll keep it safe,' he said, smiling at her.

'How long will you be here?' Lucy asked. 'Did you say you had to be back somewhere on Monday?'

'That's right. What about you?'

'Monday, too.'

'Will you have found out all you need to? From your old lady?'

'I don't know. Possibly. I'm not sure at the moment where her story is going, what it all means.'

'It's to do with your family, right?'

'Yes. To do with my father, I think.'

Just then, a young waitress with tattoos up her arms and a diamanté stud under her lower lip arrived with two huge oval plates, each heaped with chips on top of which reclined an enormous strip of battered fish.

'Wow,' Lucy breathed, and moved her camera back onto the floor. She and Anthony fell upon the food like starved wolves and for a minute or two they were silent.

After a while she paused and said, 'When you go back to work on Monday, will you go abroad again? To Afghanistan, I mean?'

He nodded. 'Looks like it. I've had three months here. They think it's enough.'

'But you don't?'

'I don't know.'

'Do you want to go back at all?' She watched him chew his mouthful and swallow before he answered.

'I'm dreading it,' he said.

She put down her knife and fork. 'Did something particular happen out there? I mean . . .' It was difficult to imagine what it was like.

She felt put in her place when he said, 'Lots of things,' rather abruptly. 'And one in particular.'

She picked up a chip and dipped it in tomato sauce whilst she considered what to say. 'You haven't been here in Saint Florian all the three months, have you?' It seemed suddenly terrible to her that she'd only just met him, right in the final week of his leave.

'No,' he said very quietly. He took a draught of his beer. 'Just a couple of weeks.'

A silence fell and they ate for a while, then they both spoke at once.

'I wanted—' he said, just as she asked, 'Why—' then added, 'Go on.'

'I needed,' he said, 'to be by myself, to try and sort myself out. I seriously love this place. It's got its memories, but they're good ones.' He stared out through the salt-sprayed window, across the twilit sea. Far out on the horizon, a fork of lightning played. 'I came here once or twice with Gray.'

'He's your friend? The one whose family owns the house you're staying in?'

He nodded slowly. She watched, anxiously, seeing that his eyes were full of pain.

He cleared his throat. 'He . . . Gray was killed.'

Lucy's breath was snagged by the little catch in his voice. 'Oh, I'm sorry,' she whispered, but her words seemed too inadequate a response to the look of distress on his face. She waited, one hand turned palm up in a hesitant gesture of openness, feeling utterly out of her depth, and yet sensing that he needed her there.

'Everything all right for you guys?' The waitress appeared between them suddenly, snatched up Lucy's empty glass. 'This one dead? Shall I get you another?'

'Thanks, yes, same again for both of us,' Lucy said quickly. 'Anthony, go on, I'm listening.'

The place was filling up now and she found she had to lean forward to hear what Anthony was saying. 'I met Gray the first day at officer school, ten years ago.' He smiled at a memory. 'It was in the queue for lunch after the first briefing. He came out with this blindingly awful joke. Gray often made me laugh. He was one of those guys who see the lighter side of everything. But there was more to him than that. He was the sort you'd want on your side when you're in desperate danger, d'you know what I mean?'

Lucy, who had never had that experience, said carefully, 'I can try and imagine.'

'We stayed best mates throughout, even though I got up the promotion ladder ahead of him. Not everyone knew what to make of his sense of humour.'

There was another pause as the drinks arrived. They'd finished their meal so the waitress cleared their plates.

When she'd finally left them in peace, Anthony leant in nearer, his arms folded on the table. She did not move away. 'Maybe you don't realize,' he said, studying her, 'how close soldiers have to live with one another. Sharing tiny spaces – tanks, trenches. We have to look out for one another whilst respecting privacy. I have had to learn to read all the different aspects of my men's characters. They know me, too: what spooks me, what pisses me off. We don't necessarily all like each other, but we have to get on, to rely on each other. Like a family, except more so; we need to trust each other in order to survive. You can't have a row and stomp out. Are you with me?'

She nodded, though she could think of no situation she'd ever been in where she'd had to rely on someone like that.

'So as an officer, you feel incredibly responsible.' He shook his head and closed his eyes. When he opened them again he said, 'Lucy, what happened, I can't talk about it easily, OK? In fact, I didn't mean to start on it at all. Sorry, I bring you out on a date and I weep all over the carpet and ruin your evening.'

'Is this a date?' she said. 'Not that I mind exactly, but I'd like to know.'

He laughed, moved closer again and crinkled his eyes at her. 'It could be if you want. Or we could just be having a meal together.'

They looked into one another's eyes and she had the strange and panicky sensation that she was falling. 'I'll think about it,' she said.

She watched him take out a packet of tobacco and roll a cigarette, though he didn't light it. Beatrice had described how suddenly and completely one could fall in love, but she still didn't quite believe it. What did she think she was doing with this man? A day or two more would pass and then they'd never see each other again. Was she setting herself up to get hurt or to hurt him? Tonight she'd seen more of the grief and damage he was grappling with; it made her wonder whether she lived too superficially, photographing the way that light glanced off the water, never looking deeper to see what swirled in the currents beneath.

She emerged from the reverie to hear him say, 'Would you like anything else to eat? No? Coffee?'

'No, I'm fine, thanks. A walk by the sea might be nice.'

'Good idea. Let's go.'

There was still light in the sky when they got outside. To the right a footpath like a pale snake led away across the headland.

They followed it a short way out to a viewpoint where they could watch the town fall into darkness, soft lights coming on, reflecting on the water, the scent of Anthony's cigarette smoke not quite masking the salty smell of the sea. There they stood for a while, separate, motionless, lost in their own thoughts, the waves booming and crashing below.

He laughed suddenly and she said, 'What?' Smiling.

'I was just remembering our first sailing trip together,' he said, and soon they were both laughing. Then he took her hand and drew her to him.

'Have you thought about my question yet?' he asked, his lips at her ear.

She knew immediately what he meant.

'It kind of might be a date,' she replied, enjoying teasing him. She closed her eyes as he kissed her and again she felt as though she was falling. But this time she knew that he was holding her safe.

'Tomorrow's Thursday,' he said, when they came up for air. 'I have to drive back to London on Sunday. And then . . .'

'Don't talk about it,' she said. 'Let's enjoy the time we have.'

'I'm up for that,' he said quietly. And he kissed her again.

Chapter 20

London, July 1941

Three weeks after Angelina's wedding, Beatrice found what she'd been looking for. She overheard a fellow FANY driver complaining that her lodger was leaving.

'I need somewhere,' Beatrice told her. The other woman, Dinah, who had a way of looking down her nose that made Beatrice feel uncomfortable, studied her with surprise as though she hadn't really noticed her before, then seemed to come to a conclusion.

'Good show. It's not much of a room, I'm afraid, but the last girl didn't seem to mind. You can come and see the flat for yourself.'

The bedroom was indeed 'not much', being a long narrow room right next to the bathroom. This meant that the noises of the whole house's plumbing system often woke her early, but Beatrice came to find the clanking of pipes and rushing of water comforting, and she liked the view from the window onto other people's back gardens; a busy mosaic of vegetable beds and air-raid shelters criss-crossed with fencing. The flat took up half the first floor of a converted Victorian house in Primrose Hill, and looked out towards Regent's Park. On a still night, strange bird cries and the roars of big cats could be heard, which gave Beatrice the delicious fancy of being somewhere more exotic than exhausted old London. The drawing room and kitchen were light and airy, even in the summer heat, and a flat roof at the back, accessible by the nimble from the kitchen window, was, Dinah assured her, just the place for sunbathing, though Beatrice didn't think she would be crawling out there any time soon. Next door, a fox terrier, who made Bea think of dear old Jinx, barked rhythmically at the sky for an hour each evening after the air-raid warning, doing its bit to ward off the bombers.

One of the best things about the flat was that Dinah was only there half the time. Another FANY driver was quick to inform Beatrice that Dinah was having an affair with a senior officer, who lived in Knightsbridge while his wife, in blissful ignorance probably, kept the home fires burning in Suffolk. Beatrice found the burden of this knowledge uncomfortable and never discussed it with Dinah. At the same time, she was aware that her own predicament meant she was hardly in a position to judge others. She liked Dinah all right. Five or six years older than Bea, tall and blonde, she was straightforward and, despite her cool manner, at heart unsnobbish and often kind. Although the two women had little in common, it worked for them to share digs together because each was fairly considerate of the other whilst not taking an unhealthy interest in what was plainly private business. That said, Beatrice took the precaution of telling Dinah about the baby immediately. After all, she would notice very quickly anyway. All Dinah said in her understated way, was, 'Poor you. Well, at least you get better rations.'

One morning, when she'd been in her new home for five or six weeks, Beatrice was shocked to catch sight of herself in the long hall mirror as she was getting ready to go out. Five months pregnant and it was as though her belly had grown overnight. She'd already had to let out the waistband of her skirt, but now the hem rode up in front and the buttons of her jacket looked fit to burst. In short, her condition was starting to become obvious. Arrangements of some sort would have to be made.

Still she hesitated to say anything to her Commanding Officer, fearing her reaction. In the end it was Sandra Williams herself who called Beatrice into the tiny windowless back room that she called her office, and asked if she was all right.

'Yes,' she said automatically. 'Why?'

Williams bit her lip and frowned. She was a plain but hearty woman, whose forehead shouldn't be so furrowed in her early thirties. The girls were responsive to her down-to-earth manner and caring disposition. Beatrice had long ago gauged that coming to work was a welcome relief from living with an ailing widowed mother in Surrey.

'Well, you don't look your usual self.' Sandra waited and, struck to the heart by her kind look, Beatrice promptly burst into tears.

When she recovered sufficiently to speak, she explained everything. 'I don't know what to do,' she finished up. 'I haven't heard from my fiancé at all. He'd have written if he'd got my letters, I'm sure he would.'

'What about your parents, can they help?'

'I haven't told them about the baby yet. They still haven't even met Guy. I daren't break it to them, they'd be so upset.'

'I expect they'd help you, though. You ought to try.'

After that, things moved quickly. Williams, being her Commanding Officer and hence in charge of her welfare, promised to get Beatrice put onto lighter duties – office work, most probably. 'After all, you won't be able to fit behind a driving wheel soon!'

Beatrice wrote to her mother and was touched by the response she received a few days later.

I cannot hide the fact that your news has come as a terrible shock to us, particularly your poor father, though we are doing our best to remember that situations are different in war-time and that in normal circumstances you would be happily married to your Guy Hurlingham. I pray with all my heart for his safe return. In the meantime we will help you all we can in this difficulty, though I think that it will be very hard for your father to have a young baby in the house. These days he does require absolute quiet *for his writing and is* easily *upset. We will, of course, inform our neighbours that you are married. I think it would be the best thing as there are some who have small minds. We have very little spare money, but I enclose a cheque from your father to help you buy a few things for the baby. Please write and tell us when you plan to come.*

She was moved by her mother's kindness, but also by her honesty. It would be a terrible pressure on her parents if she went home with a baby, even one born safely in wedlock. She remembered the episode with the evacuee and how it had poisoned the atmosphere of the household for weeks. And yet how could she do anything except go home, given that she had no money? She pinched open the cheque her mother had sent and her eyes widened. From what she knew about her parents' finances it was a generous amount. She dreaded to think what they would have to do without. Still, it was only a tiny proportion of what she had calculated she would require in the months she wasn't earning.

Her next decision was one she'd put off making for a long time: to write to Guy's parents. In the end, she decided it would be most tactful to write two letters, the first asking if they'd had any information about his whereabouts.

The reply to this, from his mother, was friendly enough, if cautious. Guy had mentioned Beatrice to them, but Mrs Hurlingham didn't seem to know that they'd become engaged. Beatrice tried to see it from their point of view. After all, they'd never met her and who knows what kind of person might have taken up with their son and what stories Beatrice might be spinning? However, they'd heard nothing from Guy or about him for as long as she had and, like her, were desperately anxious. They hoped that she was well and looked forward to meeting her one day with Guy when he was safely home.

Beatrice caught his mother's uncertainty, and she wrestled with herself long and hard before writing the letter she knew she had to write, that Guy would want her to write. It was knowing that he'd be upset if she didn't ask them that in the end made her overcome her scruples.

I find that I'm having his baby. It's due in November. I felt you ought to know.

There, she'd written the words. She sealed the envelope and stamped it, but didn't have the courage to send it. She wasn't quite desperate yet. She'd write to Guy one more time, in case her other letters had gone astray.

A few days after this, she was loitering in the sunshine outside an office in Whitehall, waiting to see if Michael Wincanton or anyone else needed driving, when one of his aides emerged. He was in the company of a man she'd seen once before, the middle-aged Colonel of compact build to whom Michael had spoken about Peter. The Colonel's voice, when he greeted her, had that lovely Scottish burr, and she liked the straightforward way he looked at her.

'I want you to get me to Baker Street by twelve,' he said, as she opened the door for him to get in.

When they turned off the Marylebone Road into Baker Street he directed her to an unmarked building of no obvious significance, where he got out, with a nod of thanks.

She was about to get back into the car when a man's voice said, 'Beatrice!' and she turned in surprise to see a dark thin man in khaki smiling at her. It was Peter Wincanton.

She hadn't set eyes on him for a year and a half, for he hadn't been able to make Angie's wedding, and she was struck immediately by the change in him. He looked much older, though he must still be only twenty-one. It was the uniform, partly, but something else too. His bearing was more confident, and although he still wore his habitual expression of watchfulness, his eyes met hers as he shook hands, instead of sliding away.

'What are you doing up this way?' she asked.

'Oh, a meeting,' he replied vaguely, and she knew not to ask any more. 'What about you? Still driving my father about? I hardly see the old man these days. Or any of my family, in fact.' His expression hardened. 'How's my sister, do you know? I was sorry I couldn't attend her nuptials, but I simply couldn't get away.'

'I think Angie's enjoying life, though not seeing Gerald much, of course.'

'Still, she has better luck than some. I say, if you're going back into Town is there any chance of a lift? I've an hour or two to fill and there's a concert at the National Gallery. Do you ever get to them?'

'No, but I've heard they're wonderful. Can one just turn up?'

She was free herself, as it happened, so she dropped the car off as pre-arranged with another driver and went with him. She knew little about music, but the great waves of Beethoven

piano chords vibrated through her thrillingly. Beside her, Peter
sat rapt and still. She followed his example, closing her eyes,
allowing her spirit to soar.

Afterwards he took her to a Lyons Corner House café, where
he bought them tea and lumpen scones and told her he'd been
bombed out of his friend's place and was living in officer's
quarters in North London and hating it.

'I keep to myself most of the time. I'm on the look-out for
somewhere. Met a chap in Albany who might have a room
coming up. How about you?'

She explained about Dinah's flat and then, warily, about
her engagement to Guy, looking to see how he'd react. She'd
never been sure what Peter thought about her. There was a
link between them, some recognition of each other's loneliness,
perhaps, but she couldn't be sure of the nature of it, indeed
found it difficult to relax in his company. He could be called
attractive, no doubt about it, with that glossy, near-black hair,
the shadow of beard beneath the pale skin. In fact, she realized
with a shock, he reminded her of Guy – but there was something about the air of unhappiness and anxiety he wore that
warned her away.

'I heard there was someone,' was his reply. She thought
there was a new tautness about his mouth but he said,
'Congratulations,' easily enough, and asked her about Guy, his
regiment, the part of the country he came from, and nodded at
her answers.

'Bit of a bitch, my sister Angie,' he said, and she stiffened.
'Your poor friend Ashton. I warned you what she was like. No
news of him, I don't suppose?'

'No,' she said, angry now. All this time, she had persuaded
herself that no one but Angie had known about her hopes of
Rafe, had thought she'd buried them deep and stifled them,

and here was Peter, stripping away the winding sheet to reveal her secret with a ghastly casualness. She looked away. 'No one's heard anything of him for over a year now. Even if he's still alive.'

'I'm sorry. I didn't mean to upset you,' Peter said quietly. 'But this chap Guy – I hope he's everything you want.' He eyed her thoughtfully, but if he recognized her condition, he didn't say anything about it.

'Thank you,' she said. 'He is.' Peter had always had that knack of making her feel awkward, unhappy, as though he saw right through her. She didn't want to know what he saw. She pulled on her gloves and forced herself to put out her hand to shake his. After all, she thought he meant to be kind. 'Thank you,' she said. 'The concert was most enjoyable.'

'Perhaps you'll come again sometime,' he said, a bit desperately, seeing he'd hurt her, and she left him turning an unlit cigarette in his fingers, all the misery of the world in his face.

Outside in Trafalgar Square, clouds raced across the sky and a cold wind blew. An old man with a crooked back swept the pavement with slow, awkward movements, the wind whipping up eddies of dust, so her eyes began to smart. No one showed any surprise these days at a woman weeping in the street.

'Cheer up, love,' said a skinny old woman in a ragged black dress and headscarf, who was sitting on the steps feeding the pigeons. 'There's them with troubles worse than ours.'

A few days after this, the very end of July, she woke feeling sluggish, but forced herself to get up. She felt better after she'd breakfasted on dry toast and went to work as usual. This was to be her last week of driving and she could hardly wait to be shot of it. Lately, she hadn't seen Michael much anyway, and when she told him she'd been seconded for desk work and would welcome the change, he looked surprised, but thanked her warmly enough and told her to be sure to call in to see them whenever she could. Oenone would love to see her, he said. Beatrice honestly didn't think he guessed a thing about her condition. Someone would tell him soon enough, she imagined. He was a man who got to know things.

When she arrived home that evening, tired and with an aching back, there was a packet waiting in the hallway, addressed to her in unfamiliar handwriting. She opened it in the kitchen and was horrified to see half a dozen envelopes slide out onto the counter. They were all letters she'd addressed to Guy, returned unopened. She stood looking at them, the truth gradually changing her. Even before she picked up the folded sheet of Army-issue writing paper she knew that Guy was dead.

He'd been lost in the withdrawal from Crete ten weeks before, but for some reason only recently had this fact been established. This Lieutenant-Colonel Burton, who wrote, had been alerted to the fact that Guy had a fiancée and now returned all the letters that had never reached him. She turned them over and saw that they were all there, all unopened, her return address written neatly on each one. So Guy had never learned that he would have a child, never had the joy of that knowledge, and, very pertinently, had never had the chance to put in place any arrangements for support of mother and child. Worst of all, she had to face the terrible fact that Guy was never coming home.

For several days she was struck down by grief, hardly able to leave the flat. It was Dinah who helped her, making sure that she ate, telling her she must go on because of the baby.

* * *

As soon as she felt able, she wrote to her parents with the awful news. There would be no marriage. The baby would have no legitimate father. She tore up the letter she'd originally written to Guy's mother and wrote a new one to say that she'd heard the news and how devastated she was. Still, she lacked the courage to mention the baby. After weeks went by without there being a reply, she gave it up as a bad job. She'd write again after the birth, offer to bring the baby to see them if they wanted. She wasn't sure what she feared: cold rejection by them, shock, the assumption that she was trying to get money out of them. Perhaps she wasn't being fair. If Mrs Hurlingham had been warmer, more welcoming, it might have been different. Or if she herself had been less proud . . .

In August, nearly six months pregnant, Beatrice had been found a place at the FANY HQ in Knightsbridge, answering the telephone and dealing with general administration. She felt much relieved. One Tuesday soon after she'd started, she left work early to shop for food, and was looking forward to a quiet evening in. She felt so tired these days, tired and uncomfortable and worn down by grief.

'Still no butter,' she said, arriving home and dumping her shopping bag on the table.

'I'll make tea. You look done in.' Dinah, in housecoat and slippers, her face glistening with homemade face cream, was scraping baked beans from a saucepan onto a plate arranged with four plain triangles of greyish bread. Her look of disgust at her supper was comical. 'No cheese either, I don't suppose. What *did* they have?'

'A few carrots and potatoes, none of them up to much.' Beatrice started pulling items out of the bag with a magician's flourish. 'The last two eggs in the shop, a tin of herring roe, milk powder, of course, and, *voilà*, some brawn! That's your lot until Thursday, madam.'

'You're welcome to the brawn.' Dinah poured boiling water onto dried-out old tea leaves in the pot, laid out two cups and saucers and sat down before her meagre supper. 'I'm out for dinner tomorrow anyway. I say, do you mind if I get on and eat or I'll be late for the theatre? I'll bag my egg, though, if there's time.'

'I'll cook them when I've got my breath back.'

'Mmm,' Dinah said, swallowing a mouthful. 'Oh, by the way – someone was waiting for you outside when I got home. A young chap, fair hair, rather a dish. I told him you were out and he said he'd call again.'

'Oh? Who was it?' Beatrice said, an irrational part of her hoping it might be Guy.

Dinah shrugged. 'He wouldn't give his name. Said he wanted it to be a surprise.'

Later, Dinah shouted goodbye, slamming the door as was her habit, leaving behind a cloud of Lily-of-the-Valley. Beatrice washed some clothes and was sewing a button on a jacket when she heard the doorbell buzz downstairs. She pushed herself up from the settee, but on hearing the well-bred tones of Mrs Elphinstone, the widow who lived beneath, drifting up from the hallway, she sat down again. A moment later came a soft knock on the door of the apartment.

At first, when she opened it, she thought there was nobody there, then a man separated himself from the shadows. As the light from the doorway fell on his face and she recognized him, she could only stare in shock.

'Bea,' he said, his voice low and urgent.

She cried out, 'No!' then, 'Rafe? Rafe?' She gave a laugh, light, hysterical.

'It really is me.' He stepped forward and hugged her, and she threw her arms round his neck. 'You're trembling,' he said, and she nodded, starting to cry.

'I can't believe it's you.'

'It's me all right, though I have to pinch myself sometimes.'

'We thought . . . we all thought . . .' she wept.

'That I was a gonner?' He released her, glancing at her body curiously. 'I nearly was. Any number of times.'

'When did you get back?' Beatrice asked shakily. 'How? Does your mother—'

'Yes, yes. Calm down. I'll tell you all that. Bea, how are you? Something's different – your face is different. Bea, are you . . .?'

'Oh, let's not talk about that now,' she said quickly. 'It's you I'm concerned about.'

As she showed him into the drawing room, she saw that if pregnancy had altered her appearance, there were myriad ways in which Rafe had changed. He was broader in the shoulder, but how thin he was, how careworn. Perhaps it was the uniform, but in the evening light he looked five, ten years older than his twenty-two. He was clutching his cap before him and, noticing his hands, she exclaimed in horror. She reached out and took one into her own. There was a long red scar across it and the nails were broken. The palm against her soft one was callused and dry.

'Oh, Rafe,' she said, grieving. 'What have they done to you?'

Chapter 21

'We were taken captive by a Panzer commander whose tanks overtook us on the road to Dunkirk,' Rafe told her. May 1940, it had been, fifteen months ago. 'For several days they kept us penned in a nearby barn with other prisoners, French as well as British. We were given only scraps of food and little water. After that we were made to march. We knew right away that we were going to Germany. It was a pretty grim feeling.' He stopped to light a cigarette and Beatrice saw his hands were shaking. 'Christ, they were brutal, some of their soldiers; they seemed to hate us British, I don't know why. The French were given an easier time of it – not so many beatings and better rations.

'We marched for weeks, walking all day and sleeping in churches and farm buildings by night. We crossed the German border and I thought, *This is it*, and it seemed so wrong that the countryside was so lovely, vineyards everywhere. At Trier they put us on trains to a transit camp, God knows where that was. They split us up after that. I was sent to an Oflag in Eastern Germany and that's where I've been most of the time. They told us the camp was impossible to escape from, but after ten months of trying I managed it.'

Rafe described how another officer had received a Red Cross parcel in which, against the rules, had been secreted a map and a compass. Over time they conceived a plan that involved stealing uniforms and money. Another prisoner fashioned false papers. Towards the end of June, two months ago, they had sauntered out of the camp in broad daylight dressed as guards, their plan to head for neutral Switzerland. In the event, their route was barred and Rafe's companion was recaptured. Rafe went into hiding then was forced to take a tortuous route back through France with the help of the Resistance. Finally, one moonlit night a week ago, he'd been picked up by a British plane from a hillside in Normandy.

'I was taken to Dover, where I presented myself to the authorities and was given a hearty welcome. Less so when I rang home. My stepfather answered. He wouldn't believe it was me for a while. Thought it some elaborate joke.' Rafe laughed.

'You've been back a week. And nobody told me.'

'Nobody seemed to know where you were living. It took me a while to find out. In the meantime there was a lot to catch up with. And when I discovered – well, you know – I didn't feel like seeing anyone much for a few days.'

'Angie.'

'And my brother, yes.'

'Who told you?'

'Angie's father. As a matter of fact it was he who got me your address.'

'I didn't know he knew it.' She didn't remember ever telling Michael Wincanton. Why should she have done?

'Oh, he can find out all sorts of things. Anyway, I'd tele-phoned the Wincantons' house as soon as I got to my mother's, and asked after my fiancée. Michael said she was living down in Sussex and I'd best ask her myself. I mulled over the mean-ing of that and thought in the end I should see her face to face, get the truth. So I got a train down to Sussex and surprised her.

It was me who was on the wrong end of the surprise. My own brother.'

'Oh, Rafe.'

He sounded so bitter, so unlike the Rafe she remembered.

'Gerald wasn't there, of course, and after I'd seen Angie, I didn't know what to do with myself. I went back to the station, got on what I thought was a train for London and ended up down at Brighton. I couldn't care where I was, to tell you the truth. I stayed there two or three nights, drinking an awful lot of whisky and sleeping in a cheap little boarding house, until my money was all gone. I eventually came to and managed to get myself back home; thumbed a lift with a couple of ATS girls driving a truck to Wimbledon. From there I walked the rest of the way. Since then I've been at my mother's place, sleeping most of the time. Then I knew I'd got to see you. Damn it to hell, Bea, the thought of home kept me going all this time, but this isn't the place I left. Hitler's blown it half to bits and everyone seems to have gone mad.'

'I'm the same, Rafe. The same old Bea.'

'No, you're not. Look at you.' Bea wrapped her arms around her belly, defensively. 'Angie's father told me of your loss. I'm so sorry. I didn't even know you had a fiancé.'

'Guy,' she said. 'Yes, it's knocked me back a bit.'

They were silent for a while and she could see his thoughts were drifting, his gaze wandering about the room. He looked so tired, she thought again, tired and worn, as though he'd packed twenty years of suffering into the past eighteen months.

'What was it like?' she whispered. He looked up, uncomprehending. 'In the camp, I mean?'

'As bad as you can imagine.' He spoke haltingly of the deprivations, the humiliation and the casual brutality.

When he'd finished, an expression of deep weariness settled over Rafe's face, a face that had lost the glow of youth like a bud blighted before it could bloom. He sat staring at his hands, lost in his thoughts, and she felt a terrible sense of alarm that something vital inside him had gone, or retreated beyond her reach. She couldn't think what to say to him for fear of it being inadequate, so stayed quiet until he came to himself and saw where he was, not in a prison camp but in a shabby room in London. It was growing dark and chilly, though the evenings weren't cold enough yet to merit a fire.

'Can we go out?' he asked. He stood up. 'I'd like to walk. If you would, that is.' He was glancing at her body again curiously now.

'Of course,' she said. 'I'll go and change.' Once in her room, she pulled on a pair of slacks that she'd had to let out and a bulky cardigan, then powdered her face and searched out some remnants of lipstick.

He seemed to cheer up once outside in the rough gusts of wind that set the trees dancing and the leaves falling around. She held his arm and they ducked through a gap in a hedge into the park.

At that moment some distant searchlight sent its beam across the sky. He flinched, then slowly relaxed. 'I didn't appreciate how free I'd been,' he said, 'until that freedom was taken away.'

He threw back his head and stretched his arms. 'Do you know what helped me? I used to picture myself walking on the cliffs by Saint Florian, watching the sea break against the rocks, feeling the wind on my face, trying to remember the taste of salt on my lips and the scent of the gorse – you know that smell.'

'Like coconuts.'

'Yes. Oh, what I'd give for the taste of a coconut.'

'I dream about food,' she said. 'It's absolutely maddening. Do you remember that chocolate cake your aunt's cook used to give us?'

'Those cakes to die for? Begone, temptress,' he said, laughing hoarsely, as though he hadn't laughed in a long while and was out of practice. 'I'm just glad to have had steak and kidney pie again, even though it was all gristle and suet. And fresh bread.'

From time to time they passed other people, a courting couple, a shambling old man hauling a suitcase, an air-raid warden. At the top of Primrose Hill they sat on a bench and looked out over the city, where the silhouettes of bombed buildings etched an alien line across the darkening sky. There had been no raids for many nights now. How tranquil it all looked. A sickle moon was rising. For a long while they were silent.

'Are you still staying at your mother's?' she asked him and when he nodded, said, 'She must be so happy you're safe.'

'Of course she is. They both are. They're just very bad at showing it, that's all. They're embarrassed about my brother and Angie. Anyway, my stepfather keeps asking me what I'm going to do with myself. I fear I will quickly be outstaying my welcome.'

'What *are* you going to do with yourself?'

'Another week's leave and I'll be back with my regiment, I expect, but there'll be plenty of faces gone. I'm learning not to ask questions. People look away and shuffle their feet. I'm a bit of an embarrassment, turning up out of the blue like Rip van Winkle.' His tone was so bitter, it struck her to the heart.

'Rafe, it's so wonderful you're back. I'd almost stopped believing.'

'No, you hadn't,' he said, patting her hand. 'Not you.'

She didn't think Angelina had exactly stopped believing. Or had she? If there hadn't been a war and Rafe hadn't disappeared, would she have found Gerald anyway? The question was of course unanswerable, but Beatrice sensed that Gerald was more than a replacement for Rafe. Perhaps Rafe had been a sort of preparation for Gerald. Angie certainly seemed to be content with him.

'Perhaps I shouldn't be so cut up,' Rafe said, plucking fiercely at the grass. 'We were all so young. It was asking too much of her to wait.'

Only a year and a half ago, but how innocent they'd been. Back then, Beatrice had still believed she and Rafe were made for each other. But Rafe had fallen at Angelina's feet as though worshipping a goddess. Looking back now, part of her couldn't blame him. She, too, had been fascinated by Angie, had longed for the girl's approval. There were no goddesses now, only ordinary people under pressure, trying their best to survive, all glamour stripped away. And, believing Rafe to be gone from her life, Beatrice had picked herself up and done her best to find happiness. And she had been happy. Guy. His image flashed on her inward eye and she felt a swell of sadness.

Back at the flat, she hung up their coats and poured Rafe a glass of whisky from a bottle Dinah kept in case of male company. She reached to replace the bottle on its shelf and when she turned back she saw he was looking at her again curiously; that same look Sandra Williams wore when she was working out the most tactful question to ask.

'Bea, forgive me for intruding, but are you all right?' The same question as Sandra.

'Yes, of course I'm all right. Why shouldn't I be?'

He stole another look at her fullness, opened his mouth and closed it again. She smiled to herself, thinking of all that he must have been through, and now he was daunted by this little thing, didn't know what to say.

'If you're in any kind of trouble,' he said, 'I can help. Money and so forth. You know.'

'Thank you,' she said gravely. She knew she should be grateful, so why did she feel angry with him? No, not with him, but with the situation in which she found herself. 'I'm fine at the moment.'

'But you'll ask if you're not. Do you promise?'

'I promise, Rafe.' She smiled at him, at his dear face, so anxious and concerned for her. 'It's so wonderful that you're back,' she said. 'I can still hardly believe it.'

They met again the following week. He took her out for dinner in a quiet restaurant near her flat.

This time he seemed a bit more relaxed, though there were signs of his trauma. He laid out his napkin carefully, almost marvelling at it, and ate and drank slowly, as though wanting to taste every mouthful. He started at the guncrack sound of a falling metal pan in the kitchen. The elegant waitress was French, the wife of the proprietor, and Rafe spoke to her in her own language without effort, though Beatrice smiled at his English schoolboy accent.

She told him what had happened to her grandfather. He watched her as she talked and his eyes were full of sympathy and pain.

He reached across the tablecloth to touch her fingers. 'I'm sorry,' he said. 'That's how it is there. Most people watch out for themselves. They see no other way. I was lucky to find some to help me, despite the danger. And there is a network there.' He glanced around as he spoke to check no one was listening.

'Rafe, it couldn't happen here, could it?' she whispered. 'The Nazis, I mean.'

'Ssh. No. We'll make sure it doesn't, don't worry.'

She finished her meal, remembering what the old French soldier had told her when she'd shown him the letter from Thérèse. To do her best and believe. Some nights she'd lie awake, feeling the baby move within her and dark thoughts would swirl in her mind. What kind of world was she bringing this child into? What kind of a life would it have? On such nights the dawn was a sign that she'd survived. None of this she felt she could tell Rafe.

She knew Dinah would be home, so after they left the restaurant, Beatrice didn't invite Rafe in and they said goodbye on the doorstep.

'I'll come to see you again as soon as I can,' Rafe said, 'but I might not be around for a little while. I'm sorry, I didn't like to tell you before.'

'Oh, Rafe.'

'But I'll write. Promise you'll let me know if I can help you.'

'I will.' She felt she was losing him all over again.

Sensing that she was trying not to cry, he wrapped his arms around her, kissed her forehead and held her close.

'Goodbye, Bea,' he said, and was gone.

She unlocked the door, walked very slowly up the stairs and let herself into the flat. Dinah was in the kitchen making a hot drink. When she saw Beatrice's woebegone face she said, 'Whatever's the matter?' and Beatrice burst into tears.

It was everything, losing Guy, the prospect of the baby, the thought of losing Rafe again.

It was Dinah who helped her see clearly. Dinah, with her crisp cold manner that wasn't uncaring but which went straight to the nub of the problem.

'You don't have to keep the baby. They make you give it up if you go to one of those places, you know,' she told Beatrice. 'It happened to a friend of mine. You have it, then they take it away and give it to some grateful married couple who can't have children, then you can forget about it, get on with your life.'

'I am not giving the baby away.'

'Beatrice, it's much the best thing. It's what your mother thinks, too, isn't it?'

'Yes.' She felt a terrible sense of betrayal over this, though she knew Delphine meant well. 'You're probably right, but I can't.'

Dinah shrugged. 'You'll feel differently after it's born. All that messy business and you won't have a nanny to look after it. Absolutely frightful, if you ask me.'

'Dinah, I don't know how I'll manage, but if I can I will.'

'You're a stubborn old thing, aren't you? But I like that. So let's work out what's best to do. Is there anyone else you could ask for help?'

'I won't ask Guy's parents, I can't. And my father's family would be terribly shocked if they knew.'

'Friends, then.'

Her mind flew like an arrow to Angie.

Chapter 22

It was early morning, a few days before Christmas, 1941. Snow fell in soft thick flakes that iced the laurel hedges and the shaggy lawn, blotting out the sky and the countryside beyond the gate. Watching from the window of her bedroom, Beatrice, for the first time in years, was amazed actually to feel safe. The snow made it possible to believe there was no world beyond this house and garden, and most of all no war. Surely no planes could fly in this. Sussex had been given a merciful respite.

She turned as the baby mewed in his cradle and smacked his lips, but he did not come to full wakefulness, and soon sank once again into deep sleep. She noticed how he lay with his dear little fists thrust above his head like a pugilist and she smiled tenderly as she moved past him on her way to the bathroom. With luck he'd give her enough time to wash and dress.

Out on the landing the smell of toasting bread wafted up the stairs with the comfortable chinks and thuds that meant Nanny was laying the table for breakfast. Less soothing was the whine of Hetty's voice, though what she was complaining about this time, Beatrice couldn't make out. Across the way, Angie's door stood firmly shut. She liked to lie in most mornings, even if Gerald was away. They had hopes that he'd come home on Christmas Eve. This is what he'd promised.

In the bathroom she washed quickly and efficiently, trying not to look at her body, which she found ugly with its great milky breasts and slack belly. Four weeks it was since the birth, and Nanny still insisted on feeding her up, as though she were a cow in calf. The woman referred to her now as Mother all the time, which was infuriating, though she tried not to let her annoyance show. She was, after all, she reminded herself, grateful to them, all of them, for taking her in and helping her, for supporting her decision to keep the baby when even her own mother had advised her to give it away. She remembered with amusement Delphine's open adoration when she'd come up to visit when he was only a week old, how she'd held him, crooning little French endearments as she must once have done to Beatrice. It was a side of her mother that she'd forgotten.

It had been a long and difficult birth, but the staff at the hospital had been calm and caring, and Beatrice had recovered surprisingly quickly, so she'd been told. The council offices where she'd registered the birth, on the other hand, had been chaotic after a stray bomb had exploded nearby.

Back in the bedroom, she pulled on a thick skirt, a clean blouse and her cardigan, and was rolling on a pair of much-mended stockings when the baby stirred and began to wail. She reached into the cradle and pulled him, a warm, damp, struggling bundle, into her arms, the milk already burning its way through her breasts in a rush of love. She'd feed him, she told herself, as he clamped his mouth to her breast, then give him to Nanny to change and dress while she had breakfast. The room being chilly, she climbed with him back into bed, and settled herself to enjoy the peaceful sounds of him drinking, the gamey fragrance of him.

She'd first seen this child as an inconvenience, then she'd wanted him furiously, the more so after the news of Guy's death, but she'd still not been prepared for the fierceness of her love for him, the strength of her determination to protect him and provide for him. He let go of her nipple suddenly, turning his head to stare up into her eyes, unblinking, as though learning her by heart. She was locked into his gaze, unable to look away even if she'd wanted to. 'Oh, you little sweetheart,' she whispered, and the spell broken he began to drink once more.

She lay back against the pillows, loving this intimate moment with her child, the pleasant calm of the room, the comforting sounds of domesticity going on below, the world beyond the window, still and silent. They were safe in a cocoon where she wanted to remain for as long as she could.

Despite the make-do-and-mend of it, 1941 was the loveliest Christmas Beatrice could remember. A neighbour had given them a small goose, which in the end Nanny had to pluck and prepare, since Angie made such a terrible fuss about it. There was a Christmas pudding of sorts, and Beatrice went out herself and cut down a small fir tree that Hetty decorated with home-made paper lanterns and scraps of ribbon. Gerald arrived as darkness fell on Christmas Eve, having managed to cadge a lift from a senior officer, and they spent a merry evening playing games with Hetty, lighting some candles on the tree and fixing two large socks, one for each child, to the mantelpiece for Father Christmas to fill.

They were woken early next morning by Hetty's cries of delight, for Father Christmas had managed to procure her an orange and some nuts, and Nanny had used an entire week's sugar ration to make peppermint creams. The baby's stocking contained a pair of mittens and two pairs of bootees, knitted by Nanny, and a toy dog with button eyes that Beatrice's mother had made out of an old pillowcase and stuffed with cut-up nylons.

'Are you sure the old chap can't have a sweet?' Gerald asked, peering at the boy on Beatrice's lap with a mixture of wariness and wonder. It was after lunch, and they were sitting round the fire in the drawing room as the light dwindled outside. Hetty and Angie were playing Beggar-My-Neighbour at a small felt-topped table whilst Nanny washed up, which she insisted she wanted to do now that she'd heard the King's speech.

'No, he cannot!' Angie cried. 'Honestly, Bea, quite what Gerry's going to be like when we have children I simply daren't imagine. He hasn't the slightest idea about what's suitable. Hetty, you can't do that, it's cheating.'

'But you've got all the good cards and I can't go.' Hetty rounded her shoulders. At thirteen, she was turning from an awkward child into an awkward adolescent. She'd been out sledding that morning after church, but she didn't know the local children yet and hung about on the edge of their games. Beatrice felt a little sorry for her, always stuck with adult company.

'I expect I'll be all right making them little carts and teaching them how to shoot,' Gerald said. 'It'll be rather jolly.'

'If they're boys,' Beatrice pointed out, 'and old enough.' She'd noticed he didn't take much interest in Hetty.

'I wonder if the war will be over by then?' Angie said. Hetty shrieked in triumph as her sister let her win a trick.

'Now America's in with us it'll make all the difference, you'll see,' Gerald said. He jabbed at a log on the fire with short, savage thrusts of the poker. She wondered if he had ever had to attack a man bare-handed like that, and if he would hesitate. She shivered. As far as Beatrice could tell, he'd not seen any real action since before Dunkirk. She wondered, not for the first time, what his present role was.

When Nanny brought in a tray of tea, Hetty took it as a sign to rush over to the Christmas tree and start to distribute the newspaper-wrapped packages arrayed underneath.

Beatrice, laying the sleeping baby on the settee beside her, was touched to see Mrs Wincanton had sent something for him, a matinée jacket and leggings knitted in navy wool that looked as though it had come from an old jumper. The Wincantons had really been so kind to her. Shortly before the baby's birth, a cheque for a considerable sum had arrived from Angie's father. It was the only indication she'd had until then that Michael Wincanton knew of her predicament. She supposed Angie must have told him.

When the boy was a week old she'd written to Guy's parents and told them they had a grandson. Several anxious days passed and then a letter arrived from Guy's father. It was guarded, very guarded. He offered money, but the offer was phrased in such a negative way that she took it to be some kind of test: if she took the money she would have failed. She was particularly cross about this as, in her letter to them, she'd specifically said she wasn't asking for money, but perhaps they'd taken the mere mention of money as a hint that she *did* want some, so she had only herself to blame. It was like a ridiculous game.

Worse was yet to come. Not long after this letter a parcel of baby clothes arrived from Guy's mother. Beatrice was touched by this, especially since they seemed to be ones once worn by the Hurlingham children, but the short letter accompanying them, though it asked that she let them know if she needed help, suggested that it might be the best thing if Baby were to be raised by a respectable family. Beatrice had destroyed the letter, but the clothes she put away for when her son was big enough. It pleased her to think that he'd wear something of his father's.

It was astonishing, really, that when the Hurlinghams and her own parents had judged her and found her wanting, the Wincantons, who were no relation to her at all, had welcomed this tiny collateral victim of war without question. She would always remember and love them for that, she vowed, laying the little outfit on her lap.

'And, it's not fair, another for you.' Hetty held out the package from under the tree.

Beatrice took it carefully and stared at the dear familiar hand. When it had arrived the day before she'd tried to take it away to open it in the privacy of her room, but Hetty had put a stop to that, insisting that it go under the tree with the rest of the presents to be opened on Christmas Day.

It was the first time she'd heard from Rafe since September. Once, when she was still at Dinah's, he'd sent a postcard of the Lake District and she'd hastily written him a letter back, not acknowledged. After the baby's birth she'd written again, telling him where she was, but had received nothing until now. He must have received that letter, because he knew to send the parcel here. She tried to guess what might be inside. It was small, about the weight of a book, and knotted up with many pieces of string. Nanny handed her a pair of sewing scissors and she cut it open. She drew out two wrapped bundles. One was marked for her and the other for her son. There was a letter, too.

'What have you got?' Hetty asked, leaning over the arm of the sofa, and putting out a commanding hand.

'Hetty, we don't have rudeness,' Nanny said.

Beatrice turned her bundles over, hardly daring to open them in case she was disappointed.

'Oh, do hurry up, Bea,' Angie said.

She opened the baby's first.

'Good Lord,' Gerald said.

'What an extraordinary gift for a little child,' were Angie's words.

'You may say that, but I happen to know,' Gerald said, 'that Rafe was a baby when he was given it. By his paternal grandfather, I think.'

It was a small antique silver pistol, the handle beautifully inlaid with mother-of-pearl. Beatrice turned it over in her hands, admiring the craftsmanship, then Gerald asked to have a look. She handed it over thinking, not for the first time, that if Gerald felt any guilt for taking Angie from Rafe, he never spoke of it.

'Sending it in the post, too!' Nanny tutted. 'It might have got lost or fallen into the wrong hands.'

'What's your present?' Hetty asked, impatient.

An ornate silver photograph frame emerged from the second bundle. The picture was of Rafe in uniform, his face handsome, boyish, smooth. She contemplated it for a moment or two, then showed it to the others, but its presence, as though he himself were suddenly in the room, seemed to disturb everyone.

'I wonder where he is,' Angie said.

'I don't know,' she replied. 'I hope he's all right.'

Gerald said, 'I expect he will be. He's proved himself a survivor, our Rafe.'

Nanny pushed herself to her feet and said, 'Isn't it time for Baby to be woken now, Mother? He'll miss his tea.' To Bea's chagrin, she scooped up the sleeping child. Instantly he woke and began to yell.

Bea took advantage of the distraction to hide Rafe's letter in her pocket.

'I'm taking him upstairs for you,' Nanny called behind her. Bea bundled up the gifts and took them with her as she followed.

Some time later, after Nanny had bathed the baby and laid him down to sleep, and Beatrice was alone with him, she lay on the bed and read Rafe's letter in a pool of light from the bedside lamp. It was characteristically short.

Dear Bea

I am so sorry not to have written before, but I assure you that it's hardly been possible. I can't tell you where I am or what I'm doing, indeed, I don't know what it is myself yet, but I'm determined to play my part to defeat Hitler and all he stands for. Now the Americans are in I'm convinced we will win this war. I'm very glad to hear of your son's safe arrival, and I shall think of you and of him and it will help me be courageous.

My grandfather gave me this pistol when I was christened, and I like the thought of passing it on to another little boy now in case I never have one of my own. I've no idea who gave me the picture frame, but you might think it pretty and I want you to have it and sometimes to think of me. Keep yourselves safe, whatever you do. You can try writing, but I can't promise I'll receive your letters or be able to reply.

All my love, Rafe

It was a strange letter, alarming. It gave the impression that he was distributing his personal effects in case he never returned from wherever he was going. She got up and went over to the chest of drawers and picked up the gun, examining again the engraved patterns on the silver, the snug little chamber where the bullets went, though there were no bullets there. It really was a pretty piece. It spoke to her of Errol Flynn, of the swish of silk dresses, of derring-do and adventure. The handle fitted snugly in her palm. She gripped the weapon and pointed it at her reflection in the mirror, screwed up her eyes to aim, rasped,

'Your money or your life.' And in the glass caught sight of the cradle behind her. Horror and shame at what she was doing washed over her. She lowered the gun and swung round to look at the baby who slept innocently on.

Quickly she opened the top drawer of the chest and shut it inside. Angie was right. The pistol was a peculiar present for a baby.

Boxing Day morning, and although there was no hunt, the brave and the proud held stirrup parties. Gerald and Angie set out in stout boots to the home of some friends, taking Hetty with them. It was too cold to venture anywhere with a newborn, but Beatrice was glad of the excuse to stay at home. Angie's friends were always perfectly civil to her, but in such situations she was visited by those old feelings of inadequacy. Besides, she loved the prospect of a tranquil couple of hours with just Nanny, preparing soup in the kitchen. Whilst the child slept upstairs she tried to read a book, but her concentration these days was shot to pieces, and her mind couldn't help turning to anxious thoughts of the future.

It was so warm and peaceful by the dancing fire, the snow starting to fall again outside. She snuggled up under her rug and tried once more to read.

Nanny's heavy footsteps could be heard overhead and her voice, talking to the baby. Soon she appeared in the drawing room with him struggling and grizzling in her arms.

'I thought he'd slept long enough and that Mother might wish to feed him.'

'Oh, Nanny, yes, of course,' she sighed, putting away her book.

'I could make him up a bottle.'

'No, I'll have him here.'

'It is time he got used to a bottle. You'll spoil him.'

'Just a little while longer,' she said.

'Then we'll change his napkin again, won't we, my little man, then after lunch, Nanny will take you for a little walk in the perambulator.'

'Oh, no, Nanny, it's icy out.'

'A little fresh air never did Baby any harm.'

It was so hard to argue with her, though Beatrice tried. What did she, Beatrice, know about looking after babies? And she was grateful to Nanny, for washing his clothes and nappies and bathing him and playing with him when he was fretful, as he often was lately in the run-up to bedtime.

The day following Boxing Day, Gerald took a train back to Devon. Warmer winds were blowing in from the south, and in the days that followed, melting snow dripped from the trees or slid, with sudden alarming thuds, from the roof. The country-side became brown and sodden and the sky was rent by planes once more. 'At least they're ours,' Hetty said.

Early one morning in January, Beatrice was woken abruptly by the sound of Angie's door bursting open and Angie's voice pronouncing in hollow tones, 'Oh, God'. The bathroom door slammed and the sounds of violent retching could be heard. Hetty banged on the bathroom door. 'Angie, are you all right?'

'No. Go away.'

Later, when Hetty had left for school, Bea was eating break-fast when Angie staggered into the dining room. The colour of her skin made Bea think of dirty dishwater.

'Tea,' Angie gulped, dropping onto a chair. 'No milk.' And her head sank onto the table.

'Are you sure it's something you've eaten?' she asked Angie, with heavy irony, placing the cup and saucer in front of her.

'It is the third day running.' She was lucky not to have felt nauseous herself, but she recognized the signs in others.

Angie shook her head. 'You know damn well what it is,' she said. 'I'm having a baby.' She tried a sip of tea.

'Angie, that's wonderful. Does Gerald know?'

'Yes. Eearghh,' Angie said, and rushed out of the room.

Later she said, 'I don't know why they call it morning sickness. It lasts most of the day.'

'I never had it. Do you feel better now?'

'Much, thanks.'

They were huddled by the fire in the drawing room. Nanny had gone to bed early complaining of a cold starting, so Bea had guiltily brought the wakeful baby downstairs instead of leaving him to cry, which was what Nanny would have made her do. She'd fed him and now he was happily staring round the room at the lights and the fire and the fascinating faces of the two women.

'But you're pleased. About the baby, I mean?' she asked.

'Oh Bea, of course I am. And we're so lucky to have Nanny to help us. She'll be busy with two, won't she? It'll be like old times for her. I do hope she'll still manage.'

'I don't think we should expect too much of her. How old do you think she is?'

'Nanny? I've no idea. She's always seemed exactly the same to me.'

'And Hetty will be an aunt.'

'Poor thing, she's not very happy here. I wish she'd make some friends of her own age. It's not good for her to be on her own so much.'

'I suppose it's my fault that we needed Nanny,' Beatrice said. 'Hetty would have been happier staying with her cousins.'

'She didn't want to be there without Nanny. I think it's too bad of Mummy not to have Hetty. The poor girl misses her.'

'But she can't live in London. Your father spends all day advising mothers to evacuate their children. It would look bad if he kept his with him.'

'Mummy should come and live down here then.'

'You wouldn't like that, you'd quarrel.'

'No, we wouldn't. Though I suppose there isn't room for her really.'

Angie, more spirited now she wasn't feeling so sick, was, Bea thought, looking particularly lovely, her pregnancy imparting an ethereal fragility instead of her usual healthy glow. She had changed since her marriage, Bea could see that. Gerald had settled her as no one else seemed to have been able to do, and she clung to him, and spoke of him often when he wasn't there. She seemed happy in this small rented cottage, though there were no luxuries and they had to scrape together the basics of daily existence. And now there would be another small baby to look after.

'Angie,' she said gently, 'there would be room for your mother if you wanted her. I can't go on staying here with you for ever.'

'Why ever not?' Angie said, putting out her arms for the baby. 'Let me have a go with him now.'

'I need to get a job. I've no money.' Bea passed the child over and Angie sat him on her knee where, with his head sunk into his neck wreathed by the shawl, he watched her so gravely that she burst out laughing. 'He's just like a little old man,' she said. 'Oh look, he's smiling, Bea. Look – he's really smiling.'

'He did that earlier,' Beatrice said, but sullenly. He'd not smiled like that before, not for her.

Angie's face was radiant. 'Yes, you smile for me, don't you, you little darling.' And he smiled at her wider than ever.

*   *   *

Bea broached the difficult subject of her departure again a few weeks later. They were walking back from the station on a muddy February day, having been shopping in the local town. It was the longest time she'd left her child with Nanny and her nerves were on edge the whole time.

Worse, the trip had brought home to her quite how penniless she'd become. Apart from Michael Wincanton's gift, her only income was the ten-shilling cheque her mother sent her every week or so, and although her ration card came in useful for the household, she couldn't afford to pay for much – and just suppose one of them became ill? How would she pay for a doctor? She couldn't keep on expecting Gerald and Angie to cover the extras. But it wasn't just that; it was the growing sense of restlessness she felt.

The road started to slope steeply upwards. She glanced at Angie. She looked tired, so she wrested one of the handles of Angie's shopping bag from her to share the load, though she already carried one of her own. It was odd. If there hadn't been a war, Angie wouldn't have been shopping for food but for dresses, and in a car. She didn't feel sorry for the Angies of this world, exactly, but she did acknowledge the adjustments the girl had made, largely uncomplainingly. And she saw how Angie was coming to rely on her. Surely this wasn't good for either of them. She couldn't, she felt, go on forever living here with Angie, being her poor companion.

She'd been thinking quite a lot about what she should do. She still wanted desperately to be useful in this war, not to sit back and let others win it for them. After all, Guy had given up his life, and Rafe was goodness knows where, risking his. Maybe if she was doing something more active to help she wouldn't fret so much.

'Can we sit down for a moment?' Angie said. They'd reached the top of the ridge, where a tranquil view of fields and trees and little houses stretched away into distant mist.

'Is that your place over there?' Beatrice said, pointing to a tiny house about a mile away.

'Yes, and that's Nanny hanging out washing! Everything looks so ordinary, doesn't it?' Angie said, but even as she spoke, far away, half a dozen flashes of silver shot into the sky: planes trailing plumes of black smoke. The plumes merged together into a single poisonous cloud that floated in the still air.

'Nothing's ordinary any more,' Bea said bitterly. 'A cloud hangs over us all. Aren't you aware of it? Look.' She pointed far ahead. 'The sea starts there somewhere, and then it's just a few miles to France. So close, Angie, so close. We can't wrap ourselves in our life here and pretend it's not happening, that we don't have to do anything about it.'

'I know,' Angie snapped. 'I didn't mean I wanted to shut myself away. It's just we've got different ways of managing things, you and I. Gerald needs me here, and Hetty does and soon the baby will. There have to be some people doing the ordinary things, Bea, or what kind of world will there be when it's all over?'

'I don't know. But I feel I can't go on being here, doing nothing, that's all. Angie, I don't know what you're going to think, but I want to go back to London. Dinah's room is still free, I wrote to ask.'

Angie looked puzzled, then angry. 'Bea, it's not just you now. How will you cope with a little baby? Someone has to look after him if you're working.'

'I'll find someone. People manage, you know – lots do.'

Angie stared at her for some seconds before speaking. 'You're different from how you used to be. Harder somehow.'

Beatrice felt hurt by this. Eventually she said, 'I'm not, you know. I'm the same as I've always been, but I'm surer of myself now.'

'I wish you wouldn't take Baby away. I'll miss him and I know Nanny will, too.'

'That's sweet and I know you will. But you're having your own child, Angie, and you'll both be busy enough. And when you have him, you'll love him so much you'll want to do anything for him, even fight for him.'

'You're sounding quite fierce, Bea. But there are other ways of fighting, quieter ways. You may not think much of me – no, don't say it – but I can be strong too. I'm just different from you.'

Beatrice was quite surprised by this. Angie rarely revealed this more serious side of herself.

Chapter 23

London, April 1942

The bus journey home was one of the times Beatrice felt happiest. If she left the office at five, she was usually safely on the bus at five past for the sleepy stop-start journey from Trafalgar Square to Camden High Street. It was partly the anticipation of seeing her baby that made her happy, but sitting on the bus was also one of her few opportunities to be quiet and think. In the mornings she struggled with the guilt and misery of leaving him, never mind the anxiety that she'd be late for work. Something always held her up now she had a young child to get ready, too.

At least it was still light now when she reached Camden. It was only a short walk from the High Street to the side road of Victorian workers' cottages where Mrs Popham lived, but she didn't like it much in the blackout. When she'd first moved back to London, in February, it compounded her misery that they always left home and returned there in darkness.

Mrs Popham's was a convenient ten-minute walk from Dinah's flat in Primrose Hill. Mrs Popham, though gentle with young children, was otherwise a prickly sort. For a start, she disapproved strongly of working mothers, which was perverse considering that she gained her income from them. And she had odd rules, one of which was that the children in her care (there were three) should each arrive with clean bottles and bowls each day, because she didn't want the bother of washing up. The children, she insisted, must be picked up by 6 p.m. and the bills be paid in cash in advance. Beatrice didn't think that the woman would actually cast the babies out on the street if their mothers failed to meet any of these orders, but she decided it was best not to risk it.

So far, by a miracle, she had always made it there by six, but she dreaded the day when something unexpected made her late. The aforementioned bills were the hardest bit, and she'd had to take a loan from Dinah until she finished her typing course to pay for the first two weeks' childcare. Dinah seemed delighted to have her back, and was awfully sweet about the baby, who endeared himself to all in the house by sleeping most nights through after his busy days with Mrs Popham. His cot, though, only just fitted into Beatrice's bedroom.

The job itself Beatrice found boring. She'd applied for clerical work in the War Office thinking that in some small way she'd be contributing to the war effort, but all she did all day was sit in a room full of other women, copying out orders for uniforms. This wasn't in itself unimportant work – after all, service people needed to be clothed – but the mundane nature of the job didn't engage her. What was more, it was difficult to form friendships with the other girls, who were mostly footloose and fancy free. To them, as to Mrs Popham, she was 'Mrs Marlow', a widow with a baby, living life in the shadows, and they left her out of their social plans.

At lunchtime, now the weather was warmer, she'd take her meagre sandwich and sit on the same low wall in St James's Park to eat it. It was here, on one warm spring day, when clouds were chasing across the sky and wild daffodils nodded under the trees, that she noticed a young officer sitting on the steps by a statue of some long-dead General, and realized with a skip of her heart that she knew him.

'Rafe?' she said, standing up, her sandwich falling forgotten to the ground. 'Rafe!'

Finally he looked up. 'Beatrice?' he said wonderingly, leaping to his feet. He came at once and grasped her hands. 'How extraordinary.'

They stared delightedly at each other for a moment.

Rafe said, 'I didn't know you were in London. What are you doing here?'

'I might ask the same of you. Nobody's heard from you for months. Where have you been?'

'I know. I'm sorry. It hasn't been possible to write and I never know how long I'm going to be anywhere.'

This jumbled explanation disappointed her. She was angry and yet she told herself she was wrong to feel that way. He couldn't help it, the secrecy, but she hated it all the same. It was as though he was distancing himself from her. Like some awful game of chess in which the other side was an enigma, and always a move ahead.

'I really am sorry,' he said again, and it was his turn to look anguished.

'It's only . . . we worry about you so much. Gerald and Angie, they're always asking if I've heard.'

'Are they?' He looked and sounded miserable.

'Yes.'

'How's the little one?' he asked with more enthusiasm. 'I say, this is silly. Do you have a moment? Shall we walk?'

'I must be back at work in twenty minutes.'

'You're not a FANY any more, I see,' he said, glancing at her ordinary suit as he took her arm.

'No, clerical. The job's dreary but it keeps us going, just.' Michael's gift and the money her mother was still mailing her were helping her pay the bills. 'And, since you ask, he's the best and brightest baby in the world.'

'He must be quite big. Is he walking?'

'Oh, Rafe, he's only five months, of course he's not. Don't you know anything about babies? I wish I had a photograph to show you. You must meet him.'

'Where is he?' Rafe said, and Beatrice burst into peals of laughter, for he glanced behind him as though expecting the baby to pop out from behind the statue. 'He's with a child-minder, of course. You don't imagine he comes to work with me, do you? She's awfully good with him,' she added, with the guilt she always felt when admitting this.

'And what about the work? Is it terribly secret?'

'Oh no, I'm just making myself useful at the lower levels. Typing, filling in forms, that sort of thing. I have to tear up anything I've done twice before I get it right. I don't know why they keep me on really. A shortage of people, I suppose.'

He laughed. 'I'm sure you underestimate yourself. You always did.'

'Did I?' She was surprised at this new view of herself.

'God, I've gone and offended you now.'

'No, you haven't. It's a sort of compliment.' They smiled at one another more easily now. 'Oh, it is good to see you, Rafe. You look so much better, you know.' It was the first time she'd met him since the summer, when she'd been pregnant and grieving, and Rafe himself so low. Now he'd put on some weight and it suited him. His face was fuller, too, and his colour healthy. She felt a rush of affection. He was so dear and familiar, but . . . she realized he'd cleverly said nothing about himself, had adroitly turned the conversation back to her. *I know so little about him,* she thought, suddenly hurt. They had once been so close.

'Where are you living?' He was regarding her tenderly now.

'With Dinah again, I told you. Did you get that letter?'

He shook his head. 'I think some of my mail must have gone astray. I've already endured a severe ticking-off from my mother for not answering letters she swears she sent me. It hasn't been easy.'

'What hasn't been easy?'

'Where I've been. What I've been doing.'

'I want to know more. Rafe, I must go back now. Are you in London for a bit? Do you have time to come and meet the baby?'

'I most certainly do,' he said, and this time he smiled like the old Rafe.

He came to the flat the following evening, bringing a mass of fragrant narcissi and a child's picture book.

'Where did you find flowers? And – oh, look, darling!'

The baby stared, large-eyed, from his mother's arms, and buried his face in her bosom when she tried to hand him to the stranger.

'You're a very handsome little chap,' Rafe said, taking him awkwardly. The child promptly reached back to Beatrice with a passionate cry. 'But I think he wants his mother.'

'He's a tired boy, aren't you, sweetie?' she crooned, taking him again.

In the drawing room she settled herself in a chair and gave her son a bottle of milk. On the table was a tray with a whisky bottle, a water jug and two glasses. A clothes horse full of little sheets, nappies and baby suits was drying by the electric fire. 'Help yourself to a drink, Rafe. I must put him to bed.' When the baby had finished she bore him away, tucked him into his cot and sang to him until he succumbed to sleep.

When she returned, Rafe had removed his jacket and was drinking whisky and frowning over the evening paper. It was as though he lived there, she thought. She badly wanted to reach out and stroke his hair.

'Have you seen this?' he asked, tapping a blurred photograph of a plane with Japanese markings.

'Oh, don't, Rafe – there's never any good news.' She diluted her drink, still not really liking the stuff.

'It sometimes seems like that,' he said, folding the paper and putting it away. 'But we don't have to talk about it. He is bonny, your boy.'

She brightened. 'He is, isn't he? And thank you for his book. He'll love looking at the animals. I mean to take him to the zoo.'

'I'd no idea what to get for a baby. There's nothing in the shops.'

'My mother makes him stuffed toys and finger puppets. And Mrs Elphinstone downstairs brought up some rattles her son played with when he was a baby. She's so anxious about her own boy. Thinks he's in Africa but she hasn't heard for months. Oh, I'm talking about the war again.'

'So let's change the subject again. How are your parents?' he asked, sipping his whisky.

'The same as they always are,' she said. 'I took the baby down to see them in January for a few days.' In fact, the visit had been very successful. Her father, who had recently had two stories accepted by a magazine, was in an unusually cheerful state of mind. '*Maman*'s busy with knitting groups and fund-raising. They have their routines and still argue about the usual things.'

'My mother drives an ambulance,' Rafe said, in a disbelieving tone, and Beatrice, who remembered Amanda Armstrong, languid and elegant, at Angie and Gerald's wedding, immediately understood his amazement.

'What about you? Have you been in this country all this time?' she asked him, trying the more direct approach.

'Mostly. There have been long periods of training. Scotland, the Lakes.'

'And are you expecting to be going . . . away again somewhere, soon?' She waited, dreading his answer.

He downed the dregs of his drink and tilted the glass carefully back on the table. 'It's looking that way. I'm afraid I can't tell you anything at all about it, Bea. I'm sorry, but that's the way it is. They'd probably shoot me.'

'Oh. I suppose that means it's very dangerous?'

'It might be. Yes.' His expression was unreadable now and it frightened her. It was as though someone else was there, looking out from behind his eyes. How quickly they'd had to grow up. St Florian, when she visited, had hardly changed. But they had.

'The horses have gone,' she said suddenly.

'What horses?'

'When I was in Cornwall a year ago, Jezebel and the ponies were still at Carlyon, though troops are billetted at the house. But this time I walked up there, just to see, and the horses had gone.' There had been no one guarding the gate, and she'd walked all the way up to the stables unchallenged. 'The stalls had been cleaned out and were being used for storage. The soldier I spoke to there didn't even know who Old Harry was, let alone where he might be living.'

'Harry will be all right. He had family round there, didn't he? I remember him telling me once. It's the horses. I don't like to think what might have happened to them.'

'Nor me,' Beatrice said, remembering the horses at the depot. 'They have no power at all over their lives.'

'Sometimes I don't think we have much more than they do,' Rafe said. 'It's a nightmare world we live in. And yet it's horrible how used to it we've become. It's normality, all of this now, what we have to do. The boredom of so much of it, the waiting around. And yet every day it seems there's some new horror to read about.' He indicated the newspaper. 'Do we get immune?'

'It's how we survive, I suppose. Accept that things happen, carry on.'

'But it's important that we're angry, don't you think? That we stay angry. We're not dumb beasts. In our own way we can fight back.'

'I wish I felt I was doing that.'

'You are, in your way, Bea.'

'Filling in forms in an office?'

'Someone has to do it. And think of your son. You have to look after him.'

'Yes,' she said, somewhat sadly. 'The darling boy. It's so dreadful that he never knew Guy.'

'I think you are very brave, Bea.' They were quiet for a moment.

'I wish I could do more. It might stop me feeling frightened. If only I could do something about the future rather than waiting for others to do it for me.'

'Are you frightened?' He leant across and took her hand. 'I do care, you know. I think of you often, what you're doing and whether you're all right. I meant what I said. You were awfully brave about Guy and—'

'Don't feel sorry for me, Rafe. The baby's wonderful. And it wasn't brave of me at all. I got on and did what I knew I had to do. It's you who's brave. You and all those who have to go and risk your lives.'

Being so close to him like this was a torment. For it was apparent that, even when they were together, so many things still stood between them. She could see that part of his mind was far away, on something else – the whatever it was he had to do. There was the past, too. She wondered if he knew that Angie was expecting his brother's child? She hadn't been brave enough to raise the subject.

And with her own circumstances, as an unmarried mother, she dared hope for nothing. She still thought of Guy, often. How could she not when she saw him in their son all the time? But she knew, too, that her feelings for Rafe were the same as ever, although she was more wary now, tougher, and she had her baby to consider.

It was a big thing, to take on another man's child. Rafe knew all about that from the child's point of view, had himself suffered from losing his father and gaining a stepfather. No, she told herself not to hope for anything from Rafe.

They arranged to meet again, and over the next few days at work she found it difficult to concentrate for thinking of him. Saturday afternoon came, and they tucked the baby in his pram and went to the zoo in Regent's Park. Although there were some empty cages, it was surprising how many animals were still there.

'Do you suppose they're on rations?' Rafe joked, when the sea lions all emerged from their pool and trailed hopefully behind them round the enclosure.

'If they're eating what's considered inedible by us they must be in a bad way,' Beatrice said, thinking of the gristly chops Dinah had recently wrestled out of the butcher, part of their meat allocation for the week.

'You don't suppose he finished up on our dinner-plates, do you?' Rafe whispered, seeing that the giant panda's cage was empty.

'Eugh! That's horrible,' Beatrice cried. She lifted the baby out to see the monkeys, but regretted it when some primal instinct sent him rigid with fear. She cuddled him into her shoulder.

For lunch they ate thin soup and rice pudding at a café near the park. The waitress, a maternal-looking woman with a pillowy bosom, cooed at the child and told Rafe, 'How very like you he is.'

'That would be a miracle,' Rafe retorted without thinking. Beatrice was hurt by this casual rejection and by the shocked look on the woman's face.

Outside, she turned away, angry with Rafe, to clip the boy into his pram.

'I'm sorry,' Rafe said, contrite. 'He is particularly handsome. It would be natural to note a likeness.'

'Oh, you,' she said in a dull voice. She pushed the pram briskly ahead, her heels clicking on the pavement. How could he still have this power over her? She thought she'd come so far, grown up so much. But despite all that had happened, he'd spied the hole in her armour, and through it pierced her heart. This time, she would not lie bleeding and helpless. She'd survive.

Still she couldn't hide her hurt and, as she scrabbled for the front-door key in her handbag, he reached out and touched her cheek.

'What's the matter?' he said.

'Why should there be anything the matter?' she said, pushing him away. She couldn't work the key in the lock and smacked at it angrily, then rested her cheek against the door and closed her eyes.

'Let me,' he said, his voice firm, and he took the key, unlocked the door and held it open for her to wheel the pram inside.

She shut the door and in the dark and echoey hall, he took her in his arms and held her close. 'I'm sorry, I'm sorry,' he whispered into her hair. 'I can't help saying the wrong thing.'

'Oh, don't be stupid,' she said fiercely, holding him tight. 'It's just everything's so difficult.'

'Are you all right?'

'No, how can I be? You'll be going away.'

Behind them, the baby started to wake and she scooped him from the pram. Tired and cross, he threw up his arms and butted her with his small head.

'You'd better go,' Beatrice said, trying to calm the child. 'I'll see you soon, shall I?'

'Tomorrow,' he replied, opening the door. 'Can I come tomorrow?'

Dinah would be out until the evening. 'Come in the afternoon,' she said. 'Is two o'clock all right?'

He was nearly an hour late. She went to the window a dozen times to look up the road, whipping herself into a state of worry at the thought of all the things that might have happened to him. The baby, who was teething, rolled fretfully on the rug, batting at his rattle with angry cries. When the bell of the street door rang at last, she picked him up too roughly and the stair-well echoed with his wailing.

'I'm sorry,' Rafe apologized, when she opened the door to him. 'Family visitors. I couldn't get away.' There was tenderness in his expression and sadness, too. 'Hello, you,' he said to the child, tickling the tiny naked feet. The baby whimpered and buried his face in her shoulder.

Upstairs, when she'd put the baby down to play once more, Rafe came to her and kissed her; her mouth opened to his in astonishment. His lips moved over her face. He drew the tip of his tongue down her neck, which made her whole body tingle. Slowly they drew apart.

'If you'll watch him, I'll put the kettle on,' she said, not trusting her voice to be steady.

'Of course.' He peeled off his jacket, threw it over the back of a chair and knelt down by the child, waving the rattle a few inches above his face. The baby stared at it with solemn eyes then slowly reached a starfish hand towards it. Rafe moved the rattle slowly to one side, so the child had to roll to reach it. Beatrice laughed, watching them together for a moment, then went to make tea.

When she came in with the tray he said, 'Oh, I forgot,' and stretched up to pull his jacket from the chair. It fell, and a pen rolled out. He shoved the pen back, then burrowed in a pocket and drew out a cylindrical paper packet. 'Mother's American cousin brought 'em. This is my whack. Would he be allowed one?'

She set the tray on a side-table, lifted the fallen jacket, and laid it once more on the chair as he unfolded the packet.

'Chocolate cookies. Oh, Rafe, how marvellous. Why not?' she said. 'Who knows when he'll get another.'

'Here we are. One each to start with.'

She sat on the sofa holding her own cookie, breathing in the scent as though it were some rare, expensive spice, too precious to actually eat. Together they laughed at the baby's attempts to suck his and the wondrous expression in his eyes at his first taste of chocolate.

'Who's the American cousin?' she asked, closing her eyes in delight as she bit into hers and the butter, sugar and chocolate melted over her tastebuds.

'A Lootenant George Kennedy from Montana,' he said, mimicking the accent. 'His grandmother's sister married my mother's grandfather. Something like that. He was told by his mother to look up his English relations and I'm very glad he did.'

'A useful man to know if it means biscuits.'

'Yes – it's just a shame I won't be around to benefit.' He said this lightly. There was a silence whilst Beatrice took it in.

'The summons will come soon, Bea, very soon.'

'Oh, Rafe. Where are you going?'

'I can't tell you. I wish I could. I'm sorry, but that's all there is to it.'

'It's something frightening, isn't it? I can see it in your face.' The sweetness of the biscuit was treacherous now. She stared at it, forced herself to eat.

'Bea, this is hard for us both. I can give you nothing, promise you nothing. It would be wrong of me.'

He turned around until he knelt at her feet and laid his head on her lap. She stroked his dark gold hair, felt his soft warm breath on her thigh, tasted the sugar in her mouth. Then she bent and wrapped her arms around him, holding him tight.

'You won't go without saying goodbye, will you?' she whispered.

All covered in wet biscuit, the baby managed to roll over twice and wedge his leg under a table. Astonished to be trapped, he let out a yell, so Beatrice never heard Rafe's reply.

It was after he'd left, and she was sweeping up crumbs, that she found it, caught in the lace of the chair cushion. A small embroidered badge. It was in the shape of a pair of wings, the symbol of a trained parachutist. It must have fallen out of his jacket. She knew at once what it meant. That he would be passing into terrible danger.

*   *   *

At work, two days later, Daisy, the petite receptionist, came across to where Beatrice was frowning over her typewriter and handed her a note. With one wary eye on her supervisor, Miss Goodwin, she read it quickly. It was from Rafe. *Meet me at lunchtime at the statue.*

She thought it was him in the distance, sitting on the steps where she'd seen him before, writing on a pad balanced on his knee. Then a group of office girls milled past her, blocking her view, and when she looked again he was gone.

Had it been Rafe or someone else? She waited there, looking around, wondering if this was indeed the statue he meant, so she walked round the others she could see, in an increasing panic. He did not come, and finally she had to return to work. It was the longest afternoon she had ever spent. She tried to reassure herself that he'd contact her again, that he wouldn't go without seeing her. Three times she made an excuse to go out to ask Daisy if anyone had been asking for her. 'I promise I'll come and tell you,' Daisy insisted, troubled that someone as quiet and collected as Beatrice Marlow was in so anxious a state.

When she arrived home in the evening there was no note waiting. She cursed the silence of the telephone in the hallway below. Eventually, she rang Angie, and got the number for Rafe's mother. When she dialled, it was Rafe's stepfather, Colonel Armstrong, who answered.

'We've not the blindest idea where he is. Who did you say you were? Wait a minute, will you, I'll fetch my wife.'

After a moment she heard Rafe's mother's elegant drawl: 'Amanda Armstrong here. Who's that, please? Oh, Beatrice Marlow – yes, I do remember you. My dear, we know nothing, only that he's gone.' The woman sounded so composed. 'Yes, it was very sudden. I'm so sorry if he didn't get to say goodbye.' Only on the last word did that elegant voice tremble.

Chapter 24

Days passed, weeks passed. There was no letter from Rafe, no phone call, no message via Daisy from reception. The spring of 1942 was changing into summer, but Beatrice hardly noticed. As the hope of hearing from him faded, fear sprang into its place. She avoided reading the casualty lists in the papers; she hated answering the phone if it rang. Every time the post came, the faithful letters from her mother, with whatever she could afford that week, it brought back that awful day when she heard about Guy.

'What happened to your young man?' Dinah asked, and when Beatrice told her, 'Oh, you do have bad luck.'

She was around more lately. Beatrice wondered if she'd quarrelled with her lover.

'Why don't you give yourself a few days away?' Dinah went on. 'You don't look well.'

Staring at herself, whey-faced and spotty, in the bathroom mirror, Beatrice decided Dinah was right. She was under-nourished. It wasn't just the limited diet but the long days at work followed by childcare and housework that were wearing her down. And with Rafe's disappearance, the spark he'd rekindled had been snuffed out.

In June she took the baby on the train to stay with Angie. She'd negotiated a whole week's holiday, largely on the basis of poor health.

Angie was six months pregnant now and possessed a glossy sheen that Beatrice rarely saw in the city any more.

'It's those awful eggnogs Nanny makes me drink,' Angie told her. 'I can hardly get them down.' There were plenty of eggs, for they kept chickens now, also rabbits, which it was Hetty's job to look after. She kept heartless little notes in a book of their names and broods and dates of slaughter. Even Angie could wring a hen's neck now without being squeamish.

They were all delighted with the baby, so that Beatrice hardly had him for herself. He found Angie enchanting, and they smiled and chatted at each other like lovers. Nanny looked after feeding and naps, and when she was allowed, Hetty would bear him away to look at the animals or to play on the grass.

There was something magnificently contented about Angie, these days. She was loving being married to a man who adored and cherished her, and full of joy about the baby. 'I know people say it's a terrible world to bring a child into, but life has to go on, don't you think? There has to be *hope*.' Gerald came home for a couple of days every fortnight or so. Angie told Beatrice he was working at something *terribly important with the Americans* but she couldn't breathe a word, even if he told her anything, which he hadn't anyway.

There did have to be hope, Beatrice agreed, but she found it irritating how insular Angie was becoming. Perhaps it was to do with her pregnancy, a sort of survival mechanism to protect the baby, but she allowed little to ruffle her serenity.

Beatrice avoided speaking about Rafe. Angie could no longer be regarded as a rival, but her feelings about him were too deep and precious for exposure to anyone, let alone Angie, who might not be able to resist interfering in some way.

'I do wish you'd come down more often,' Angie said, at the end of their stay.

'I will, of course I will,' Beatrice said, pressing her cheek to Angie's. She did feel protective of her friend. That's how Angie always made people feel.

'Goodbye, little sweetheart,' Angie said, kissing the child as she strapped him into the pram. 'Be a good boy, won't you? And come and see Auntie Angie soon. Oh, he is sublime, Bea, you're so lucky. You know we'll have him anytime if you need a break.'

'He's no trouble, are you, little poppet,' Nanny declared, 'but he must keep his little sunhat on as Nanny tells him.'

It was hard returning to the routine. She felt much better physically, but the break made her see how frustrated she was with everything. She hated Mrs Popham's disapproval, the boredom of the job, the powerlessness of her position. She was learning to live with the fact of Rafe's absence, but lately she'd lain awake at nights thinking about Guy, realizing she'd never had a proper chance to mourn him, and wondering how his family were getting on without him. Perhaps she'd write to them again.

She was considering this one lunchtime in July, walking back to the office up Whitehall, when a car drew up on the opposite side of the road and a man put his head out of the back window and called her name. It was Michael Wincanton. Asking his driver to pull in, he stepped out and waited for her to cross.

Michael, in his fifties now, she guessed, was still handsome in that broad-shouldered, square-faced kind of way.

'Mr Wincanton – how do you do? And how is Mrs Wincanton?' she asked.

'Very well, I think. She and Hetty have been staying in Cornwall – that little house in Saint Florian she's rented while Carlyon Manor is being requisitioned. It's useful having her down there, to be honest. I can't get down to the constituency myself much these days and she keeps an eye. Also, she needs a rest from London.'

Poor Oenone. 'And Peter? I haven't seen him for a long time. I hope he's not in any trouble.'

'Not that we know of, though he has some queer friends – some of these greenery-yallery types. It doesn't look good, not in his line. Not that I'm suggesting he's up to anything unBritish, but there are some communist sorts about.'

'Oh,' she said, appalled. 'Well, I'm sure Peter isn't one of those.'

They chatted briefly about Angie and the forthcoming baby. 'It'll steady her, having a child,' her father said. 'Gerald's a good husband. They talk most warmly about your little boy. He's well, I hope?'

'Oh yes,' she said. 'We're going down to visit them again shortly. He loves it down there, he gets so much attention.'

'How are you managing with money? It can't be easy.'

'It isn't always,' she said, standing up straighter. 'But I assure you he's being well looked after.'

'You're a plucky girl,' Michael said quietly. 'I don't know that you made the right decision keeping him, but part of me admires you for it, you know.'

'Thank you, but I don't need admiration.'

He laughed. 'Damned if you don't,' he said, almost to himself. Then 'Tell me, do you ever hear from that boy Rafe?'

'Not for ages,' she said, astonished at the change of direction. 'I'm quite worried about him, actually. I don't know where he is or what he's doing, but I think it's something very dangerous. Do you know anything?'

Michael Wincanton ignored her question. 'You're very fond of him, aren't you? Saved his life once, I recall. As I say, you're a plucky girl. What is it you're doing now?'

'Typing at the War Office. I should be looking around really. Seeing if I can't be more useful.'

'Oh, it's all useful, my dear. God knows, we're all cogs in a giant wheel. And that wheel will turn to crush the Nazis, we're determined.' He took her hand, kept it for longer than was polite. 'Please convey my best wishes to your parents. Can I offer you a lift? No? Well, goodbye.'

She watched with a feeling of unease, as he got in and the car pulled away. Their conversation had seemed on his part purely a courteous act towards a young family friend. Yet beneath the surface it was as though he had been testing her responses. What his purpose was she had no idea, but he'd stirred up something in her, a troubled feeling. She turned and set off in the direction of the office.

Several weeks passed and life went on as before, until late one evening, Beatrice was woken by the faint but insistent ringing of the phone downstairs. It stopped mid-ring, and a moment later there came a knock on their flat door. 'Mrs Elphinstone says it's for you. Hurry up,' came Dinah's muffled voice. Beatrice crawled down to the end of the mattress to avoid jolting the cot and stumbled downstairs in the soft darkness to the phone.

'Beatrice, it's Gerald, can you hear me? I've some bad news, I'm afraid. Damn, this place is so noisy, you'll have to speak up.'

Gerald was telephoning from a hospital in Sussex. Early the previous day, a month earlier than expected, Angie's labour pains had started and once they'd gained in strength and regularity, Nanny had called the hospital. What followed was a nightmare of pain and panic, for what no one had known until then was that Angie was carrying twins.

'Something wasn't right – the poor little blighters were the wrong way round, something like that. Beatrice, the pips are about to go, there's no time to explain.'

'Is Angie all right, Gerald? *Gerald*!' Beatrice had slid down the wall, was now crouched on the floor, her eyes closed in anguish.

'What? No.' Gerald was almost shouting, against a clanking sound somewhere in the background. 'That is, she's alive, thank God, but she has to stay in hospital. Bad way. Lost a lot of blood. Look, it's pandemonium here. Can you tell her parents? Their line was engaged.'

'Yes, I'll try. But, Gerald – the babies?'

His reply was the last thing she heard before the call disconnected. Still holding the receiver, she stared into the dark recess of the hall, trying to assimilate what he'd said. 'The babies didn't make it.' Poor, poor Angie.

A few days later, she left her son with a grumbly Mrs Popham and went down to visit Angie. Though out of danger now, she lay very still in her hospital bed, her complexion bloodless, tears seeping from beneath her closed lids. Gerald hadn't been able to stay long, but Oenone and Nanny now took turns to sit with her at visiting times. Today they left Beatrice alone with her.

'Angie?' she whispered. The eyes fluttered open and met hers. Huge, pleading eyes, like those of an animal caught in a trap. 'Angie, how are you? I'm so sorry . . .' The eyes closed. Angie's forehead wrinkled, her mouth turned down and she gave a small moan that seemed to have been ripped from somewhere deep inside.

*   *   *

St Florian, 2011

'I felt so desperately sad for her,' Beatrice said. 'If only the doctor had realized that she was having twins, they might have made better preparations.'

'How could they miss it?' Lucy asked, horrified.

'There weren't the modern methods. You would have thought that a midwife would have discovered it was twins by examining her, but if the babies were small and not presenting in the right way . . .'

'Poor Granny. I had no idea . . . no one ever told me. Do you think she ever told Dad?'

'I wouldn't know,' Beatrice said, as though she hadn't considered the idea.

'It's so strange, thinking of it,' Lucy cried out suddenly. 'That Dad had these siblings he never knew. Oh, I can't bear it, it's so sad.' She put her hands over her face.

'Don't, dear,' Beatrice said. 'I know it's sad, but it was a long time ago.'

Lucy thought, not for the first time, how calm and controlled Beatrice could be. Not unconcerned about the suffering – far from it – but as though she herself had been dealt so many blows in her life that suffering didn't surprise her. She suddenly realized that she didn't know the name of Beatrice's baby. Beatrice hadn't said what he was called.

And now the old lady was rising from her chair and making her way across the room to stare out at the garden, which was falling into late-afternoon shadow. Silhouetted there, lost in her thoughts, she looked a very lonely figure. And Lucy knew that it was time to slip away.

*   *   *

She walked down to the harbour to look for Anthony, though she'd arranged to meet him later at the bar. There was no sign of him, and *Early Bird* was bobbing gently in her mooring. She sat on some steps, out of the wind, and took her phone out of her bag.

'Mum?' she said, when Gabriella answered.

'Lucy. Where are you?'

'Still in Cornwall. Mum, it'd take too long to explain much now, but I've been talking to an old friend of Granny's. Someone called Beatrice. Ashton, used to be Beatrice Marlow.'

'Who? I didn't hear.'

'Beatrice Ashton.'

'I've no idea who she is.'

'So Dad never mentioned her?'

'He might have done, but I can't remember.'

Lucy thought for a moment. What was it she wanted to know? Oh, about the babies.

'Did Dad or Granny ever mention her having any other children? Before Dad, I mean.'

'Lucy, who is it you've been talking to?'

'Her name's Beatrice, Mum. She was a friend of Granny's when Granny was young. At Saint Florian. That's where I am now.'

'How peculiar. I thought you were at Penzance. What are you doing in Saint Wherever you said?'

'*Mum.*'

'No. The answer's no, they never said anything. Did your granny have other children? She didn't misbehave, did she? Now that *would* be a turn-up.'

'No, Mum, she didn't. But—'

'I don't know why she only had your father. It was never the kind of question one could ask her. They were so close, she and your father. I shouldn't think there would have been room in her life for a brother or sister.'

'Were they close?'

'Oh yes. She adored your father. That was part of the trouble. She disapproved of me . . .'

'Yes, Mum.' Her mother had told her this so many times. Lucy wondered how true it was; whether both sides in the matter had become over-sensitized.

'That's why he married so late. She had her claws in him.'

'Couldn't it just have been he hadn't met anyone he wanted to marry until you, Mum?'

Her mother gave a gentle laugh. 'It would be nice to think that,' she said. 'Lucy, I must go now. Lewin's coming and I'm not dressed yet.'

Lucy ended the call, smiling, and put her mobile away. She sat thinking for a while, feeling reassured by the phone call. Probably her grandmother had felt particularly close to Tom because of her lost babies. He must have been so precious to her, and how loved he must have felt.

As she stood up, she saw Anthony coming round the corner. When he spotted her, his face brightened. She'd never felt like this about anyone before, certainly not about Will. He came to stand close to her and it felt so natural for them to slip their arms round each other and just be, without speaking.

Chapter 25

The next morning was Friday. As Lucy took her seat in Beatrice's sitting room, the old lady said, 'How are you today? I was worried that I'd upset you.'

'I'm all right. It was the shock of everything, that's all.'

'Today won't be easy, either.' Beatrice sighed. 'The next part of my story is the most difficult for me to tell. I don't want to deal with questions until I've finished, but I think you'll understand why.'

'That sounds a bit worrying,' Lucy said. 'But I still want you to tell me.'

'It starts,' Beatrice told her, 'after that chance meeting with Michael Wincanton . . .'

London, August 1942

One Monday, two weeks after Angie's tragedy, an odd letter came for Beatrice. It was signed *E. Potter* and asked her to attend an appointment at an address in Westminster in three days' time. There was no official letterhead and she wondered briefly if it was a trick. She daren't ask for more time off work and the letter said she should tell no one about the appointment, so when Thursday came she called in sick.

Number Three, Sanctuary Buildings, when she found it, did not look promising, being an ugly, many-storeyed building of grey stone in the maze of streets behind Westminster Abbey. It was home, a notice informed her, to the Ministry of Pensions. Seeing this, her heart sank. More clerical duties, she supposed.

When she asked the commissionaire for directions to Room 55a she was shown not into a busy office, but upstairs to a small room with boarded-up windows. It was furnished only with a simple wooden table and two folding chairs, and lit by a single, naked ceiling light. There she was left alone to wait.

She sat carefully on one of the chairs and looked round for any clue of what the room was used for, but apart from a list of air-raid regulations that she'd read many times in other offices, there was nothing. The minutes ticked by and she started to feel uncomfortable, as though she was being watched. Eventually there came a brisk knock and the door opened to admit a slight, clean-shaven man of forty or so, wearing a lounge suit and an apologetic smile.

'I'm so sorry to keep you, Miss Marlow – it is Miss Marlow, is it?' He peered at a paper in his hand.

'Yes, it is,' she said. 'Are you Mr Potter?'

'Yes, that's right.' He shook her hand with his long cool one, took the seat behind the table and extracted a small notebook from his breast-pocket.

'I expect you'd like to know why I've invited you here,' he said.

'Well, yes,' Beatrice said. 'You see, I've not the least idea.'

'Your name has been passed to me, as somebody possibly suited to assist in the work in which I'm engaged – very important work, vital, in fact, to our success in this war. And it's for this reason that I must urge upon you complete secrecy concerning what will pass between us in this room.'

He looked up at her. In the silence that followed she felt first of all a sense of complete unreality, then a low throb of excitement.

She said, 'I have no trouble agreeing to that condition. Please do go on.'

He folded his hands together on the table, sat very straight in his chair. 'Before I explain further, I'd like to ask you some questions, if I may.'

'Yes, of course,' she replied, but a little uncertainly.

'I've been led to understand that you are fluent in French. Is that right?'

'Yes, I am – that is, I lived in Normandy until I was ten. My mother's French, but my father's English.'

'And you're twenty – no, nineteen.'

'Twenty in two weeks' time.'

He made a note in his book. 'In good health?'

'Yes.'

'And you're a FANY.'

'I was, though I was let go . . . on compassionate leave.' She was struck by a keen awareness that she shouldn't mention her child. And in telling the lie, felt instantly that she'd betrayed him.

'Compassionate leave?' Potter asked, studying her.

'My fiancé was killed in Crete. I'm afraid it knocked me back a bit.'

'Ah, I'm sorry to hear that. Do you feel, as far as it's possible, that you've recovered from that?'

'Oh yes. I loved him very much, please believe that, but we hadn't known each other very long, and I suppose that's why I was able to get myself back on my feet quite quickly. Does that sound very hard of me, Mr Potter?'

'Not at all,' he said. 'You didn't return to the FANY, then?'

'No, I wanted a change. In working for the War Office I thought I'd be doing something more directly useful than the driving work.'

'Tell me about what you mean by being directly useful.'

'It's something I started thinking about after Guy died. I couldn't see why it shouldn't have been me out there taking the risk. I know women are told to be brave here, at home, keeping everything going, but it didn't seem fair somehow. I might not be as strong as a man physically, but I have courage and stamina.'

'I see. Those are certainly important qualities. Now tell me more about what you did in the FANY, Miss Marlow.'

She told him about her work during the Blitz, and he asked detailed questions about situations she'd found herself in and how she'd dealt with them. There followed further questioning about her family and her schooling, and her brush with polio.

'You have recovered your strength fully?'

'Yes,' she said. 'I made myself exercise until I did.'

'Very commendable. And what do you know of the situation in France?'

'My mother and I follow it closely. We got word that my grandfather had been killed,' she explained. 'It's such a short distance over the Channel, isn't it? The Nazis are so near. Sometimes I lie awake at night and think of them being so close, and how important it is that we win this war.'

'My sentiments exactly,' Mr Potter said. She was aware of him watching her intently, as though she were an interesting insect. Not unkindly, though.

Finally he came to the end of his questioning. How long had she been here? An hour, perhaps more. And now he asked if she had any questions.

'What is it you want me for?'

'I was thinking that your knowledge of France and the language could be useful to us,' he said. 'But there would be some risk involved.'

'Is it spying?'

'No,' he said. 'But it involves similar skills and training. We need people to go into France who speak the language and will be invisible to the enemy. Who will fight this war from within their camp.' Mr Potter was quiet and mild-mannered, and yet the force with which he spoke was chilling.

'What would my work be exactly?' Beatrice asked.

'To put it simply, we are trying to make things as difficult and unpleasant for the Germans as possible. This involves working with local Resistance groups, sabotaging lines of communication, troop trains and arms depots. It is dangerous work, and if one is caught, well, the reprisals can be brutal.'

Beatrice felt horrified and strangely thrilled at the same time.

'We find women are particularly good as couriers,' he said. 'They can move around more freely without suspicion.' They talked some more about what couriers did and then he said, 'I should like you to go away and think about it all very seriously, then contact me. And, of course, now that I've met you, I need to think about everything you've said about yourself, too.'

'Are you all right, love?'

She looked up in a daze. The waitress was about her age, a skinny little thing, with a small round face and front teeth that crossed.

'Your tea's gone cold,' the girl said, her eyes full of concern. 'You've been sat here for hours. I thought there might be something wrong.'

'There isn't,' Beatrice said. 'I was just thinking. Oh, is that the time?' She laid a few coins on the table, feeling the girl's

puzzled stare, then buttoned up her jacket and hurried from
the café.

All the rest of the day she wandered about without noticing
her surroundings, her thoughts a seething tangle. She was in
a state of shock, that was it; hardly believing that she'd been
picked out like this, plucked from her ordinary routine into
some parallel world. How had it happened? she wondered.
Who or what had brought her to the attention of the enigmatic
E. Potter? Her thoughts always led back to the same place: it
could only be something to do with Michael Wincanton. And
yet that was difficult to accept. Michael knew about her child;
he knew, but he'd still put her into this terrible quandary. And
it was a quandary.

What she had to confront about herself was the fact that
she had chosen not to mention to Mr Potter that she was a
mother. Why not? Her son was the obvious reason why she
shouldn't step forward for this role that he was offering her,
but she'd allowed the other part of her, the part that wasn't a
mother, to listen enthralled as he described the work of his
department – secret work that took its agents into the heart
of danger.

Sitting on the bus to Camden, the shock began to fade. Now
the image of her little boy filled her mind. She couldn't leave
him, couldn't put herself in danger, because what would he do
without her?

When she reached Mrs Popham's, heard his shout of joy,
saw the way he crawled across to her crying with relief, she
almost wept herself. To think she'd ever, even for a moment,
considered going away. She snatched him up and hugged him,
inhaling the familiar smell of him.

It was after the baby had gone to bed that this resolve crumbled. She was alone in the flat. Dinah was on a tour of night

duties at the moment. The house was silent, except for the distant sound of a wireless. Downstairs, poor Mrs Elphinstone would be sitting alone, hoping to hear news that might suggest what was happening to her son. Restless, Beatrice turned on their own wireless and the Prime Minister's voice crackled into the room. 'Everybody is making sacrifices,' he said. She turned it off again quickly. Everybody was indeed making sacrifices. She squeezed her eyes tight shut and images of Guy and Ed Wincanton and Rafe came into her mind. Her friend Judy. And now something important was being asked of her. Michael Wincanton had as good as picked her out. She was being chosen.

Pictures spooled through her mind, newsreels she'd seen in the cinema, of marching soldiers, lines of refugees, huge-eyed children, families pushing cartloads of belongings, men covered in burning oil, screaming in the sea. She thought of her mother's family in Occupied France, of all the other families like them who were suffering. She was being given a part to play to win this war.

And yet here at home her innocent young baby needed her.

She dropped her head into her hands and wept.

The worst thing of all was that she could speak of this matter to no one. Each day for the next week, she went through the usual motions, dropping her child with Mrs Popham, going on the bus to work, shopping in the lunch-break or the early evening, putting the baby to bed. She hardly saw Dinah. And her thoughts raked deep and agonizingly into her mind.

She tried to imagine what the work Mr Potter had alluded to might mean. Would she be brave enough? It was impossible to say; only that she had no fear of the idea. She knew she was strong, physically and mentally; she had always had an innate sense that she'd get through. The important thing in life, she'd already learned, was to put one's head down and get on with the next thing. This had always worked for her. If they'd asked her, they expected her to be able to do it, whatever it was. People got on and did things; she'd seen the most extraordinarily brave people in this war, people pushed to the limits of their endurance. Why should she be excused?

She was a little shocked to find excitement in the idea. She wasn't sure how to regard this aspect of herself, whether with horror or delight. All she knew was that she wanted to meet this challenge. She wanted a more active part.

Yet as she gave the baby his bottle and watched his dark dreamy eyes as he drank; as she cuddled his strong little body, felt his chubby arms tighten around her neck, she knew she couldn't bear to be separated from him.

Gradually she started to be able to rationalize it. Perhaps she could go a little further, see what might be involved. She could always pull back; Mr Potter had given her that impression. It would be the least she could do.

Her supervisor, Miss Goodwin, a trim, efficient woman, with short greying hair and black-rimmed spectacles that she wore on a ribbon, called her into a side office one morning and said, 'Mrs Marlow, I understand your difficulties, having a young child, but I am beginning to question your commitment to your work here. You are frequently absent, and when you are here, it seems to be in body rather than in mind. One or two of the other girls are complaining that you're not pulling your weight. Now I do like to try and help if I can, dear. Is there anything that's bothering you?'

'No, Miss Goodwin. I'm sorry. I shall do my best to remedy the situation.'

'Good. I don't expect you to enjoy the job, an intelligent girl like you, but I do expect you to try your best. We all have to do things we'd rather not if we're to win this war.'

When Beatrice returned to her desk in the airless room she shared with the other girls, no one raised their eyes to smile at her. She wondered which ones had complained. *I don't belong here*, she thought, as she mis-fed a blank form into her type-writer and ripped it out again.

That evening she began to make plans.

She spoke to Mrs Popham, said she might be changing her working hours. The woman agreed to look after her son over-night very occasionally, if necessary, for a higher rate. That had to be good enough for all of them at present.

From a public phone she rang the number Mr Potter had given her, and was put through first to one switchboard, then another and another, before she heard his voice.

'Yes,' she told him, when he'd greeted her by name. 'The answer's yes.'

'I'm very pleased to hear it,' he told her. 'Now listen carefully to what I have to say. I'm going to give you some instructions. You must remember them, not write them down. It's important that you learn to do this.'

The next week was full of purpose. She had a second interview with Mr Potter, after which she resigned from her job at the War Office. 'A terrible nuisance, frankly, Mrs Marlow, but given your general attitude, perhaps it's for the best,' Miss Goodwin sighed. There were forms to sign – the Official Secrets Act – and Mr Potter said her new role required her to be a FANY, so there was a fitting for another uniform.

At this time, she learned something that strengthened her belief that Michael Wincanton had been involved in her new appointment. It was that the organization she was joining – the Special Operations Executive – had its headquarters in Baker Street. Michael knew someone senior there; she remembered driving the grey-haired soldier with the twinkly eyes. She wasn't invited to visit these offices – agents were kept away for security reasons – but she remembered they'd had no name or number. She'd met Peter outside that time. That was something else interesting.

Dinah was intrigued when Beatrice came home with her new uniform, but she was a girl who'd learned at her aristocratic mother's knee not to ask too many questions, so she accepted Beatrice's explanation – a new driving job that might occasionally mean she was away – with a shrug of the shoulders. 'I'm sorry I can't offer to look after your baby for you, but I just can't,' she said. She was filing her nails, which were always getting chipped from messing about with car engines.

'I wouldn't ask,' Beatrice said. 'You couldn't anyway, with your hours. I just need you to keep the room on for me.'

'Of course,' Dinah said. 'As long as the rent gets paid I don't mind if you're here or not.'

Anyone who didn't know Dinah might think that rather off-hand, but Beatrice was used to the way she avoided ever expressing her feelings.

Two weeks later she was idling at home when the letter she'd been waiting for arrived. It delivered a shock. She must report for a further interview, it told her, and if she passed this, she should be packed and ready to leave for several weeks' training, no mention of where. She looked across the table at the child, who was slamming his spoon on the tray of his high-chair and crowing with laughter at the noise. Several weeks. How could she leave him for that long when she'd only left him overnight once before, the time she'd had to visit Angie in hospital? She put the letter back in the envelope and thrust it into the rack. She could not imagine how she was going to be able to do this task. But as the day passed, her confused thoughts grew clearer. She would have to do it. It was her duty. It would not be for ever. But it was important in the meantime that she do her best for her child.

The more she thought about it, the more convinced she was that Mrs Popham wasn't the best person to leave him with. After all, the woman would only reluctantly have him overnight. And she'd thought of a better solution.

That evening, after he was asleep, she sat down and wrote to Angie. When she read the reply that came two days later she packed a suitcase with her son's clothes and toys and ration book, and took him down to Sussex. She returned home the next day, alone.

On the train back, the well-dressed elderly woman sitting opposite leant forward and dropped a clean handkerchief into her lap, for tears were running unchecked down Beatrice's face.

Chapter 26

September 1942

It was as though she entered another world, one in which, after a few days, her son faded into a comfortable place in her memory. He was always there, she always thought of him, but she didn't worry. Now she wasn't Beatrice any more, but Simone. In this shabby country house in Surrey with its rambling garden, or running through the fields and woodlands around, she was learning to be a different person, one with no life but the one she was being trained for, surrounded by people she was never to get to know in any proper sense, with whom she must live and work. She spoke to them in French, the complexities of which she'd half-forgotten and which at first came thick on her tongue. They were people with whom she must laugh and play and compete, but about whom she was allowed to ask nothing, and from whom she was not to expect even friendship. She shared a room with the three other women, came to know their individual habits, the position they lay in to sleep, what they muttered in their dreams, but not what their real names were or what they kept hidden in their hearts. It was a little like boarding school, but even more lonely.

She knew she was being watched, her conversations overheard and noted; she knew she was in some way being judged. And so she guarded herself carefully, as she'd learned to do since she was a child. The Wincantons had taught her well. She'd learned to fit in, to soothe friction where she found it, to be faithful and to demand little, to cheerfully endure. But she'd learned passion and determination, too. Duty for her was mixed with love. The observers couldn't see the secrets of her heart, but they saw the strength of character, her watchfulness, her powers of judgement. And she thought they were pleased.

She learned things that thrilled her: how to shoot, how to fall safely, how to set explosives, how to find her way by map and compass, but also, if needs be, by the sun and the stars. How to send coded messages by wireless, how to follow tracks whilst covering her own, how to pass unnoticed, how to answer if picked out for interrogation.

The first time she was given a revolver, she hefted its chilly weight in her hand with awe, recalling the only other time she'd held a gun: Rafe's antique pistol at Christmas in the Sussex cottage bedroom, while her babe slept and the snow fell outside. She'd felt repulsion then. Now, in one of life's ironic twists, she must learn to live with one and to master it.

The first time she fired it, she was shocked by the kick-back and dismayed at how wide of the target the bullet flew. To her surprise she found she enjoyed the challenge and quickly improved. The rifle was easier to aim, held steady on her shoulder, the sights right against her eye, but the resulting ache up her arm and neck kept her awake at night until she was used to the weight. There were other nights she went to bed covered in bruises after a wrestling bout or a bad fall.

Her weak point, as she'd feared, was running. She found she had neither the speed nor the stamina for long-distance, possibly because of her past illness, but she determined to do her best. Morning after morning, she joined the others in the cold dawn to run through misty fields or sometimes along a ridge of hills where a plain rolled out beneath. She liked it up there, not least because she fancied she could see right across to Sussex, the only time she ever allowed herself to think of her son. She was not allowed to use the telephone which, perversely, helped – and because any letter she sent out was read by someone in authority, she dared not indicate that the boy to whom she sent her love was her own child, in case they sent her home.

'It will help if you don't think about your family,' one of them had told her, not ungently, at an interview before she came, an elegant straight-backed woman with a strong, handsome face. Her name was Vera Atkins which, as far as anyone could tell, was her real name. 'We are here to support you,' Miss Atkins assured her, and somehow, Beatrice trusted her.

Beatrice strived to please these people with every ounce of her being, to run when she was past exhaustion, to shoot straighter than any of the others, to show cunning when cunning was required, and never, ever to cry out with pain. She tried not to think ahead, about how she might be required to use her training in situations of extreme danger. She'd think about that nearer the time.

One night she was awoken by the sound of weeping, and was surprised that it came from the bed of a quiet, proud-faced young woman known as Françoise. Bright moonlight illuminated the room. Some instinct told Beatrice to do nothing so she lay still, listening to the soft sobbing, wanting with all her heart to go to her and whisper words of comfort but sensing the girl would not like it. She would never know whether or not she was right. The next day, Françoise packed her case and was gone. Beatrice never saw her again.

The month raced past and the band of recruits were told they should go home and wait to hear if they were wanted. Beatrice imagined she'd stay with Angie, so she gave them the address. First, though, she returned to her flat to repack. There she found Dinah, who greeted her with unexpected warmth. She slept for fourteen hours, exhausted beyond all measure. Then she boarded a train down to Sussex.

Nanny was standing in the doorway of the cottage with the boy in her arms. When he saw his mother he gave a shout of anguish. Beatrice dropped her bags and tried to take him, but he kicked and fought and howled, and this cut her to the bone.

'He's such a good quiet boy normally, I can't think what's the matter,' Nanny cried. 'Shh, shh, little man.'

Beatrice knew. He was angry at her for leaving him.

After a while, his rage abated; he reached towards Beatrice with outstretched arms and, when she took him, buried his face in her neck. Nor would he let her go. They clung to each other as though they wanted to be one.

When she looked up it was to see Angie, leaning against the doorway to the living room, her arms folded, a curious expression on her face. She came forward and they embraced.

'Bea, you do look marvellous. Oh, sweetheart, what a silly fuss. Come here, my love.' But the child burrowed tighter into his mother.

'Darling, don't be like that,' Angie said, stroking his soft dark hair.

'He'll be all right, the love,' Nanny cooed to him. 'Such a good boy he's been whilst Mother's been away. You'd hardly know he was here most of the time. He never cries, you know. Now I remember Peter, when he was a baby. Just the same. Whilst you, missy . . .' she told Angie, with a benevolent look, 'you always made your feelings felt.'

'Oh, Nanny. What else should I have done when Ed and Pete got all the attention? Well, Ed did, anyway,' she said, moulding her lips into a soft, downward curve as she spoke his name. She looked quite thin – thin and elegant, Beatrice thought, following her into the living room.

A fire crackled in the grate, for October had brought cold winds. A clothes-horse full of little clothes and nappies stood next to the fireguard. There were toys strewn about the floor, toys Beatrice had never seen before. She sat the child down and tried to interest him in some wooden bricks, but he batted them away and crawled quickly into her lap. He'd changed so much, she saw, now he was calmer. His movements were sturdier, his expression more purposeful. 'No,' he kept saying.

'No what, darling?' she asked.

'Oh, he says "no" to everything,' Angie laughed. 'Even when he means yes.'

Beatrice could hardly keep her eyes off him the whole day. The things he could do. Walk his way round the room, if he held onto the furniture, try to put a spoon to his mouth. She'd missed seeing him learn all these things. It was painful, too, submitting to his new routine.

'He's used to sleeping by himself now,' Nanny said sternly, when Beatrice saw she was expected to have Hetty's room, Hetty still being with her mother in Cornwall. Nanny, it was, who knew the times of her child's naps, who ordered the afternoon walk with the pram and who said that he was to have no milk during the night and forbade her to pick him up when he woke briefly during the evening.

'Oh, Gerald loves him to bits,' Angie told her when she asked if he minded having him. 'He'll be home in a few days, he says, if he can get away.'

Beatrice slept like the dead again that night without remembering her dreams. Woke early, as she'd got used to doing, and let herself out in the morning darkness to run. Otherwise, she tried to lose herself in being a mother again, but all the time a part of her mind was still with the group in Surrey. She felt alert to what might happen next, restless. When she was supposed to be building a tower for her son to knock down for the twentieth time, her thoughts drifted. If they didn't want her back, then her old life could resume. But she felt disappointment at that idea, too. Her boy was all right, she told herself. He'd be all right if she left again.

Angie noticed her distraction. 'Let me have him,' she said. Now that he was used to his mother being there again, he was content to go to Angie. And Beatrice was disturbed to find that her jealousy at this was tempered with relief. She felt sorry for Angie, too. She'd noticed the girl was thin, but as she put out her hands to take the child, she saw quite how loosely her clothes hung on her. How unhappy she must be after the loss of her babies.

When she asked Angie how she was, the reaction was brittle, defensive, though she admitted that yes, the doctor said they could try again. There was no reason not to hope.

After a week, Beatrice received a letter asking her to report for another training session in a further week's time. Part of her felt a dragging reluctance, but something pulled her onwards: she knew she had to do it. She was needed. She might make a difference.

'Could you bear to keep looking after him?' she asked Angie.

'We'd be desolate if you took him away,' was Angie's reply. 'But where on earth are you going?'

'I don't know exactly. It's just training,' Beatrice said simply.

October 1942

This time Beatrice and some other agents were sent on a long and tedious train journey to Scotland. At Glasgow they changed onto a small local line, finally being told to alight at a tiny country station where a lorry waited for them. From there they were driven over unmade roads to a handsome granite house overlooking a freezing, pewter-coloured sea. In this desolate but beautiful landscape she was to spend a month undergoing a physical training that would test her stamina beyond endurance.

There was only one other woman in the group, a sturdy, plain-faced girl known as Geneviève, a year or two older than herself, with whom Beatrice shared a room – not that they were to spend much time in it.

'You girls, you're the same as the men,' was the clipped instruction of the officer in charge. 'No whining to me for favours.'

'He'll have you peeing standing up,' joked his NCO, a small dark Welshman who clearly relished his job of goading on the freshers. The women made an unspoken pact to ignore his comments, which proved the best possible course. They knew they had to be as good as the men, if not better, and not to make a fuss about it. How they peed would be the least of their problems.

It was full commando training. Twenty-five-mile treks across mountains in the dark, scaling the most impossible cliff-faces whilst weighed down with great coils of wire and weaponry, sleeping out on hilltops without blankets in the pouring rain, dragging equipment through icy rivers. In addition, they learned how to shoot a wide variety of guns, handle grenades, make bombs. Geneviève had reserves of energy and endurance that drew open admiration, even from the Welshman. Beatrice stumbled through, never quite as fast as the others in the most exhausting expeditions. It was sheer determination that got her through and it was that that they noticed.

Rarely did she have the opportunity for reflection. If there was ever the time to sit down to write a letter to Angie, or her parents, which was practically never, she could think of nothing she was allowed to say. What was more, the distance between her world and theirs was so great, she could hardly visualize them and ended up merely sending her love. More often than not she simply gave up and went to sleep. Sleep was what they lacked, and became the thing they most desired. She was amazed by the circumstances under which she found she could catnap, in the freezing cold or leaning against a tree. Even twenty minutes would restore her.

There was no time, no reason to think of her child, but there was to think of Rafe.

Once, when she battled to launch a canoe in choppy seas to lay a depth charge, a picture of that awful stormy Cornish sea flew hard-edged into her mind.

Another occasion was the climactic event of her training, the parachute jump. For this they were transported to a Parachute School in the north of England. Exercises in falling – hands in pockets, legs together, on impact rolling to the left or right – were followed by jumps in a hangar from platforms of increasing height, whilst attached to a cable. Finally, she and the others were taken up in a plane and made to do what every nerve in her body screamed against doing: dropping into empty air. The initial sensation was every bit as bad as she had feared, but she managed to jerk open the parachute and euphoria followed as she floated quietly down to a peaceful English landscape spread beneath her. Then the ground was rushing up and she hit it, rolling over into a patch of nettles, a humbling end to all the hubris.

Still, as she rolled up her silken cradle and queued to return her equipment, a sense of satisfaction swelled in her.

'Well done, girls,' the young airman said, taking her harness. 'Here's your prize.' He pushed an embroidered badge into her hand. When she looked at it she was shocked. It was an identical badge to the one that had dropped out of Rafe's pocket.

Rafe had been here before her – if not at this location then somewhere like it. And that meant – well, who knew what it meant – but she understood now what the nature of his most secret work might be and the measure of the danger he'd passed into ahead of her.

This time, when she saw her child again, he was waiting inside the door when Nanny opened it, still wobbly on his feet, but definitely standing. She crouched and opened her arms to him, the rush of love for him overwhelming.

'Sweetheart?'

He looked at her, and glanced up at Nanny who said, 'Go on, give your mother a kiss.' Again, he waited, then gave a big sigh and stepped forward into her arms. 'Mar Mar,' he moaned, pushing his arms round her neck.

'Oh, my darling,' she spoke in his ear, almost crying with relief. She hadn't realized until now how much she'd missed him.

She knew, as soon as she set eyes on her, that Angie was pregnant again.

'I'm a bundle of nerves,' Angie told her. 'Something, anything I do, might make me lose it.'

'What does the doctor say?'

'That I shouldn't exert myself in any way, and should eat well. Hah! It's all very well saying that, but I feel sick all the time.'

Angie was tired, Beatrice could see that, and since she had a whole two weeks off until her final bout of training, she decided to go home to Cornwall.

The boy was fretful on the train, unused to the noise and the people, perhaps missing Angie and Nanny for, twisting and struggling on her lap, he'd sometimes turn and look at her with puzzlement as if to say, what are you doing here? He threw the food she gave him to the floor and only settled when he had his bottle. Finally, he dropped off to sleep in her arms and she watched the passing countryside as the train travelled towards the setting sun. How ordinary this was, she thought, a mother and her child. She could hardly believe that last week she'd jumped from an aeroplane.

January 1943

'You are no longer Béatrice or Simone. Your name is now Juliette Rameau and you are a children's governess. Here, take these and study them carefully.'

She was at another country house, this time in Hampshire. At the end of the first day, Miss Atkins and the man in charge of the French operations, Major Maurice Buckmaster, arrived from London. Beatrice was summoned to see them in a comfortable book-lined room with a view across the front lawn, where she sat in front of a big desk as Major Buckmaster described her new role. Tall, slender and athletic, Buckmaster was physically like an older version of Rafe: the same fair hair, but thinning, the same sensitive, slightly puzzled look. Miss Atkins sat quietly behind the desk but he was sitting on it, swinging his legs and perusing Beatrice with a shrewd eye. She looked down at the documents Miss Atkins had given her: a French identity card bearing a photograph of her face, coupons for food and clothing, and a faded picture of two slender, dark-headed girls, presumably Mademoiselle Rameau's pupils.

'Your immediate task, *mademoiselle*,' Buckmaster said, 'is to rehearse the story of your entire life. We will help you, of course. You must know everything there is to know about yourself, the names of your grandparents, the pets you had when you were a child, where you live, what your father did . . . the list goes on and on. You must know these details so well that you will answer as Juliette Rameau, even under the greatest pressure.' He said the last two words with emphasis and they chilled her.

'That's very clear, sir, I see what I must do.'

'Do you?' he said, folding his arms. 'Do you grasp that you must learn to act as Juliette always, even if the Gestapo drag you from your bed at midnight and question you? You must automatically answer as Juliette. In effect you must *be* Juliette.'

She nodded, looking at him steadily now. 'I'm ready to start work on it as soon as I'm told,' she replied.

Miss Atkins stood with a reassuring smile. 'Come,' she said. 'We'll begin immediately.'

Chapter 27

February 1943

Four weeks later, sitting in the little Lysander as it flew over Normandy, nauseated by the smell of fuel and the vibration of the engines, Beatrice remembered this conversation. Concentrating her thoughts on what she had to do kept her mind focused and calm.

The pilot turned his head and shouted, 'There are the lights, Pickard, look,' and the man sitting beside Beatrice pushed himself up and peered over the pilot's shoulder.

'Right we are,' Charles Pickard said to Beatrice. 'Ready for landing?'

The plane slowed and began to descend.

'Easy does it,' Pickard whispered. Torch beams flashed, the plane hit the ground with a bump, bounced once and, scraping over the grass with a long sigh, drifted to a halt. Pickard was already getting the door open.

A man and a woman waiting on the cold hilltop greeted them with hugs and soft murmurs of welcome. Beatrice knew they were Pierre and Lorraine, a middle-aged couple, farmers.

Pierre dragged bicycles out of a nearby copse, and Pickard helped Beatrice strap her suitcase to hers. Then he shook her hand and wished her luck and stepped back into the plane. As they waited to wave it off, she looked about her, trying to match her surroundings to the details of the map she'd pored over back in England. They were looking down over a moonlit valley, patchworked with fields and farmsteads.

Her immediate instructions were clear. She was to return home with Pierre and his wife and try to get some sleep. Early in the morning she was to cycle the twenty miles to Rouen and board a train to Paris. 'The last time I went to Paris I was followed,' Pierre explained. That's why Beatrice had to go instead.

They cycled in the cold winter air along winding country roads until Pierre turned suddenly down an unmade lane, across a little bridge and into a farmyard. She was haunted by a sense of familiarity, and it was a moment or two before she realized it was because it was similar to her grandparents' farm. That must be thirty miles or so north of here; there was no chance at all of her being able to go and find it even if she were permitted. She pushed thoughts of her family away and concentrated on avoiding puddles.

Inside the farmhouse, as Pierre poked the fire and set a pan of onion soup to heat, the feeling of recognition came again, but this time it was accompanied by a sense of rightness that she had come. When, an hour later, she lay down in her cot-bed under the eaves, she was sure she'd be unable to sleep for nerves. Yet it seemed only a moment later that Lorraine's harsh whisper roused her. It was time to go.

She dressed quickly, in the worn navy suit they'd given her, and checked her clutch bag once again for papers and money.

'*Dieu vous bénisse,*' Lorraine muttered, as she kissed her forehead.

'*Et vous aussi,*' Beatrice replied softly. Pierre had told her the night before, whilst Lorraine had been busy upstairs, that their grown-up son, their only child, had been conscripted by the

Nazis and sent to Alsace to work in a factory, making shells. Six months ago, word had come that he had been killed – in a drunken fight, they were told. This explanation, Pierre did not for one moment believe. Raoul had been a gentle boy, not that sort at all. His death decided them. They'd volunteered for the Resistance.

Beatrice wheeled her bicycle out of the farmyard, mounted it, and wobbled off down the road. She knew where to go; she carried the map in her memory.

Some miles down the road, behind her in the distance, she heard a vehicle engine. Dismounting quickly, she wheeled the bike behind a wall and hid. It was a car, and as it passed she peeped out and saw Nazi soldiers, four of them. It was her first encounter with the enemy and it shook her somewhat. She leant back, closing her eyes, then, quickly recovering, set off down the road once more.

The country lane fed into a wider one, that eventually met a trunk road. She knew she must leave this quickly to follow a route where it was less likely she'd be seen. The sun climbed in the sky. Sometimes she passed signs of the Occupation. A burnt-out house, a dog shot dead in a ditch. Of the people she passed, some were friendly and wished her good day. Others avoided her eye. She never stopped to make conversation. It was her job not to be remembered. 'You're Juliette,' she told herself. 'It's perfectly natural that you're here, going to Paris for a few days to stay with your aunt.' All she had to do was be Juliette. They'd have to tear the lining of her jacket to discover the precious piece of folded silk she'd brought from London, or the little pill she must take if she were captured and unable to endure it.

At the station she parked her bike, but when she went to the window to buy a ticket, she saw a young soldier lounging by the door to the platforms. '*Paris, billet aller-retour, s'il vous plaît,*' she said to the woman behind the window, trying to sound confident, but her fingers shook as she searched her purse for coins.

When she passed the soldier she thought, *He'll see my fear*, but he gave her a bored look and let her through.

On the train, an old lady with a basket on her lap chattered about her daughter, whom she was going to visit because she'd had a baby, and Beatrice listened politely. Actually, the talking took the edge off her nervousness. The others around her remained quiet and watchful. When two Gestapo officers came along the corridor, looking into all the compartments, she understood why.

Leaving the Gare St-Lazare, she forced herself not to stare about her as though she didn't know what she was doing. She bought a newspaper at a kiosk, then, since there was no hurry, set off on foot for the Luxembourg Gardens. She had visited Paris only once, as a girl of seven or eight, and remembered gay accordion music, and the pretty trees of the Champs Elysées, the groups of men sitting outside the cafés laughing and chatting over carafes of wine and games of draughts. Now the atmosphere was subdued, and there were men in Nazi uniform everywhere. She knew not to meet their eyes and was alarmed when one stopped her and tried to chat, offering her a cigarette. She refused politely, as Juliette Rameau would have done, smiled and hurried on.

She reached the gardens at a quarter to three, and visited a public convenience nearby where she locked herself into a cubicle. There she cut several threads in the hem of her jacket and wormed the precious silk out of its hiding place. As she was straightening her clothes, someone tried the door and she held her breath. '*Pardon,*' said a woman's voice and she relaxed.

In the park, she found the small fountain as she'd been directed. Nearby was the bench she wanted, but an old man was sitting there. She walked on for a while, pretending to enjoy the sun and the flowers, and when she returned was relieved to see that he'd gone. She sat down on the bench, peeled off her gloves, shook open her paper and tried to read.

After a few moments, a stranger sat down next to her: a quiet, serious-faced young woman whose severe black suit complemented her graceful figure.

'*Un bel après-midi, n'est-ce pas?*' the newcomer murmured. She had lovely creamy skin, Beatrice saw as she lowered the paper. It was beautiful against the black. She noticed too that the pulse at the woman's collar beat too quickly; she, like Beatrice, was nervous.

'*Bonjour,*' Beatrice replied, as though making polite conversation. '*Vous avez lu le journal aujourd'hui?*'

'*Non, j'étais trop occupée, mais j'aimerais bien le lire.*' Good, she was definitely the expected contact.

'*Voilà, prenez-le. J'ai fini.*' She folded the newspaper and offered it to the woman, who took it, and with it, the little piece of silk hidden inside. On the silk was a hand-drawn map that another agent had brought back to London. By this circuitous route, the Resistance could plan an act of sabotage.

'*Merci, madame. C'est très gentille,*' said the woman, glancing at the headlines in a casual fashion, before putting the paper in the shopping bag at her side.

'*Je vous en prie,*' Beatrice responded politely and stood, picking up her gloves.

She forced herself to walk away slowly, though she badly wanted to distance herself from the map and the woman. The job she'd come for was done, and she felt quite light-hearted, but knew she must still be vigilant. Tomorrow night, all being well, another plane from another hillside near Rouen would take her home, but anything could happen to prevent that.

It almost did. At the gates, on some strange impulse, she paused and looked back, only to be dazzled by the sun. Walking on again she collided with someone, a man. 'Oh!' The 'S' of *sorry* was on her lips, and she realized to her horror he was a German soldier. He gripped her arm to steady her.

'*Excusez-moi, Fraulein,*' he said, and smiled at her.

She smiled back shyly, then set off once more, her mouth dry, a pulse thudding in her ears.

'*Fraulein!*' he called and she made herself turn round. He was holding up one of her gloves and there was an expression of amusement in his eyes.

'*Ah, merci,*' she murmured, going to take it from him. He was a pleasant-looking youth of nineteen or twenty and had dealt with her kindly, but this made no difference to the strength of her revulsion.

She took a different route back to the station, as she'd been briefed. She passed along a side street by the rue de Rivoli, lingering by the shopfronts, fascinated by all the beautiful things for sale. It was a toy shop that caught her eye. There in the window was a wooden engine, painted bright red. She stopped and stared at it for a moment. Why not? She opened the shop door and went inside.

'Presents! Oh, Bea!' It was worth it to see their faces.

The little boy grabbed his train with both hands and put it to his mouth. 'No, like this,' Bea said, extricating it gently and showing him how to push it along the floor. 'Woo woo!'

'Oooo,' he said, snatching it up and banging it on the ground, an expression of pure joy on his face.

Angie cried out as she unwrapped her gifts: an enamelled powder compact and a lipstick. Even Nanny had something: a warm scarf. There was soap for the household, too, and hairgrips.

'Bea, where did you get these things?' Angie asked, staring at her friend in wonder and suspicion. 'They're French.'

'It's easy if you know the right people,' Bea said, enjoying herself. How easy it was to lie now, even to friends. But she couldn't tell them the truth. It was her duty not to.

'What is it you're doing?' Angie persisted. 'Where have you been?'

'Somewhere exotic, that's all.'

'Where?'

'Miss Angie, how often have I told you not to look a gift horse in the mouth?' Nanny said, stroking the soft wool of her scarf. 'It's not for us to know.'

'I'll take them back if you don't want them,' Bea said, smiling. She'd known that she risked being conspicuous by buying the gifts, but she hadn't been able to resist.

'You will not!' was Angie's indignant response. 'But what have you got for yourself? You must have something.'

Beatrice brought out of her suitcase a tissue-paper package. She opened it and shook out a long silken dress, a lovely fragrance of Chanel wafting through the air.

'Oh, how beautiful,' Angie breathed, fingering the soft fabric. 'It's the wrong style for me, but it'll look perfect on you.'

Beatrice had stared at the dress in the shop window for some time before plucking up the courage to go inside. It was a black and gold evening dress, made of some filmy material that folded up to nothing in her luggage. When she tried it on in the dressing room, it had fitted exactly, as though made for her. 'I'll take it,' she'd told the unsmiling shop assistant. She paid for it in a cloud of elation, trying not to think that she was handing over half the money they'd given her for emergencies. She'd pay them back for it somehow, she'd told herself.

Later, she heard her mission had been important. As a result of her delivering the map, the Resistance had succeeded in blowing up a bridge over the Seine, thus destroying a vital route for the movement of German tanks.

She also learned that the shop where she'd bought the dress was frequented by Nazi officers buying gifts for their mistresses. No wonder Madame had looked at her so frostily.

During March and April 1943, Beatrice flew through moonlight on two further missions to Normandy. The first time she posed as Juliette again. She was there for a month as courier for a British agent known as Henri and his wireless operator Georges, her job to carry messages between two local Resistance groups who, she finally worked out, were in the final stages of plans to destroy a Nazi arms depot.

Two Gestapo officers who noticed the regularity with which the pretty dark-haired girl cycled to Rouen from a town fifteen miles away and back again later in the day, stopped her once and examined her papers. They found no reason to doubt her story – that she was going to her place of work, teaching the children of a lawyer in a well-respected firm, and let her go. When, the night before the raid was to be carried out, she was flown back to England, she wondered whether, after the explosion, these policemen would notice that Juliette Rameau had vanished and visit the law firm she'd mentioned to find that Julien Defours, whose name was still over the door, had in fact died, a childless widower, the year before.

The second visit was much shorter. She had to meet the

surviving members of a network that had been infiltrated, and collect a list of coded names. Radio contact was deemed unsafe, so the only way the list could be got out was by giving it to Beatrice, who this time carried false papers in the name of a farmer's daughter, Elise Fontaine.

Between missions she stayed in Dinah's apartment, paying snatched visits to Sussex, but since she was often expected to be in London for briefings or debriefings, or, once, was sent away for further training, she couldn't stay long. It was a strange existence, completely without routine or any sense of past or future. Everything was about living for now.

In the evenings she'd socialize with some of the other agents, often wearing her Parisian dress to go dancing or dine out, not caring about other women's jealous looks. They didn't know how she was risking her life. She wasn't going to dress dowdily just to please them.

These were occasions of fun and laughter. A group of them would start the evening at one of several favourite restaurants, then after dinner they'd go on to a nightclub or two, sometimes not returning home until the small hours. They were an ever-changing party, its members conversing usually in English, and known by whichever names they volunteered. Sometimes a face would be seen regularly for a couple of weeks, then simply vanish, sometimes without a goodbye. If they appeared again weeks later, they'd be greeted warmly, but no one asked where they'd been or what they'd been doing. She was always on the look-out for Rafe, but never saw him, and it was frowned upon to ask questions.

Geneviève, the sturdy-looking girl she'd met in Scotland, was a regular for a while. Beatrice knew little about her, except that her family were French refugees, but she was a pleasant companion who spoke fluent English and was an excellent mimic. She had them in stitches when she portrayed Hitler, Churchill or Lord Haw-Haw.

But there came an evening in early April when she took Beatrice aside and said, 'It's my turn again tomorrow. Wish me luck. I'm awfully nervous.'

'Oh, Genny,' Beatrice sighed, embracing her. 'Keep yourself safe, dear.'

It was the last time she ever saw her.

Her friends talked very little about their personal lives, but sometimes she'd glean little bits of information. In turn, some seemed to know that she had a child, though she'd taken care not to tell anyone except, finally, Vera Atkins. Somebody asked after him once and she said, 'He's very well, thank you,' in surprise, half-expecting him to raise the question she constantly asked herself: How could she bear to risk her life when she had a son? She had privately rehearsed an answer. It was for his future. She guessed each agent had their own reasons for being part of these special operations, each had their own private anguish, was making their own sacrifices in the fight against this great evil that lay like a poisonous cloud over the world.

There was always a majority of men in the party, and Beatrice was never short of dancing partners, but when invited to dine *à deux* she usually politely demurred, and, indeed, as the news spread that she had a child, the invitations became fewer. She supposed it put some of the men off or they made some assumption or other about her in order to placate their vanity. Respect or disdainfulness. Whichever it was she didn't care. There was none who particularly appealed to her anyway. For the truth was that that part of her, the part that enjoyed flirting and being wooed, was in suspension. She was waiting for Rafe.

It was strange to her that they never met, if, indeed, he was definitely involved in this kind of work, which she still thought he might be. Gerald said that their mother received occasional notification that he was alive, but no more. Of course, he might have been sent anywhere in Europe – or the world, for that matter.

Chapter 28

It was early in May 1943 that she was surprised and not a little disturbed to receive a telephone call asking her to go to the offices in Baker Street. She'd only ever seen these from the outside – that time she'd driven there and seen Peter Wincanton. The policy to keep agents away from the nerve centre of the organization was really very strict, so it must be something quite serious for them to summon her there.

When she announced her arrival, the receptionist sent her to an annexe across the road, where she was met by another FANY and taken up to the second floor. The lift stopped and through the latticed gate she could see a man waiting. When the FANY wrenched back the bars, Beatrice was astonished to find herself face to face with Peter.

'Peter . . .' she said. 'What are *you* doing here?'

'Bea, good heavens!' he replied. They waited for the FANY to step past. 'I work here – F section. I know all about you, of course.'

'Oh! I'd no idea.' All sorts of little clues and hints started to slide into place in her mind like so many drawers in a Chinese box. This was the mysterious job that Peter was doing. It could have been another kind of 'hush-hush' department he was working for, but by a miraculous coincidence, it was hers. But was it coincidental? she asked herself, as she said goodbye and followed the FANY down the corridor. There would be no point in even asking.

The other girl stopped and knocked on a door and Beatrice was admitted to a cramped office where the head of F-section, Major Buckmaster, welcomed her with a vigorous handshake and introduced two colleagues – a man named John Hudson, who wore a Major's stripes, and one of the clerical staff, Yvonne Andrews, a graceful girl with an expression of appalling misery on her intelligent face.

'Do have a seat, Miss Marlow. Yvonne, be a good girl and go and see that the latest message has been sent.'

Yvonne Andrews nodded obediently and left the room.

'I know this is a little irregular,' Buckmaster said, taking up a sheet of paper and perching on the edge of the desk. 'Miss Atkins would not approve, if she were here, but she isn't. We wanted to ask your advice.'

'Of course,' she murmured. 'What is it you want to know?'

'This came in yesterday,' he continued, passing her the paper. It was a teleprinter message, already decoded. 'We believe it's from our man Georges, who you met with Henri out in Rouen, but Hudson here is casting some doubt on it and we wanted to ask your opinion since you know the local set-up.' She read it quickly.

'He should have used the check code,' Major Hudson told Buckmaster. There was clearly a disagreement rumbling on between the two men.

'He should have done, I agree,' Buckmaster said smoothly. 'But the question is, was he in a hurry and simply forgot?'

'He's never forgotten before. And we issued a particular instruction about check and bluff codes only last week. You know the Germans have picked up a few people in the operation since the depot went sky high. He missed his last two scheds, too.'

'So I say he simply forgot.'

Letterbox unsafe stop, the message read. *New letterbox address 19 rue de Beauregard, repeat, 19 rue de Beauregard stop. Monsieur Vincent. Otherwise all well. Ta ta for now goodbye.*

'How do you think I can help?' Beatrice said, uncertain. The message implied that Henri's circuit was basically safe, just that new agents and equipment arriving would have to report to a new address. The question to ask was, of course, would they find the Gestapo there waiting for them?

'For a start, do you know Monsieur Vincent and the address mentioned?' Buckmaster asked. 'You spent enough time in the town.'

'I remember the street.' Off a sleepy square, lined with plane trees. 'It had several shops.' Was number 19 the boulangerie, perhaps? 'But the name Vincent doesn't mean anything to me.' She looked at him, anguished. If she made the wrong judgement she might be responsible for sending agents straight into the Nazi net.

'You probably wouldn't have been told his real name,' Buckmaster said briskly. 'At least if the address is genuine . . .'

'What did Home Station say about the Morse-code transmission?' Hudson broke in.

'Ah. They think it was Georges sending it all right, but his tapping was hesitant.'

'So maybe someone was standing over his shoulder.'

'The Gestapo?' Beatrice asked, with a prickle of unease.

'He wouldn't have used the sign-off we gave him if that were the case,' Buckmaster said.

'He might have had to, if they'd found out he was supposed to use it,' Beatrice put in.

'Possibly,' was all Buckmaster said to that. There was silence in the room. The seconds ticked past.

Finally he declared, 'Well, I say the message is genuine,' and put out his hand for the paper. Beatrice returned it to him, feeling unhappy. Major Hudson, she saw, was having difficulty suppressing his rage.

'Someone had better speak to Hugh about getting something organized,' Buckmaster said, picking up a phone. 'Hello?' he said into the receiver. 'Will you show Miss Marlow out, please?' A moment or two later, the FANY reappeared.

On the way to the lift Beatrice asked the girl, 'Would you mind if I visited the cloakroom?' She was hoping she'd have an opportunity to slip away and speak to Peter. Surely he wouldn't mind her asking about Rafe?

'Of course not. It's down this way.'

She was washing her hands, when the woman she'd been introduced to earlier, Yvonne, came out of one of the other cubicles.

Beatrice glanced at her, and saw that she'd been crying. 'Is there anything I can do to help?' she asked. 'I noticed in the office that you didn't look very happy.'

'What did they decide?' Yvonne burst out.

'I . . . I'm afraid I'm not at liberty to say.'

'Buckmaster thinks it's genuine, doesn't he?' She appeared to read the answer in Beatrice's face. 'He's wrong, I know he is. It wasn't Georges's style. He always puts something in for me – I always see it when I file the messages. You know, something personal that only I'll understand. And there wasn't anything.'

'You know him then?'

'He's . . . a friend, yes.'

'Well, why don't you tell them?'

'There'd be no point. They wouldn't listen to me. I'm not important, you see.' She stumbled out of the room. Beatrice was horrified. If Yvonne was right, whoever was sent on the next mission to Henri's circuit would be flying straight into a trap.

Miraculously, the corridor was empty. The FANY who was supposed to see her out had disappeared. Beatrice saw her opportunity and took it. She walked quickly along the corridor, glancing at all the offices until, through a half-open door, she spotted Peter sitting in a small room sifting papers in a wire tray. She knocked and slipped inside.

'Bea!' He got up, put his head out into the corridor briefly, then closed the door. 'What are you doing here?' he said, nervous.

'Shh. Listen. They're making a dangerous decision,' she said, and repeated what Yvonne had told her.

Peter listened carefully then whistled under his breath, commenting, 'Well, she's right, they wouldn't ask her. Not their style. And Hudson's very dismissive of what he calls womanish opinions.'

'But that's ridiculous. He listened to me.'

'He had to. You've been there on the ground. He'd respect that.'

'But not other women.'

'Vera Atkins, maybe. But then wait until you hear him on the subject of Jews. Very unpleasant.'

'Vera's Jewish?'

'Yes, though she wouldn't thank anyone for noticing. A dicky bird told me she's not yet a British subject and she'd be worried the authorities would force her out of her job if they knew.' He thought for a moment and said, 'But on the subject in hand ... Tell you what, I'll have a word with Buckmaster about it myself.'

'Will he listen to you?'

'I don't know. If he gets a bee buzzing in his bonnet, well, it's difficult to dislodge it. He's always liked to believe the best, old Buckmaster, you need to know that.'

'Oh, I'll remember. Well, thank you, and good luck.'

He went to open the door for her, but she placed a restraining hand on his arm. 'Peter,' she said, 'there's something else I need to know. Rafe – is he, you know, one of us? In the French section, I mean?'

'Bea, you know I can't tell you anything like that.'

'He is then.'

Peter said nothing.

'Is he in awful danger? I can't bear to think—'

'*Bea.*'

'No, of course you can't tell me. It's so awful, though, not knowing.'

'They write to his mother. She'd hear if things ... weren't going well. You're still very fond of him, aren't you?' He said this with some bitterness, and she saw, with sudden clarity, that he minded.

I carry him in my heart all the time, she thought, but all she said was, 'Yes, I'm sorry.'

He came along with her to the lift and shut her firmly inside. To make sure she was safely off the premises.

'Goodbye, Peter,' she said, through the diamond-shaped bars.

'Take care of yourself, Bea,' he said softly as the lift began to fall.

She tried not to think about Rafe and Peter, just to get on with what she had to do. Naturally, she wondered what had happened in Rouen, but there was no one she could ask – or rather there was, but she wouldn't have been given any answers. Sometimes, she knew, life was a waiting game. Her role was always vital, or at least she was led to believe this, but it was an unspoken rule that everyone involved recognized. You were only told what you needed to know. What you didn't know you couldn't betray.

She was dispatched on another training course. Three weeks in the Hampshire countryside where the hedges were radiant with hawthorn blossom and the fields lush green. As she ran down the English country lanes a sense of exhilaration coursed through her, a delight in her strength and the beauty of the world around her. She slept well, too. The important thing, she was coming to learn, was not to think of what might lie ahead but to live for the minute. Only her dreams betrayed her – dreams of darkness, of suffocation, above all of trying to run and not being able to.

She mentioned these dreams once to Miss Atkins when she visited as they walked in the grounds of the mansion.

'It does not surprise me,' Miss Atkins said. 'It's natural. But on the surface you are so calm. That is good. We cannot see what lies ahead, but we can best confront it when we are calm.' Beatrice was surprised and pleased to see admiration in the older woman's eyes. Some spoke of Vera Atkins as being self-contained, hard even, but Beatrice could sense warmth; that she cared deeply about the young girls she sent off into danger.

'Last time we met,' Miss Atkins said, 'you asked me about arrangements for your child.' Beatrice bit her lip. The woman had encouraged her to be practical, to make a will, for instance. 'Please rest assured that there would be money for him if . . .'

Though she was told nothing more, there started up in her a thrumming tension, like an electrical charge.

Miss Atkins touched her shoulder, pulling her out of her

reverie. 'Why don't you go and spend a few days with your family when you've finished here? Then come back to London fit and refreshed.'

She tried to read some hint in Miss Atkins's steady eyes, but she saw there only concern.

'Why don't we all go to Cornwall?' Angie said down the tele-phone. 'Oh blast, the line is dreadful. Can you hear me?'

'Just about,' Beatrice said. 'But where would you stay? There isn't room with my parents for all of us, I'm afraid.'

'Oh, Mummy's kept that rented house on. We'll all come, there's plenty of space. He's such a big boy now, aren't you, darling? I'll put him on if you like. Oh – too late.' They'd had the three minutes the authorities allowed, the pips had gone and the line went dead.

St Florian in May. The sky an infinite blue across which sailed glorious puffs of pure white cloud, casting their shad-ows on a glittering sea. The beach, once so dear and familiar, was now spoiled by coils of barbed wire. An old sailor showed them a safe way down to the water.

At eighteen months, her son was running for joy across the chilly sand to the sea. She chased after him, snatched him up and swung him round to dip his toes in the lapping waves, his excited shrieks lost to the wind. Precious days of joy before the lurking shadows fell.

They all stayed in the rented house on the quay. Angie, round with pregnancy now, slept every afternoon, and Beatrice took that time to climb the steep steps with her child to visit her parents. Hugh had been ill, and still had a hacking cough. He looked ten years older than his age. He still shut himself in his study after breakfast.

'What does he write now?' she asked her mother, who

fastened her with a long meaningful look and shook her head. 'I don't know,' was all she said.

They didn't press her about what she was doing, though she knew her employers must have requested their permission for her to go abroad, with her being under twenty-one. Her mother had heard nothing more of her family, but they must have been in her thoughts for she'd look at the boy and say, 'He looks like my brother at that age,' or '*Viens, mon petit* . . . Do you speak French to him? You should, you know.'

The holiday was over all too soon. The little household was to stay on, but Beatrice must return to London.

'Don't upset him when you say goodbye,' Angie told her. 'It's difficult to stop him crying sometimes after you go.'

Beatrice stared at her, tears pricking her eyes, then turned away to hide her hurt.

It was decided she would walk up to the station with her mother. When the time came she took her son in her arms and held him close. Angie was watching.

'Mummy's going for a ride on the train,' she told him.

'Train,' he said, pushing himself back to look at her. 'Train,' he said, twisting to look at Angie. 'Woowoo.' He often played with the little wooden train she'd given him.

'So you be a good boy, won't you, and Mummy will see you soon.'

'Mmm,' he said, and for one last moment he laid his head against her collarbone, his fingers clutching her shirt.

'Here we are,' she said, distangling him gently, and passed him into Angie's waiting arms.

At the station her mother did something very rare. She hugged her. '*Que Dieu te protège*,' she murmured into her daughter's hair. 'Please write if you can.'

Chapter 29

June 1943

There were two men already sitting in the room in the flat in Orchard Court when Miss Atkins led her in, Major Buckmaster and a man she hadn't met before, introduced only as Chrétien. Whether this was his first name or his surname she didn't know, but he didn't need to speak for her to know that he was French. He smoked American cigarettes throughout the meeting, lighting each one off the last, studying her with a thoughtful expression. He was a compact man of thirty or so, with thinning hair. Buckmaster didn't explain what his role might be in this interview, for it *was* an interview, she felt it in the formal way that he greeted her, and the fact that the room was arranged so she sat facing the three, the big leather-covered desk between them.

'Thank you so much for coming,' Buckmaster began. 'As you might have guessed, we have another mission for you. We've talked at some length amongst ourselves about who would be right, and your name came up. But it's something more dangerous than anything you've done before, and you'd need to be sure you think you can do it.'

He went on to explain that, as part of future plans to invade France – about which he spoke only in the vaguest terms – it was important for the Allies to prevent German Panzer division reinforcements coming up from the south. Hence certain

SOE circuits were working with the grassroots resistance in the south-west to stop the tanks.

'They're a hot-headed lot, the Maquis,' he explained. 'They're brave, no doubt about that, but they're difficult to control. There's some nasty rivalry between groups and some of them are frankly Communists.'

'What is it you'd like me to do?' Beatrice asked.

'There's a circuit that needs a courier – someone we can rely on. But I must stress that you don't have to go if you don't want to. You've already done your bit.'

'More than your bit,' Miss Atkins murmured.

'Do you worry that I might not be good enough?' she asked them.

'No, it's not that at all,' Buckmaster said. 'It's . . . well, we've lost some good people. I need to tell you this.'

'You must think about it carefully,' Miss Atkins reiterated, 'before giving an answer.'

Beatrice considered. *Your name came up.* 'I'm not seeking compliments, but may I enquire why you thought of me? Are there particular skills that you're seeking?'

Buckmaster glanced down at the paper on his desk but Miss Atkins continued to look at her steadily.

'*Mademoiselle.*' Chrétien spoke for the first time, in a deep, smoky voice. '*Savez-vous la région Limousin?*' When she answered, '*Non, Monsieur Chrétien*', he chatted with her for a while in French about her experience and training. *But they already have all this information*, she thought.

Finally, he said to the others, 'Her accent.' He blew through pursed lips. 'It's just about good enough,' and she understood that he had been testing her French.

Chrétien stubbed out his latest cigarette, stood up, gave her a little bow and left the room.

'Who is he?' she asked the others.

'He was out there till last week. We had to pull him out,' was all Buckmaster said. 'And he knows Florian.'

'Florian?' She was instantly alert. *St Florian*.

'He would be your organizer.'

'That's . . . not his real name.'

'Of course not. It is, however, believed that you might know him.'

'I think I do,' she breathed. She felt strangely dizzy.

'That could be useful in this particular case. You'd be living at close quarters.'

She knew for certain now. It was Rafe.

She would have said yes anyway, before she'd learned about Rafe. But knowing made her sure.

'You must think about it overnight,' Buckmaster said.

'I don't need to,' she replied. 'I'll go.'

Beatrice had never been more certain of anything in her life.

Victor pushed the crate to the edge of the hatch and tipped it out into empty air. Together they watched its parachute open, far below. Beatrice readied herself to follow.

'*Now!*'

And closing her eyes, Beatrice let herself drop. Felt terror as the air rushed past, then, after her silk cradle ballooned out and she was floating down, exhilaration. She opened her eyes. Spread beneath her in the moonlight was a wide plain patterned with fields and hamlets. Snaking across this vista was a river, glistening silver. The sound of the plane's engine had died away now. All she could hear was the wind. And now the ground rushed up, slamming into her legs, knocking the breath from her as she rolled. She sat up and, unbuckling her harness, looked about; was relieved to see Victor, his parachute collapsing as he landed, a hundred yards away. There came a cry; she stood up quickly as two figures separated themselves from a dark line of hedge. She tensed, then relaxed as Victor called, *'Salut!'* and each man echoed his greeting.

The older man made his way across the muddy wheatfield to help her. Victor and the other man hunted for the crate, which they located and loaded onto a waiting handcart.

The moon had begun to sink in the sky by the time they reached a farmhouse several miles away. Once inside, a smoothly rehearsed operation saw the contents of the crate unpacked and whisked outside somewhere. A sturdy woman, the wife of the older man, set out bread and bowls of vegetable soup. When they'd eaten, she beckoned Beatrice upstairs and showed her into their bedroom to change. On the wall above the bed a wooden Christ hung in agony.

'Dépêchez-vous!' Victor called up the stairs. They were to move on at once to another farm where they would be able to sleep for a few hours. Then Beatrice was to go on alone.

'J'arrive!' she called back. She breathed an entreaty to the crucifix, glanced at her face in the mirror, seeing it small and pale and set, and went forth.

Nobody found anything odd about seeing a strange face on market-day, which is not to say she wasn't noticed, especially by the men, despite her plain dress and black cardigan and the fact that she was dusty from riding in the haycart. Beatrice ignored them, instead wandering amongst the stalls, testing the fruit, haggling for some strawberries, which she bought to appear normal. Even here, in this small town, there were German soldiers loitering, or passing down the line of stalls, stopping occasionally to buy a trinket. Beatrice saw how most people moved out of their path, refusing to look at them.

It was getting towards late morning now; the heat was building and some of the stalls were packing up. Beatrice slipped away, heading for a street on the far side of the square. She was looking for a certain small café. There it was, with the picture of the cockerel over the door and a couple of kitchen chairs lined up outside. She parted the bead curtain and stepped inside.

It wasn't much of a place, being poky and dark, but at least it was cool. Two old men were playing cards at a table. A thin dog lying beside them got up, stretched, and came over to sniff at her, in a rather bored fashion, before returning to its place. She went over to the bar where a woman of forty with a big round face and heavy black hair in a net was polishing glasses. She looked Beatrice up and down with an impassive expression.

'Bonjour, madame,' Beatrice said. 'Je voudrais parler avec Madame Girand, s'il vous plait.'

'Attendez, mademoiselle.' The woman's face was still stony, but she laid the glass on a shelf and went off readily enough through a doorway behind. As she waited, Beatrice glanced around the café. It was then she noticed someone sitting in the darker recesses of the room. He was a youngish man, clean-shaven with cropped hair, and wearing an office suit. A small leather briefcase was propped against his chair. His glance rested briefly on her then slid away again. Its effect was disturbing and she wondered what he was doing in a shabby place like this, rather than the smarter café on the square.

The dour-faced woman returned, and behind her came another, this one wiry and friendlier, her greying hair tied up in a bun. She came straight round the bar and embraced Beatrice as though she were a long-lost cousin. 'Paulette, ma petite!' she cried. 'Comment vas-tu, mon ange? Et ta mère – elle va bien?' She hustled Beatrice, or rather Paulette, through a small kitchen, along a hallway, and through the back door into a shaded yard with a couple of dustbins.

'We're almost there,' she whispered, leading Beatrice out into a dusty lane that ran along between two lines of buildings. She knocked on the back door of the house opposite and they waited for what seemed a long time.

Finally the door was unbolted and opened to reveal an old man in shirtsleeves and braces, whose sad jowly face reminded Beatrice of the French General she'd once driven in London. '*Entrez, entrez, mesdames,*' he murmured, and once they were inside, pumping Beatrice's hand, he added 'You are very welcome. My name is Gaston. Brigitte, some coffee for our guests, perhaps?'

Mme Girand, Brigitte, took Beatrice's small bag, whilst her husband, who limped slightly, showed Beatrice down the hall and knocked on a door at the front of the house. '*Elle est arrivée,*' he called. Then he opened the door and stood back to let Beatrice go in.

She walked into a small sitting room. A man was rising from his seat at a desk. When he saw her he froze, his face a mask of shock.

'Hello, Rafe,' she said, in English.

'Bea,' he said finally, his voice full of horror. 'What the hell are *you* doing here?'

'I came to help you,' she said. 'You don't seem very pleased to see me.'

With a sudden cry, he crossed the floor and took her in his arms. They clung to each other as though to life itself. She closed her eyes and breathed in the familiar smell of him.

After a few moments he gripped her shoulders to stare into her face. 'I am pleased to see you, of course I am, but I'm horrified, too. I can't believe that they sent you.' His voice was rough, passionate. 'You must go back. We'll tell them it's too dangerous. How did they put you up to this?'

'They didn't. There was no pressure. They explained that it was a courier job and I told them I wanted to come. When I heard it would be with you . . . there was no other possibility. I had to, Rafe.'

He dropped his hold of her and said harshly, 'You must go back.'

'Why? I can't, anyway.'

'Charles will be here soon. He can send a message.'

At that moment there came a tap on the door, and Brigitte entered carrying a tray of coffee. 'I will show you your room when you're ready, Paulette, and perhaps you'd like to sleep.'

'Thank you, *madame*, but I'm not at all tired. It is so kind of you to have me here.'

The woman smiled, but Beatrice saw the tension in her face. 'You must call me Brigitte.' She poured milky coffee for them and withdrew.

Rafe took his cup and went to stand at the window, which looked out onto fields, apparently deep in thought. He looked sad, she thought, sad and worried. His gold hair was lustreless, and his face had a greyish tinge as though he didn't see enough sun.

He turned back to her and tried to smile. 'How are you anyway? And the boy? I still can't believe you're here . . . it's a miracle.'

'He's well, thank you. Shouldn't we speak French? Are we . . . are we safe here?'

'Is anyone listening? I shouldn't think so, but who knows these days. It's been awful – I can't tell you, Bea. It's difficult to know whom to trust. Oh God, you shouldn't be here. I'll feel so responsible . . . if anything happens.' He covered his face with his hand.

'You'd feel responsible no matter who I was,' she pointed out.

'Yes, of course,' he muttered.

'Rafe,' she said, touching his arm. 'Listen to me. It was my own decision to come here. Your circuit needs me and I shall help you. It's as simple as that. Do you think I can't do the job, is that it? It's not my first mission, you know.'

'No, it's not that, Bea. Damn it – Paulette. I can't imagine how you got yourself into the show in the first place. It's all too bloody dangerous, I tell you. You've no idea what they'll do to you if you're caught.'

'Yes, I do,' she replied. 'Those little pills they gave us aren't sweets, you know.'

'God in heaven,' he breathed. 'Don't even think about that.'

'Of course I've thought about it. I've thought and I've thought and I've thought. If they catch us – well, it would hardly be a tea-party, would it? They'd want to know everything we could tell them. That's what the pills are for, in case we found we couldn't stop ourselves telling. But I don't think I would take mine. I'd want to stay alive. For the boy.'

'But you know their methods?'

'I think so,' she said, her voice faltering.

'Well, you're a fool to come, then. You'd have done your best for your son by staying at home.'

'That's a cruel thing to say. Don't speak like that!' she cried. 'I can't bear it. You mustn't even mention his name to me. I won't have him connected with anything to do with what's happening here.'

'I'm sorry,' he mumbled, looking startled.

'At bottom I'm here for the same reason you are. To win this war. And I can be as good as you are here. Better, in fact. They won't question a girl. That's something I noticed immediately

– there are so few young Frenchmen here that if you see one, he stands out.'

'True. They've sent them all off east, to work in the factories. You're right – I'd be stopped if I go out, so I don't. But, Bea, surely you know what happened to your predecessor?'

'They didn't say.'

'They should have told you. Well, listen . . . I sent Genny down to Périgueux with a message for a Resistance cell there.'

'Genny,' she echoed. 'Geneviève?'

'Yes. A tallish, well-built girl with heavy eyebrows, quite a self-possessed type.'

'I knew her, Rafe. Oh, you'd better tell me, I suppose it's awful.'

'The Gestapo walked in on their meeting. One of the Frenchmen went crazy and started shooting. That's all our informant could tell us. But she's dead. I'm sorry.'

'Poor Geneviève,' Beatrice whispered. 'How did they find out? The Gestapo, I mean.'

'That, of course, is the question, and I wish I could answer it.'

'They don't know about you – us, I mean.'

Rafe shrugged and turned his attention to the view, his breath misting the window as he said, 'We told London, naturally, but they don't seem to think there's a problem. At any rate, they've gone ahead and sent you.'

'Oh. I'm hurt that they didn't tell me. About Geneviève.'

'I'm not surprised they didn't,' was all he said.

Chapter 30

June 1943

One evening, Beatrice stood at the back door, watching the bats flit amongst the trees. She felt as though she'd lived on the edge of this little French town for a long time, with its houses of shabby grey stone that were shuttered into silence in the midday heat, and its marketplace where the old men played boules between the rows of pollarded trees in the late afternoon. Once or twice she'd stepped out with Brigitte to buy food, to make her presence seem ordinary. Her cover was that she was the daughter of Brigitte's cousin from nearby Nexon, come to help Brigitte and the other woman, Marie, in the café, now that Gaston was finding it too much.

She'd met some of the others in the cell, too. Charles, the wireless operator, lived in one of the tiny rooms over the café and, like her, was half-English. Stefan, whose ugly scowling face hid a shrewd mind, owned the garage. He brought to the operation an extensive knowledge of the area, a rich vocabulary of profanities and an ability to strip down a gun and clean it with remarkable speed. She'd been introduced, too, to a couple of men from surrounding villages, and the local doctor, who would get into long, time-wasting arguments with Stefan about who in the wider group could and couldn't be trusted. The two men hated one another for some reason that Beatrice had never got to the bottom of, but that Rafe thought concerned Stefan's wife. The two Frenchmen were bound into loyalty to one another in their loathing of the occupying forces, but Rafe found it very difficult to manage them. Beatrice, whom they called Paulette, was the only woman. She sat silently in the long candle-lit sessions, listening to their plans, for the moment lacking the knowledge to comment. Yet they treated her with a rough respect for they needed her, needed her badly, to take out messages across the surrounding region.

She'd only been on one such mission so far, on Brigitte's bicycle one morning, with two baguettes sticking up out of the basket, to take instructions to the farmhouse where Victor was hiding out. It was about the onward movement of the cache of weapons they'd brought with them on the plane. The journey there had been entirely uneventful; on the way back two young Germans on motorbikes had made catcalls to her as they passed, but she'd ignored them and they sped off without bothering her further.

In general, it was seen as quite natural that Brigitte Girand's young cousin should be seen out on errands. She played the part of a shy young thing, which excused her from saying much. At some point it would be natural that she'd want to take the train to visit her family back in Nexon, perhaps, or even her great-grandmother, Brigitte's aunt, in Limoges. Even someone with a suspicious mind was unlikely to make much of the matter.

In the daytime it was a useful cover to be seen working behind the bar in the café, bringing carafes of wine for the old men and listening to the gossip.

Café le Coq wasn't a place the Germans cared to frequent; it was too homely, and too tucked-away. They preferred the more stylish place opposite the tiny town hall in the square, where they could see and be seen. Mostly it was the same old locals who frequented the Coq, but still, Beatrice's nerves were always as taut as piano strings.

This particular June evening, watching the sun dipping over fields, and little dots of glowworms beginning to shine in the grass, Beatrice's mind began to wander. She started to think of home, and she knew she mustn't, for the rush of longing was overwhelming. She hastily went back inside to her room. It depressed her, with its bare floorboards, the narrow bed with its lumpy mattress, the cracked bowl and ewer on the chest of drawers and the wooden chair that wobbled noisily if she sat on it. Worse, it was lit by a dim ceiling bulb that flickered maniacally. Sometimes the electricity supply would cut out altogether, leaving her with a candle that smoked horribly and made her head ache, so that it was almost preferable to go to bed in the dark.

She had just finished washing her face when there was a soft knock at the door. 'Dinner's ready,' came Rafe's voice.

'I'm coming,' she replied, but by the time she opened the door he'd gone downstairs.

She frowned. Since that first meeting, he'd been avoiding her. Well, not avoiding her, exactly; after all, they had to work together, and he certainly spoke to her and took every care. But he was aloof, withdrawn, and this hurt her. She couldn't understand it. She knew he was under a terrific strain – that greyish pallor never left his face, and tiredness and anxiety were etching furrows on his forehead.

She sensed that life here was worse for him than for her. After all, he could never go out without attracting attention because all the young men had been sent away into forced labour, and, yes, she had to admit it, he was English-looking. He had only to open his mouth to confirm that he wasn't French. And there were things he couldn't tell her; she knew it was policy even here, in the midst of their activities, not to let others know more than they needed to play their own parts, in case they were picked up by the Gestapo. What they didn't know, they couldn't tell. Rafe would know everything, she guessed, and he kept it from her. For her protection, yes, but it was hard having so much between them.

After that first day he'd been punctilious about speaking in French to her. He rarely talked to her about anything to do with their normal lives. Here they were Florian and Paulette, and she felt terribly, terribly lonely.

She pushed her feet into the pair of house shoes Brigitte had given her – worn slippers bulged out by Brigitte's bunions – and went downstairs.

'That man came into the café again today', Brigitte told her husband.

'What man?' Gaston growled. He mopped his face with his napkin and broke off another piece of bread, which he dipped in his stew.

'You know who I mean.' Brigitte addressed Beatrice, who nodded. It was that smartly dressed man she'd seen on the day she arrived, sitting in the shadows. Today he'd ordered coffee in French that was fluent enough. No one knew his business, but Marie said she had seen him coming out of the police station, so they suspected the worst.

'There's something wrong about him,' Brigitte declared, shaking her head. 'Anyway, I don't like him.'

'You don't like all sorts of people,' Gaston said.

'Being suspicious saves lives,' Brigitte riposted and started collecting up the empty plates with unnecessary bangings and fumblings.

Gaston winked at Beatrice, who smiled politely and looked at Rafe. Rafe looked more worried than ever, but, *'C'était deli-cieux, merci,'* was all he said as he passed his plate to Brigitte and looked up at the clock on the wall. There was to be a meet-ing tonight.

Later, they sat round that same table over tumblers of red wine: Rafe, Beatrice, Charles, Stefan, the doctor and a couple of others. Stefan had brought along a man only he and Rafe had met before – a great burly type with a handsome hook-nosed face, thick dark hair and eyes that flashed in the lamplight. Beatrice wondered if his ancestors mightn't have been Mediterranean pirates.

'There are difficulties.' The *maquis* leader rapped his fingers on the dining-room table as he spoke. 'The others want to do things differently.'

Rafe sighed and said, 'Somehow we have to work together. You know the plan; you'll have to talk them round. This is not something I've come up with – I've got my orders from further up. They must know that.'

Stefan swore violently under his breath. 'They're a lot of country bumpkins,' he almost shouted. 'Concerned with their own petty quarrels. How can we stop the Nazi pigs if we all think of ourselves, huh?'

The stranger's eyes flashed dangerously.

'Thank you, Stefan,' Rafe said quietly. 'It won't help to insult others. But I have to tell you, Charles heard again today: we're to continue with the plan, no changes. Now perhaps we could look at the details again.'

Beatrice didn't know the exact location of the bridge that was to be blown up, but problems had arisen because of tighter German security, and it seemed that there was a certain hot-headed proposal from this Resistance cell, whose job was to carry out the mission, that involved storming a German position. This was almost certain to end in failure, if not in exposure of the entire operation. They had to be dissuaded from doing this at all costs.

She listened to Rafe's quiet but firm voice as he soothed the visitor, praised his cell's courage, appealed to the man's pride, then twisted his words in such a way as to make the man not only accept the official line, but also make him believe that he'd come up with the idea in the first place.

'It's important that your group be seen to succeed in this mission,' he told the *maquis* leader. 'When the war is over, the people will look to men such as yourself for leadership, not only because of your bravery but because of your cleverness.'

'Yes, yes,' the man said, 'and we will make sure that they do not look to us in vain. The needs of the ordinary working man will be met. First we'll deal with the enemies within our ranks, and the collaborators. You know —'

'Of course you will. But that is for the future,' Rafe said, a tad impatiently. 'Now we must address the present, so you will go back to your men and tell them that the original plan is the one to follow. Is that understood?'

'Yes. You can rely on us.'

'I know we can. Now, that girl who told you about the shift changes, can you go back to her . . .?'

When the official meeting broke up two hours later, Beatrice crept exhausted to bed, leaving Rafe, Stefan and the *maquis* leader still talking below.

A week later, Beatrice got off a train in Périgueux and walked down a long shadowy street to a square in front of the cathedral. She was supposed to turn up one of the smaller roads off its north side in search of a particular address, but she did not dare because as her journey had progressed she'd become more and more certain that she was being followed.

It was the man she'd seen on the day she'd arrived at Café le Coq; today he didn't have his briefcase with him, but she'd noticed him pass her compartment in the train, and that's when she'd started to feel uneasy.

By the time they reached Périgueux she'd almost dismissed her worries, but then she saw him ahead of her on the platform and had hung back, waiting until she thought he'd gone. But walking up the long boulevard to the cathedral square she'd turned round a couple of times and seen him. She'd quickened her footsteps and decided she'd stop at a café to see what he would do next. Outside the smarter of the two cafés in the square, two Nazi officers stood talking and laughing with an elderly but elegantly dressed Frenchman. She passed on to the smaller, shabbier establishment, sat at a table outside, ordered coffee and, while she waited, contemplated the cathedral, a rather astonishing building that combined a square, pineapple-capped bell tower with a roof of nipple-like domes. She was just thinking how alien it was after English Gothic when she caught sight of the man who'd been following her. He was standing at the edge of the square, looking straight at her.

What he did next was surprising. He came over to the table and asked if he could join her. She looked about quickly. The café was busy, so it would have been rude to say no, and anyway she couldn't think of a reason that wouldn't rouse his suspicions. So she shrugged and, as he pulled out a chair, stared out across the square.

'You think it's ugly, *n'est-ce pas*? I see it in your eyes.' Brigitte had been right about his odd French with its hard rolling Rs. She wondered whether he might be German.

'Excuse me?'

'The cathedral. You don't like it.'

'What's wrong with it? It's just the cathedral. I was daydreaming. Is it a crime now to daydream?'

The waiter arrived with her coffee and the man ordered some for himself. 'I will pay for the lady's coffee,' he said.

'Oh, no.'

'Ah, why not. I wanted to talk to you. I've seen you in Café le Coq.'

'I work there.' She was watching the Nazi soldiers, who were now shaking the hand of the elegant old gentleman and walking away.

'My name,' he said, 'is André. And you, I've heard them call you Paulette.'

'Yes,' she said. 'The café belongs to my cousin and her husband.' If she tried to sound outraged at his audacity then maybe she wouldn't sound nervous.

'But she is not really your cousin.'

'What a thing to say! Of course she is. Not first cousins. That is, she and my mother were.' She was worried now.

'No. You don't need to say anything more, but I think we both know what I am talking about.'

Beatrice gathered her things and stood up, trying to look very young and very shocked, but he put a hand on her arm and said, 'It's all right. Your secret is safe with me.' His eyes flickered across the square to where the German soldiers now stood watching a group of children playing hopscotch.

'I must go,' she said. 'You are being very rude.' The grip on her arm became more forceful. She sat. There was nothing else she could do.

'Now, Paulette,' he said. 'There is no need to do anything silly, is there?'

'I ought to go,' she repeated. 'My mother said . . .'

He threw back his head and laughed, a rolling, carefree laugh. Then he leant forward and whispered, 'Your mother is a long way away, is she not? In England, perhaps.'

She grew still and he released her arm.

'Let me make myself clear. I am not one of them.' Again, he glanced at the soldiers. 'Nor am I one of you, if you get my meaning. But I want to be. I want to get to London and I need you to help me. I help you and you help me, do you see?'

She looked at him blankly.

'I need to get to London,' he repeated.

'Why?'

'You don't need to know that. I have been watching and biding my time. I would like your friends to telegraph London for me and say that I have vital information and that I need to be flown to England.'

'I don't know what you're talking about,' Beatrice said. 'You're frightening me.'

He gave her a freezing little smile. 'I think you do,' he said.

'I must go now. I have an appointment.' She opened her bag and from her purse laid out several coins on the table. Meeting his eyes she said, 'Goodbye. If you follow me, I . . . I will call for help.'

He smiled again and fear shivered through her.

'What did he want?'

'I've told you. He said he wanted to get to London, that he has information.'

'Well, this is a disaster. He's guessed who you are.'

'Not who I am, just that I'm not who I say I am. Oh, I don't know.'

'You did the right thing, at least,' Rafe said. He was trying to soothe himself, she thought, as much as her. They were in the small parlour, where she'd found Rafe when she returned. It was here that he spent most of his time fretting over papers on the desk or, like now, pacing the floor, or sometimes just standing by the window, his hands in his pockets, staring out over the fields.

'What else could I do?' After she'd left the man who called himself André, she'd picked at random one of the small streets that led off the square and hurried up it, then turned left and right several times before getting thoroughly lost and having to ask her way back to the station. It had not been possible to deliver her message.

'What should we do?'

Rafe thought for a while. 'We'll have to get a message to Buckmaster, see what he says. And we'd better find out all we can about this chap. I'll get Stefan to put a tail on him. And in the meantime . . .'

'What?'

'We'd better carry on as we are. He might just be a bit mad, or operating on his own, as he says. We've no reason to suppose he knows about anyone except you.'

'Well, of course he must, or he wouldn't have been sitting there waiting when I came in through the door on the first day. Oh, Rafe.' She stood before him, staring down at his unhappy face. 'And no, don't tell me I shouldn't have come. That's not what I'm worried about. It's the success of the mission that concerns me. I've only just got here and I seem to have ruined it already. It makes me boil.'

'It's hardly your fault,' Rafe said, hands in pockets, his expression grim. She longed to reach out and put her arms around him, to comfort him, but something in his demeanour warned her away. Nothing felt natural here; there was always the sense that they were being watched, that the enemy could knock on the door at any time and they'd be discovered. It had already happened once or twice in the town. There'd be some hushed conversation in the café about this or that family or individual arrested or sent away somewhere. People would be taken without warning and sometimes without trace.

In the end, the vital message to the house in Périgueux was delivered by other means. André was not seen in the café for several days, but even this made Beatrice nervous. The report came from Stefan that the man was living at a hotel in Limoges. The Germans seemed to let him come and go without harassment.

Just as she was starting to tell herself that he'd given up on her – decided he was wrong about who he thought she was, or accepted her rejection – there he was, sitting at his usual table and smiling at her as he ordered his usual coffee and glass of water. She acted as her alias would have done, tossing her head and refusing to meet his eye, then hid in the kitchen and considered what to do. 'Act normally,' was her decision. However, when she ventured out once more, he'd gone, leaving her a ludicrously large tip.

'Here, you have it,' she said to Marie. 'I don't like him.' Marie put the money in her purse in the twinkling of an eye.

After that there was no sign of André for a long time.

'They don't think anything of it in London,' Charles told her one afternoon, showing her the message he'd transcribed. 'Just that we must watch and see. The man is probably a maverick and not dangerous.'

'How do they know that?' she wondered aloud.

'Perhaps that is what Rafe thinks, too,' Charles replied with a shrug. But Beatrice was not reassured.

It was hard keeping the peace between the different ideologies in the movement. One of the cell near Périgueux had befriended a woman cleaner at the big guardhouse near the bridge, and she'd found out useful information about night patrols. The other members of the cell were impatient to go ahead, but Rafe was trying to persuade them to wait. There was a wider timetable that should not be jeopardized. The atmosphere of the meetings was dark with argument, and sometimes Beatrice, feeling her presence wasn't important, avoided them and crept away to her room, though her sleep was broken by the rumbling of voices below. Once there was a crash, as of a chair falling.

Her dreams were troubled. Often there was that old one of trying to run and getting nowhere. Sometimes she was trying to save Rafe, sometimes her child, sometimes just herself.

There were quieter evenings, too, when the five of them – the Girands, Rafe, Charles and herself – sat together in the kitchen talking after supper was cleared away, or in the parlour, airless, for they had to keep the windows closed, trying to tune into the BBC on the wireless. Finally, there came a message they'd been expecting. 'Antony to meet Cleopatra tomorrow night,' the announcer said. Stefan was dispatched with a second man to the field where Beatrice had landed, to pick up another crate. The mission passed without incident. Beatrice was sent off into the countryside the following day on her bicycle with a message for the *maquisards* about its arrival. The contents of the crate were moved on.

The weather grew hotter, the air thick and heavy. Faraway thunder rumbled, the tension in the air was palpable. It was impossible to sleep and she felt constantly headachey.

One hot night she lay restless, the window open, a net stretched across to keep the insects out. Nothing could keep out the moon, though. It shone through the crack in the shutters onto a gecko splayed motionless on the opposite wall of the room. Some small animal scrabbled in the roofspace above. She listened to it patter about its business across her ceiling and thus didn't hear other footsteps, outside on the landing. But she did hear someone knock lightly on the door, and sat up, her heart thumping with fear.

The latch was sprung and the door swung open. 'Bea?' He came quietly into the room, his lithe figure in the long nightshirt striped with moonlight. The door closed softly behind him.

'Rafe. Is something the matter?'

'No. Sorry if I frightened you. I couldn't sleep.'

'Nor can I. It's too hot.'

'I got up for a drink of water, then I thought, well . . . I'd see if you were all right. It's oppressive, isn't it?' There was a huskiness in his voice. She heard him swallow.

'Come over here,' she whispered, and he came and knelt on the floor by her bed so that he was looking into her face. His, she saw, glistened with water, or was it sweat? She wrapped her arms around him and drew him close and they sat like that for a while until it grew too uncomfortable, so he got onto the bed and lay beside her. Gently at first, then with increasing passion, he kissed her. His hands began to move over her body and she rolled towards him, wanting him desperately, hardly believing that the moment had come at last.

Later, as they lay in each other's arms, she said, 'I've wanted this for so long.'

'Have you?' he said, his eyes glinting. Eventually he said, 'Me too.'

'I didn't know,' she whispered. 'All I could see was that you were tense and unhappy.'

'There's no one I can talk to about it, Bea. Not even you.'

'You don't have to reveal secret things, but you can tell me about how you feel.'

'No. I want to be strong for you, not make you frightened.'

She laughed at that. 'How could I be more frightened than I am? Rafe, I know exactly what could happen to me. There's no point trying to protect me from it. We're in this together all the way.'

'I want to protect you,' he said.

They lay together, not feeling the need for any more talking. The creatures in the roof settled into silence, perhaps aware of the coming storm. Outside, the little rolls of thunder were grumbling louder and closer, and though the moon no longer shone, the room was periodically lit by lightning. Then came the first urgent taps of rain.

Rafe drew the sheet up over her shoulders and together they lay listening to the storm as it passed overhead. The air became cooler, less heavy, and eventually she slept.

After that night he often came to her. Her room had the advantage of being further away from the Girands', but his had a double bed. Once they were embarrassed to meet Mme Girand in the corridor, but she merely murmured, *'Bonne nuit,'* and retreated to her own bedroom.

They went downstairs the next morning feeling very nervous about what might be said, but the woman was exactly the same with them as she always was and the matter was not mentioned, so after a while Rafe's room was where they spent the night. It was, Beatrice thought, like being in a sort of haven together where they could, for a short time, be blissfully happy.

At first they didn't talk much; it was as though they lived entirely in the present – alive to a creak of the stairs, or the distant sound of a vehicle or the warning bark of a dog a mile away. Here, at least, the weight of the past had fallen from their minds. There was only the work they had to do, and the delight of exploring each other.

'Do you think of home?' she asked him once, but he shook his head.

Once she woke in the small hours to find he was awake, too, lying quietly, just watching her in the half-darkness.

'What is it?' she whispered.

'Nothing,' he said. 'I like to see you sleeping. You look so peaceful.'

Rafe, on the other hand, was a restless sleeper. There was another time she awoke in pitch darkness to find him gone. She panicked, got up, found the door was open and slipped down the stairs. It was such a relief to glimpse him outside at the edge of the cornfield, pacing up and down, the tip of his cigarette glowing fiercely. Not wanting to disturb him, she padded upstairs again to bed.

Once, after they'd made love, he clung to her so tightly it hurt. 'I love you,' he mumbled. 'I still can't believe you're here.'

'Oh, Rafe, I love you, too. But I worry . . . will it be different when we're back in England?' If they ever got back, said a little voice in her mind.

'All I know now is that I want to be with you always,' he said, and she was almost but not quite comforted.

July 1943 moved slowly by and something in the air was changing; Brigitte and Gaston sensed it, the old men in the café felt it. German patrols passed through more frequently; there was a house-to-house search one market-day, ending in a whole family being taken away, their crime being to hide a Jew. Then Stefan brought word that the man he'd had followed, André, had vanished, and enquiries at the hotel led nowhere. He'd simply paid up and left.

'The tide is turning out there. They're getting frightened.' Gaston's solemn pronouncement followed the news filtering in of the Allied invasion of Sicily.

'They'll tighten the screws here, then,' Rafe replied, and indeed the hope in people's eyes was tempered by fear. The Resistance might be growing bolder, but everyone was afraid of reprisals. And so the tension grew.

Chapter 31

'Bea, get up!' Rafe was shaking her awake. There was the sound of banging, shouting all around, coming from downstairs. A woman's voice – Brigitte's – could be heard, high-pitched, screaming. Beatrice knew what she had to do. Her hand closed on her pistol under the bed, her ammunition belt. Then her jacket – she pulled it on – and shoes. Rafe, already dressed, wrenched open the shutters. He said, 'You first – hurry.'

It was all familiar from the training. Step on the chair, swing over the windowsill, hang down, jump, knees together, into the darkness. And she was rolling amongst the weeds, getting to her feet, then stumbling over a low wall and away, running through the cornfield. She could hear Rafe behind her, then his jacket brushed against her arm. 'Over there,' he gasped. She swerved towards the hedgerow and a copse of trees, blacker shapes in the blackness.

Bright beams of light, the crack of gunfire. Now they were out of the cornfield and treading on loam. When they reached the copse she looked back. Half a dozen torchbeams were searching the field; the man with the gun was out in front.

Beyond the copse lay another field, then, she knew, dense woodland and, some distance off, the river. 'This way!' she cried. Into the field she ran, Rafe just behind her. A bullet sent earth flying up into her face. She cried out, brushed it away, still running. Her breath came in heavy gasps now. The ground changed again under their feet and they were dodging past trees, their clothes catching on undergrowth. She mustn't look behind or the torchlight would blind her.

She was beginning to see quite clearly in the darkness. They found a path and ran along it, all the time alert to the sounds of pursuit. They came to a lane, crossed it, and cut along the side of another field under a line of poplar trees.

To the right, the land began to slope downwards. Rafe overtook her and veered out into the open and down the hill. The response behind was more cracks of gunfire before the dip took them out of sight of their pursuers. There was a brighter sound, the rush of running water. The river! Her heart leapt with hope. On they ran.

They crossed another lane by an old farmhouse, setting dogs barking, then climbed a wooden fence and struck out once more into scrubby woodland. The rush of the river was all the time growing louder. There must be a weir. Now she saw Rafe's purpose. She remembered from her briefing that the river was quite wide at this point, and shallow, with lots of forested islands; surely there would be plenty of opportunity to hide. And now they were nearly at the water. She could hear it, frothing and churning. She was right, there must be a weir, though it was too dark to see it through the trees.

Pain ripped through her ankle and the ground slammed into her chest. 'Bea, no, get up!' Rafe cried, and she felt his arms around her, hauling her to her feet.

When she put her leg down the pain in her ankle was excruciating. 'I can't,' she sobbed. 'You must go on.'

'Don't be stupid.' He tried to drag her, but she resisted.

'Leave me, Rafe. It's your only chance.'

'No.'

'Rafe, this is not about us,' she said, struggling. 'I'll be all right; I can talk myself out of it. Go, for God's sake, or they'll get us both.' And the whole thing would be doomed.

'I won't leave you.'

Torchlight strafed the trees above and shots exploded all around. Rafe bucked and cried out, and it was with a sense of desolation that she saw the darkness claim him. She prayed he'd not been badly hit. She rolled over behind a tree, stood up on her good foot and fumbled for her gun.

When the first white-faced figure came at her, she took steady aim and pulled the trigger.

It was his expression in the torchlight before she fired that fixed forever in her mind. He was a young man, as young as Rafe, with Rafe's gold hair, and his face showed utter terror. Then it flowered with blood and he fell.

She was aware of someone behind her, felt a great crack to her head and for a time knew no more.

She came to on her back in an open truck. Her head ached, her ankle burned with pain, her wrists were bound tightly behind her. Something heavy pinned her legs to the floor. When she moved her head to see, she realized with horror that it was the body of the poor boy she'd shot.

'*Get down!*' came the order in German and a vicious jab in the chest cut off her breath. She lay still, aware of her tormentor's rifle still hovering above, waiting for an excuse to hit her again. The vehicle changed gear and roared on, bumping over the country roads. Soon the vibrations changed and she saw the passing silhouettes of buildings. Eventually the truck rumbled to a halt. Another soldier came to help remove the body, then they seized Beatrice and tried to make her stand, but her ankle crumpled, making her scream with pain. They half-carried her through a small door in a huge, dark building. For the first time she felt real fear.

They dragged her down a dimly lit corridor past a row of cells, all of them closed, until they reached an open door at the end where they took her in and laid her on the concrete floor. There they untied her and retreated. She sat up as a wardress appeared, a muscular German woman, who stripped her of her jacket, trouser belt and shoes, and searched her with rough hands. Then she, too, left, locking the door behind her.

Alone for the first time since her capture, Beatrice inspected her ankle gingerly, wondering if it was broken. It was certainly swollen and, when she tried to stand, it wouldn't take her weight. Her head still ached from the blow.

She took the measure of her surroundings. The cell was about three yards square. The only window was too high to see out of, though it threw stripes of pale dawn light across the floor. No chance of escape there.

A thin straw mattress lay against one side wall, a metal bucket at the other. She crawled over to the mattress and curled up to gather her strength and to think. *Rafe*. She prayed that he was still alive; that he had got away. But what had happened to Charles, and to the Girands? Desolation crept over her. She didn't know where she'd find the strength for what would happen next. Whatever that was. It struck her that the suicide pill had gone with her jacket. That decision had been made for her, then.

She must have slept for some hours, despite the pain, for suddenly the light from the window was brighter and sound from the street came to her ears.

A few minutes later, the cell was unlocked and two policemen were admitted.

'Get up,' one said in English.

'*Excusez-moi?*' she responded, slipping into her part.

'I said get up.' He hauled her to her feet. She cried out, but found she could just about stand if he held her.

'*J'ai mal à ma cheville,*' she cried. '*J'ai besoin de voir un medicin.*'

'Later,' he said. 'I think it's not broken.'

Each taking an arm, they conveyed her out of the prison, across the square and into a grim three-storeyed house that was guarded by more Gestapo.

She was taken to a room where a senior officer with a broad fleshy face sat behind a large desk, and was helped into the chair opposite. The man pulled a notepad towards him and took up an expensive-looking fountain pen.

'Good,' he said in English, surveying her calmly. 'Now, we talk. Tell me your name.'

'*Je ne parle pas l'anglais,*' she replied, looking him in the eye. His eyes were very pale blue; the whites reddish from tiredness. Now he grew irritable.

'It is useless to pretend. We know you are English.'

'*Je ne comprends pas. Parlez en Français,*' she persisted.

He sighed. 'So we play it your way. *Bien. Parlons français.*' His next question threw her. 'You know André Mansart.' He spoke in French now.

André. The man in the café. He could only mean him.

She pretended to consider. Every nerve in her body was alert. What was the best answer? 'No,' she replied.

'I think you do.'

'I don't.'

'What is your name?'

'Paulette,' she told him.

'Paulette,' he repeated, shaking his head. But he removed the top from his pen and made a note on his pad. 'Paulette who? And where do you live?'

She remained silent, deciding that she must still pretend to be Mme Girand's cousin, but that she shouldn't let out information too eagerly.

'*Mademoiselle*, I should tell you that we already know more about you than you think we do. If you give me correct answers, you will find that everything will be simple and straightforward and you may go home very soon.'

Bea thought this very unlikely, but perhaps it was worth pretending to go along with this line for a while and see what happened.

'My name is Paulette Legrand,' she said hesitantly. 'I live in Nexon with my family.'

'Then what are you doing living with er . . .' he consulted an earlier page of his notepad '. . . the Girands in Saint Pardoux? It is no use denying, since that is where they said you were last night.'

'I am staying with her for a while to work in the café. Her husband is unwell and can no longer do much. She needs help, and my mother sent me.'

'And your mother's name is . . .?'

'Félice.'

'And her address in Nexon?'

'Nineteen rue Saint Juste.'

He put down his pen and said, still in French, 'I think we will find that there is no road with that name. Now why don't you drop this pretence. We know you are English.'

Her head began to pound harder, but she forced herself to keep looking at the German.

'No. You are wrong. I'm Paulette.'

'And what was Paulette doing, running away with a British spy? And why did she have a firearm, hmm? Where did she learn to use it?'

'I'm not saying any more,' she replied. 'You talk in riddles and won't believe me when I tell the truth.'

'What is the truth?'

'That I'm French. That my name is Paulette.'

'Yes, yes, and Paulette has killed a hero of the German nation. You are not the innocent young girl you try to make out.'

'If you won't believe me, then I will say nothing more. Except that I need to see a doctor. My ankle really is very swollen.'

'Yes, yes. So, you will not be unduly alarmed then, when I tell you that the body of the man you were with was pulled out of the river last night.'

Beatrice froze, a voice screaming in her head. *He is dead. Rafe is dead.* No, it was a trick, it had to be. She forced a shrug and heard herself say, 'I don't know who it is you mean.'

At this the man appeared to give up. He screwed the top back on his pen, stood up and went to the door. He opened it and spoke to someone waiting outside. In the brief moment that his eyes were off her she struggled to master herself. Rafe was not dead. She refused to believe it. It was the only way she could go on.

They returned her to her cell and dumped her on the mattress, but it seemed they were determined not to let her be. Every few minutes someone came to disturb her. First the woman who'd searched her the previous night. She brought water, bread and a bowl of fatty soup that Beatrice could not eat. Then a guard, who walked in and stared round the cell, as though checking that she couldn't escape. Then, at last, the doctor arrived. He was an old Frenchman with thinning silvery hair. He was fearful of the guards and wouldn't look her in the eye. First he examined her head, where she'd been hit, then tutted at the state of her ankle, manipulating it and getting her to stand.

Finally he said he didn't think it was broken and ordered a cold poultice to reduce the swelling. The wardress tried to stop him giving her a bandage. 'I'm not going to hang myself with it,' Beatrice said, angry, and eventually the woman gave in. 'Take these aspirin for the pain,' the doctor murmured, before packing up his bag. 'I will ask to see you tomorrow.'

Tomorrow. She was losing all sense of time. She lay down to get what sleep she could. What seemed only a short time later, but was probably late afternoon, the Gestapo officer summoned her for interview again. She held stubbornly to her story.

This time, when she returned to her cell she was pleased to hear the soldier who escorted her say the word 'Resistance' to the wardress. If she'd instilled a doubt that she was English then she'd done well. Her life might still be on a thread, but she hadn't betrayed the others and the Germans might just deal more leniently with her if they thought she was a rebellious French girl than if she was a British spy.

Her feelings of relief were quickly stifled. The next morning when she awoke she was taken from her cell to a waiting car.

They told her she was being transferred to Paris.

And so the nightmare deepened.

A gruelling 200-mile drive across France, then the car turned down a long avenue of trees ending at the heavy gates of a monstrous prison building. Once inside she gave her name as Paulette Legrand. They wrote it in their book. A dumpy woman in grey SS uniform marched Beatrice down an underground passage, then up a long metal staircase off which ran floor after floor of corridors caged with iron bars. They went down one of these to a wretched little cell. There the woman stripped her naked and searched her, then gave her different clothes of a coarse material, ordering her to put them on. When she asked to keep her underclothes, the woman answered her with a slap across the face. The door clanged shut and she was alone.

This cell was worse than the last, draughty, for the tiny window was broken. Plaster peeled from damp walls. There was an iron bed with a lumpy mattress, a broken chair and a dirty bucket. That was all. Beatrice lay down on the bed and wept.

The next day, the process was reversed. Along the corridor, down the staircase, through the underground passage and out into the fresh air, where a long black car awaited. And so, once more, Beatrice entered Paris. There were the lovely gardens, the long boulevards, the elegant shops, but none of these for her now. Yet the building in the grand street running off the Arc de Triomphe where the car drew to a halt was not as she expected. This was no dark prison or functional police head-quarters, this looked like a grand palace. How appearances can deceive.

They took her up a wide staircase to the fourth floor, and into a splendid, high-ceilinged office. The man behind the desk, who stood at her entrance, did not have the appearance of the monster she expected, instead being young, good-looking and dressed in a tailored suit rather than uniform.

'Come and sit down,' he murmured in English, and dismissed the men who brought her. She sat on an upholstered chair and looked about, her fear temporarily allayed. It really was a beau-tiful room, with silk curtains at the windows and old paintings on the wall. All this spoke of civilization, of graciousness.

'I expect you know why I've asked you here.'

'*S'il vous plaît, parlez français.*'

'I think you must give up this pretence. I can assure you that we know all about you.' There was something about this voice, suave, assured and dangerous, that inspired fear. He laid his fingers on the edge of the desk, very lightly, like a pianist poised to play. It was a gesture of total control.

'Miss Marlow. It is Miss, isn't it? I believe you are not married.'

She couldn't stop herself staring at him in horror. *'Comment? Qu'est-ce qui se passe?'* she managed to whisper. She waited for him to mention her son, but thank God he didn't.

'You see? We know everything about you already. We know about your operator, Rafe Ashton, we know the man you call Charles. We know a very great deal, Miss Marlow. Your mission is, how do you say, full of leaks. Your leadership too trusting.'

She pressed her lips together and said nothing, but knew her dismay must show.

He pulled a folder towards him and, opening it, took out a small rectangle of card. This he passed to her. 'You know who this is.'

She found herself staring at a picture of her mother. Her mother at twenty, riding a hay-wagon, laughing. 'Pretty, no?' The officer's eyes sparkled.

'What does this prove?' she said in French, but a sense of dread stole over her.

He sat back in his chair as though to enjoy the full effect of his words. 'We paid her family a visit,' he said, and she almost gasped. 'Your grandmother and your Cousin Thérèse are, shall we say, enjoying a little holiday with us.' His thin pale lips curved in a smile and she stiffened and stared down at the photograph, trying to control herself, aware that he was watching her like a leopard with its prey.

Finally she said, in English, 'My family are nothing to do with this affair. It is me you must deal with, only me.'

'Then in your hands lies their fate,' he said briskly. 'But, please, things are not so bad. If you help us then you, too, may return home. Since we know so much already, there is no point in withholding anything else from us. We will find out somehow.'

'I won't tell you anything,' she said.

'I think you will. It is obvious that your masters care nothing for you, since they have been so lax about security. There are these, for instance . . .' From the folder he withdrew two sheets of paper and gave them to her. 'We have copies of all the radio messages.'

She read them quickly in growing alarm. How did they get hold of these? Did this mean they'd captured Charles? One was a transcription in which Charles had asked London what to do about André. The reply seemed to her now horribly glib: *We know nothing of Andre, stop. See what you can find out about him, stop. He may be useful.* Useful, yes. But to whom? Had he been acting by himself or was he working for the Nazis?

The police officer chuckled, as though enjoying her discomfort. She pushed the papers back on the desk.

'What we want from you,' the man told her, 'is names. Names and the details of plans. Where the stocks of weapons are kept, which targets are involved. By telling us these things, you will save lives. These rebels are but a fly on our operations, but they are a nuisance and we are determined to stamp out this kind of trouble. In the long run you will see it is for the best.'

'I don't know anything about plans and targets,' she told him. 'And I wouldn't tell you even if I did.' She looked down again at the photograph of her mother, still cradled in her hands. 'So you see there's no use trying to get at me through my family.'

He put out his hand for the photograph.

'No, I'm keeping this,' she told him, with a lift of her chin. She would rather tear up the photo in front of him than return it into his keeping.

'Have it,' he said. 'Maybe focusing upon it will make you see reason.'

'I am already clear in my mind,' she said. 'Did you not hear me? I know little and will tell you nothing.'

The man's smiling expression did not change. He rose and shook a little bell and two soldiers came in. For a moment she wondered what was happening but he merely put out his hand and said, 'Thank you for coming to see me, Miss Marlow. I'm sure we shall meet again very soon.'

She ignored the outstretched hand and turned to go. Then remembered something. 'One thing,' she said, turning back. 'The wardress in the prison. Last night she struck me in the face. It was cruel and quite unnecessary. I would ask that someone speak to her about it.'

'I am sorry to hear this. Leave the matter with me,' the officer said, unblinking.

Beatrice wondered if anything would be done, but she felt better having said it.

As the door of her cell clanged shut, Beatrice sank down on her bed and for a moment gave in to an attack of wild despair. What was she to do? She had no idea whether Rafe was alive or dead, no idea whether she should concentrate on helping her family. She was quite sure the officer was telling the truth, that her cousin and grandmother were in custody. She imagined this prison contained others like them, hostages. She tried to think calmly. Where should her loyalties lie?

If the enemy knew as much as they seemed to about the activities of her operation, would she really be betraying her country to fill in a few details and save her family? Her whole operation was blown, and surely safe houses would have been closed down by the remaining members, and people sent into hiding – if they hadn't already been arrested. And yet . . . she thought of Stefan and the doctor and the pirate-man. They all had families, too, and yet they'd struggled against the occupying force in such a brave, almost reckless fashion. If she said anything that put even one of them into danger, it would be the same as saying that their sacrifices were worthless. In what book was her family worth more than theirs? At least her child was safe in England.

Her thoughts were broken by a heavy trundling noise, then came a bang on the door. The peephole opened and a bowl of something steaming was pushed through onto a little ledge, followed by a lump of greyish bread. She went to fetch it, not realizing until now that she was ravenous. She forced herself to eat the horrible stew slowly, moistening the bread with it, silent tears pouring down her face all the while.

Afterwards, still hungry but too exhausted to care, she lay down and slept, a fitful sleep full of terrible dreams. Once she woke and it was pitch black and her ankle was throbbing. She needed to turn over but she couldn't move. It was as though the darkness were pressing down on her, stopping her from breathing, stifling all hope.

She must have slept again, because she was woken next by a man's shout beyond the tiny square of window, where pale daylight now gleamed. Another shout came, then a shock of gunshot and a thin, animal cry that tore at her soul. She staggered over onto the chair and tried to see out of the window, but the only view was of the brick building next door. Marching footsteps and men's guttural voices echoed upwards from the yard. Then came other cries. For a moment she couldn't make them out. In her inward eye she saw the soldiers untie the bodies and take them away. She slumped on the chair and raked her hand through her hair, again gripped by a terrible despair. The cries came from all around now, from other cells, she realized. *'Vive la France!'* they were crying and her heart leapt.

On the wall by the chair someone had written something in tiny faded handwriting. She had to twist her head to see, and after several attempts managed to make out the words.

Quand j'etais jeune, je gardais les vaches.
Maintenant les vaches me gardent.

When I was young, I watched over the cows.
Now the cows watch over me.

It was the last time she was to laugh for quite some time.

Later that morning – she was already losing a sense of time – the wardress came to fetch her. There was something in her eyes that made Beatrice wonder whether she hadn't indeed been spoken to, but there was no repetition of the rough treatment. Beatrice was taken to the same office in the Gestapo Headquarters in Avenue Foch, to meet the same man, but this time the atmosphere was different. Although the man spoke as quietly and politely as he had the day before, there was an underlying tension.

Again, he asked her to give him names and the details of Resistance operations in Southern France. Again, she said no.

'I'd like to show you something,' he said, going to open the door. 'Come.' He waited courteously for her to go through first, then led her up a flight of stairs to another part of the building. Here he opened some double doors with a flourish, and she was shown into a beautiful chamber that was clearly used as a conference room.

Her eyes were immediately drawn to a great map of France on one of the walls, and it was this that the officer had brought her here to see. As she got close enough to read, her resolve almost left her. At the top of the map was Major Buckmaster's name, and spreading out beneath it, like a great spider web, was a chain of command that named all his circuits in France, their organizers and wireless operators. So it was true. They knew everything. But no, they didn't. Again, the thought of Stefan and his comrades-in-arms kept her strong.

'And you will recognize this, perhaps,' the man said, going to a sort of sideboard, opening it and bringing out a heavy object the size of a shoebox. Of course, to an untutored eye one wireless set might look very much like another, but Beatrice knew where she'd seen this one before: in Charles's room over Café le Coq.

'I know what you're telling me,' she said in a colourless voice. 'Is he still alive?'

'I'm afraid it is I who asks the questions. Now, are you ready to talk to me?'

She looked up again at the chart, at Charles's name under Rafe's, and decided.

'No,' she said.

Although he said nothing, merely turned on his heel and told her to follow him, she could tell he was furious. Back in his office, he picked up the telephone and rapped out something in German. Soon, two guards arrived and again she was led away.

'This is not the way to the prison,' she said in French to the man sitting next to her in the car. 'Where are we going?'

He ignored her as the driver took a route through a mass of side-streets, finally stopping outside a grim-looking concrete building in a narrow, shadowed road.

'What is this place?' she asked in increasing alarm, but again she was ignored. She was hustled out of the car and inside the building. There, two guards escorted her up several flights of stairs, along more corridors, until they stopped outside a door and without further ceremony, pushed her inside. She stumbled, but when she turned to ask where she was, it was already too late. The door slammed shut and she was alone.

Alone – and yet, in this shadowy room she sensed the presence of others, those who had been here before her and whose pain and sorrow had been absorbed into the atmosphere. And as she glanced about, the voices of the ghosts began to speak through writing on the walls. Above the bed someone had pencilled in English *Never confess* and *I am so afraid*. By the door: *Catherine, je t'aime. Adieu, mon amour*. Almost worst was a simple calendar labelled July 1943, marking off the days in crossed-through blocks, each completed block meaning five. Four vertical lines: on 29 July it had ended. She tried to calculate the date and thought it must now be . . . no, 30 July! She stared at it in horror, wondering what had happened to the unknown person who had been here until yesterday, then searched around for something that would make a mark. Finally, she found a bit of soft grey grit that enabled her to complete the block, gaining a tiny satisfaction from the task.

She'd just laid the grit down on the floor where she could find it again, when there came the urgent sound of footsteps outside, then of a bunch of keys and the lock turning. The man the guard brought in was her interrogator from the Avenue Foch.

'Ah, Miss Marlow. I hope you are comfortable in your new premises?' His manner was the same as ever: polite, suave – even warm, as though he really did care whether she was comfortable.

'What do you want?' she asked.

'You will come this way, please.' She stood and made to follow him, but suddenly her limbs felt terribly weak. She concentrated on the hot throb in her ankle, finding it gave her courage.

The guard opened a door to a large square room with windows all around. A tall figure of a man was silhouetted against the light. And at the sight of him, Beatrice felt a terrible animal fear. She could not, would not enter, but stood obstinately, her hands on the doorframe, until the soldier pushed her over the threshold. She fell against a table. On it was laid a collection of cruel-looking metal tools. And the wall above it was splashed with red-brown stains.

Firm hands pulled her up and sat her in a chair. The guard tied her wrists to the armrests and her legs together above the ankle. The face of her interrogator filled her line of vision. She stared into those calm blue eyes, knowing he could save her. He said, 'Miss Marlow, Beatrice, all you need to do is tell us the things we wish to know. The names, please, you know the ones I mean. And details of the plans. It's very simple.' His voice was low, reassuring.

Her lips quivered. Part of her wanted to tell him. She couldn't see the man standing behind her, but every bit of her body sensed that he was there. Finally she gained enough control of herself to say, 'No. I'll tell you nothing. NOTHING.'

His face suffused with anger. 'Miss Marlow, by whatever means, we will get this information from you.'

Her response was to spit in his face. He recoiled, wiped his face with a handkerchief, then gestured to the man behind her, who moved over to the table by the door so she saw him clearly for the first time. Under his white doctor's jacket he wore a suit. The trousers had sharp creases and his black shoes shone. When he came towards her he carried a pair of cruel-looking pincers.

The guard stooped and pulled off her shoes. She struggled but they held her down; she went rigid with terror, and swallowed her breath.

The pain, as they ripped out her toenails, was worse than anything she'd experienced. She tried to scream, but the guard clapped a hand over her mouth. She bit the hand as hard as she could. A man's high cry of outrage and the hand smacked her.

'Give me the names of the people who helped you,' the interrogator said very gently. 'One name and we will stop. Come, Miss Marlow. *Bitte.*'

She shook her head frantically and closed her eyes, rocking herself against the waves of agony. Someone seized her other foot and again came the torture. This time she heard the ripping of her flesh.

But still she would say nothing.

She made no mark on her cell calendar for the next few days, for light and darkness merged and faded as she lay in agony on her bed. She was aware once of a man with careful hands anointing her feet and dressing them with bandages, but mostly they left her. The food came and was taken away uneaten. She could not sleep, though she'd doze, and when she did, the lost voices in the cell spoke to her, soothed her, bade her be strong.

And then the Gestapo officer came again. Two soldiers seized her and back they took her to the torture room. This time the man in the suit took an electric branding iron. He lifted the shirt from her back and pressed the iron to her flesh, and she shrieked at the most exquisite pain. After that she sank into kind oblivion. When she swam back to consciousness, it was only to pass out again with shock, the smell of burning meat filling her nostrils.

And still she would not tell them what she knew.

They took her back to her cell. Now she could only lie on her front and sob as the doctor treated her wounds with something that stung. He murmured soft phrases in German as though she were a child, and she sensed that he was doing his best in the midst of the horror. The whole world was pain and confusion and she did not know who she was any more. She'd wake from visions that she was looking down on herself from above: a slug-like creature on the bed, black and naked. She had no identity, only a single will – *that she would not speak.*

Twice more they took her to that room, but the second time was different from all the others. The white-coated man held a syringe and thrust its needle into her thigh. She must have passed out, because the next thing she knew she was again in her bed, the blanket flung across her. After this, they did not come for her any more and she supposed they'd given up. So she came to wonder what the injection had been, and what she might have told them under its influence.

Chapter 32

Once the worst of the pain receded, dread poured into its place. It took many days for Beatrice to train herself not to tense at every footstep in the corridor, and as daylight drained from the cell each evening, she threw up a prayer of acknowledgement that she'd survived.

But darkness brought different terrors. Tomorrow, it might be her turn to be seized from her sleep and marched down to the yard below at dawn, tied to a post, blindfolded and shot.

She tried to calm herself by imagining that she was somewhere else; riding Cloud over the cliffs by Carlyon in the wind and the rain, kneeling amongst the rockpools looking for mermaids' palaces. Tasting salt upon her lips, stroking Jinx's oily hair and feeling the wet roughness of his tongue. How happy she'd been there, she knew that now. Her spirit roamed every part of St Florian; her feet walked the cobblestones by the quay, her fingers twisted the wiry sea grass. She remembered the chalk and leather smell of Carlyon's schoolroom, the view of the croquet lawn, Angelina's bewitching laugh.

She tried to think of them all now, of her son running around, but he would look different, she couldn't imagine how, and this upset her.

They'd be worried about her. Miss Atkins might have written to her parents. She tried to project her thoughts to let them know she was still alive. This made her feel a little better.

She had no idea if Rafe was alive or dead, in prison or free. She'd done all she could for him, to the utmost of her being, but she dreaded the worst. Since they had Charles's radio and if, under the influence of some chemical, she'd given out names, then . . . she didn't dare to think.

And so she'd sink into a restless sleep full of dreams of falling, or trying to run. Sometimes she'd see the face of the young man she'd killed, his face naked with fear before it bloomed red. She often thought of him; tried not to think of his mother, opening the telegram with the news.

And she remembered that snowy Christmas in Sussex, when she'd taken up the silver pistol and pointed it at the mirror. How different she was now from the Beatrice she'd been then. *Thank God the future is shielded from us*, she thought as she lay in the post-nightmare dark. And now, though her memory focused on the crucifix on the wall of the Limousin farmhouse, she could not pray.

August 1943

One morning there were no executions, and she woke late and listened to the far-off clamour of the city and the clanking of the pipes, then sat up and listened more intently. There was a pattern to the clanking. Someone was spelling out letters and words in Morse. *'Il y a quelqu'un?'* was the message she strung together. She waited, listening, wondering if it were a trick, or if the message was for another prisoner, but after half a minute the message tapped out again.

She rolled over, loosened a small key from the chain that helped hold the bed together and quickly tapped on the pipes with it. *'Oui.'*

A silence then, *'Where are you?'* also in French.

'I think third floor looking west.'

'Me too but second floor.'

Her downstairs neighbour!

She was ready to tap again, but a message came quick on the heels of the last. *'Careful, the pigs might be listening.'*

'Yes,' she replied, eager. What should she say? *'What shall I call you?'* Real names could be dangerous. On the other hand, if she gave a name recognizable to the Resistance, she might learn of others she knew.

'Michelle,' said the pipe.

'Paulette,' she replied.

'How long have you been here?'

'A fortnight, maybe. And you?' She was getting faster doing this now, more confident.

'Three weeks, I think. What have they done to you?'

She didn't reply for a moment, then tapped, *'It's better now.'*

'Me, too,' came the reply, then the rapid tap, *'Go now.'* Someone had come.

Beatrice felt strangely elated after this conversation. She had a friend. Someone who had suffered as she was suffering.

In the weeks ahead she had many conversations with Michelle and gradually learned nuggets of information about the progress of the war: the Allies had bombed Hamburg and Rome. Mussolini had been ousted by his own monarch. There was information, too, about others in the gaol. Her own pipe, it seemed, was at some cul de sac of the plumbing system, because she was never able to 'talk' to anyone else. Michelle however had contact with the cell next door, and through the woman there to a wider network, including some of the men. There were mostly French here, although she had heard of an Englishman known as Alain who had some sort of spyhole in the wall of his cell from which he had a view of the main staircase and, through which he somehow managed to pass notes. The name Paulette seemed to mean something to Alain, though Beatrice had never heard of him, and occasionally there would come up to her via Michelle news of someone familiar to her from the agent training school, or from that social time in London. Through the metallic grapevine she asked for news of Rafe and of Charles. Charles, she was told, had been seen in the Gestapo lock-up in Limoges, but not after that. There was never anything about Rafe.

One very awful morning she was woken by the sounds of activity in the yard below her window, followed by the cracks of gunfire. She at once tapped a message on the pipe for Michelle but there was no answer. She tried several more times that day, but there was nothing. She never heard from Michelle again. In her honour, she wrote on her wall with the little scrap of grit: *In memoriam Michelle, my friend from the cell downstairs. Never to be forgotten. Vive la France.* And the date, *2 September 1943.*

Two days later, it was her turn to be taken from her cell. 'Where are we going?' she asked the guards in panic, but as usual they ignored her. She didn't know whether or not to be relieved when they escorted her out of the front door of the prison and to where a bus full of prisoners stood waiting. They were being taken to Fresnes, the word eventually got round. They were driven out of Paris, back down the avenue of trees to the great prison. The same cell with the broken window, the same rough wardress, the door was slammed shut . . . and Beatrice was alone with her despair.

She started a new calendar on her wall with a stub of pencil she picked up in a corridor. Months passed. September, October. There were no books for Beatrice to read, no paper to write on, nothing to do but play games in her head. The only contact with others were the sporadic Morse code messages, the occasional outbreak of community singing, usually brutally cut short by the guards, and the longed-for daily exercise in the yard, where the prisoners were not permitted to speak, but sometimes managed to.

None of this was enough. Her wounds had gradually healed, but in November she became ill with depression. She could survive the bad food, the harshness of her captors, got used to the winter nights shivering under a coarse blanket, having stuffed the broken window with cardboard. It was the fear and the loneliness that gradually undid her. In the depths of the night, voices started up in her head, mocking her. No one who valued her knew where she was. She'd been dumped in this prison because the Nazis didn't know what else to do with her. The Gestapo officer had been right. She'd been forgotten. It was the ultimate betrayal.

Christmas came and went and the prisoners stubbornly sang carols to the chagrin of the guards. She pencilled in the new year, 1944, with a feeling of desperation. At the end of February she sensed the nights becoming milder.

One day in March she was lying on her bed thinking of nothing, lacking the will to move, when a bee began to fly around the room. She raised her head, wondering where it could have come from, and realized the card on the broken window had slipped. The insect circled about a few times then came to rest in a patch of light on the wall above her bed.

She sat up and studied it closely as it cleaned its wings. It was a honey bee, its pouches heavy with nectar, and she wondered where it had come from and so early in the year. On the bus journey to the prison in September they'd passed orchards dotted with late-summer flowers, and the bee brought back the memory. She thought too of the faithful Wincanton heraldic bee, and Mrs Wincanton's attempts to bind her to the family. Beatrice believed she'd done her best by Angelina. Yes, she'd been that faithful bee. She'd been faithful to others, or tried to be, as far as she could. To Rafe, and when she thought Rafe was lost, to Guy. She thought of her son, of how she'd kept him, not given him away. There might be some who thought she'd betrayed him by leaving him to do war work. 'We all have to make sacrifices.' That's what everyone had said, the government posters, the women in the queues for rations, the men who went away to fight . . . Only her son might not understand that. He might just feel betrayed.

She hadn't often wept here, fearing they'd see her tears as a weakness, but now the little bee was blurred by them. Suppose she never saw him again, or Rafe, or her family? After that first meeting with the Gestapo interrogator he'd never mentioned her grandmother or her cousin, and she wondered whether he had lied; whether they were still living safely on the Normandy farm.

The bee took off again, looking for a way out. She pushed her chair beneath the window and pulled the card off. After a while the bee found the hole and flew away.

She went over to the wall and drew another line on the calendar. Eight months she'd been in captivity. Yet she knew that the tide of war was inexorably turning. Last September, the news in the exercise yard had been that Italy had declared war on Germany. In November it was rumoured that the Soviets had won Kiev, then, after Christmas, that they'd liberated Leningrad. There was a growing sense of excitement and hope.

Everybody believed that an Allied invasion of Europe was only a matter of time. And in April 1944, the Occupying forces in France started to move imprisoned British agents east into Germany.

There was no warning. After breakfast one morning in April, the wardress gave Beatrice time only to put on her shoes, and a guard waiting outside escorted her down the metal staircase, through the underground passage and into the reception lobby, where several other women had gathered, all of them dazed and anxious.

'What's happening?' one asked her. She recognized her from the exercise yard, a dark-eyed, gentle-faced woman known to her as Madeleine.

'I don't know,' she whispered back, and the guard pushed them apart with a shout:

'No speaking!'

Outside, they were herded into a battered bus and driven for miles across the countryside. 'Well, we're still alive,' she managed to murmur to Madeleine. 'Maybe they're moving us to another prison.'

'Maybe,' came the reply. 'Perhaps they're nervous. The invasion will come soon.'

The bus came to a stop outside a rail station in a small town. There was another bus just pulling away and on the platform a group of male prisoners, some wounded, all as shabby and emaciated as themselves, were being corralled onto a waiting train by armed police.

As she watched, trying to see if she recognized anyone, one of the prisoners suddenly broke away from the group and started to sprint along the platform. The police opened fire; he dodged onto the track behind the train. Three or four policemen set off in pursuit, some of the others redoubling their efforts to load the prisoners onto the train.

Beatrice was standing at the back of the group, and now everyone was looking at the escapee, running down the track, the bullets sending up clouds of dust behind him.

Then she realized. No one was looking at her. For a second, time stopped. She moved quietly like the shadow of a bird, back through the doorway of the station, and waited. Nothing happened. She glanced across to the ticket-seller's window and met the eye of the young man who sat there. Fear shot through her. But then he signalled to her, and disappeared. A second later the door to his office opened and he ushered her inside. He shut the door, and started moving cardboard boxes from under a desk. She crept into the hole he made and lay down on her stomach while he replaced the boxes. Then, through a little chink, she watched him retake his stool at the window.

Outside, the shooting had stopped but the commotion continued, with shouting and running footsteps. Train doors slammed. A whistle, a whooshing sound and the roll of heavy wheels. The train chugged away. A moment later a bus engine started up, then eventually there was silence. She wondered what had happened to the man who'd run away.

The ticket-seller chatted inconsequentially to someone out of sight; a station official came into the office, spoke some instruction about a late train and went out again. Eventually there was peace and the young man came across and moved the boxes so she could crawl out. There was a woman's coat and scarf hanging on a hook and he helped her put these on. She was shocked to glimpse her reflection in a small square of mirror next to the hook. Grey skin, sunken eye-sockets, frizzy hair. She wound the square of scarf around her head and pulled the coat collar up.

'*Allez chez ma mère,*' he said, pressing a scrap of torn paper into her hand. Then he opened the door, looked about outside, and gestured for her to go. He was a small, wiry man with a merry face covered in acne scars. Quite unremarkable-looking, but she knew she'd always remember him.

As she tried to thank him, he shrugged as though the whole matter was nothing and shut the door behind her.

She tiptoed to the door of the station and peered about. It was lunchtime on a beautiful spring day and the place was deserted. The sun warmed her face. She had no papers, no idea where she was and only one clue, on a scrap of torn paper, of what to do next. But she was alive and she was free.

The ticket-seller's mother spoke as little as her son, but she did not hesitate to believe Beatrice's story. Beatrice found herself sitting in a shabby kitchen eating fresh bread and butter for the first time in months, almost crying at how good it tasted. She watched the woman fill a bath by the fire with hot water from a copper urn, then, while Beatrice bathed, lay out some clothes and shoes she said had belonged to her daughter. Something in the way she handled the simple blouse and skirt made Beatrice wonder what had happened to the daughter, but the woman was not the sort to invite questions. The shoes, of stout black leather, fitted her exactly and the woman seemed oddly satisfied by this.

'I am sorry that you cannot stay here, but it is not safe,' she told Beatrice when she was dressed.

'I have family,' Beatrice told her. 'Near Le Havre.' If she went there she could put her worries about them at rest.

'No,' the woman said immediately. 'It is too dangerous that way. Go south. I will tell you the way to Melun. There are people there who can help you.' She extracted some money from a coffee pot on the dresser.

'I can't,' Beatrice said. 'You must need it.'

'Please,' the woman said, and thrust the money into the

pocket of Beatrice's coat, together with a packet of sandwiches. She had the same sweet face as her son.

'You are a very good person,' Beatrice said, taking her hand. 'After the war. . .'

'Yes, yes, everything is after the war. It will not be long now.' She pressed her hand against her chest and Beatrice couldn't tell whether she meant that the war would be over soon or that she wouldn't be there to see it. 'Now, go.'

She followed the woman's directions, walking, like a cat, in the shadows, so as not to be seen. When night fell she found a barn, as Rafe had once done, and slept under empty sacks, taking care to be up and away at dawn before the farmer was about. All the next day she walked. The only danger she encountered was in a village where she stopped to buy food and ask directions. The baker regarded her with suspicion, and in response to some instinct she varied the route he described to her.

Melun. Finding the address the woman had given her. Knocking nervously at the door of strangers and again finding the miracle of kindness, food and shelter. She stayed with the couple for several days, sleeping mostly and regaining some strength. The wife gave her a bicycle and they sent her south again to a village outside Orléans. There was some argument between them over this. The woman was worried that Orléans was crawling with SS, but the man insisted anyway. There was someone he knew who could get her false papers, and since these could be more crucial to her escape than anything else, she agreed that she should go.

At the country house near Orléans it took over a week for the forger to finish the papers, a long anxious stay, hidden in a wine cellar where there were rats. When they were ready, she went forth again, this time as Jeanne de Varnes, south, always south, for Hitler's eyes were turning northwards to the coast, to where the Allied invasion was expected daily, and she might just slip away through a chink in his defences while his attention was elsewhere.

She could travel faster now, could use trains with less fear of detection, though the children sitting opposite in the carriage to Angoulême stared curiously at her too-thin face and lustreless skin. She smiled back at them and turned to look out at the passing countryside, awash with longing for the time she'd see her own child back in England.

At Angoulême a doctor examined her scars, an expression of deep compassion on his face. Her toenails were growing again, he assured her, and the ointment he supplied would soothe the scars on her back. Her hosts gave her money and sent her on to Marseille.

The Germans there had bombed the Resistance out of the old city the year before, and the cells had scattered and reformed, but more strongly than before, their efforts utterly focused on destroying the roads and rail that aided the German advance north. Someone was to meet her in a café near the station, that's all she knew. They'd give her instructions about what to do next, where to go.

What went wrong she never learned. She arrived at Marseille, found the café and waited for over an hour, but no one came. She tried another café in the street, wondering if she'd got the wrong one, but there, too, she drew a blank. Marseille was as far south as she could go without help, and she was alone. She stood staring out across the Mediterranean, wondering what to do next.

In the end she took a room in a run-down boarding house near the docks. It was a rough area and she didn't like being

out in it after dark. The proprietor regarded her with pruri-
ence as she filled out the forms. When she came downstairs
the next morning, there was an SS officer lounging against
the desk in the narrow hallway, chatting to the man. She
tried to slip past, with eyes cast down, but he seized her
arm and swung her round with a jeering, 'Well, what have
we here?' Nine in the morning and there was wine on his
breath. Anger blazed through her and she pulled away, with
a '*Laissez-moi!*'

He came at her, his fist swinging, but her body remembered
what to do. She heard the trainer's voice in her head. *Grab the
hand before it hits, twist it behind his back, trip him so he falls backwards. Then run like hell.* She did all this and ran.

Flung open the door, into the street. A shout behind her.
She dodged sideways down an alley as the bullet hit the
window she'd just passed. Then left down behind the line of
houses, over a wall into a back yard, through a back door into
a kitchen. Through the house and out of the front, down a
bigger street. Behind her the sounds of pursuit. She looked
about wildly.

Coming towards her was a very old man leading a donkey
that was pulling a little cart covered with a tarpaulin. He
stopped, called softly, '*Ici, mademoiselle,*' and lifted a corner of
the tarpaulin.

'*Merci,*' she gasped, and climbed inside the cart. It was
empty, but smelt of sweet manure. The man straightened the
tarpaulin then the cart jerked forward as the donkey moved
on. The cart trundled over cobbles for some time at a slow but
steady pace, turned this way and that. She lay rigid, smelling
that familiar smell of horse. Finally, the cart stopped.

When the tarpaulin was pulled away and she sat up, she saw
they had reached the end of a quay where dozens of assorted

small boats were moored. The donkey was now tied to a ring in the stone wall. The old man stepped onto the deck of a shabby barge. He fired up the engine – Beatrice wondered where he'd got the fuel – then came back to the quay.

Five minutes later, an observer on the shore would have seen a strange sight. A black barge skirting the coast, heading west into the sunset, on its deck the clear shape of a donkey silhouetted against the sky. The old man sitting at the tiller might have been any old man going about his business in war or peace, a handrolled cigarette between his lips, his cap pulled down over his ears. But Beatrice didn't see any of this. She was hidden in the cabin.

Journey's End – the Camargue. A wild, desolate landscape where land, lagoon and sea merged in a single horizontal plain. Here Beatrice wandered, a slender, solitary figure, lost, waiting for time to pass. Sometimes as she watched, a great flock of pale flamingos would rise from the water and drift away across the sky and her heart lifted with them. Herds of bulls roamed the marshes, and blunt-nosed white horses with flowing manes, a homelier version of the noble white beasts of her childhood dreams.

She shared a lonely thatched cabin with the old bargeman's brother and his wife. There was a pair of bull horns over the door to ward off evil spirits. The brother rode the wild horses, and gradually, through the long, humid summer, she learned to master them, too. She hoped he'd come to trust her to go with him to gallop amongst the bulls, though this was man's work and he merely frowned and shook his head. His own woman was tough, work-hardened – she had to be – but she was gentle enough with the young English girl, tutting over her scars and nursing her back to health and strength with rich beef stews and other stranger, muddier delicacies found in the marshes and pools.

The war felt as though it was happening somewhere far, far away. In June the Allies made landfall in Northern France. The *maquis* rose in the south. In August came the great news of the Liberation of Paris.

Beatrice was like a dreamer awakening. Her restlessness grew. She knew it was time to leave this wild paradise where she'd been lost in time, and go home. Her son would be waiting. And maybe she would find out what had happened to Rafe.

At the beginning of September, the man with the donkey took her back to Marseilles and she presented herself to the new authorities. News of her survival was telegraphed to London. In the third week of September 1944, she boarded a great warship that was overflowing with sailors and soldiers and other flotsam and jetsam of war like herself, and set out through the Mediterranean for England.

Round Spain they went, and Portugal, and up the west coast of France. It was a journey of over a week because the ship stopped everywhere, for some to disembark and others to board – everybody was on the move – but eventually, Beatrice watched from the deck as the buildings of Southampton solidified out of the autumn mist. And disappeared again in a blur of tears.

And there to meet her on the quay, was Rafe.

For a long moment they simply stood and stared at one another. He looked thinner than when she saw him last, but he'd lost that awful strained look. Then his face broke into the most boyish of grins and she groped her way forward into his arms. They clung to one another.

'I thought I'd never see you again,' she sobbed into his ear. 'I thought you might be . . . Oh, never mind, you're here.'

'I could hardly believe it when they told me you were safe. Oh, Beatrice . . .' he murmured.

She pulled back from him and looked about. 'Where's Tommy? Where's my son?' Why wasn't he here?

Chapter 33

Cornwall, 2011

'They hadn't brought him, Lucy,' Beatrice said, her voice low and trembling. 'They could have brought him to meet me and they didn't. They knew I was coming home. Miss Atkins telephoned everybody . . .' Her voice trailed away and she closed her eyes.

Lucy sat watching her, wondering whether to speak. *Tommy*. Now that she'd finally mentioned his name, Lucy was a maelstrom of emotion.

Of course, she had known that this whole story was leading up to something important, but now that they were getting there she didn't think she wanted to know what it was. Was this the thing her father had been frightened of discovering? And yet, knowing that there was some secret, he had fiddled about on the fringes of it, trying to find out about Rafe.

'Where *was* Tommy, Mrs Ashton? Was he all right?'

'Just let me get my breath, dear, and I'll tell you.'

September 1944

Rafe said, 'He's in Cornwall.' There was something uncertain in his voice and she looked hard at him. His expression was serious, his eyes unreadable. 'Bea, there are many things we need to talk about.'

It was then she saw someone standing quietly watching them. A handsome woman in the neat navy uniform of the WAAF, very poised and upright. It was Miss Atkins. She stepped forward and took Beatrice's hand.

'Beatrice,' she said, in her lovely low voice. 'It's so marvellous that you're home. We've been searching everywhere for you.'

'Have you?' Beatrice said, not quite believing her.

'Why, yes! But it's been impossible. So many people coming and going, papers destroyed, tracks covered.' She shook her head. 'And getting our own people to give us any information . . . Well, I've already said too much. I'm so glad you're home safely. You must have had an awful time.'

'Yes, I did.'

'We need to talk, of course. There's a car waiting. Major Buckmaster is extremely keen to speak to you.'

Beatrice glanced at Rafe, who nodded imperceptibly. 'I'll come with you, naturally,' he said.

'I can't go home yet?'

'Very shortly you can,' Miss Atkins said, almost crisply. 'But there are important matters to speak of first.'

Rafe sat in the front of the car, Miss Atkins and Beatrice in the back. As the car pulled away, Miss Atkins turned to face Beatrice and said, very gently, 'First, my dear, I'm afraid I have some rather sad news for you.'

'Tommy,' she cried. 'Not Tommy?'

'I understand that your son is quite well,' Miss Atkins said. 'No, it's your mother I'm talking about.' In August, a year ago, Delphine Marlow had been visiting a friend in Falmouth. On the steep road down to the coast, the bus had lurched into a crater in the road and fallen on its side. She and another woman were crushed underneath. The other woman died at the scene. Delphine lingered on for several days but in the end her injuries proved too grave.

'She never regained consciousness,' Miss Atkins said. 'I am so sorry to have to give you this news.'

It was a blow. She sat with her hand over her mouth and tried not to cry.

Rafe said, 'Beatrice, are you all right?'

'My father?' she said, dull.

'It was he who wrote and told us,' Miss Atkins said. 'Of course we were unable to forward the news to you. We didn't know where you were.'

'No one knew,' Beatrice whispered. A picture of the man in the white coat advancing flashed into her mind. That's where she had been.

Much of the journey she sat sunk in misery, trying to remember the sight of her mother's face, the sound of her voice as she sang.

'She would have been so worried about me,' she told Miss Atkins. 'And she didn't even know that I was alive.'

The debriefing at the offices in Baker Street took all day, but while they sat waiting for Major Buckmaster to arrive, she learnt what had happened to Rafe, and to the rest of the network after her capture.

'I swam across the river. They'd hit me in the shoulder, and I didn't think I'd make it. I nearly passed out and they kept shooting at me. I still don't know how I managed it.'

'And then what did you do? Didn't they have dogs?'

'Yes, I could hear them. I stumbled about a bit in the woods, then found a log and drifted downstream where the river widens, and hid on some of those little islands for two days. It was awful. The wound got infected and I developed a fever.'

'I'm not surprised,' she said. 'It must have been awful.'

'And I was so worried about you. I felt so guilty that it was me who had got away.'

'But that's ridiculous,' Beatrice cried. 'You were wounded. We both did what we had to there.' And with the words, warmth coursed through her body. She took his hand and squeezed it.

'I still feel the same about you, Beatrice,' he said, taking her other hand. 'I'd do anything for you, you know that.'

'I know, Rafe. So what happened to you after the islands?'

'An old man came down to fish. Got a bigger catch than he imagined.' Rafe laughed. 'Anyway, he helped me.'

'I know Charles was captured, but do you know if he's still alive?'

'They took him to Limoges, like you.'

'They had his wireless in Paris. And some of his messages.'

'Beatrice, I'm afraid Charles is dead. He took his pill that first night.'

'Poor Charles.' Beatrice couldn't speak for a moment. 'What about the Girands?'

'I'm afraid it's bad news there, too. They were tried and later shot.'

'Oh, Rafe.' And now it became even harder. 'And the rest of the network? Stefan, the doctor?' She read the answer in his eyes, eyes that tried not to accuse, but she read the accusation there nonetheless.

'They're dead, aren't they? *Aren't they?* Rafe,' she said desperately, and he put his hands over his face, 'I promise, I tried so hard not to say anything, but after they had tortured me many times and got nowhere, they injected me with something. In the end I might not have known what I said.'

'I can't bear to think of it, you . . . going through that,' he whispered.

Nearby a door opened and a young girl said, 'Major Buckmaster is ready for you both now.'

Beatrice told Maurice Buckmaster and Vera Atkins the story from beginning to end. Every now and then, once of them stopped her with a question. Who did she think André was, the man in the café? What had she told the policeman in Limoges? What had she told the interrogator in Avenue Foch? Who else had she seen in the prison? What about the map on the wall – what was on it? How did she think the Germans had got the information? What had she said when she was under torture?

As she stumbled through her story, she became more and more distressed and finally angry. They didn't explain anything to her. They were trying to find answers for themselves, not least to piece together what had happened to some of the other agents, people she didn't know. Miss Atkins was very interested in the name Madeleine – the fellow-prisoner Beatrice had whispered with on the bus journey to the train station. Had Madeleine definitely got on the train? Where was the train going? Where in Germany? 'I've no idea!' Beatrice almost shouted.

She saw that Miss Atkins cared, that she badly wanted to know where some of her protégés were, whether they were alive or dead, but there was also a sense that they were wanting to cover their own backs, for they would not comment on the map on the wall in the Avenue Foch, but merely stared at one another in disbelief. As the session continued, the Major began to pace the room, not saying anything for long moments.

Her account of her torture seemed to upset him badly; she was grateful at least to see that.

As the interview began to run out of steam, at last she could bear it no longer.

'Why didn't you do something earlier?' she burst out. 'You didn't listen to us when we told you about André. You just dismissed it.'

'There seemed no reason for us to be suspicious,' was the Major's mumbled reply. 'He sounded harmless, a maverick, maybe.'

'I'm afraid we've since found out that he was working for the Germans,' Miss Atkins said. 'Whether his intention really was to come to London, or whether he was trying to get information out of you, we don't know.'

'He knew all about us, that was what was alarming. You should have pulled us out of there. You've no idea, have you, quite how abandoned one can feel. I came to believe that they were right, that you didn't care about us, that you were ready to turn your back on us.'

'That was never true,' Miss Atkins said quietly. 'You have been in our minds all the time. We tried desperately to find out what had happened to you, but we heard nothing after you were taken from Limoges. Nothing, that is, until September, when we were allowed into Paris. And then we feared you'd been taken to Germany. There are so many missing, Beatrice. You don't know how glad we are to see you safe. You have been so extraordinarily brave.'

'You certainly have,' the Major echoed. He looked, Beatrice thought, quite upset, and it struck her how decent he was. A man who expected the best of people and often got it, but who in so doing, underestimated the depths of brutality to which humanity could fall. A man too nice to go to war.

*   *   *

It was early evening when they finished with her and Rafe. She was exhausted, physically and mentally, but now duty was done there was only one thing on her mind.

'Rafe, I need to see Tommy. Where is he?'

'He's in Saint Florian, Bea. It's too late to go tonight.'

'Here is your handbag with your keys, all safe,' came Miss Atkins's voice behind her. 'We kept up the payments on your flat as you asked.'

'Thank you.' She was looking forward to seeing Dinah.

'I can arrange for a car to take you down to Cornwall tomorrow, if you like. We telegraphed Mrs Cardwell to say you were home.'

'Thank you,' Beatrice said, taking a moment to realize she meant Angie.

'It really is the least we can do.'

'I must speak to my father as well. I still can't believe . . .' Her voice broke.

'I know,' Miss Atkins said, taking her hand and looking very sympathetic. 'I really am so sorry.'

They said their goodbyes. In the lift Rafe drew her to him. 'My poor girl. Are you too worn out to have dinner with me?'

'Of course not. And you'll come with me tomorrow?'

'I can't, unfortunately. They've asked me to do something here.'

'Oh,' she said, her spirits plummeting. 'I'd hoped . . .'

'I know.' They reached the ground floor and made their way out into the sunshine. Rafe hailed a cab. 'The Ritz, don't you think?'

'That would be marvellous. Rafe, have you seen Tommy? How is he?'

'Very well, as far as I know. I saw him last month. Did I tell you they've moved back into Carlyon Manor now? Angie's mother's down there with them. Hetty's been sent away to school. Young Tommy enjoys racing around in all that space. He's a smart little chap.'

'Has he changed very much? He'll be three next month. *Three!*' She felt a surge of terrible sadness to think of all she'd missed. 'Oh, Rafe, suppose he doesn't remember me.'

He laughed. 'I expect he will.'

'I do hope so.' The more she thought about it, the more anxious she felt. 'And how's Angie? Has she had her baby? And Gerald?'

'My brother's in France somewhere. Do you know, it turns out he was involved in the invasion plans all along? He went over on D-Day plus twelve. Most of the really dirty work had already been done. He really has had all the luck in this war.'

'Don't say that. It's not over yet. What about Angie?'

'Angie's had a hard time, Bea.' Rafe's tender gaze was fixed on her now. 'She lost the baby, I'm afraid.'

'Oh no, that's so awful.'

'I think it's helped her, having Tommy. They seem very close.' She looked at him quickly and saw he was trying to choose his words carefully. 'It will be very hard for her to lose him.'

She laughed in astonishment. 'I would have thought she'd be glad to be relieved of the burden of someone else's child.'

'Just be gentle with her, Bea, that's all I'll say.'

'I wish you were coming down there with me.'

'I wish I were, too, but perhaps it's best I'm not. You'll want to see Tommy on your own. And your father, of course.'

'Yes. I must telephone him from the hotel.'

From the Ritz, she managed to speak briefly to her father, who sounded very quiet and faraway. When she gave the operator the number for Carlyon she was told there was some problem with the line. She would just have to turn up.

It was extraordinary to Beatrice to be drinking cocktails in the Ritz, bumping into people she hadn't even thought about since she saw them last, in what seemed like another life. No one asked her where she'd been, though one or two studied her curiously, and she laughed and joked with them, wanting to blot out all that had happened and finding she was unable to do so. Tomorrow she'd see Tommy and her father and, grief welled in her once more, she'd see the home where her mother was no longer. The drink burned her throat as she gulped it down, but it seemed to help. Later, in the restaurant, she ate in a sort of haze.

'You're exhausted, aren't you?' Rafe murmured. 'Shall I take you home?'

'Stay with me,' she told him, when the cab pulled up outside the house in Primrose Hill.

'Are you sure?' he asked.

'I'm not letting you go now,' she replied.

'That rather settles it then,' he said.

The flat was dark. Dinah was away – she must have been away some time, for the place had an unlived-in air and was cold, but everything looked the same, and when she opened the door of the old mahogany wardrobe, she saw her clothes still hanging there. She closed the door and turned to find Rafe. Gently, he put his arms around her.

'Rafe,' she said as he undressed her in the dimness. 'I'm frightened. I'm . . . not the same as I was.'

'I understand,' he said.

He cried out in pity when he saw the scars on her back and her poor feet. The two of them lay together in the bed for a long time, he just kissing and caressing her, until finally she gained the confidence to let him in.

Afterwards she wept and he held her close. And, as she drifted into sleep, safe for a while at least in this little world they'd made together, away from war and duty, her last thought was, *And tomorrow I'll see Tommy.*

Her plan – half-formed, for she didn't know how things would be – was to stay at Carlyon for a while. It made sense to let Tommy get used to her again. She'd be able to see her father, too, and give him any help he needed. Then she supposed she'd return to London and Rafe.

Chapter 34

September 1944

Beatrice's fears rose the moment the car turned into the drive leading to Carlyon Manor. One of the gates hung on its hinges. There were great ruts in the gravel, presumably from army vehicles, and the once-cropped lawn was a mass of earthworks greened over with weeds. The house itself had a blind, surly look due to the blackout curtains that were drawn across most of the windows. In the old days, of course, Brown would have pulled back the curtains daily, but perhaps there wasn't a Brown any more.

When she rang the doorbell it took a long time to be answered, and her nervous feelings intensified.

Finally there came the sound of bolts being drawn back and a key turning in the lock. It was late afternoon – had they already locked the front door, or had it not been unlocked at all that day? Finally it shuddered open and there stood a woman with a thin, boyish figure, dressed in dirty riding breeches. Her hair was twisted up at the back but with all the elegance of a bird's nest.

'Yes?' the woman said. It took a moment for Beatrice to recognize Mrs Wincanton, and Angie's mother seemed as surprised to see who was standing on her doorstep. One hand flew to her face. 'Oh, Bea!' She gathered her wits together and pulled the door wider.

'This is extraordinary.' She turned and shouted into the house. 'Angie, Angie, come and see who's here! I'm sorry, dear, do come in,' she said to Beatrice, and tugged her inside. 'We'd no idea you were coming. We thought— oh, never mind what we thought. You're here now.'

'I did try to telephone.'

'The line is unreliable. There's so much to do here.'

She embraced Beatrice in a vague, half-hearted fashion and Beatrice felt dismay. Why did they think she wasn't coming? Miss Atkins had said she'd telegraphed them. The sense of something badly wrong was by now leaping like a dark flame within her.

She looked around the hall. If there was something neglected about Mrs Wincanton's appearance, the house was worse. The prints were gone from the walls and the lovely carved staircase was battered and chipped.

'It's so sad, isn't it?' Mrs Wincanton whispered, following her gaze. 'Even the house is having its war.'

And now Angie appeared at the top of the stairs. 'Bea!' she cried, and hurried down. 'I can hardly believe it. Are you all right?'

She stood before Beatrice, staring at her, and Beatrice felt as she'd done on that very first day at Carlyon, lost and uncertain. She knew she didn't look the same as before, but surely her appearance wasn't that startling. They hugged each other and Beatrice breathed in the familiar scent of soap and apples and of something more earthy. Angie, too, had changed.

'Didn't you know I was coming?' Bea asked again. 'I thought they told you.'

'There was a telegram, wasn't there?' Oenone asked her daughter. 'Where is it?'

'I thought *you* had it,' Angie replied, her voice frosty. She said to Bea, 'We knew you were coming back but not when.'

'Where's Tommy?' Beatrice said. 'I'm longing to see him.'

Oenone opened her mouth, but Angie cut in quickly: 'I'm awfully sorry,' she said. 'I know you'll be disappointed, but unfortunately he's gone away with Nanny for a few days. He'd have loved to have seen you.'

For a moment Beatrice was speechless then she stuttered stupidly, 'You mean, he's not here?'

'No.' Angie gave a regretful smile. 'It's such a shame. He sometimes asks about Auntie Beatrice. I warn you, when he does see you he'll want to know if you've brought a present for him. He's a naughty boy like that.'

Beatrice licked her lips, which had gone dry. 'Is that what you make him call me, Auntie Beatrice, not Mummy?'

'I find it's less confusing for him that way. You have been away for a long time, Bea. You haven't seen him for any length of time for nearly two years. Two years! It's not easy for a little boy.'

'I think I need to sit down,' Beatrice said, feeling suddenly weak with shock.

'Of course, come into the drawing room. Mummy, would you ask Phoebe to bring tea in?'

When they'd sat down Beatrice asked, 'Tell me again, where has Nanny taken him?'

'Oh, just up to Truro to see some friends of hers. It gives me a bit of a break. There's an awful lot to do here, as you can see. They left it in such a mess.' Beatrice saw now the deprivations the room had suffered. The chandelier was broken and the wallpaper all scuffed. 'So you're back. Have you had an awful time? I expect you have. Your hair's going grey and you look . . . so much older.'

'Angie,' her mother said, looking embarrassed.

'I'm sorry,' Angie said. Why did she keep glancing at the door? 'It's been simply dreadful for us. The doodlebugs were the absolute last straw – we couldn't stand it in Sussex any more. I used to have nightmares that they were hanging over our cottage, about to drop. So when we heard the army had left Carlyon and it was empty we shot back down here. Daddy fixed it for us. Gerald's away. His chance to be a hero finally. We think he's in Paris.'

'Rafe said he was in France.' Rafe had been right – Gerald always managed to keep away from the front line.

The tea duly arrived, the trolley pushed by a maid even smaller and younger than Brown, and the wheels caught in the fringes of the rug. Mrs Wincanton went to help and for a while everyone was distracted.

Beatrice took her tea and a sandwich, which she crumbled on the saucer but did not eat. Her mind was only on one thing. 'When will Nanny be back with Tommy?' she asked. 'Did you say they were to be gone a few days? Perhaps I should go to Truro and fetch him.'

'Oh no, no. That would upset his routine. He was so looking forward to going.'

'Oh, Angie, really . . .' started her mother, but Angie gave her a cold look and she shut up.

Beatrice looked at Angie in surprise. 'But he'll want to see his mother, surely?'

'He'd find it a bit of shock seeing you,' Angie said. 'He's become rather used to me, now, the poor darling.'

'Well, he's going to have to get used to me, because of course I'll be taking him home. I'm back now. I won't be going away again. At least, I think not.'

At this, an expression of terrible anguish crossed Angie's

face. 'Oh no, Beatrice, he'll find that awfully disturbing. He loves it here. Do you remember how we played among the rockpools? Well, despite the dreaded barbed wire, we can still reach them at low tide, and he does have fun trying to catch the fish. You wouldn't believe how clever he is, and the darling is not quite three.'

Again, she glanced at the door. And now Beatrice was sure that something was terribly wrong. Had something happened to Tommy? Something awful?

She tried to calm herself. Miss Atkins had said Tommy was well. Rafe had too. She remembered how Rafe had warned her that Angie had had a bad time, but she wasn't prepared for her to seem so, well, downright peculiar. And Mrs Wincanton was staring into her tea as if her thoughts were winging far away. Beatrice asked her, 'You heard the news about my mother, Mrs Wincanton?'

The woman's eyes flew to hers and she saw pain and sympathy in them. 'I forgot to say, Beatrice. We were so dreadfully sorry to hear. Such a lovely woman, your mother. Of course, we wrote to your father, didn't we, Angie?'

'I'm sure he was touched. I haven't seen him yet. I was going to go after I'd seen Tommy.'

Angie perked up a little at this and said brightly, 'Well, you can go straight away, can't you, since Tommy isn't here. I expect you'll stay at The Rowans a day or two and maybe come down another time.'

Beatrice stared. 'I will stay with my father, yes, but I'm not going to go back to London without Tommy.'

Angie was starting to look quite agitated now. She put down her tea and it slopped onto the saucer. 'Damn.'

'Don't swear, dear,' Mrs Wincanton said to her daughter. 'I think you'd better explain properly to Beatrice.'

'Explain what?' Beatrice said. She was beginning to feel more and more that she was in Wonderland with Alice, and it was a dark and painful place.

Angie covered her face with her hands and said, 'I can't.'

Beatrice stood up and almost shouted. 'What's happened? What have you done with my son?'

'Nothing's happened to Tommy,' Oenone said immediately. 'It's just we thought you weren't coming back. You were gone so long, Beatrice. They . . . well, they had prepared us for the worst, those people. They sounded certain. We had to make arrangements, do what was best for Tommy. And Angie – well, you can see how she is. Losing her baby again . . .'

'Don't, Mummy,' Angie said, putting her hands over her ears.

'Beatrice,' Mrs Wincanton went on, 'having Tommy has been marvellous. It's kept us all steady through these terrible times. First there was Ed, then with Gerald gone – and, no I mean it, Angie – Tommy's helped you so much.'

'I'm very glad,' Beatrice started to say, 'but now, as you can see, I'm back and—'

Oenone Wincanton talked on. 'I think you have to realize that it's in Tommy's best interests to stay with us.'

'No,' Beatrice breathed. 'He's my child.'

'Then why did you go off and leave him?' Angie's eyes were dangerous pools of blue.

'Because I had to. You don't think I wanted to, do you?'

'The fact remains that you went. And that was very hard on him. He's had to adapt. We are his family now and you can't take him away.'

Beatrice could hardly believe that she was hearing this.

'Angie,' she said, 'please don't think that I'm not grateful for everything you've done. I am. All the time I was in prison I knew I didn't have to worry about Tommy because he was safe with you. I shall always remember that. But he's my child and I want him with me. Gerald will come back and you'll have your own children, I'm sure.'

'I won't, Bea, but that's not the point. Think of your son. He'll be distraught. It'll be like him going to a stranger.'

'How can you say that?' She could barely speak, her throat felt so tight. 'I'm his mother.'

'You remember how angry he was when you went away for just a few weeks? How can you expect a small boy to cope for so long without you? Bea, accept it, he won't remember you.'

'And that's why you let him call you Mummy?'

There was a silence, then Angie said, 'Of course. It's only kind. A baby needs a mother. And a father.'

'That's a low comment.'

'But it's true, isn't it? You should have given him up as soon as you had him. It would have been kinder in the long run.'

'Angie, you supported me back then. You took me in, and the baby. I tell you, I'll always thank you for that.'

'And now you must think of Tommy. You must leave him with us.'

'No, Angie. This thing is all about you, not Tommy.'

'It is not. How dare you suggest—'

'I'm sorry about your babies. It makes me dreadfully sad. But you can't have mine instead.'

'You are missing the point. I'm thinking about Tommy. *You* are thinking about *you*. If you wanted to be his mother, you shouldn't have left him.'

'Angie, I went to do my bit in this war. For Tommy.'

'No woman with a child should be expected to do what you did – and you could have said no. You could have, Beatrice. Your job was to stand by your child. Your plan now, I suppose, was to take him and for the same thing to happen again. You'd leave him with someone else in order to go off somewhere and work.'

'I don't know what I'll do yet, I haven't had time to think – but money has to come from somewhere, yes.'

Just then, a door slammed, and a moment later came the sound of voices: a woman's and the light, high voice of a child. Angie and Beatrice rose to their feet at the same moment.

There was a knock, and the door of the living room opened. A little boy ran in, followed a moment later by Nanny. The boy had a cap of straight dark hair, and his pale skin was flushed with a healthy glow. 'Tommy,' Beatrice breathed, and put out her arms. Tommy glanced at her in alarm, and instead ran to Angie, who swung him up to sit astride her hip. 'Mummy,' he said to Angie, 'we did go on a train!'

'He was a very good boy,' Nanny said. 'Oh, hello, Miss Beatrice. Nice to see you safe home. I expect you've had some adventures. Now, I'll just go and see about his tea.'

'You went on a train, my love?' Angie cooed. Her face, when she turned to Bea, was full of motherly pride.

Beatrice tried to make a sound, but nothing came and she held out her hands wordlessly to Tommy. Tommy studied her for a moment, without any sign of recognition, then nuzzled Angie's shoulder.

Beatrice turned to Oenone, who was sitting calmly, arms folded around her knees. 'Help me,' she implored.

Oenone shrugged. 'There's nothing I can do.'

'He's my child,' she appealed to both of them, but they just looked at her without speaking.

She gazed hungrily at Tommy, who was peeping at her round his hand. She smiled and put out her arms. 'Tommy, darling, come and sit with me.'

But he shook his head urgently and cuddled into Angie's arms.

'I bought you a present,' Beatrice said. She'd found it in a shop in Marseille, in the days when she was waiting to take ship. She placed the cube box on the table and unhooked the catch. The puppet shot out and lolled on his spring, his clown's face grinning crazily. Tommy's eyes widened with fear and he screamed.

'My God, Beatrice, get rid of it!' Angie shrieked.

Beatrice seized the Jack and stuffed it into the box. Her hands were shaking. 'What on earth's the matter?' she whispered.

'He saw a clown at a children's party,' Oenone Wincanton said in a weary voice. 'For some reason it frightened him. Tommy can be a nervous little boy sometimes.'

'Oh, Tommy, I'm so sorry, I didn't know,' Beatrice said, horrified. How could she have known? She went to sit by Angie and stroked his hot silky head as he sobbed into Angie's shoulder. Minutes passed and he was calmer, but still he would not go to her. And now she did not know what to do. She sensed that Angie and Oenone were waiting politely for her to go, but she did not want to leave the house without Tommy. Yet she could hardly snatch him out of Angie's arms. There would be uproar.

In the end, she saw that discretion would be the better part of valour and gathered up her things. The jack-in-a-box she slipped back into her case.

'I haven't seen my father yet,' she said. 'I expect I shall stay with him tonight, it's only fair.'

'Of course,' Oenone said, rising and putting out her hand. 'The poor man. Please convey our best wishes.'

Beatrice saw with a terrible clarity that they'd made no attempt to see him, which meant that Tommy wouldn't have visited his maternal grandfather, who only lived down the road. Now she hardly registered Oenone's handshake at all.

'Let me give Tommy to Nanny,' Angie said. 'His tea will be ready, I expect.' She allowed Beatrice to kiss the back of Tommy's head, then left the room with him.

And now she and Oenone were alone. Oenone went to the mantelpiece, picked up an invitation card that was propped up there, pretended to study it, and put it down again. Then she turned to Beatrice and said in a low voice, 'We're so glad that you're home safe, you know.'

'Thank you. And I'm so grateful for all you've done for Tommy, you and Angie – and Nanny, of course. He looks so big and fine.'

'He is a dear little boy,' Oenone said. 'Angie's had a terrible time and after the last . . . disappointment, the doctor told her it might be dangerous for her to – well, try again. It was rather a blow.'

'I'm so sorry,' Beatrice said, trying not to think of her own bad time, all the awful things that she'd been through. Oenone spoke as though the war wasn't happening, as though her family was all that mattered. Of course, they'd lost Ed, she must remember that and feel sympathy. 'She'll miss Tommy when I take him. I can see that.'

Oenone took a pack of cigarettes out of her cardigan pocket and lit one. The seconds ticked past. Finally, she glanced at the door, then said, 'Which is why you must leave Tommy with her, Beatrice. It would be the best thing for all of us, surely you can see that?'

'No,' Beatrice said, her voice rising to a squeak. *'No.'*

'Think about it for a few days. That's all we ask. I'm sure Angie would be happy for you to come and see Tommy. But there's something I have to tell you.' She balanced the cigarette on the mantelpiece and bent to explore the wooden carving, her finger stroking the little bee that still crouched, half-hidden, amongst the cherry-wood flowers.

Beatrice, seeing the bee, felt as though everything that had happened to her throughout her life was coming at her together in a great engulfing wave. She'd tried hard to struggle against this family, but she'd needed them, too, wanted them too much. She didn't wish to hear whatever it was Oenone was about to tell her.

'Beatrice, because you were missing, believed killed, something had to be done about Tommy.'

'What do you mean?' Beatrice breathed.

'It was Michael who arranged it. He knew whom to speak to. Angelina and Gerald are legally Tommy's guardians.'

Beatrice stared at Oenone in disbelief and then horror. 'No!' she cried. 'That can't be true!'

'It is true.'

'I don't believe you. It's not possible to do that, is it? To take a child from his mother?'

Oenone was silent, but Beatrice read the truth in her face. In war all sorts of things happened in response to extraordinary situations. Michael had made this particular one possible. There was a whooshing noise in her ears and her legs buckled under her. When she came round she was lying with her head in Angelina's lap and there was a smell of burning.

'Tommy,' she said, in a distant voice.

Angie said, 'He does feel a little hot, but Nanny says he'll be fine.'

Beatrice sat up. 'You haven't really done that, have you, Angie? Have you?'

'Done what? Oh, Mummy, you haven't told her?'

Oenone stood up to rescue her cigarette, tapped the ash into the fireplace and took a long drag. 'I thought it sensible,' she said finally. 'It makes things plain.'

'Show me,' Beatrice said wildly. 'Show me the evidence.'

'We don't have the document here,' Angie said. 'It's with Daddy's lawyers. Oh, Bea, Tommy will be all right. We love him to bits. And he'll see lots of you, I promise. We're so pleased that you're safe. And Rafe as well. You've seen Rafe, of course.'

'Yes.' Rafe must have seen how things were with Tommy and Angelina.

'He didn't know about . . . what you've done?' she burst out.

'No,' Angie said. She reached out and tried to hug Beatrice, but Beatrice pushed her away and stood up.

'I have to go,' she said, 'but I'll be back tomorrow to see Tommy, and I'll get to know him again, and no matter how many days and weeks it takes, I'll win him back.'

But when she left she carried with her the memory of Angelina's face. It was a mask of serene triumph.

She stayed with her father for several days and felt a stranger to him.

'Beatrice,' he'd said, in mild surprise, when he opened the door. He leaned on a stick, and it was something of an effort for him to reach forward and give her a dry kiss. His hair was completely grey now, and thin, but he was neatly dressed and, she saw, looking round, the house was as clean and tidy as ever. Part of her kept expecting to see her mother come down the stairs, to hear her light, foreign voice, and the silence mocked her.

Her father asked practically nothing about what had happened to Beatrice. He was mourning her mother, she could see that, but he was wrapping himself up in routine. Cook still came, cleaned, cooked a hot lunch, left him a cold supper. In the mornings he wrote. Someone had suggested to him before her mother died that he write a children's book, and he told her, to her amazement, that it had recently been accepted by a publisher, and they wanted another. A children's book! What did her father know about children? She supposed he'd been one himself once. In the afternoons he played bridge or took a little exercise, though not with a dog. Dear old Jinx had died of old age shortly before Delphine's accident.

That first evening, she walked about the house, remembering, mourning her mother, whose clothes hung in the wardrobe still, and the memory of whose touch lay in the placing of every ornament, and she wondered what to do about Tommy.

The next day she walked up to Carlyon and spent the day there. Nothing had changed from the day before and the air was charged with tension. Angie referred to her in front of Tommy as 'Auntie Beatrice'. Tommy called Angie 'Mummy' and did not stray far from her side. When they took a walk down around the grounds, it was Angie's hand he held, and he wouldn't take Beatrice's at all when she suggested playing 'swing'.

'It's time for his nap now,' Angie said after lunch, and Nanny led him away upstairs.

Beatrice looked after him longingly. She sat in the drawing room to wait for him to wake, whilst Angie wrote letters, but she sensed Angie's watchfulness. If she left the room, Angie followed her. She was allowed to see Tommy after his tea, and then, because of the hints Angie dropped about receiving neighbours in the evening, there was nothing for it but to go back alone to her father's for dinner. She couldn't try to snatch Tommy away because he'd be upset. She couldn't leave him, because Angie would think she'd won. It was like a war of attrition.

On the third day when she went up to Carlyon, determined to talk seriously to Angie again, no one answered the door when she rang. She walked around the house, trying all the doors. Every one was locked. There was no sign of anyone, no car either. Deeply distressed, she turned to go. All the way back down the drive it was as though the house was watching her, hostile, waiting for her to leave.

When she returned later in the day, it was to find a padlock on the gates. The Wincantons had gone, and Tommy with them.

There was nothing for it but to take the train back to Paddington. When she saw Rafe waiting on the platform, she cried out and hurried towards him.

'Darling,' he said, and she was caught up in his arms.

'Rafe, it's all so awful.' The statutory three-minute phone call hadn't been long enough to explain clearly last night.

'Come on, let's get you home.'

Cornwall, 2011

'I told him everything, Lucy,' Beatrice said, 'and he tried to comfort me, but I was beyond comfort. I'd been betrayed by the family I'd trusted, the deepest betrayal possible.

' "We'll get him back, Bea," Rafe kept saying, "we'll get him back." And we tried so hard. The police wouldn't do anything. They told us it was a matter for the courts, and so I started legal proceedings, but there was such a back-log of cases and everything moved so slowly. It turned out that Angie had gone to Scotland, to her godmother's place, and whenever I asked if I could go up and visit Tommy, I was refused. Rafe stopped me from turning up unannounced;

he said it would make matters worse. He was probably right.

'I sometimes wonder if things would have been different if I'd just gone along with Angie's plans without objection. We could have remained friends and I'd have seen Tommy, been his loving "auntie". But something in me couldn't do that – I just couldn't. He was mine and I wanted him back – that thought consumed me.

'Something wonderful did happen: Rafe asked me to marry him, and what else could I say but yes? I'd loved him from the moment I'd set eyes on him; as I said before, that might sound ridiculous to a modern young thing like you, Lucy, but there it was. Guy, your grandfather, had been very special and I'd loved him, too, but not in the way I loved Rafe.

'We had a quiet wedding in London in December 1944. My father came up on the train to give me away, combining this rare journey with a visit to his publisher. Aunt Julia and Uncle George were there, and Rafe's mother and stepfather, a few friends, oh, and marvellous Miss Warrender with whom I'd lodged when I'd worked at the remount depot and who'd got me into the FANY. She and I had exchanged letters from time to time; in fact, I kept in touch with her until she died.'

'But what happened about Tommy?' Lucy prompted.

'I'm coming to that,' Beatrice said. 'By the autumn of 1945 I hadn't seen Tommy for a year. Angie had well and truly taken care of that. My case had not proceeded much in my favour, Michael's lawyers having argued that I had been an unfit mother who hadn't even been married to Tommy's father and who had then left him whilst I pursued my own path. Since I was now respectably married, I might have countered some of this successfully, but where their case held water was in respect of the fact that Tommy could not remember any other mother but Angie. Maybe if I had continued the case, despite the considerable expense, I might eventually have won, but I was coming to see that there were other sides to this situation.

'Suppose I did win and Tommy was returned to me. What would that do to him, being sent from familiar people to a couple of strangers? I kept thinking and thinking, trying to see it from his point of view.

'And there was Rafe to think of. Rafe was supportive of me all the way about Tommy, though it had split his own family, and I could see that the strain was beginning to tell. I was obsessed about getting Tommy back and it must have been very hard for him to be newly married to a wife who was not focused on her husband. He'd have tried to be a good father to Tommy, I know he would, but the fact remained that he wasn't Tommy's father and, what's more, he had a bad experience of fathering himself and had never got along with his own stepfather.

'In September 1945, we moved into a flat in Regent's Park, quite near to where I'd lived with Dinah. Because of his experience, Rafe had been given a job in Military Intelligence, which meant occasionally returning to France, but by the summer he'd come home for good. One thing he'd managed was to contact my mother's family in Normandy. My grandmother and Cousin Thérèse were, it turned out, quite unharmed, and never had been imprisoned, though the Gestapo had paid a visit in 1943 and had ransacked the house. One of my uncles, it seemed, was keeping the farm going.

'I had not seen any of the Wincantons since going to Carlyon the September before. No, I tell a lie, because in June 1945 I bumped into Peter when I got out of a taxi by Claridge's one lunchtime. He was with a tall, scholarly looking man, but as soon as he saw me he came across. He was in civilian dress, and his face still bore that bitter, unhappy look. I wonder if he ever lost it?

' "So you got the man you wanted," ' Peter said. He'd obviously kept up with the family gossip. "I'm very happy for you."

' "Thank you," I said.

' "But I'm sorry for all the other stuff." He meant Tommy, I imagined.

'I muttered something about it not being his fault. It wasn't, of course. He was the one who had alerted me to the Wincantons' dangerous allure. He was an outsider, too, and I felt sorry for him.

' "You'll have heard about Gerald," he said.

'I had – from Rafe, of course – and was very sorry. Gerald had been returning to England the month before when his boat hit a mine. A piece of flying metal had caught him in the face, slicing it open to the bone. It was the most dreadful injury. Though the doctors had done their best he had lost an eye and he was in constant pain.

'I asked Peter what he was doing now, and he explained that he had recently started work at Sotheby's. "It'll be an interesting time," he said, and now, of course, we can see what he meant. So much looted art was to be tracked down and identified, and that became Peter's speciality.

'We'd only been in our new place for two weeks when Michael Wincanton came to visit us. I thought he looked much older, and this wasn't surprising considering the pressure that he must have been under, though we didn't yet know about this. The woman he'd been seeing during much of the course of the war, the one whom I'd had to drive to Cadogan Square, hadn't, it turned out, been quite the thing. I forget the exact circumstances, but she'd lived in Russia before the war and become the mistress of one of Stalin's henchmen. Nobody knew much about what she'd done there or whether she had contact with her lover during the war, but you can imagine the scandal when the news eventually broke, and after that, his political career was effectively over.

'Michael enquired after my father, and then he said, as if we hadn't guessed, "I've come about Tommy." Angie wanted a truce. If Tommy was allowed to remain with her and Gerald, then I would be allowed to see him regularly. The idea was that I should drop all legal proceedings and we'd all try to be friends.

'I was terribly upset about this and I'm afraid I lost my temper and it all came out in a jumble, all the resentments I'd been storing up. He must have thought I was mad. I accused him of all sorts of things, some of which I later realized he couldn't possibly have been responsible for – of using me in various ways and sending me to France and not caring about what happened to me. Rafe did his best to calm me down; even he was shocked.

'Michael just sat listening to me, rather white-faced. I don't know what he'd expected, but not this raving madwoman. He left soon afterwards.

'We talked about it for a long time, Rafe and I, and eventually I agreed to do what Angie wanted. It seemed the best thing for Tommy, and that it, after all, a mother's most important duty. But Angie did not keep her side of the bargain. I did see Tommy several times more, but as Auntie Beatrice, and Angie was very guarded. Probably my outburst to her father had not helped me. He was such a lovely little boy, Tommy, if a little shy and uncertain. Such a sweet face that reminded me of Guy. But soon after that, Gerald's regiment sent him to Hong Kong for three years, and, of course, Angie and Tommy joined him. And then I finally did what I saw to be in Tommy's best interests. I signed papers for his adoption. I did not know that after that I would not see him again until the day of Angie's funeral.'

Beatrice was silent now, her thoughts far away. After a while, Lucy said, 'I don't think I remember you at the funeral. When we first met, here, I thought you looked familiar, but I suppose that is because you are family. You are my real grandmother, after all.'

'You were very young, dear, only about sixteen, and I imagine very caught up in the drama of the occasion.'

'It was awful. I hadn't been to a funeral before, not even Grandad Gerald's. So many things took me unawares.' She recalled the electric curtain that moved round the coffin, separating the living from the dead; the morbid wreaths with their elevated messages in florists' round handwriting.

'He spoke so well. I admired your father for that.' Yet it was a shock seeing Tommy at nearly sixty, when in my imagination he was still a little boy. 'And, Lucy, it's strange. Hearing what he said about Angie, and talking to you about her, it's made me think. I can't forgive her exactly . . . but I can understand her, I suppose. And there is something I'm pleased about, which is that he and Angie loved each other. Your father was very loyal to Angelina and I think he must always have thought of her as his real mother. Perhaps that's why he didn't ever want to meet me. But that was hard, terribly hard.'

'I wish he could have met you,' Lucy said, 'and heard the story, too. I can't say that I'm not finding the whole thing very difficult to accept. That my father was your son. That Granny wasn't ever really Granny.'

'Did you really not know?'

'No, I didn't. He never said anything. Do you think she told him?'

'I sometimes wonder whether she said something, but never

explained properly. How it all came about. I wish more than anything that I'd had the opportunity to tell him the story I've just told you.'

'In some ways, though, it's not totally a shock. I think part of me guessed a long time ago that there was some secret. And this is it. Why couldn't he have told me? Even Mum didn't know, I'm sure she didn't. Or my stepmother.'

'I'm so sorry that it's been an awful shock. I still can't accept that he's . . . gone. I always held him in my mind, you know. When he was young I sent him birthday cards and presents and wrote him letters.'

Lucy had found nothing like that amongst his things and wondered if he'd ever got them. Perhaps he hadn't.

Instead she told Beatrice about how she'd been thinking about Tommy ever since Beatrice first mentioned having him, that it had gradually been dawning on her who he was. 'I see now that Dad and Granny were so unlike each other. I don't mean just physically, but the kind of people they were, their personalities.'

'That's not so unusual in families, is it?'

'And Granny was never very relaxed with Dad. There was always anxiety. But there was love, I'm sure of it.'

'I would hope that there was. That would have been the worst thing of all, if they hadn't loved each other.'

They were both quiet for a moment, then Lucy said, 'Tell me what happened next with you and Rafe.'

And here Beatrice smiled. 'Rafe and I had a wonderful marriage,' she said. 'He was a most marvellous husband, not that we didn't have our little ups and downs like everyone else, but we were very happy together. We had a daughter, Sara. Look, here she is.'

Beatrice stood up and fetched a photograph that Lucy hadn't

noticed before because it was on a shelf behind the chair. It was of a smartly dressed, middle-aged woman with a clever, lively face, standing on the steps of what looked like an office building.

'Sara is a Professor of Marine Biology in Maine,' Beatrice said proudly. 'She's due to retire next year and she's promised to come here on an extended visit. She has two grown-up sons and I've just become a great-grandmother!' She brought out more photographs now in a plastic album, of a dark-haired couple with a tiny baby girl.

'She's so sweet,' said Lucy, delighted at these new-found cousins.

'Catriona, they've called her.' The old lady stood gazing at the album a moment, a faint smile on her face.

'Do they know about Dad?' Lucy thought to ask.

'They know I had a child that I had to give away, yes,' said Beatrice. 'Lucy, I don't expect anything of you, dear,' she added. 'Angelina and Gerald don't stop being your grandparents.'

'No, of course not, but . . .'

'You can go away and never see me again. I respected your father's decision not to talk to me, you know. Nothing that happened was his fault. He was the victim.'

'But it wasn't completely your fault either, or – and you might disagree with me here – Granny's. And yet I can't suddenly pretend . . . well, I've got to get used to it all.'

'You've lived all your life without me, without knowing about me. But the strangest thing is that I recognize you, Lucy. I can see things about you that are like me. I don't mean your appearance, but your . . . well, the way you look at the world, your yearning for something.'

'I do want to get to know you,' Lucy said gently. 'What would you like me to call you? It doesn't feel right to say Granny or Grandma or Nan. Could I go on calling you Beatrice?'

'Of course you could,' Beatrice said. Her smile was light with relief.

'Beatrice,' Lucy said suddenly. 'Can I bring someone to meet you?'

That evening, over supper in the bar, she explained to Anthony a little of all Beatrice had told her.

'Will you come and meet her?' she asked. 'I think you'd like her.'

'But will she like me?' Anthony said, smiling.

'I know she will,' Lucy replied solemnly.

'Of course I'll come,' Anthony said. 'I'd like to hear some of her stories. I've read up quite a bit about SOE's role in the war. I can't believe I'm to meet a real veteran.'

'Nor can I. Beatrice would be a great subject for a TV documentary. If my boss likes the idea, I'm going to ask her. She'd be excellent in front of the camera.'

'It would be an amazing story.'

'There's something else I need to ask you, Anthony. Do you have a car with you?'

'I do. Did you want a lift back to London on Sunday?'

'That would be lovely. But tomorrow there's somewhere I want to take Beatrice first. Do you know Saint Agnes on the north coast?'

Chapter 35

'My father once offered me a penny to climb Saint Agnes's Beacon!' Beatrice remarked as the car passed a distinctive-looking hill on the right. She was sitting next to Anthony in the front seat and clearly enjoying the outing.

'Did you win the penny?' Lucy asked.

'Of course, and in record time.'

'This is Saint Agnes village, ladies,' Anthony said. 'Where do you want to go?'

'Down there, I think,' Beatrice said, pointing past a signpost for the beach, and he turned down a narrow lane dusted with sand and lined with houses on either side.

'There's The Hawthorns!' Lucy cried, and Anthony drew up outside a broad-fronted 1930s villa with the front garden asphalted over for cars.

'Are you sure you don't mind hanging about?' she asked him as he helped Beatrice out of the car.

'No, of course not,' Anthony replied. 'I'll drive up the road a little and take a look at the beach. I'll be fine.'

'We'll ring you when we're ready then,' she said, kissing his cheek. She took Beatrice's arm. Now the reality of seeing Hetty was close, Beatrice was, she thought, looking grim.

The Hawthorns' Care Home looked a pleasant place to pass one's sunset years. Lucy had phoned ahead and the young woman who opened the door to them said, 'You're to see Miss Wincanton?'

'That's right,' Lucy said, introducing Beatrice.

'Come in. She's quite bright today, so you've picked a good time.' The woman showed them into a large, high-ceilinged room at the back of the house with a distant view of sand dunes.

'Miss Wincanton, your guests are here.'

A shrunken old woman tried and failed to push herself up out of her easy chair.

'Hello, Aunt Hetty,' Lucy said, rather shocked to see how much Hetty had aged since Granny's funeral – the last time she'd seen her – and went forward to take her knotted hand. Hetty Wincanton's watery eyes looked up at her with confusion. 'I'm Tom's daughter,' Lucy said loudly.

'Ah yes, dear Tom,' Aunt Hetty said, quite clearly. Her eyes alighted on Beatrice. 'Oh, it's you,' she said. 'I didn't know you were coming.'

'Don't blame me. It was Lucy's idea,' Beatrice said haughtily.

Lucy and the care-worker arranged two more armchairs and established Beatrice in one, Lucy in the other. 'I'll bring you some tea shortly,' she said and hurried out.

Now that they were all here, nobody seemed sure how to start. Lucy bravely dived in.

'Aunt Hetty, Beatrice has been telling me all about the family and how ... well, how Granny came to adopt my father. I didn't even know he was adopted and it's been something of a shock. Could you possibly tell me – did Dad know?'

Hetty's eyes moved suspiciously from Lucy to Beatrice and back. Then she pushed herself upright in her chair and moistened her lips.

'He suspected and asked Angie once. She told him he was adopted, but asked him never to speak of it, said that it was hurtful to her and anyway it didn't matter. His real mother hadn't wanted him. She only gave him a short form of his birth certificate, which didn't have his parents' names on it. Of course, later he looked up the full version and . . .'

'I remember. It only had my name on it, not Guy's,' Beatrice broke in, her voice trembling. 'The local Register Office had been bombed and the girl was filling in for someone. She told me if you weren't married you didn't put the father's name on. She was wrong, as it transpired. I could have done if I'd wanted, but by the time I found out it was too late.'

'How sad that Granny wouldn't tell him anything,' Lucy said.

'I imagine she found it too difficult,' Beatrice said. 'But perhaps he did, too.'

'And he never said anything to me or Mum. Why?'

'I don't know. Yes, I do. He was ashamed. People used to have a proper sense of shame.'

Lucy was taken aback by this. 'You mean about being adopted?'

'About being illegitimate.'

That was an old-fashioned word, Lucy thought. She didn't think that would have been her father's reason. Beside her, Beatrice shuffled restlessly.

'I don't know what *she's* told you,' Hetty went on, 'but I'll be surprised if it's the whole story.' And suddenly, she began to ramble. 'I don't know why she ever had to come to Carlyon in the first place. Nobody asked me, not little Hetty, no.' Lucy quickly realized that Hetty was talking about her childhood. 'They thought I didn't matter; shovelled about, I was, from house to house, always in the way. My mother didn't want me, you know. She as good as told me once. Said she'd finished having her family and then I came along.'

Lucy stared at her, bewildered, then looked at Beatrice, whose horrified gaze was absolutely riveted on Hetty.

'So along comes Miss Prim here and nobody notices poor Hetty any more. She pretended to be nice to me, but I knew what she wanted – to be like one of us – and she wasn't.'

'Hetty,' Beatrice said to her, 'that's plainly ridiculous. It wasn't like that at all. They *did* care about you. They always did.'

'Did they?' Hetty said. 'Well, it never felt like it. It was always Ed this and Angelina that. Even Peter had a better time than I did. And then,' here Hetty addressed Lucy, 'she goes and has a baby and there's no father, though we knew who the father was, didn't we? Angelina's young man.'

'*Who?*'

'Rafe – Gerald's brother. She took him. Beatrice took Rafe from Angelina.'

'No I didn't,' Beatrice said. 'Stop it, that's nonsense.'

'It's not nonsense. You gave the baby to Angelina and went away and Angelina had to look after him. And then you came and wanted him back and Angelina wouldn't give him to you. Serves you right.'

There was a silence and then Beatrice said to Lucy, 'I don't think she's quite right in her head.'

Hetty heard her and looked mutinous.

Lucy was thinking about something else. She said, 'Auntie Hetty, do you really believe that Tom's father was Rafe?'

'Oh yes.'

'Did you . . . is that what you told Tom?'

'Yes. Sometime after Angelina's funeral he came to see me. I told him the truth, the whole story. How *she*, Beatrice, had abandoned him. Angie would never speak about it to me or to anyone, but I knew the truth.'

So that's why Dad was so interested in Rafe, Lucy realized.

Beatrice said tiredly, 'Hetty, you weren't there a lot of the time. You only knew bits and pieces of what happened.'

'That may be, but I was always watching and listening. I could work it out. I saw what kind of person you were. Even afterwards you kept trying to get him back, didn't you? By sending all those birthday cards and letters. Angelina never gave them to him of course. He found them when she died and opened them. Brought them when he came to see me.'

Beatrice gave a little gasp. 'Why didn't she give them to him? Oh, that is cruel.'

Lucy said gently, 'Perhaps Granny was afraid, Beatrice. That he would reject her and go and find you. I think she loved him so much.'

'He said that, too,' Hetty remarked.

'Do you mind telling me what you mean?' Beatrice asked.

'It's what he told me. He couldn't go and look for you because that would be betraying Angie's memory. He was surer of this after what I told him, about you abandoning him. Much surer.'

'I haven't found those letters,' Lucy told Beatrice. 'They weren't among the things my stepmother gave me.'

Hetty muttered something.

'What? Do speak up,' Beatrice said, frowning.

Hetty repeated triumphantly, 'I took them from him and I burnt them.'

After this there was another long silence.

Lucy glanced at Beatrice and was astonished to see that the old lady's eyes were swimming with tears. She placed a hand on Beatrice's arm. 'Oh, don't,' she whispered.

'It's all right,' Beatrice said, finding a handkerchief. 'I'm used to the fact that he never came to find me. It's the thought . . . well, I have a picture in my mind of him finding all those things

I sent him – the birthday cards, the airmail letters, oh, with the little drawings I did – and reading them all, and perhaps learning that I loved him.'

The care-worker returned with a tray of tea. She took one look at the anguished expressions of everyone in the room and said to Hetty, 'Are you getting upset again, Miss Wincanton? It's not good for you, you know. I'll get your medicine.'

Lucy followed her outside. 'She does seem very worked up. Is this normal?'

The young woman checked the label on a bottle and shook out a pill. 'It's worsened, I'm afraid, since her little stroke,' she said. 'Early stages, they think.'

'Dementia? But she sounds so lucid. It's *what* she says that's so worrying.'

'She does say whatever comes into her mind, that's the trouble. It can be a bit rude or hurtful sometimes. I really shouldn't be telling you this. You ought to speak to her doctor.'

'I understand,' Lucy said.

When she returned to the room she was astonished to find that the tenor of the conversation had changed radically. Beatrice and Hetty were chatting quite amiably.

'Do you remember the picnics on the beach?' Beatrice was asking.

'And fishing in the rockpools,' Hetty said, her eyes shining. 'And the secret steps from the cove.'

'To Carlyon.'

'Ah, Carlyon,' Hetty said. 'I can't bear to think of it being gone.'

'Nor can I,' Beatrice said.

'What happened to Carlyon, Hetty?' Lucy asked softly.

'Burnt to the ground,' Hetty said, her expression clouding like a child's. 'And Mother with it.' After a moment, she said, very slowly and clearly, 'She was living there by herself, after the war when I was away at school. The doctor had given her pills, to help her sleep. She often complained she couldn't sleep. She must have taken them and forgotten her cigarette. She sometimes did, you know.'

'I remember, she did,' Beatrice sighed. 'Poor Oenone.'

'That's so dreadful,' Lucy whispered. 'And it's never been rebuilt. Who owns it now?'

'Peter,' Hetty said. 'Though he never wanted it.' Then she looked straight at Lucy. 'Peter told me he was leaving it to Tom, but Tom's dead. So, Lucy, Carlyon will one day be yours. Not long now, I shouldn't think – poor old Peter.'

In the car on the way back to St Florian, Beatrice surprised Lucy by remarking, 'You know, I'm thinking that I'll drive over and see Hetty again. It might help her to talk more. She's a crusty old thing, but she must be lonely. And she remembers, Lucy. It's so nice when you're old to talk to others who remember.'

Epilogue

That evening, after supper at the hotel, Anthony and Lucy took the narrow path over the headland to the beach as the moon was rising. She let him help her down from the rocks onto the sand. He put his arms around her and kissed her. Later they found the path over the dunes and walked back to the house where he was staying and up the stairs to his room. There, very gently, he made love to her.

It was as they lay together afterwards in the darkness that he finally began to tell her what he'd been through, hesitantly at first, but with more certainty, as he relived the events. She supposed it was the dark that freed him to speak. She lay very still, just listening; some instinct told her that he did not need her to ask questions or pass comment, only to listen. And anyway, she thought, compared to what he'd been through, what did she know about anything?

They'd been in Helmand Province, he said, guarding a dam. The area was particularly dangerous, everyone knew that, not only because of insurgents, but because of unmarked areas of landmines. They were of the type, it seemed, designed to maim rather than kill, and every few days there came some awful new tale. Who, after all, can stop children treating ruined buildings as a playground or taking a short cut home across the fields? Everywhere these things were hidden, undetectable until too late.

It was in response to an urgent call that they set out that afternoon, he driving, Gray next to him in the armoured vehicle, bucketing down a mountain road to rescue a patrol which had gone where they shouldn't to help such a child – and had paid the price.

He should have seen it – how many times had they been warned, after all? – and he did, but not until it was too late. The glint of a wire stretched across the road teased his awareness for a split second. Then they were upon it.

The blast threw the vehicle up in the air. Somehow he was tossed clear, but Gray, poor Gray, was engulfed by a fireball. He didn't stand a chance. Anthony would remember his friend's screams for ever.

As Anthony lay in the field hospital, recovering from minor burns, from broken ribs and shock, he played over in his mind again and again what had happened, trying to make sense of it. He couldn't.

Things he'd done or hadn't done tormented him. If only he hadn't been driving so fast. If only he'd been concentrating harder, maybe he'd have seen the tripwire in time. Worse, worse even than this, was the fact that some automatic instinct had made him turn the wheel – not consciously, he wouldn't ever have done that – but he'd swerved, all the same, and it was Gray's side of the vehicle that caught the full force of the blast.

They sent him to talk to someone. It helped, but not much. Eventually they'd packed him off home on three months' leave and here he was, at the end of it, still bewildered and hating himself.

'They've all been so bloody kind; I've been tortured by kindness,' he said.

No one had blamed him, not even Gray's family. Their acceptance and forgiveness were extraordinary. When they'd suggested he go and stay in their holiday house in St Florian he'd gratefully taken up the offer. Here he could feel a connection to Gray from happier days.

'Do you feel ready?' she felt able to ask. 'To go back, I mean?'

'In some ways yes,' he replied. 'I'm in a vacuum here. I need to do something.'

'But in other ways . . . ?'

She watched him draw on his cigarette. For a while he said nothing, just lay thinking.

Finally he said, 'Did Gray die for a just cause? It's very hard to know. But I have to believe so or else I can't go back. How could I?'

'Do you have to go back? If you don't want to, I mean?'

'I do want to,' he said. 'I feel I owe it to Gray – and to all of them. It would be like deserting if I didn't. I have to do it.'

Lucy sighed. She didn't understand properly, how could she? But she thought she had an inkling. The things he was saying, well, it reminded her of Beatrice. It was all about duty, yes, but about love as well. About not putting yourself first.

'Will you be all right?' she asked.

'I think in the end I will.' In the dark she felt his hand find hers. 'It's odd. We hardly know each other,' he said, 'and yet I feel at some deeper level we do.'

He rolled across and she found herself looking into his face, felt his breath on hers. She reached up with her other hand and touched the sandpaper skin of his jaw, the softness of his lips.

'Lucy, my Lucy,' he whispered, taking her hand and kissing the fingertips. Then he bent his head and joined his mouth to hers. She drew him to her, and for a while there was no need to say anything.

Afterwards, falling asleep in his arms was the most natural thing in the world. She felt she was where she belonged.

Author's Note

Beatrice Marlow is a fictional character, but inspired by various real-life SOE agents, including Violette Szabo and Odette Churchill, who were mothers of young children. I am indebted to the many books that I consulted about the Second World War, and in particular about the SOE F-section (headed by Maurice Buckmaster with Vera Atkins), and the FANY. Among them are: *A Life in Secrets* by Sarah Helm, *Carve Her Name With Pride* by R J Minney, *Odette* by Penny Starns, *Debs at War* by Anne de Courcy, *In Obedience to Instructions* by Margaret Pawley, *London at War* by Philip Ziegler, *How We Lived Then* by Norman Longmate and *Cornwall at War* by Peter Hancock. An article I found at *www.kentfallen.com* about the Pluckley Remount Depot was helpful, as was Emma Smith's excellent memoir about growing up in Cornwall between the wars, *The Great Western Beach*.

Thank you to Bill Etherington, whose article in Eaton Parishes Magazine about the FANY set the hare running; to Frank Meeres of the Norfolk Record Office who was kind enough to read my script; to Sarah Hammond and Roger Pearson who advised me about sailing; and to my mother, Phyllis, who brought me up on stories of her wartime childhood, when the family had goats and, like Hetty, she kept a Rabbit Notebook.

Very many thanks to Sheila Crowley and her colleagues at Curtis Brown Literary Agency and its associates, to Suzanne

Baboneau, Libby Yevshutenko, Clare Hey, Florence Partridge, Kerr MacRae, Jeff Jamieson and the rest of the team at Simon & Schuster, and to copyeditor Joan Deitch. Endless love and gratitude are due as ever to my husband David, and to Felix, Benjy and Leo.

Rachel Hore
Norwich, 2011

Rachel Hore
A Place of Secrets

**THE
RICHARD AND JUDY BOOK CLUB
BESTSELLER**

The night before it all begins, Jude has the dream again ...

A successful auctioneer, Jude is struggling to come to terms with the death of her husband. When she's asked to value a collection of scientific instruments and manuscripts belonging to Anthony Wickham, a lonely eighteenth-century astronomer, she leaps at the chance to escape London for the untamed beauty of Norfolk, where she grew up.

As Jude untangles Wickham's tragic story, she discovers threatening links to the present. What have her niece Summer's nightmares to do with Starbrough folly, the eerie crumbling tower in the forest from which Wickham and his adopted daughter Esther once viewed the night sky? With the help of Euan, a local naturalist, Jude searches for answers in the wild, haunting splendour of the Norfolk woods. Dare she leave behind the sadness in her own life, and learn to love again?

'Rachel Hore's intriguing Richard and Judy recommended read ... is layered with a series of mysteries, some more supernatural than others' *Independent*

ISBN: 978-1-84739-142-1
PRICE: £6.99

Rachel Hore
The Glass Painter's Daughter

In a tiny stained-glass shop hidden in the backstreets of Westminster lies the cracked, sparkling image of an angel.

The owners of Minster Glass have also been broken: Fran Morrison's mother died when she was a baby; a painful event never mentioned by her difficult, secretive father Edward. Fran left home to pursue a career in foreign cities, as a classical musician. But now Edward is dangerously ill and it's time to return.

Taking her father's place in the shop, she and his craftsman Zac accept a beguiling commission – to restore a shattered glass picture of an exquisite angel belonging to a local church. As they reassemble the dazzling shards of coloured glass, they uncover an extraordinary love story from the Victorian past, sparked by the window's creation. Slowly, Fran begins to see her own reflection in its themes of passion, tragedy and redemption …

'Fans of *Possession* and *Labyrinth* will recognize the careful historical research Hore has undertaken and enjoy the seamless blend of past and present narratives into one beautiful story' *Waterstone's Books Quarterly*

ISBN: 978-1-84739-140-7
PRICE: £7.99

Rachel Hore
The Memory Garden

Magical Cornwall, a lost garden, a love story from long ago...

Lamorna Cove – a tiny bay in Cornwall, picturesque, unspoilt. A hundred years ago it was the haunt of a colony of artists. Today, Mel Pentreath hopes it is a place where she can escape the pain of her mother's death and a broken love affair, and gradually put her life back together.

Renting a cottage in the enchanting but overgrown grounds of Merryn Hall, Mel embraces her new surroundings and offers to help her landlord, Patrick Winterton, restore the garden. Soon she is daring to believe her life can be rebuilt. Then Patrick finds some old paintings in an attic, and as he and Mel investigate the identity of the artist, they are drawn into an extraordinary tale of illicit passion and thwarted ambition from a century ago, a tale that resonates in their own lives. But how long can Mel's idyll last before reality breaks in and everything is threatened?

'With her second novel, Rachel Hore proves she does place and setting as well as romance and relationships. Tiny, hidden Lamorna Cove in Cornwall is the backdrop to two huge tales of illicit passion and thwarted ambition ... Clever stuff' *Daily Mirror*

ISBN: 978-1-41651-100-7
PRICE: £6.99

Rachel Hore
The Dream House

Everyone has a dream of their perfect house ...

For Kate Hutchinson, the move to Suffolk from the tiny, noisy London terrace she shares with her husband Simon and their two young children was almost enough to make her dreams come true.

Space, peace, and a measured, rural pace of life have a far greater pull for Kate than the constantly overflowing in-tray on her desk at work. Moving in with her mother-in-law must surely be only a temporary measure before the estate agent's details of the perfect house fall through the letterbox.

But when, out walking one evening, Kate stumbles upon the beautiful house of her dreams, it is tantalizingly out of her reach. Its owner is the frail elderly Agnes, whose story – as it unravels – echoes so much of Kate's own. And Kate comes to realize how uncertain and unsettling even a life built on dreams can be: wherever you are, at whatever time you are living, and whoever you are with ...

'A beautifully written and magical novel about life, love and family ... tender and funny, warm and wise, the story of one woman's search for the perfect life which isn't quite where she thought she would find it. I loved it!' Cathy Kelly

ISBN: 978-1-4165-1099-4
PRICE: £7.99